Copper Tales:
Vedian

Copper Tales: Vedian

Written By

Steve Casbourne

World & Characters

created with

Neal Wixele

To my son Pippin –

Time will not diminish

my greatest respect

and everlasting love.

To my wife Louise -

The best thing I ever did

was be there the day I met you.

To my friend Neal -

For your huge role in creating

the world and the people in it.

Without you Vedian would not exist.

To my godson James -

My only advice:

Never listen to anyone who does not

agree with your heart.

Chapter 1 - The Luff

'If in my earlier sessions I misled my learned colleagues in my interpretation of the free will, then I would take this opportunity to expound it here.

It is not free will that creates imbalance but only the misuse of it. I would have all men choose their own destiny and follow it as they will, but I would not command every man do so. For balance to be maintained there must not - as some of my contemporary students have supposed - be dictation. We do not seek the path of purity, that path is for the self-righteous. Man must regulate himself and his kin, his balance comes from within and only in this way can free will bring about a productive equilibrium.

So, we as a race: the Scholatic, have been selected for the task to assist man in the education of self-regulation and this my friends is not an easy road. For at times we witness his anger and pain but also his aptitude for compassion and tolerance. Believe me, regulation is not imparted by halting his polarisation. In many ways it is through this combination of extremes that man will have his greatest victory. Only through witnessing his nadirs and zeniths will he ever learn balance.

Do not confound yourselves with words like 'good' and 'evil', these terms are mere toys that are easily bent. They are not absolutes but pressures of circumstance, we must step back from the detail and look to the whole, the cycle of birth, death and rebirth. We will not sit in condemnation of his rights and wrongs but stay true to the hope that he will regulate himself through judgement.'

'Judge No Other but Thyself The Proceedings Vol III, Session V' - MonPellia - Vedian 675

Another wave crested and beat itself hard against the creaking boards of the stern. The foam of the wave washed across the name plate on which the words 'The Dusk Returner' were painted in gold. The old ship had seen the sea's wrath and might hold against those burdens for a while longer. The dock came in sight where men waved and readied for the imminent arrival of cargo. The waters settled to a murmur around the hull as the modest harbour wall lent it's protection to the vessel and the air was suddenly full of the whipped up spray from the waters below. The top sail beat noisily too high to benefit from the wind shadow of the breakwater.

Brisk orders were shouted out by the first mate to reef the last sail as the inward current was left to take her the final league. From the dockside she looked a fine ship: long and sturdy, crafted by master shipwrights, but she had been abroad many years and too often without a refit. The sea had climbed upon and scoured her decks while the rocks scraped her tough hide. In truth she was a dream of yesteryear, a shadow of what had gone before, her captain knew her time was running short.

Captain Pike stood at the helm, the first mate attending at his shoulder ready to amplify and enforce any orders the captain might mutter. His hands guided the great wheel, bringing her carefully into port. The sailors hurried to and fro, reefing and hauling, but he was a calm in the middle of their actions. He concentrated solely on the job at hand. The wind touched his back, gusting a slight easterly, while the captain peered across the bow which now pointed toward the low fish yard at the west of the dock.

The Returner came about and as if by willpower alone the stern came leeward and brought the ship alongside: a manoeuvre he had performed many times. As the men on shore came within hailing distance he nodded to the young bosun on the main deck and the athletic man went about his business. He moved to the bow and shouted for the ship's hands to secure the fore and aft lines being thrown ashore, ensuring the tenders that protected the ship's side from the abrasion of the jetty were set at the correct height. The bosun in his long oil coat moved quickly, checking the seating of the devil's claw on the anchor chain as he passed along with the many other small things that make the difference between a ship's hand and a master sailor.

Pike smiled at the youth who had come such a long way in past year, he was an able seaman now and respected as a valued crewman by the experienced sailors. The gang planks were unshipped and the mooring ropes were secured to the bollards to hold the ship steady. Had it really been thirty years? He wondered. Thirty years since he had first walked upon her decks

8

with the smell of cut wood still strong in his nostrils. She'd been a fine ship then - a princess amongst her kind and a horde of sailors had wanted to be on her crew. Her revenues had been opulent in those days but times had changed. He examined the lower deck before him where a weeks stock, perhaps less, was opened up through the cargo hatches. A good few tillers and many of the smaller stickma that were prevalent in these waters, but none of the great po-tails and orndykes that she used to fetched up, they had long since gone to new waters, the catch had become lighter and the fish smaller. There would barely be enough to reimburse the crew and set aside a few coppers.

There were ways to earn a better living and many captains would cut short his original promises to a crew, then hold back profits for his own purse. But he was no cheat, the long years hadn't hardened him to friendship and fairness. He would make do with what he got and everyone would receive the share they had been promised. It was the proper way: the same way they had agreed all those years ago and he would never go back on his word.

Pike wasn't an unhappy man by nature but found himself wondering if things had been different would today be just a little easier for it? Manuo Caedron was his greatest friend and companion: they had grown up together in the Luff and followed their fathers into the trade. Manuo was a fine sailor, always ready to help his companions, even though many of them were jealous of his talents. He rose quickly up the ranks and got a good name for himself even outside the Luff. Happy years had passed and the town was as rich in trade as any could hope to be, so Manuo saved enough coin to place an offer on a new ship. Manuo made himself an equal partner with Pike even though Pike's money was not half of his. Manuo had said he would rather be right than rich, so they were always on an even footing.

"Captain." Pikes' thoughts were interrupted by the crew about him. "The catch is loaded in the carts and the ship is stowed proper. We'll take our leave, it's been a long sail. If you'll be so kind as to make payment ready?' The sailor wore a gutting apron that hung down to his dirty boots.

The captain looked at the half dozen faces around him - they were so old. He tried to employ the crew that he trusted, the men that had sailed with him time and again. It was safer that way when you dealt with the sea: she didn't care for what should happen or how respected you were. With the many fates that could strike a man on the oceans, having reliable, resourceful men made your chances of surviving far better.

"Joseph", the captain called the bosun to him, "time for us to give out the shares - go fetch the purse.'

The tall lad stood in high black leather boots and leather leggings, a dirty cotton shirt was about his torso and at his neck hung a pendant with a picture of a mariner holding a trident carved upon its face. His hair was dark black and his eyes brown and deep set, he looked once more upon the ocean before waking from his trance and acknowledging the captain. He climbed to his feet and traversed the short distance to the hut which stood at the end of the walkway. It was a small two man hut, woven reeds and mud, sufficient shelter in these parts and useful to keep the hot sun at bay. Upon its roofing a small sign was written in red, 'The Minter'. This post had existed for longer than he could remember, a precaution against those that would chance their luck. His father had told him that in past days, crews would mutiny against a captain, steal the copper and throw him overboard. So all payments were held before sailing at 'The Minters', he was employed by the town and paid a small fee for each holding. From this wage he employed three guards, one inside and two out. It was a good system and kept the opportunist away, although this was a problem more prevalent in larger towns, the Luff was just a village holding only five hundred who called it home.

He nodded to the guards and stood against the hut for an arms check. The taller guard began to examine his clothing, 'Evening to you Master Caedron, how was the catch?

'Not bad Rayme, not bad at all. Perhaps the seas are beginning to show us some kindness.' The boy had learned a long time ago it was not a good idea to show disappointment in a bounty. Fishing trade was crucial for the Luff as its main export, word would spread quickly through the town if things looked to be suffering.

The tall guard motioned him to enter the hut through the opening. It was cool inside, a candle burned on the desk that he stood in front of. The third guard stood slightly crouched due to the small roof, to one side and behind the desk sat the Minter.

'Name?' the man barked. He was dressed in leather tunic and trousers and atop his head sat an oversized helm. The guards did not act as a deterrent to all thieves it would seem.

The young man replied, 'The Dusk Returner, Captained by Pike and copper collected by Joseph' The man's long moustache twitched as he rummaged into the small chest by his side. He pulled out the coinage and placed it into a small pouch, in return Joseph gave him the seal that he had received when the copper had been deposited prior to sailing.

Joseph nodded and smiled at the nervous man, 'Good day to you Minter. I'll take your leave until our next meeting.' The young man ran from the tent, he was looking forward to going home now, two weeks had passed slowly and he wanted to check on his mother.

He ran up to the Captain and tossed him the small pouch, if there was enough left over, perhaps he could buy her a small gift. A token of his....friendship. No, he thought, shaking his head, perhaps not, somehow he did not think she would appreciate that.

Once all the crew had been paid and departed for home the Captain turned to Joseph and placed twelve copper in his palm, 'There you go Joseph, a little extra for you and Goodwoman Caedron.'

Joseph shook his head, 'It's not right Captain, the others would be mightily peeved if they knew I got more. I wouldn't feel right.' He offered back the extra two coins.

'My boy,' Pike put his massive hands on his hips, 'You will take the copper for your service. The sailing earns you ten and then one more for each trip to the minter. There are few men I would trust with that task. The older man took a seat on a mooring post on the dock.

'I promised your father long ago Joseph, that if anything ever happened I would look after you. You are a man now Joseph and as able a sailor as your father was, you do not need my help anymore, my last days abroad are drawing near. I wish that I had children and a wife, but that time never seemed to come. I watched you grow up and I thought for a time that would be enough, I have tried to be the man your father was, but I will never be him.'

Joseph leant down and crouched behind Pike holding his shoulders, 'You have treated me as any father would have these past six years Pike. My mother and I owe you everything, few men would have made the sacrifice you made.'

Custom was a strange thing but it ruled the Luff with as strong an arm as any monarch or council. When a man died in partnership, all his possessions in work passed not to his wife or young child but directly to whomever the contract had been sealed with. Pike had been passed the Dusk Returner and he could have been a well-off sailor. At that time many woman of the village had flocked to his side hoping to wed, but Pike had not tarried with them long. He could not actually give back the share so he employed Joseph at only eleven years to his crew. He had him run errands and do small jobs and in return paid him a crewman's wage. Much outrage had been caused in the village but Pike had stayed firm with all that he promised his friend. In truth Pike would have taken Goodwoman Caedron as his wife to seal the future and protect her from idle tongues but she would not have it so. She had often thanked him for all he had done but held the thoughts of her husband too deeply in her heart to take another.

'Pike. Speak to me again of my father's final voyage, there are still questions I wish to ask you. Will you tell it once more?'

Manuo was a good and honest man but he would not have his son brooding so long over his demise, Pike thought to himself. He had recounted the tale many times over the years, how they had drifted out from the waters of the bay under a heavy storm and found themselves in the Great Seas themselves. Few had returned from such a journey but Manuo would have, had it not been for a monstrous serpent that had attacked the boat. He had held the mighty creature at bay while he ordered Pike to crew them back into calmer waters. At the last he had fallen, the beast knocking him limp from the vessel and into the waters. There had been no way to save him and no chance to search the icy depths. The memory was not a pleasant one even years hence.

'Not tonight Joseph, for I tire and would have by bed as soon as we finish at market. Perhaps tomorrow, now lad let us depart and ensure they do not ruin all our fish!'

The pair rose and left the docks as the sun set upon the waters. They followed the track into the village passing the huts that lined the way. It was quiet now and the children had been called in for supper so they hastened on to the market which lay at the centre of Kearn Luff. On reaching the stalls they saw the carts being unloaded and packed in crates lined with sea-water mud to keep them fresh. The loads had to depart before night was ended to ensure they reached their destination for tomorrow's buyers. Pike walked over to a stout man, dressed in a white apron sullied with grime from a hard day's toil, a fiendishly sharp filleting knife dangled by a thong around his waist. 'Good evening to you Comlay, how goes the preparation for departure?'

The man's cheeks puffed out as he spoke, 'Yes, all is well. My men have the bounty almost packed, we should load the caravans before midnight and reach the town by dawn. Now old sailor, leave a poor market man to his work and get ye off home.'

Pike smiled at Comlay, he was an honest worker and he gave a fair price for the catch. It was not an easy trade as it had once been, the smaller bounty's and caravans being raided on the road had left him with a difficult position. He would pay half the copper on departure to the Captain of the catch and half if his men returned safely with payment from the town. Vagabonds and curs roamed the land in these times and such deliveries were easy prey to them. Comlay, drew a purse from his apron and passed it to Pike who tucked into his belt.

'Seventy five coppers now as is agreed and the same on the morrow if all goes well. I bid you goodnight Captain and to you Master Caedron.'

Joseph smiled at Comlay and turned with Pike to depart the market.

'I fear Joseph, there is scant enough to start the repairs we spoke of. The price of boards has risen again from Kanegon due to the accursed raidings. She will not last many more trips without them and I would not risk a crew with an unfit vessel. I am unsure what is to be done.' The older man's head dropped slightly, the spring in his step lessened as his thoughts turned to the problem. Wood was in scant supply through all of Vedain, no tree that could be harvested grew in these lands, the dirt wood trees which had grown in Vedian since time immemorial got there name from the carpenter's opinion of the heavily knotted, hard and brittle wood. Supply could only be reached by boat onto the mainland forests, where great trees grew in abundance, but it was a long and perilous trip to journey on barge and only few experienced sailors knew the course through the Straits Of Reslin to the west of Kanegon. Prices had always been high but the caravan raids of late had increased, pushing the cost higher still.

"Worry not." Joseph turned to Pike, patting him on the back, "A way will surely present itself to us. The Dusk Returner will not sail her final voyage this year."

They walked from the market heading south to the edge of the village, passing the Mariner's Retreat, the local tavern which served as a friendly meeting place for many of the local folk in the long evenings. It was a large wooden structure, one of the few in the village, the tavern master was a well respected man in the community and sat on the governing assembly that watched over the Luff's day-to-day activities. A few people wandered up the track, nodding politely to the pair, some shouted briefly asking for information on the catch. Pike always answered the same, "A fair bounty," he would say, "worse and better but fair enough for this journey."

Finally they came to a row of small huts that marked the edge of the village border, the lights shone from his home and Joseph motioned to invite the old sailor inside.

"Perhaps just a quick drink," Pike replied, "just to reassure your mother I have not abandoned you."

Joseph smiled to himself, he knew that Pike was fond of his mother and harboured him no ill-will for such thoughts. He knew that a union would be of great help to her in later years and had often asked her to take Pike up on his offer of marriage. They entered the hut, his mother sat upon a large stone seat, it was covered in bright fabrics woven by her own hand. She smiled as she saw him enter and rose to greet him.

"I heard from one of the children that you had returned, it is good to see you safe Joseph." She turned to Pike, "Has he behaved himself and worked hard?"

Joseph snorted, "Mother! I am not a boy. I crew as hard as any man."

The old sailor smiled at the woman, "He has worked well and I am pleased to accompany him to you safely Goodwoman Caedron. It does my heart good to see you in fair health."

"As seeing you does mine Pike. Now sit I have prepared a broth to warm you through, it must be an age since you have had a good meal inside you both."

The men did not take long to wolf down the hearty meal and chatted with Joseph's mother, telling her of the trip and asking of events in the village since their departure.

"I would say this", she interjected over Pike's long tale of the voyage, "more strangers are travelling through the Luff of late. I have heard that men in the village have taken to carrying arms as a precaution against thievery. It is a poor state of affairs, they say these men come from Kanegon where lawlessness is rife. I for one would wish they stay there."

Pike nodded, "Aye, tis a sad state of things when a man must carry dagger or staff to protect what he has worked for. Have the assembly made any comment on the matter?"

"No. I think they see more guards as just a further cost to them. There is a meeting tomorrow in the tavern apparently, something will surely be said then. Perhaps they will try to petition the duke for more patrols."

They washed the meal down with two large mugs of ale, shortly after Pike thanked Joseph's mother for her hospitality and departed for his home. He stopped and turned at the opening of the hut and smiled, "Do not forget my offer Goodwoman Caedron - it still stands."

"I have not forgotten my dearest," she smiled at Pike, "perhaps one day you will not ask and I will rue what I have missed out on but for now I am of similar mind as I have been. You have my thanks forever though, if that be some consolation to you."

"It is." He replied and then left.

15

Joseph retired to his room, a small mattress of feathers laid upon the floor. He thought of Pike's words concerning the repairs and lay thinking of how he could raise the coins needed for such a venture. His final thoughts before sleep took him, were of the serpent. I will have me that creature one day, he thought, I will avenge my father's memory and bring its hide to the Luff for all to see. He woke late in the morning, sailors sleep patterns being dictated more often by the duty of watch than daylight, sometimes it took a whole week to get back to the normal village routine. The children were playing outside the huts, chasing each other around the grasses. He dressed in his leather leggings and put on the clean cotton shirt his mother had laid out for him.

Yawning and stretching, he blinked his eyes venturing into the morning sunlight, it was a hot day as most of the them were in northern Vedian. He walked around the back of his home, avoiding the children running past him and knocked on the hut at the rear.

"Come in." a familiar voice echoed out from the inside.

Joseph entered the hut, very similar in style to his own home, the stone chairs and table, walls adorned with tapestries and triangular openings to allow light to enter with hide flaps pinned above in case the rains came. A small lad sat in the chair at the far wall, his back to Joseph. He was reading a large book, which was remarkable in that manuscripts were rare. Joseph supposed it was possible this was the only book within forty miles.

"Good day to you Master Lucent," Joseph said to the lad, "how do I find you today?"

The young man placed his book down on the table and stood up, turning to face the visitor. "You find me waiting Joseph. Your mother said you were asleep, I thought you had lapsed into a coma! The middle of the day is nearly upon us." The young man, moved towards Joseph and grasped him by the forearms. "I have missed you Joseph, it has seemed like an age. You must tell me all of your tale and I will share a few of mine that you may find interesting."

'That we will Speck, but come, let us venture out into the light and leave your book behind. We do not want unfriendly eyes upon us today.'

16

The youths walked outside and sat on the lush grass. They had been friends since forever, sharing in many adventures as boys do when they are young. Speck looked up to Joseph like a brother, he was all that Speck was not. Strong, reliable, generous to all. As they had grown older Speck had stood out in the village but Joseph had always protected him against the others who would bully him and call him names.

It was in fact one particularly unpleasant lad that had christened him 'Speck', his real name was Lucent Symeon, but only his mother called him that now. Joseph had given the boy a black eye and sent him home in tears, yet the name had stuck. He was a small in height and stature but he had other talents that emerged as he had got older. The one that stood out was his ability to read, he had never been tutored, as few were, but he read and wrote as if he had sat in classes for years. This in itself made him unpopular to adults and children alike, the younger men envied his talent and the adults were somewhat fearful of the way he had acquired it. His father had died before his birth at sea like Joseph's, but he knew little of him and his mother had to be hard pressed before she mentioned his name. She also had never remarried but, unlike the Goodwoman Caedron, did not have a patron to help her son. So she made a livelihood by travelling from the Luff to Pluris, the capital of Vedian, purchasing various unusual items for the kitchen at the large market there and selling them at the Luff.

She was not popular to men or women in the village, by tradition women did not work for keep, if such a tragedy occurred that they became widowed they would be expected to marry swiftly to ensure a future for their children. It was true of all women considered in their prime, only the elder women would be cared for by their children, or if there were no offspring, by the assembly. Yet Speck's mother would not remarry and so set about her tasks to ensure her son was cared for. Joseph's mother would help her at times, as they too had become friends over the years, she would assist preparing herbs and spices that had been brought back from Kanegon.

Speck despite his size, was constantly trying to prove himself to Joseph as a fighter. He would pick fights with boys twice his weight just to try and persuade his friend that he was not a coward. Often he would come home battered and bruised when Joseph was at sea and unable to protect him, but it never stopped Speck. The boy had a fire inside him that Joseph could not understand. He was fascinated by his friend, with his gold curling locks of hair and staring green eyes. He too was a little concerned of the lads exceptional gift with the books but unlike others it didn't frighten him. His friendship meant more than anything else, as it had to his father and Pike before.

"I saw that girl, yesterday," Speck said, half smiling, "at market, when I was fetching vegetables for the table."

"What girl?" Joseph tried to be dismissive but turned so as not to make eye contact with his friend.

Speck laughed, "You know full well which one. The scully who lives there, the one you keep trying to impress with your tales."

"I do no such thing!" Joseph protested, "I think she shows much interest in the affairs at sea, so I merely try to enlighten her further."

"Ha!", Speck snorted. "She is interested in nothing, she is a waif and a thief. Why she has not been thrown from the village borders I know no reason."

"You know fully well Speck. She is an orphan of the Luff, therefore she has right to live within its borders, even though she has no right to shelter or supplies. It is an outrage that a small child should be left to fend for herself because her parents are either dead or have abandoned her. We punish the wrong people Speck, our traditions bind us too tightly."

The small lad jumped to his feet, "Well I think the sea has soured your brains Joseph! You are almost beginning to think for yourself, what will become of you?" Speck laughed out loud then took one look at his friend and began to run. Joseph leapt up and raced after him, jumping upon his back and dragging him to the grass, they fought like playful titans. As Speck had Joseph pinned to the floor kneeling on both arms to keep him from moving a voice reached the young men from above.

'Well, well. Another brawl little Speck? And this time you seem to have the better of your opponent. What manner of man are you battling that has not the strength to raise himself against your will?" Both lads, stopped their contest and stood to see a handsome man, almost ten years their senior standing with hands resting on a long spear. He was of middle height and dressed in the light green garb of the master hunter's men.

Joseph smiled in recognition, "Arn! I thought it was you. How are you my friend? How has the hunt been? Where is your father, is he not with you?"

Speck sat down again, smarting at the mans ridicule. The huntsman pushed his hand forward in a halting motion, "Hold on, hold on lad, one thing at time. I am fine and the hunts have been good since you departed last. My father is leading one now to the eastern plains." Arn turned to examine Speck sulking on the ground. "Come now little master, do not take my words so quickly to your heart."

Speck huffed but stayed and listened to the hunter. He had first met Arn six years ago through Joseph. He was much older, though Speck could never make out his age on account of a timeless element to his face and Joseph did not seem to know himself, he was skilled in the ways of animals and the hunt. His father was the master huntsman of the Luff. An important position, he was responsible for tracking prey and arranging hunts for the village men to gather food. It was, as were most professions in the Luff, one that handed down from father to son. Arn was a good hunter but lacked the dedication and commitment that his father required. Speck had often seen them arguing in the tavern at nights, Arn enjoyed practical jokes and his father thought this type of thing misplaced in such an important village role. The time was coming closer now when Arn would take the role of master huntsman for his own, his father was ageing and would retire soon to his wife and home. In truth, Speck liked the hunter, but he would never say so, he was amazed at the clear synergy the man had with animals, a true understanding, it was fascinating to him. Too often though had he teased Speck, though never with malice, it was just the way he was. A man that had or would not grow-up the villagers said. Yet for all the respect his office had within the village, Speck often thought that there was something out of place with the hunter. Externally he seemed all he should be, strong and capable as was his father, but a veil hung over the hunter that shrouded some other purpose, it perplexed Speck but made Arn all the more interesting for it.

Arn continued talking, "Have you heard. There was a fight in the tavern last night, with outsiders. Apparently they arrived late and began to cause trouble with Herm and Pudd the butchers boys."

"Ha! Those two have caused more trouble in this village then any strangers," Speck shouted, "they probably started on the visitors, it would be just like them."

"No Speck. It was the travellers, Old Man Talon saw them, he told me this morning and he is as honest as the day is young. Apparently so he says, they drew knifes on the butchers lads, gave them quite a fright and cleared the tavern a bit sharpish to. My father says that we must protect ourselves, we should carry arms to deal with such ruffians." Arn, held aloft his bow, is if to back-up his fathers words.

"You two should do the same, mark my words. There are more and more of these strangers coming up from the big towns like Kanegon. I could get you a dagger Speck and what about you Joseph what weapon do you wish?"

Joseph looked sheepishly at Arn, not wanting to disappoint the man, 'I..I do not wish to fight. So I do not think I will need a weapon. Brawling and fists are one thing, but this is different. He paused and looked again at the huntsman who he had such great respect for, 'Perhaps I will ask old Pike for a staff with a hook on that we use for gutting the big fish. That way it would be like carrying a useful item, but I could still turn it to my defence. What about that Arn?'

Arn smiled ruefully, "That would do just fine my friend, I'm sure you will save many lives with your sailing stick. Now come on. The assembly is meeting later, lets go and query Old Man Talon again in the market and see if he knows what they are going to say."

The three young men, raced up the north track to the market, the tavern was quiet now as opening was not allowed outside evenings. On arrival at the market edge they were met with the bustle of many folk, some buying and others selling, some just looking to see what others were buying. It was a close type of village and many spent time concerning themselves with others business, however insignificant it might be. The group pushed through the crowd who congregated round the many stalls that lined the market way. Joseph eyed Comlay presenting a well sized stickma, fresh from the catch to a wary purchaser. He waved to the stout man, who paused his fervent haggling routine to smile and shout pleasantries to Joseph. They pushed their way further through the crowd, passing the well stocked tanners, hides draped over the tall stone stall. To the left Speck saw his mother's small stall being surrounded by a group of busy women, pushing and pulling each other in an effort to reach the front of a unregulated queue. For all the traditional dislike of his mother's status in the village, it was becoming known to many that she had a nose for sound and rather fashionable ingredients and spices. It was one thing to be traditional but another entirely to be unfashionable in a small village. Beyond the stalls a ring of villagers stood about a man perched on a small mound, at his side upon a simple wooden stool, lay a fragment of leathery parchment. The man was as round as he was long, dressed somewhat comically in leather britches and a bright red shirt which threatened to come apart at his stretching midriff. Upon his head there was a hat of green, which leant conspicuously to the side.

If any had thought to smile or chuckle at the chubby man's appearance, the sight of his belt would have soon returned them to their senses. His belt was black leather and wide, at its centre a buckle crafted from copper and representing a trident of the Luff. This symbol was one only born by those of the assembly, only two other men in the history of the Luff had been given leave to wear the belt without being in active service to the village. The first being The Mighty Kearn Baylak founder of the town and forger of the symbol and second, Senior Rayne an especially unusual man who had served upon the assembly for thirty years prior to retirement. It was normally true that a member would only be granted two terms of 5 years, but Rayne had proved so popular in the village, that they had begged him to continue standing. His early decisions to allow tavern opening in the village and reduce trade taxations to families who had at least three Luff generations may have had a partial effect in this matter. Nonetheless the village had deemed that he should be allowed to wear his belt of office, even until the day he passed to the ground. The symbol of the Luff was a mark of great respect even to those who appeared in such outlandish attire.

Arn pushed to the front of the circle and turned to the other two following close behind, "Hey. It's an auction and by the looks of the crowd an expensive one at that, let us see who bids."

Joseph turned to Speck and whispered, "I thought the assembly had decided to dispense with all auctions in favour of a fair distribution of commissions?"

"Your time at sea has left you behind events," Speck replied authoritatively,"that is only for commissions below the ten copper threshold. Above that the old rules apply, although this is the first that has passed through the Luff in a good while."

The group quietened down as the fat man announced the beginning of the auction.

"The auction is open to all. Let those who would bid for its commission, stand forth and present themselves before its contents are made available to all present." Carefully shifting his weight, so as to not topple from the mound, the announcer bent to lift the parchment from its resting place. In front of him five villagers moved forward to begin the bidding. He nodded to each in turn and then unrolled the parchment and began to read its contents.

"The following commission is offered to the Luff by the University of Asten and its esteemed servant Lamentor, Low Lore Scriptor." Pausing to clear his throat from a low gurgle he continued. "To retrieve and bring unto Asten University a relic of the Bannermane site from the archaeologist who holds it in his keeping. The duty to be performed by no less than three and one skilled, to ensure said items protection upon the road from Bannermane to Asten. Maximum payment rests in the assembly hands and I start the bidding at the threshold of one hundred and fifty coppers!"

Arn shouted at his companions, "Bannermane! Could you imagine a more exciting journey my young friends. What secrets and tales lie upon that road I wonder."

"There is naught on that road but old skeletons and thieving rogues. It would be a fool to take such a reckless journey. The bandits would smell its delivery from a mile off. I would not take such a trip for a thousand coppers." Speck retorted indignantly.

The pace of the bidding began to pick up and the surrounding crowd began to grow excited by its potential. Two of the bidders who had begun separately now stood offering one bid as was their right. The price had dropped to one hundred coppers and two other villagers had sat down to signify their exit from proceedings. The surrounding areas were not the lush and friendly fields they had once been, a trip through the hills to the old town and returning to Asten with an item of value was not a commission to be taken lightly. The two men were waiting on a bid from the final opponent, who stood very silent seeming to contemplate the newest bid.

"Speck, Arn, look its her, its Febra! I hardly recognised her, it has been too long that I have been abroad, has she not turned lovelier since last I laid eyes upon her my friends?"

The girl stood in tight breeches and loose cotton shirt, her hair cut short and ragged was as dark as her eyes. Thick bushy eyebrows sat ominously above them, scowling against the malicious sunlight. Her small figure dwarfed by the large cut of the cloth she wore.

If that is beauty, then may they forever frame my face in the great City Of Pluris for all to marvel at its handsome features, thought Speck.

It was true that the girl, short and slightly rough, was not of classical looks or pedigree, even in the Luff's eyes. Yet within, a child like expression lay and a deep sense of loss which accosted her a feeling of protectiveness. Not all men would perhaps save her for love but many would do the same for pity. She was a curious creature, standing there slowly counting to herself, her fingers moving up and down as another ten coppers were accounted for.

Joseph stood and stared, he did not see pity and felt none either. To him, a sailor of the Luff she was a girl of great beauty and strength and one that he had designs on, since the day he had first set eyes upon her.

"Eighty copper pieces!" the girl exclaimed, excitedly jumping up and down on the spot and pointing at the two men who would take her prize.

The men groaned and scoured at the girl, they huddled together whispering under hot breath. The announcer motioned to the men, "The bid is upon you gentlemen. Do I hear a lesser offer, or is the commission with this scully?" The final word was offered with little affection.

The villagers called orphans 'scully'. Children who had lost parents to sea or sickness were left to fend for themselves under the eyes of the village. While kept within the borders from which they were born, they had no right to food or shelter than that they could find themselves. It was a tradition of worthiness, those that

23

could survive would do so and be reintegrated into village life, those that did not were products of unworthy parents, it was said. Village realities were harsh but not without fairness. Scullies often would turn to thieving at the market and many were known to the traders. Yet, unless they were directly apprehended then no action would be taken against them, it was deemed fair under the traditional laws. So a few such children survived the harsh conditions, sleeping rough under the canvassed protection of the market and feeding from its scraps. As they grew older they often ran errands for traders or sometimes less scrupulous works.

The two men finished their discussion and turned to face the announcer, shaking their heads. They reluctantly sat down upon the ground and began to argue with one another over bidding tactics. Febra walked towards the announcer and bowed then stretched out her thin arms to receive the parchment.

The man observed the girl carefully and asked, "You have the companions the commission speaks of to fulfil its request?" A harsh smile crossed his thin lips.

The girl looked up at him, "I ave 'em fat man, now give me the words."

With a large huff the announcer passed the girl the parchment and five copper pieces, "Full payment at Asten on receipt. Non compliance to be referred directly to the assembly for due consideration and punishment."

The girl nodded, snatched the parchment and wandered into the crowd smiling at Joseph as she left the scene.

Commissions were not a small consideration for any village. They were important to relations with larger and important officials from other locales. The assembly would take a healthy percentage from all dealings and the commerce was an integral part of their funding. Subsequently any commissions not carried out to satisfaction of the offerer were looked on seriously by the assembly. Floggings or beatings were not unknown sentences to be dealt out on those not fulfilling their promises.

Speck turned to Joseph, "What companions could she possibly have, unless it is the rats under the butcher stall? She has taken leave of her wits, those few that she had left to her. What idle rabble will follow her on that foolhardy quest?"

Chapter 2 - Fifty Pieces Of Copper

'We have heard from so many notables, that man is not worthy of our consultation in determining the relevance of his own existence. He is comforted in the knowledge that we do not blame him for this, it is simply that we do not believe him to be equal to the task of understanding. While we debate and write, discussing the fabric of his society and arguing the merits of his strength and weaknesses, we the Scholatic, do not at any time consider that the achievement of his balance could be realised by his own philosophy. At no point would my learned colleagues consider or open their thoughts to the painful truth, that the natural state of man is good and wise. Have we become so blinkered in our debate, that we are closed to even the possibility that as an individual, or as a race; he may have something to contribute? Even MonPellia himself realised that man could only fulfil balance through self-regulation. I then would ask you to take just a small step further into the philosophical unknown, if he has the potential within himself to command balance, can he not be part of the understanding that engenders that process?

If my words and actions have caused embarrassment to my peers, then for this I apologise, it was not set out to be such. Yet I feel we are on the breakthrough of unrealised understanding and my hand will not be stayed by the narrow thinker or self obsessed politicians that grow like a fungus within our council. The Scholatic were bred as a race to purify the mind, to allow us to understand and protect the common man that threatened to destroy himself. I believe now that man will never capitulate into the void, as he has a natural survival instinct within his core. An underlying understanding that will ensure his continuance.

To fathom this from mere observation could take an eternity, only in allowing man access to teaching, lore and philosophy can we hope he will discover these truths for himself.'

'The Noble Savage Philosophies' - Pionor Saban – Vedian 844

The old man, walked slowly though the long hallway. Its heavy stone walls narrowing to a point far into the distance. He paid little attention to the carefully woven tapestries that adorned the passageway, depicting the many faces of those that had gone before him. His gnarled stick, carved from trees that had long since departed the shores of his country, offered him the only assistance to a tired and weary body. Knowledge and writings could not replace the pleasures of youth, he thought. The tapping of the stick on stone, echoed through the hall, announcing his arrival to those that waited at its end. He knew his time was coming to an end, with hindsight perhaps he would have done things differently. He had been too outspoken, allowing his personal beliefs to cloud the greater goals. Yet he would trade all those mistakes to be made right for just one other. His greatest failure.

Reaching the end of the hallway, a tall ornate door rose up to halt his progress. Raising his stick, he tapped twice on its thick wooden panels. He stood quietly, waiting for an answer. Leaning the support aid against the door, he reached up to remove the hood that shrouded his face in darkness. The cloth folded down and rested about his shoulders, revealing a strong face, lined and racked with time but tempered with eyes that age could not wither. His thinning hair, wispy and white fluttered in the cool air that breezed through the passage. He breathed slowly in, then out and reached once more for his plain stick. The faintest smile crossed his face as the heavy door began to open. There was always hope of another he thought and shuffled into the room.

The guard could not be seen who stood behind the door but he heard his heavy footsteps as he moved to seal the exit behind him. The chamber was over sixty foot in length and its ceiling stretched up to the very top of the university itself. They had always met here, long before Gru-Staedak had walked within these walls. The chamber had been forged as part of the original building under the instruction of its founder MonPellia. The first of the true Scholatic.

Time had taken a toll on many parts of the university but the chamber was just as it had been all those years ago, magnificent as it was cold and forbearing. The old man reached within the confines of his heavy robes, pulling from a long pocket a small book. It was bound in copper and upon the cover was set a tiny symbol. It had no text or writings on either back or front.

He approached two guards who wore the cloaks of the Council Protectorate. They were armed with long swords which one held in the left hand, the other in the right, standing close enough together that the tips of the blades crossed on the stone floor. The guard on his left held out his hand and the old man placed the book upon it, the cover was opened then closed and passed to the second guard.

The process was repeated and the book returned to its bearer. Both men moved their arms from the floor and parted, ushering the man into the centre of the chamber. In great contrast to the rest of the bare and empty hall, the central area was richly adorned with a hexagonal table. It was crafted from a dark wood with heavy legs at its base, supporting a ten inch thick top that was covered with a hide stretched about its corners. The great rivets that held the material in place were of copper, each bearing a shining jewel within.

About the six sides were tall backed chairs, forty seats in total, seven graced each of the five sides that were nearest to him. The final side at the top of the central chamber had only five, similar in every way to the others with exception to a dyed red covering of leather pulled about the back.

He walked around the table, acknowledging those who were already seated with a nod or an occasional smile. Finally he came to the side on the right nearest to the five and sat between two others cloaked in a similar fashion to himself. He rested his stick upon his lap and turned to face the central seat where the five sat. Upon that focal chair sat a tall wiry framed man, he too wore robes, but his were of a deeper hue, a dark blue, almost black in the poor light of the chamber.

His hood was pulled back and revealed a determined face, concentrated eyes that scanned the table continually, seeking out information and above all knowledge. Allowing the final arrivals to sit, he rose to his feet and addressed the council.

"May those that sit now do so in the grace of knowledge and enlightenment." He stretched his arms out in a semicircle to encompass the audience. "I must first offer apologies for two of our number," he said pointing to the empty seats, one opposite him at the other end and another on the side of the old man, "Lamentor is unwell and bound to his Asten house, DeFache is extremely busy with urgent matters at the High Council's request and so has been given leave from this meeting."

A few murmurs went up from the council, sickness was one thing but they were all hard pushed at their universities, why was DeFache any different. The man, pushed his hands downwards to calm the voices, "Let us move directly on to matters of this calling. We have gathered on this day, because word has reached the Highs of a great danger in Vedian. No simple enemy, or issue of state is this of which I speak. Yet it is a danger that could threaten all of the lands. While I have little doubt that many of you know the tale of which I must recount here, I offer no apologies in telling it again. For to truly understand this peril, we must once again give reference to 'The Days Of Impurity'.

Much head turning and shuffling came from the council members, some staring at colleagues, others dropping their heads in acknowledgement of the tale about to be told.

"I do not tell this tale lightly and I only voice it here away from the soft minds of the common man, for in this it is he and his brethren that I do feel most sorry for. Yet I your duly elected leader and Head of The High Council am responsible for the charge the Scholatic have been set, and I will not waiver in that purpose as I know it to be right."

From the left hand side nearest the five, a voice came from a middle aged man, "I would not hear this tale again Shel-Toro Master of the Balanced Lore. Did we not ensure many years ago the end to this saga? Were the writings not lost to the world or burned to ensure such peril does return? What purpose can such recounting serve but remind us of these times?"

The man offered his hands up to the Council Leader. Shel-Toro turned to the man and smiled, nodding at the words, "I more than any, would have it another way venerable SanPollan. I respect your words in this matter and all around should pay homage to your intellect, yet I fear there is no other course for us, to ensure we are of one mind in the dealing of this peril."

SanPollan acknowledged his leader and bowed his head, he grinned to himself knowing it would not be long now before his place within the highs was ensured.

"Shel-Toro continued his address, "We must go back many years now to find these times. We can not recount their source and no text will tell of them, many philosophies have been considered but those are for another day. Within the council at this time, a few years after its original leader had passed to the earth, a keen and ambitious young man was in residence. He had proved himself within the 'Pulpit' and progressed quickly into the council proper.

While criticism could be given to its then highs, I will not spend the time to do that here. Years had passed without great incident until reports began to arrive at the council of Pionor Saban's teachings. It was being rumoured that Saban had strayed from the path of schooling and had been offering his time to the common man. Some had even said that he had employed some of them within his classes under the disguise of manual labourers.

Disturbed by this news, the Council sent word to Saban to attend an emergency meeting at Pluris, within these very walls. Here he was questioned and officially warned to stay clear of any such future gossip. Yet the rumours did not depart and indeed turned to clear fact when some of Saban's writings were presented to the Council by worried members. Within them they talked of the common man's need for teaching and ideas relating to man's own philosophy. Clearly he had passed beyond the council's aide and there recourse was to call him once again. This time Saban did not in any way attempt to deny his actions, instead addressing the members and actively promoting his views.

A vote was taken and Saban became the first and only member in its history to be sent down. His title and his belongings were not only taken away but he was dismissed from the Scholatic. Removed from the race he was born into and left to reside with those he sought to corrupt. Yet the council was ill advised in this matter, for this only angered Saban and turned him to darker pursuits. He forged his own cult, to be known as the Saban Monks, they were made from the common man and he went about teaching them and learning them beyond their control. He rallied many to his impure cause and his followers erected a school which he called a monastery, and he labelled it 'the School for Believers'. Intimating that any could attain the highest peaks of scholarship if their belief was true.

These lies and half truths had to be stopped before the infection spread through man's easily led race. Finally the council took a definite action, calling upon the Protectorate to attack the building and end this terrible tyranny once and for all. It was clear for all the Scholatic to see that Saban would drive down man into a well trodden path of destruction and despair were they to attain the teachings which he offered. They would fight amongst themselves once more, warring and killing until none remained!", Shel-Toro's voice echoed through the chamber, he was animated now, his eyes wide and hands clenched.

"The Council planned to capture Saban and thereby leave his followers without direction, they would return to their flock and forget quickly of these perilous lies. Yet no one was prepared for what they faced. Some ancient arts had been studied by the followers, the power to control the mind and even spirit summoning it was said. The Protectorate was massacred, only a few escaped to tell of the ghastly events that befell them on that dreadful day. Our Captain now," he turned motioning to a man that stood in the far corner of the chamber, his face obstructed in the light, only his chain mail could be seen reflecting off the candles, "he is the only true descendent of the Protectorate of old because of Pionor Saban."

Shel-Toro turned again to face the council, his voice now dropping to a whisper that remained piercing in its tone, "Then as the Council began to amass their defences with the King, for fear of an attack on Pluris itself, Saban and his followers vanished. The monastery was found empty, left with only the blood stains of the Protectorate as proof that life was ever there. No follower was ever found, though many believe they just went back to their homes, fearing Saban had indeed gone mad. Saban himself was never found but stories and rumours were rife of his demise. I am but a simple man at heart, I do not attempt to understand why he disappeared when he did, I hope...perhaps, that he saw the true future that faced the common folk and something within himself could not bring them to that terrible end. That is what I hope."

Shel-Toro slumped down into his chair and for a moment sat silently with head in hands before once again resuming.

"You all know the events that came after. We tried to ensure all teachings and writings were laid bare from Vedian. That no trace of this matter ever arose to trouble our fair country again, we were forced to burn all texts in reference to this period and set to the fire everything that had been built in his name. Banished was he from ever existing on the Vedian lands, wiped from its history a name that would stick in the throat of even the oldest bard. We thought our task done. How wrong we were my friends."

Once more Shel-Toro erupted from his chair, his tall frame leaping away from the table and coming to rest behind the tall wooden seat. Resting his hands on its back he stared solemnly at them all, "An item has surfaced, an artifact of the old days. It is said that one who is strong of will and blessed in the ways, can see days of yesteryear within its aura. I have heard of such an item but until now never truly believed it existed.

The texts suggest that such an artifact can bear the characteristics of its creator. This item, this cursed throwback to a savage age, it could reveal too much to those that are not ready for its knowledge. We can not allow this to happen and we will not!"

His final words dropped like stones on the chamber floor, resounding and unyielding. "The recovery of the artifact must be made with caution and in secrecy, we do not wish to draw unnecessary attention to the issue. I will ask our Captain to send for some able men, to assist in the relocation of the item, if it is the councils wish."

A brief vote was taken and and behind Shel-Toro, in the alcove of the chamber, the shadows shimmered and the Captain departed to carry out his sworn duties. He did not wait to confirm the details, he already knew the word had been given. The Protectorate was no simple military gaggle, it was a unit formed through bloodline and maintained through sacrifice, he would carry out the orders and he would never question them. It had been his destiny to carry out the duties of the council, as did his fathers before him. He did not consider actions to be right or wrong, he did not consider them at all. Yet for the first time in many years, he relished the task to be undertaken here, the Saban Monks had laid bare his people for many generations. He would send enough men to ensure the deed was done on the road or if that failed at its final destination in Asten.

Shel-Toro continued, his manner urgent still, "Go now and research in your private libraries. Discover any information that may shed light on the origin of the artifact, I have placed with each of you the details my informants have gathered so far. Do not speak of this to anyone. The fate of the common man may lie in your hands, do not forsake him, do not condemn him to the fate of Saban"

He motioned to the assembly that the meeting was ended and they ushered from their seats, whispering and muttering, some to each other, some to themselves as they walked from the chamber. The old man raised up his stick and began to take leave of the ancient hall, his mind was troubled now and he knew something must be done. If only DeFache was here, he thought, he would know what action to take. His limbs ached and his joints creaked, the cold air of the chamber infested his body. The tale had been known to him, he had heard it told many years before, but not entirely as it was told here. Key factors had been amended and some parts left untold. He wished to return to the sanctity of his university and consider the matter at greater length as was his way. A voice came upon him as he turned to leave, "Stay now Gru-Staedak, the Highs would speak with you." The tone was instructional and cold and he turned to see Shel-Toro sitting again between the other four men.

"What matter would we speak of Master of the Balanced Lore?" The old man was not comfortable, warning signs raised hairs on the back of his neck, yet he ignored them.

"You know that we do not hold rumours and gossip in high place at this table. Yet words have reached us and their content has the highs worried." The men about him nodded in agreement.

"It is said that you have been witnessed conversing within University boundaries with the common man, it is also said that the matter of these discussions were philosophy related. We also hear that your writings give mention to the 'purity of man'? You must surely understand our fear in this matter?" The council leader did not move, neither did his eyes ever leave Gru-Staedak, his gaze locked like an arrow on its target, watching and waiting for the kill shot.

"I fear you have been misled. The context of my writings too has been misconstrued, I feel it is a minor misunderstanding, I can assure the Council such matters should be of little concern." The

32

old man smiled, yet he knew what was to follow, it was inevitable DeFache had told him in their last heated meeting. They had sat within the walls of the Sanctuary of Bridges at DeFache's University, discussing and debating as they had for many years. DeFache had talked as he always did of balance through non-interference, just as MonPellia had many ages before. But it had felt right, all this time, these long years of teaching and philosophising, for the first time he had felt what he was doing was right, the common man had a right to realise his potential, not to be dictated to by self serving politicians. It had not always been like this, the council had been a source of wisdom and guidance in years gone, but things had changed more recently, new members had been installed who's lore followed that of Shel-Toro's. He and DeFache had been the only voices in opposition to the changes and now DeFache had withdrawn from debate, preferring to stay within his own halls disillusioned with the councils new policies.

The High's stood as one man, Shel-Toro held a hand out and addressed Gru-Staedak in a formal tone, "We cannot take this offering, we will not accept these words. The mistakes of our forefathers are lessons to be learned, not actions to be repeated. In respect of your long service to the council, we do not cast you down old man. You are dismissed from the Council of Lore and as such may no longer teach at the University of Asten. Yet your place in the Scholatic will stay and you may continue residence until your death. We will not allow another cult arising in our lands, the people do not deserve such poor leadership."

Gru-Staedak withdrew the small book from his robe and placed it in the palm of Shel-Toro's outstretched hand, "Perhaps you are right, to dismiss me Shel-Toro, for old I must be. I thought the Scholatic was birthed to guide men, not to rule them."

The back of the inn was lit solely by the light that escaped the long tavern windows. Arn, Joseph and Speck sat on driftwood logs around a makeshift table. Though they could have sat inside, and sometimes they did when there was a good song or tale to hear, something brought them back to the spot where they had been forced to sit when deemed too young by the tavern master. The three drank deeply from the clay mugs of black ale that was brewed in the large barn behind the tavern.

"My round.", noted Speck.

"I can get them if you like Speck, I got a bonus from the captain.", offered Joseph. He often worried about how the other boy got by, his mother made so little and Speck himself only got occasional work writing notes for the village council and a few merchants.

"I said it's my round!", erupted the boy, quickly standing and marching in a black mood through the back door of the tavern.

Arn leaned toward Joseph and said in a low tone, "Next time try - 'Speck I'm feeling good, I got a bonus and we should all get drunk on me!', you'll spare that fearsome pride the lad has."

Joseph nodded knowing that Arn was right, as he invariably was in matters of diplomacy. His own straight-forward approach didn't always work. When he looked up from his brooding he saw a familiar grin spread across the hunter's face. "Ral's coins?", offered Arn.

Ral's coins was a common tavern game, taking it's name from a legend in which a thief won back his freedom from a demon king by playing him at the game. The tale goes that the cut-purse and the beast played with jewels but for obvious reasons coins or stones were used in the bar version. Two lines of ten coins were laid out and the players had to remove the coins from the table and drop them into a cup one at a time. If a player is fast enough he can get ahead of the opponent, slap his hand over the others and he wins. If all twenty coins get into the two cups then the coins are laid out again and the players continue until someone wins. Arn was the village champion at the game and rarely lost a match, in fact few ever got past the eighth coin before they felt the weight of his hand on theirs.

"I'd like to keep some of that bonus. I was thinking of buying a gift for someone with it."

"I'll play." Came a feminine voice carried by the night air.

Arn looked out into the dark and replied, "Step up to our table then my beauty!"

Joseph peered out to see who had called but could not make the figure out, until to his surprise, Febra stepped into the circle of light from the tavern windows. Her ragged dress came down just below her knees and a wide leather belt was wrapped around her waist, it was quite obviously made for a man several times her size since she was forced to wind the tongue back around and tuck it in. The belt had telltale slots cut into it for dagger sheaths but being empty they just added to the peculiar look of the girl. She sat down at the table and cocked her head to one side, seemingly weighing up Arn with a lascivious look.

"What's the stake then?", she asked.

"I think a copper would make it interesting,", Arn sidled into his tavern entertainment style, "pick your own ten stones and we'll let the fun begin."

Whilst the girl was wandering around finding ten suitable stones, Speck emerged from the inn grasping three large mugs. An unabashed look of disgust crossed his face when he saw the orphan girl.

"I see we're letting the riff-raff join us now are we?"

"That's quite enough from you Speck, bring that beer over and we'll start our little match of Ral's coins between myself and the lass." Speck's face lit up at the prospect of watching the girl thrashed by the hunter and plopped himself into a seat, waiting for the action to begin. Febra sallied back to the table and laid down ten round bean sized pebbles, Arn nodded in appreciation, had she selected smaller or larger stones than her ability to get a swift grip on them would have been impaired. It was all to do with the relative size of the stone to the players hands, as the demon king in the legend had discovered to his cost.

"Money on the table?", chimed Speck.

"I'm good for the money", glared the dark-eyed girl.

"Good. Ah yes, we often go about taking the word of unemployed village skullies for sums of money - even the well-off round here have so little, where are you going to scrape up money? Or perhaps you weren't thinking of earning or lending eh? Perhaps you were thinking of lifting the coin from some passer-by?"

"That is enough Speck!", Joseph raised his voice in an uncharacteristic show of anger. He immediately felt strange about the outburst but continued, "We're all here for a bit of entertainment. Her word is good until she breaks it OK?"

Speck mumbled darkly to himself but stayed quiet, if the truth be told even he was feeling a little guilty about the way he had talked to the girl. That was Speck's way though, the anger took him first, then the brain kicked in to tell all the minute details of what he had done wrong.

"Ready hand.", Joseph commanded. Arn had laid out ten stones of similar size to the ones Febra had chosen from the ground, the only difference was that these were a little more consistent in size and that Arn had grown sentimental about them and carried them in his pocket wherever he went.

Following Joseph's instruction both players held their hands hovering over the first stone, just far enough away to be certain that they weren't touching it.

"Go."

The stones dropped into the cups with phenomenal speed, and though the expectant crowd of two watched for the usual slap of Arn winning the game, it never came. The pair finished at precisely the same time and as each dropped in their last stone their eyes locked on each others in a maniacal competitive glare. For long moments the staring match continued between the two, each waiting for a telling reaction from the other. Slowly in a kind of mental truce, both broke into a composed grin.

"Well then.", said Arn.

"Well indeed.", responded Febra.

"It seems we shall have to set them out again if I am to claim my copper off you."

"It is I who would be claiming it off you I think. But I confess, you are quite quick." The girl grinned at Arn, her eyes widening like saucers. "I always give a worthy opponent the pleasure of my smile before knocking them in the dirt." This made Arn break into a cackle, this young slip was beginning to impress him. As he reached for the cup to pour his stones back on the table, Febra's hand covered it.

"Before we play again perhaps you and your friends here would like to hear a proposition I have. A venture that might require men with quick hands."

Arn glanced at the other two, who both gave unhelpful shrugs. Frankly the scully girl with a shady scheme was a little bit out of their experience. Arn turned back to Febra.

"Let's hear about it then."

"I could see you were the kind that cottons on quick to a good thing. I have won the bid on a real jewel of a job, the pay is excellent and the risk minimal but I need to get together a party of four to pull it off."

"It isn't illegal is it?", inquired Speck.

"It is quite legal!", Febra sounded genuinely annoyed, "this task has been hired out by the nobles of the dukedom through the traditional auction. I have the mandate for it. As well you know I suspect, for I saw you there earlier today. Now, do you want in?"

"How much is our cut?", this comment from Joseph surprised Arn a little, as in all the time he had known the fisher boy he had always been unconcerned about profit and such. Joseph however had suddenly thought of the Dusk Returner and wondered just how much it would cost for a winter refit.

"You would receive 20 copper pieces each, and all that for just a few weeks work, a month at the outside."

Even the hunter looked marginally impressed by the figure. Twenty copper over a month or sooner outstripped what any of them could make in that time. It sounded too good to be true.

"The auction gives better money for more dangerous missions I've heard.", said Arn defensively.

"Not this one, it's an academic mission. All it requires is care. You look like a man who could care well about something. I'm afraid the cut might have to go down a few copper's though because we may have to hire a scribe."

At this the three faces on the other side of the table from Febra mysteriously lit up and Speck spoke in a vague manner, "A scribe you say?

The young lad leant back into his seat and folded his hands behind his head, "Perhaps I know of such a man. A quite brilliant young theologian, a perennial master of lore, some say."

"Who is this man? I would meet with him, tell me of him now." Febra's eyes widened again at the chance to fulfil her quest.

A long arm came out and pushed Speck, he toppled unceremoniously from the stump landing on the sawdust laden floor below. The perpetrator piped up, "What this silly young fellow is trying to say, is that he can help you. There is no lore master in these parts and for that we are all the more pleased. Yet in essence he speaks the truth, he does know of words and books, though I for one have warned him against such. Yet I would say Febra, he can help you." Joseph would have continued but instead found himself staring into the girls eyes, dreaming of far off hopes.

Speck dusted himself down and snarled at Arn, who had found the whole matter of great amusement and was still laughing hard.

"Why a scribe though scully?" he said in a terse tone, "You were correct, we did see the auction on the afternoon, there was no mention of a scribe. What requirement could you have for one, I wonder?"

Febra ignored his tone and spoke as pleasantly as she was able, in the knowledge that his kind were hard to come by, "Within the words that were passed with the quest, they say that three and one are required to travel..."

Speck butted in "Yes, yes we heard all this, but what of the scribe silly girl."

Febra's face was turning scarlet and she was not used to holding her tongue, yet she needed this task for her longer term plan, so taking a deep breath she continued, "As I said, three and one, the one specified as a scribe. Apparently the item to be collected must be verified by identification. Certain inscription within the item must be read and married with the scroll I have been given."

Speck grinned and spoke in a voice like he had heard the merchants from Pluris use, "Well girly, that is of interest indeed. Yet I must ask, how did you read such words when clearly you cannot?"

That was the final insult, Febra stood up and shouted at all of them, "Old Man Talon read for me, if you must know. Now I have run short of patience. To journey we need supplies, I have an advance to pay for some, we may need to acquire the rest. I will wait at the market square at dawn tomorrow, if you are there, we will all make good coin, if you are not I will go alone."

Her face was crimson with anger, the three opposite her sat back in there seats, stung by the ferocity of her words. Then in a swift move, she leant over the table and clumsily planted a kiss on Joseph's cheek. She then turned on her heels and began to leave for the road, as she turned the corner she shouted back, "At least the dreamy fool, may accompany me now!"

Arn's belly ached with laughter, clearly the girl had no experience in the art of affection and her recipient was none the better. Poor Joseph had frozen to the spot and hardly moved long after Febra had departed the scene. He slapped Joseph on the back, "Come now my friend, it was but a little wound, you will heal in time. I will fetch more ale to calm your nerves."

As Arn left, the smile dropped from his lips and his mind turned to thoughts of the offer. He did not need the copper, he earned fair wage assisting with the hunts and soon his father would retire and he would take over as master. It was a good and respectable position, he should have been glad, yet he felt a longing. A longing that he had not seen enough or done enough, the felt that from the moment he was born the pattern of his life had been decided for him.

His father was a fair man, but rarely a gentle one. He demanded much and Arn had worked hard, yet he wished just once that he could turn to him and say 'no'. Just for a moment to be his own man, that would be worth more than all the copper in Vedian. Perhaps his father would grant him a leave of absence to take up the task. No, he was fooling himself, his father did not like straying from the plains that surrounded the Luff, he did not see why there was need to do so. Arn had heard of towns like Pluris and Kanegon but he could only envisage them in his mind from the tales that were told by firelight. Now to have the chance to witness the great site of Bannermane, it was too much to turn away. This would be his final chance, by the next summer he would have to take up his duties full time, it must be now.

He ordered the tankards from the bar and leant against a central pole. He would go on this quest and he would be damned if his father would deny him this opportunity. He would return in ample time to take over the hunt, no harm would be done. He would take a beating for sure, but the old man wasn't as strong as he used to be, it would be worth it.

He collected the ale and walked back outside to their seats, his resolve was set, he would take the quest and he already knew Joseph would come with him. The boy was smitten, he would follow the girl into a blazing fire and scarcely feel the flames, he was not the problem here. He sat down and offered an ale to Speck, "So young word master, what a fabulous opportunity this must be for you."

Speck looked at the hunter curiously, "In what way Arn?"

"This is your chance Speck. The chance to get a name for yourself in the eyes of the village, to gain respect. A scribe and translator who visits Bannermane and perhaps even Asten University would surely be held in high esteem by the assembly. You would be, a sort of ambassador of the Luff, a statesman wandering from town to town, spreading your skills to the nobler men."

The small boys eyes lit up, "Yes, yes. You could be right, I will show them all, I will bring books to the Luff and they will thank me for it. In time perhaps I will be asked to join the Scholatic."

Joseph awakened finally from his fixation, turned to Speck, "You can not be invited in like it was a party Speck, you have to be born into the Scholatic, you know that. I ask you, who would want that, it is said that they do not work but sit and think for days on end, whoever heard of such strangeness. Do not veer too far from your roots Speck, you are different I grant and I respect you for it, but you are still of the Luff, be proud to be so."

Speck spoke quietly, "Should I be proud of the taunts and beatings, proud of the way they look at me from across the path? Am I proud of the way my mother is regarded and treated in the village? Perhaps born of the Luff I am, but not proud to be so. If I am proud it is because I call you friend, that is all and nothing more"

He turned to Arn, "I will go on this quest, not for money or for the Luff, or indeed for fame but I will go for friendship."

Arn stood up, "Then my comrades it is decided, for I too would wish to travel for my own reasons. So the girl has her three and one."

Joseph turned his head from side to side, looking at both men, "Why has no one asked if I will go, are you not be presumptuous?"

Arn smiled at Speck and he grinned back at the hunter, "I think good Joseph," Arn offered whimsically, "that we already know your mind in this matter. For it clearly is being controlled by something other than your head."

Joseph blushed and nodded, he would go and bring back money for Pike and the refit, he would make his father proud. Yawning, Arn began to start the trek south to his home, "Don't forget, dawn tomorrow at the market, the girl is right, we will need plenty of supplies, the wilderness will not be a hospitable land past the plains I think."

"What will we meet out there Arn," Speck shouted after him, "are there beasts and enemies to fear? I do not worry you understand, yet I would like to know."

The hunter shouted back, "You read to many tales, young master. Sleep soundly and do not be troubled by beasts or foes. Heat and drought are the travellers greatest enemy. Goodnight friends, rest in the arms of the Luff."

Arn wandered down the winding path thinking to himself, rest soundly my friends for the Luff will not protect us out there and a hot sun will doubtfully be the greatest of our hurts.

Chapter 3 - Unrest In The Council

'Earlier in this work, we looked at some examples of my predecessors attitudes towards the theory of balance within Vedian society. I do not believe that such masterful scholars as these would contest the principle of symmetry in nature. Therefore I go so far to take that as given, in the hope that all before me would have me do so.

So if we are to believe that the common man and his brothers whom claim home to Vedian's shores, are to flower through achieving this stability, we must next ask ourselves a simple but inextricably difficult question.

At What Cost?

To answer this we must first look into the past to discover the price of man's self-regulation. Prior to the birth of the Scholatic, it is well documented that man warred within his homeland. Fighting not only with external races but more often with his own. Our precious world was brought close to extinction and such examples as the poisoning of the tree soil which has created our current wood shortage or the demise of the Huskian race is proof of this fact.

MonPellia himself realised that man would quickly self destruct if he was not aided by a more learned body. So the decision was taken to begin creating a new race. A people able to understand the limits of man and help him to ensure he does no further harm to himself. Over generations the Scholatic have stayed pure as a race to allow us to grow our philosophy, for the good of all Vedian's peoples.

Yet for all our knowledge and for all our hard work and guidance, the truth is simply that man continues failing himself. I understand that some of my learned brothers do not wish to openly admit to this failing and as a scholar myself I fully understand their stance in this matter. It is never easy to say that we have not fulfilled our potential or to admit our mistakes in the building blocks of our understanding. Now though, as the newest Master of the High Council I feel I must speak out before all is too late. It is clear that we do not wish or attempt to be rid of good deeds or foul. For these are within all men, but what we must ensure is that the scales are not tipped too heavily in favour of either.

Society is growing lawless, man has lost respect for himself and all others. We are drifting into a void of danger, our guidance has failed to bring man from its dark walls. So what must we do I have asked myself? Time and again I have returned to the only possible answer. Yet in its nature, I find it in opposition to some of the greatest minds of an age, even MonPellia himself. Perhaps, I then surmised, it is not in opposition to their thinking but just a further step that they did not take. Perhaps because in their time it did not need to be taken, but I know now, it must. If the child will not be guided from the dark by a helping hand, then he must gripped firmly and led. For if he does not, he will surely fall into the abyss that is crafted by his own making.

'The Price Of Achieving Equalisation ' - Shel-Toro - Vedian 985

Madistrin was dwarfed by the room around him, the hearth was half again his height and the massive woven rug that covered the floor of the regal hall made him seem almost child-like. He had learned patience in his role over the years and yet he had never learned to actually enjoy waiting.

Raised in the noble ranks and born into the House of Pluris, he was as powerful and commanding as any man in Vedian. Long illness and fatigue had however taken its toll, too many hours spent discussing politics and administrating matters of state had left him weak.

He was never meant to be the one. His departed parents had known that, his elder brother Laferious should have been the rightful heir. He had fallen by accident from the world. A tournament of arms had ended in disaster over twenty years ago. His brother had been an adept rider and natural warrior, a true man of his people. Perhaps at times he could have been overconfident but he had inspired the hearts of men and that was a small price to pay for such a gift. Tall and elegant, strong with sword and quick to anger, he would have taken up the crown in time, the Council would have made him King. Few had doubted that eventuality. He had always been second to his brother, in the peoples eyes, definitely in his fathers eyes and always in his own. Yet for all the beauty and success, he had loved his brother. He had loved him as a child and as a man; never envying his talents or finding jealousy in his natural social grace. He did not harbour this love because his brother protected him or looked after him but because he had done what no other had, treated him as an equal.

Laferious had never offered him quarter, never held back his skill in tournaments. Madistrin had lost to him time and time again over the years, but his brother had never looked to his illness or weaknesses as an excuse to dishonour him. He had treated him as any other soldier, as any other man and that had ensured Madistrin's eternal love. Laferious had fallen under his mount on the tournament, the beast had inexplicably become panicked and threw it's rider, he was trampled on the field. He remembered his brother looking up at him as the last breath of life escaped from his broken lungs. There had been no remorse, no pity.

Vedian had mourned the loss of his brother for many years and the role of Crown Prince had passed to him for a new cycle of five years. Upon such time the Council would decide the legitimacy of his leadership for King.

Three times the cycle had come and gone, still the council refused his petition for Kingship, as was their right. So Vedian continued to be run regionally by its nobles and at its centre by the Council in agreement with himself. Madistrin smiled to himself, in truth he had no power over Vedian and little say within the Council. They ensured he was kept busy with small matters of state in Pluris, issues of taxes and levies. He had given up ever fulfilling the role, believing as the nation did that he was never meant to be King.

The office had died with his brother and the Council now controlled Vedian. For many years he had thought this to be a fair decision, the high Scholatic had members of great distinction and respect. Men like Gru-Staedak and Umberto DeFache he held in the highest regard but times were changing, new faces had entered the Council and the election of Shel-Toro as the new Lore Master had troubled him deeply.

He paused his nervous pacing and slumped down into the long seat that seemed scaled to fit the hall. The warmth of the soft fabric made him feel sleepy and he pulled his legs upwards. His strength was ailing, his coughing had worsened this year and the accursed heat played havoc with his breathing. He was not old, only forty two in years but sickness had withered him showing a man twenty years more advanced. He moved with aide of a stick whilst in his halls but not in front of the people. He often walked amongst them, even dressing in their plainer garb, shunning the robes of office.

They loved him, as he was a fair and kind man, who legislated well and made few enemies. He was a friendly face, not a warrior or King like Laferious but a good man none the less. They would bow and curtsey, though he had often asked them not to, he had gained their respect through his service and actions but they were not moved by him. He had thought that he would drift on quietly in life, slowly slipping away as the sickness took him, hoping that no one thought ill of him after he was gone.

Two years ago, a rising level of disorder had come to his attention.

Thieves and bandits had entered Pluris, some said they came from Kanegon others said it was the Huskian's from the south. A plague had begun to slowly work its way into Vedian, in more recent months he had sent loyal scouts out to the other towns to seek reports of this activity. They had returned with similar stories, raids of caravans were rife and lawlessness had grown throughout Vedian. He could not persuade himself that these events were unconnected. He had requested audience with the council, finally receiving their ear at the third time of asking. He had sent his personal guard the last time to ensure they understood the urgency of the matter. Shel-Toro had listened as always, sympathetic and patronising in equal measures.

"Do not fret yourself, my fair Prince. We are aware of these matters, though we offer you great thanks as always for bringing them to our attention. Be assured that if this small rabble continues to trouble the good people of Vedian then we will guide your subjects to end the situation. Yet, I feel it is but a passing phase, it will surely blow over and peace will again bless our land for many more years. Rest now Crown Prince for you look pale and I speak for all the council when I say that we would fear for your health. Why don't you leave this matter in our capable hands?"

Yet after he had departed the Council chamber and left the walls of the University Gru-Staedak had approached him, warning of

45

dangers that may lie ahead. Asking Madistrin to not abandon his post or his people in the hour of their need. The words had given new life to him, he had begun on a covert plan to ascertain consistent updates of matters all around Vedian.

Sending those that were loyal to seek out information and return it to him. For the first time he had felt as though he could earn the role passed to him by his brother. The pain had dulled his strength but never his mind. He began to learn more history of the land and had grown in understanding of Vedian's past. He nestled his head further into the softness of the cloth, the time for action was nearing now and he would need all his strength for the hard days ahead.

As sleep took him images began to form in his mind, he dreamt of an army of riders standing atop a hill looking down on the plains beyond. Behind them stood a great fortress and at its crest a lone tower flying a flag. He could see in his mind the crest of the King of Vedian upon the banner as it fluttered in the wind. As a deeper slumber took him, his final impression was of the horses departing from the hill, not together but each moving separately away from the tower.

Darkness took him and the dreams departed.

Febra crouched under the cover of the fish market stall, she had become accustomed to the stench and hardly noticed it now. Others often brought it to her attention, though she did not care. She had survived too many hard years in the town to be upset by a few churlish words.

She hummed to herself, rocking backwards and forwards as the rain fell hard on the stall above, dripping water down onto her bare toes. It had rained most of the night, a heavy downpour not uncommon this far north in Vedian, the weather would often change from dry and humid to wet especially this time of year.

The marketplace was her home, sometimes she had shared it with others but most of the time she was alone. She survived because she had the will too. In the early years she had relied on scavenging from the traders, some had caught and beaten her, but not all. Comlay the fishmonger had ignored her stealing for years, not even complaining when he arrived early morning finding her asleep under his stall. He had no children of his own and he felt sorry for the girl, often he had thought of taking her in to his own home but the town rules were strict and he was not a rash man, merely a kind one.

Comlay was rather the exception than the rule, most treated her with contempt and as she grew older she encouraged their attitudes. She did not hate them, not as individuals anyway. Yet she was angry, sometimes so full of it that she thought she might burst. As she grew older she began to channel that anger, finding a focus that allowed her to carry on surviving in the Luff.

Her mother had died at childbirth, she had learned that much from Old Man Talon and her father had abandoned her, choosing to leave the Luff and orphan her to its care. In all the years that passed he had not returned to claim her, or seek out news of her well being. He simply had left her to a life of sorrow and hardship. So she began to hate him, a little more each day. More with each drop of rain that chilled her and every hand that beat down upon her.

Then as she neared adulthood, she took the anger and realised that she could mould it into revenge. The girl knew he was alive, somewhere, she just knew it. She began to ask questions, taking tasks she could get, for money and for the chance to meet with outlanders. She exchanged her favours for information with husbands far from home on trading business. Mostly she discovered nothing and was left with only her own rage for company.

Last season a man had come to the Luff, a sailor from Kanegon trading wood with the tavern master. He had stayed at the Inn and Febra had found opportunity to offer herself to him, he was a disgusting burly man, cold and spiteful and yet she had not really noticed. Her intent was focused on the one question, where was her father?

The sailor, whose name she could not remember, if she had ever known it, told her of a man that had come to Kanegon and worked the boats through the Straights of Reslin. The dates seemed correct and the man's age, also a rough description seemed to tally with the information she had gleaned from Talon.

Knowing she would need assistance in Kanegon, she had hatched the plan to recruit some local help to see her to her goal. She knew exactly what the boy Joseph thought of her, he was easy to ply to her will but she knew he would not be enough on his own. So she had devised a strategy, a quest that paid money which few could turn down in the Luff. A simple test of their mettle and to gain their loyalty, then if all went well she would move them on to her true goal.

If she cared for them she was unaware of it, they were a means to an end. She bore them no love or hate, she seemed empty to such emotions where people were concerned.

Her eyes looked down at the gutted orndyke that lay in the crate next to her, the small beady eyes staring back at her, she fell asleep glimpsing her own reflection.

Arn sighted the two boys as they reached the top of the road, he shouted out to them and they paused for him to catch up. Dawn was upon the Luff and the market traders were readying for the early trade, carts were parked all around, offloading goods that had arrived overnight.

"Sleep well?", Arn questioned as he approached.

"No," Speck grumbled, "blasted rains kept me awake half the night."

"Excellent!" Arn smiled, "You will no doubt be a natural wilderness camper my small friend."

Joseph motioned the others to carry on, shaking his head at Arn as Speck continued to mumble and complain about this and that.

They sighted Febra purchasing provisions from the butchers stall, she was arguing with one of the brothers, Herm by the looks of it, Joseph thought.

He had never got on well with the butchers' boys. They were a troublesome pair at best and often had picked on Speck in their younger days. Febra had a heavy backpack upon her shoulders and she removed it to slip in the cuts of meat after finally settling on a price. Joseph almost thought he saw a smile on her face as she saw the three of them approach.

"Right", the girl instructed motioning to Arn, "you are in charge of weaponry. Joseph, you take the little one and purchase camping equipment. I have provisions and herbs already."

Speck drew himself up to his full height, keeping a careful eye on Herm who was leaning against the stall eyeing him, "Perhaps we should inspect these wares if we are to survive by them, I don't intend to spend the next weeks eating rodents and rotten leaves."

Joseph placed his hand on Specks shoulder, "Come on Speck, Febra knows what she is doing, leave her be. Lets go and find Old Man Talon and purchase stick and tinder. How much do we have to spend?" He glanced at the girl.

"I have one copper for you and two for the hunter, the rest you will have to find yourself. The rest waits at our successful return." She handed the copper to Joseph.

They ambled northwards to seek out the general stalls, leaving Febra and Arn discussing the merits of knifes and spears.

Febra glanced at Joseph, "I hope Old Man Talon is in generous mood, I can not see him parting with all we need for one copper and.." Speck continued talking quietly, "...I have no more coins left to aid us."

"It's ok, I gave most of my wages to mother but I still have a couple of coins left should we need it."

The three stalls at the north of the market were selling a large range of wares for the traveller. Furs and clothing at one and herbs and ointments at the second. The last stall was laden with sticks and cuts of wood of all shades. Behind the trellis stall sat an elderly man, he was bent over his stool as still as a statue, his hands coupled together in his lap gripping a small leather pouch.

"Good morning young fellows," the gravelled voice announced, "what help can an old man be for you today. Something for the mothers kitchen? Or are thy requirements farther afield perhaps?"

He looked up from his perched position and smiled at the young men, he had a kindly face streaked with lines and age. His hair was white but thick and hung long over his shoulders, his eyes squinted to focus in on their faces.

Joseph grinned and winked at the old man, "Nout for the kitchen today Talon, we are after a few supplies for a journey. My friend Speck and I are off to find our fortune and become famous throughout the land!" Talon nodded and observed them closely forcing him to squint further.

"No doubt you will find both. The question is will you like what you find? You would do well to take care, the road is hard these days and it will not be easy to travel. You will need wood for fire and to cook." He fumbled through various bundles of sticks, eventually pulling a large bunch out from beneath the stall.

"Here, this wood will light in even the dampest conditions. It is not the bark cut from the lands away, it is Vedian wood."

Speck turned his head and whispered to Joseph, "The old boy's really lost it, there's been no wood in Vedian for hundreds of years."

"Correct young master," Talon smiled at Speck, who turned a scarlet colour, "at least no living wood. This bark was taken from the Forests of Malevolence, of which even those in the Luff have heard I'll warrant." The boys stood in astonishment, the forests Talon spoke of were indeed known to them. Many a time had they been told tales and stories of the forest as children. It was said to be the home of spirits and demons and no man ever visited its borders let alone entered into it. Tales to frighten children Joseph had thought, yet he did not recall ever meeting anyone who had been to the place.

Talon continued, "I purchased these long ago from a traveller, I do not recall his name. I questioned his story at the time but I tested the wood and its properties are true."

He handed Joseph the bundle and then began to rummage in a sack at his side, "You will require a tinder box as well." The boys nodded in unison.

His long fingers retrieved a small silver box, ornately engraved with letters on its face. It was unusual for anything in Vedian to bear letters as few in the land understood them.

"What do the words say Talon, I can not read it, is it Vedian?" Speck peered across the stall trying to get a closer look at the box.

"The language is Vedian but it is very old, older than even I, if such young goats as you can imagine that! The words read 'Free Will' and the box belonged to a pipe smoker I would warrant.

There are still a few leaves crunched in one corner." Talon opened the box and pointed at the contents.

"Free will what?" Joseph asked puzzled by the words.

"Perhaps nothing. I really do not know, not anymore. I have had it for such a long time, yet today seems like as fair a day to part with it as any. Now my payment for such luminary wares." The boys huddled closer together and Joseph jangled the few coins in his pocket.

"One copper piece is my price and not one less!" Talon smiled at them and handed the box to Speck.

Joseph looked at Speck and quickly passed over the copper to Talon that Febra had given him earlier, "Thank you Talon, it is a fair price indeed." Talon nodded, "You thank me now, perhaps one day I will thank you. Now I have other customers, a days work is ahead, move on lads and good journey to you." He waved them off with his long fingers and returned to his perched posture.

They turned to leave but a voice interrupted their exit, "Oh one last thing, I remember his name now. It was Cyrus." Speck turned and blankly looked at the old man, "Should that mean anything?"

"No. I suppose not." Talon replied, "Farewell then, fair luck with you both." Confused the pair ambled back towards the centre of the market to seek out Arn and Febra, the area was busy now and the Luff was bustling with its daily business.

They spied Arn at the arms ring, he was gripping a short spear in one hand and a rope net in the other. The stall was equipped with targets at the rear, they where thick butts, woven from straw standing upon large rocks.

Each were distributed back every twenty paces and prospective purchasers were encouraged to test the wares prior to buying. Arn was lining up the spear for a throw, he drew back his arm and turned his chest so it was facing sideways to his legs which turned to the target. Then he uncoiled and projected the spear forty feet at the second target. It buried deep in the straw, just landing left of centre.

Joseph and Speck applauded loudly as they approached, shouting and cheering so that a few faces close by turned their way.

Arn grinned and motioned them over, "Its weighted too heavily on one side, that's why it landed off centre. Nonetheless, a fair weapon."

"The only thing weighted too heavily to one side is you, huntsman. Too many nights in the tavern no doubt." Speck prodded Arn in the ribs, he found it impossible not to like the fair hunter.

"Perhaps you are right my friend. Now, I have purchased arms for you both, as I notice you did not yet heed my words of yesterday. I hope that you will not have need of them on the road but I will feel better if they are by your side." He turned to face Speck, "For you a knife, conceal it within your robe, it is forged well and is true. It will serve if the need arrives."

Speck took the short blade and tucked it inside his robe, being careful to point the blade away from his body should he choose to sit down.

"For you Joseph a slightly more unusual weapon. I know you are uncomfortable with bearing arms, so I purchased a hook from Comlay and had the smithy bind it to a spear pole. It is an odd tool but I think it will suit you." He handed the crook like weapon to Joseph.

Joseph nodded, "My thanks Arn, I feel more at ease with a sailor's tool than a warrior's."

"Now Febra will meet us outside the tavern, have you explained the journey to your elders?"

They both nodded.

"What about you Arn, what did your father have to say of the journey. I am surprised he was in agreement with your leaving in the middle of the hunt season." Joseph said.

"He has said little to dissuade me. Though I feel that my decision not to inform him may have played a part in that. It is my wish and it is decided, now let us depart."

As they journeyed from the market ambling slowly down the south road, Joseph thought of all the times he had played in the market as a child.

It was always a hive of activity, colour and sound, it held a fond place in his memories. It seemed to Joseph as though things were changing, he had never really wanted anything different from life at the Luff. Yet it was slipping away and he was doing nothing to halt its departure. He reassured himself that the copper earned would go a long way to refitting the Dusk Returner, so he and Pike would sail on for many years to come. In the back of his mind, for the first time in as long as he could remember, he could no longer visualise the serpent he would catch in memory of his father. He tried to focus but the image was no longer there. It disturbed him but regardless he carried on.

As promised Febra was waiting patiently outside the tavern, she was sat upon the ground, with her short legs pointed out in front of her. Her head was tossed back as she breathed in the morning air, catching the sea breeze as it moved across the Luff.

She seemed to Joseph to be a statue of beauty, a timeless siren that called to him. The cotton shirt draped loosely about her, the sunlight revealing the outline of her figure for all to see. For all her ragged appearance and almost boyish looks she had a feminine and nubile figure that even caused Speck to cough and turn his head in embarrassment.

"Ah my good friends, you have returned. I trust all is well with our purchases." The girl offered this as a statement not a question. She sat up and began to divide up the provisions she had purchased earlier.

She smiled, turning to face each of them in turn, "If my manner in any of this has been of upset to you, I am sorry. I was not raised as a lady."

Speck held back the urge to raise an eyebrow.

Febra continued," I would apologise to you most of all Speck. To show my good nature in this matter, I give you now the letters to hold in your keeping. Although you will not need them until we reach Bannermane, I offer them to show my trust and friendship." She pulled out the scroll given to her at the auction and handed it to Speck.

"Thank you." Speck tried to think of something else to say but could not.

Instead he took the scroll and slipped it into his pack, startled and surprised by the girls kind words. He felt somewhat ashamed of his earlier feelings towards her and thought to hold his tongue in the future with matters concerning her.

Arn, short spear in hand and net strapped on his back motioned for them to begin.

"We must follow the south road from the Luff and turn east after we exit its borders. From there the path will be over the Brillmon Plains in a north-easterly direction. We should meet up with the main Pluris to Asten road which we can follow for perhaps another two days march north-west.

It will take us slightly off the more direct route but will be an easier passage I think. From there we must decide to either cross the ravine or take time to go around it to the east. That decision is for another day." The tall hunter adjusted his backpack and prepared to rejoin the path south.

"Where after that Arn? After we cross the waters." Speck asked inquisitively.

Arn turned and replied to the lad, "I am honestly not sure Speck. The direction is generally northwards as I have heard folk tell. Yet I am unsure of exactly the path to follow. Once we pass the waters I suspect it is still another weeks walk, if all goes fair."

Speck asked Febra, checking his tone against any hint of malice, "Did you not seek directions or details from the quest provider?"

"They had little information to give, only as far as the Asten road. I do not think any from the Luff have made the journey. We will trust to our hunters directions." She smiled at Arn warmly leaving Joseph with a strange feeling in his stomach.

As they left to depart, a figure approached from the southern path.

"Now then my boy." The voice boomed at them as it approached.

"You did nay think you would get away without a word to old Pike, did ye?" The stocky sailor came into view, a broad smile crossing his wide lips.

"You know the punishment for mutiny boy! The Dusk Returner will not have traitors in its midst."

Pike grasped Joseph's arms and pulled him close almost squeezing the life from the slim lad.

"I'm sorry Pike, I left word with mother. I did not know how to tell you, so I thought perhaps I could slip off quietly." In truth Joseph was happy to see his Captain, he had wanted to visit him and explain the reasons for his venture but had thought Pike would not accept his aid in repairing the old ship.

"The Goodwoman Caedron explained all Joseph. A young lad needs to stretch his legs on occasion tis sure. And you seem to be keeping good company." he winked at Speck and Arn and smiled at the girl.

"Yet I would not have you leave without my good wishes upon you. Your place will wait on the Returner." The sailor released Joseph from his bear like hug.

"I ask for nothing more." Joseph replied, slapping Pike on the shoulder.

Arn moved forward to address the sailor, "Pike you have met many travellers who journey to the Luff. Do you know the way beyond the ravine to Bannermane? Is there a path that holds a direct route?"

"I'm a sailor Arn, I have little need to know the ways of the land. Yet I have heard of a man that lives to the east of the road as you near the horn of the ravine. I heard stories of him in my youth, he must be old now if he still lives. If you seek him out he may know of a way beyond. Be warned though, it was said he does not treat all travellers kindly, though I do not think he holds malice to any."

"What name does he go by?" Arn asked.

Pike paused trying to recount tales from the tavern long gone, "I think it was Rundell. Yes that's it. He was a soldier by all accounts, a hermit now. He lives alone, cut off from most and I have heard nothing of him since your fathers time Joseph. Yet a man like that may still be alive, he would be skilled in the ways of the land to survive for so long in isolation."

"Thank you Pike. Could I ask but one more favour before I depart?" Joseph looked sincerely at the sailor.

"Of course, anything you require."

"Will you watch over mother while I am away and Specks to if you can. I would feel better if it was so."

The old sailor smiled ruefully, "I shall be getting quite the reputation in the Luff. And at my age too! I will watch over them, do not fear their needs while you travel lads."

They thanked Pike again, Speck shaking him warmly by the hand for what seemed like an age.

As the group departed from the tavern, beginning their exit from the Luff to the south, the sailor watched silently. He knew Joseph's reasons for the trip, Goodwoman Caedron had told him straight. He had wanted to hold the boy from the venture but she had bade him not to do so. Seeing him now, he knew she was right. The boy must make decisions of his own, looking back he had thought that Joseph's father would have done differently. Yet he was not the boys father, he was his friend and as they departed into the morning sun that had risen from the south, he realised he may never see Joseph the boy again. But perhaps the man.

The debate and discussion had ran for so long, that DeFache began to wonder if night had fallen on the city of Pluris. The highs had called him two weeks earlier via a messenger that had arrived at the Sanctuary of Bridges. He had at first been angry, as but a week earlier he had been delivered message that he would not be required at the council moot. That had suited DeFache just fine, he had grown tired of the councils political manoeuvrings. He would be happy to sit quietly in his house teaching his philosophy and guiding those that requested his views. He was not opposed to the council directly only the way in which they went about their tasks. He did not see eye-to-eye with Shel-Toro or many of the highs but he still had friends such as Gru-Staedak within its confines.

Reluctantly he had made the long trip across the harsh waters of Vedian Bay to arrive at Pluris the previous night. He had stayed within the university walls, as did all Scholatic. Early morning he had decided to visit the library at Pluris, spending his time constructively reading some of the newer texts that had spawned over the last decade. For all he loved his own home at the Sanctuary, few sights were more humbling than the largest and most complete library of Pluris. As a child he had not had a fancy for berries or sweet pies, yet if he had he imagined it would have felt like this, to have arrived in a house packed full, all ready for consumption.

Every great purist and philosopher of this and many others ages were there. All written down in the most beautiful scribed lettering, the covers in leather and blocked in gold. Great words had to be presented as such to do them justice, so Shel-Toro often had said. These tomes of knowledge were not works crafted over days or hours. They were discussed and thought carefully over, sometimes taking years or decades to come to print. A great scholar would produce perhaps three texts in a lifetime and be considered prolific.

Subsequently those that scribed the tomes took the time and patience to do justice to the works contained within.

DeFache was not held in sway by ego or fame, within the library there where four volumes of work bearing the insignia 'Umberto DeFache' and yet he paid them no heed, rather spending his time pouring over other masters works or new students that had first tomes available to read. He was a sponge for knowledge and thought, constantly taking in writings of others so as to consider and compare, never too proud to make them part of his own philosophy. He had been one of the Scholatic's great students, an icon of his generation. A brilliant speaker in his time, many could recall his performances as a young man in the Pulpit, the haven for debate and speech in Pluris town square. For years he had actively promoted philosophy working with the council to guide the common man in co-operation with the Crown Prince. Times had changed and as they did DeFache had disappeared from the forefront of Scholatic life and debate. Preferring his home at the Sanctuary of Bridges on the island Imanis off the eastern shores of Vedian.

Everyone had said he would be a high, perhaps the youngest ever but it did not come to pass, he was a respected member of the council nonetheless.

Lately he had been reluctant to share time with his peers, rather spending days in his gardens beautiful grounds that surrounded the University. He would often sit between the plants and the flowers, just thinking and considering, there he was at peace.

The messenger that had arrived more recently had requested his presence at Pluris forthwith. This in itself was not a diplomatic request, the proper etiquette was for them to ask for his presence, never to require it. So he made the trip and found himself called from the library at midday to attend a meeting of select members. One representing each Vedian regional university and the high council themselves.

The debate had centred around the activity of Crown Prince Madistrin, word had reached Shel-Toro of his followers movements throughout Vedian. Some of the Council did not see Madistrin to be any type of threat to the balance of things but the Highs and SanPollan of Coralis argued fervently that he represented a danger to Vedian and its continuity as a stable land.

DeFache had listened, occasionally nodding or shaking his head but never choosing to speak. He was thinking back to his last meeting with Gru-Staedak, his mentor had pleaded him to see the truth of what the council were doing. He did not listen because he did not want too. Now for the first time he was beginning to see for himself that the Council were stepping beyond their boundaries. For the whole period of the gathering he could feel the eyes of Shel-Toro upon him, seeking out his mind on the matters discussed.

Finally the debate died down and Shel-Toro rose to his feet, "It is never easy, to see malice in a child. Especially when he is sick and not long for this world. Yet we can not allow corruption from any quarter, lest it seeps too far into the roots of our land. I more than any wish no harm to Madistrin, up to now he has been a fair and good ambassador for Vedian. Perhaps he is merely misguided in his actions. Let us not be hasty in our action, we will send individuals loyal to the peoples cause to watch over him. To ensure, he is not a danger to himself." Shel-Toro smiled and nodded and one by one the Council nodded back at him. As did DeFache, but he was not thinking of Shel-Toro, the council or Madistrin but Gru-Staedak.

As the meeting broke and each departed from the chamber, unfolding too quickly, he thought. He was not a man of impulse he needed time to cogitate and consider, he believed nothing was more dangerous than action without thought.

The library was quiet as always, within in its tall ceilings was held a pungent smell of knowledge. He had always identified it as such, the scent of leather and parchment, ink and dye. All rolled together in the air, giving DeFache a tangible feeling of being surrounded by wisdom. It offered him comfort. He sat in the deeply padded leather chair, sinking so far into its comforts he hardly noticed the figure sitting opposite him, smiling back.

"Rill Fortuna I did not see you there. It is good to see you in such good health." DeFache smiled and touched his own brow. It was a sign of honour that all Scholatic shared.

"It is no bad thing to be lost in thought. That is what this place is all about. But I would step quickly from gracious talk and onto more sober matters." Fortuna's brow was pulled tight over his brown eyes.

"Your tone is serious indeed Lore Giver, I implore you to deliver the information that clearly vexes you." DeFache sat forward in his chair, he knew Fortuna well, the elder was the lead scholar at the Lough University in the south of Vedian. Due to the political circumstance of the Lough Taran currently having no resident noble, Fortuna was also responsible for its citizens welfare.

The position did not sit well with Fortuna, he was a cerebral man not a statesman and he had found the task appointed to him difficult at best.

"It is not my place to discuss issues of the council that they would not have discussed. And yet I find myself seeking your ear. It is said that you have taken in to your house, one that is ordained to stay separate. I would not believe your actions are such, as I deem you as I always have, a purist of our lore." Fortuna shuffled uncomfortably in his seat, his sprawling robes getting caught under his long legs that trailed down below him.

"If I hear rightly you are suggesting that I have taken in a commoner to my University. I am unaware of any such action and would not undermine our laws so flagrantly." DeFache's tone was constant in his speech.

"It is as I suspected Umberto. I would not believe these accusations myself of course. Yet I felt it important to inform you of the suspicion that arises within our walls. They suggest that the individual is a young man of Vedian, it is clear that idle speculation has got the best of our members once again."

Fortuna settled back into his chair, an air of comfort sweeping over his face.

"Young man? They must speak of Samuel Plutaran, he is my Master of Gardens at the University. He is a herb child, no teachings of the lore is he given, he merely resides for convenience." DeFache looked puzzled.

Fortuna stood-up belying his age, "Yet he is a commoner, you imply that. It is clear that no man may live within University walls, no matter what his role. You have erred greatly DeFache in this matter. I do not query your heart, yet I judged you a wiser scholar. It is of no matter that the boy is not taught, he still may not reside in the house of lore. I implore you now, as I am of those that call you friend. Remove the lad from your house before the council moves rumour into fact. For if that happens then your fate may follow that of poor Gru-Staedak." Fortuna swept past DeFache, his robes trailing behind him. Protesting DeFache rose to question again with the scholar but it was too late he had already departed from the library.

He sat back, the leather seemed less comfortable now, resting his hand under his chin he contemplated. The council would wait in this matter, he would not bow to foolish ways of an age past. He was an upholder of the philosophy and that was not always the same as the law. The words of Fortuna at the end troubled him most, what fate had met with Gru-Staedak? He questioned now in more detail what he had foolishly ignored earlier. Why had the old man not been present at the meeting? He was after all the senior in Asten house. He had thought perhaps an argument or ill health but the tone of the words suggested something more sinister.

His impulse was to ride for Asten immediately and seek out his friend. In doing so he felt that he may forsake the boy in the long term, he was a commoner it was true but DeFache had in truth always thought there was something special about him. Something different from most of the common man he met.

Thought not action.

He sat and stared at the books around him, the volumes of knowledge. Time passed. Then he raised himself up and walked to the doorway, glancing finally at the tomes around him.

Gru-Staedak was a wily and clever old man, he would not forsake the boy, something about him gnawed at the back of DeFache's head. He would return to his Sanctuary and see him safe and then seek out Gru-Staedak, no harm would befall the old man in a few weeks.

Chapter 4 - Old Dogs, New Tricks

It would be foolhardy of I, or any other historian, to not give full reference to our final pre-600 building. Constructed under direction of King Tanistrin (362-401), this fortress was designed with the assistance of his lead chancellor, who is understood to have had a flair for the sublime, if not the ridiculous.

While the fortress was built from the finest stone masonry available at that or in any time, mined from the northern borders of the Inpur Desert, its' innermost walls were only laid twenty feet in height; immediately ensuring it would be indefensible against any determined aggressor. It is this point without exception that has troubled historians over the past two hundred years, made even more curious when we see what was held within the walls.

From the central keep of the fortress to the first outer wall, the distance is approximately fifty paces. The first wall measures twenty feet in height. From the first wall to the second it is one hundred paces and the second wall measures thirty feet in height. From the second wall to the third and final outer wall the killing ground measures 150 paces and the wall forty feet in height.

Now, a set of walls gradually decreasing in height from outer to inner is perhaps acceptable if the keep is positioned at the top of a hill, the gradient making the inner walls taller. Yet this is not the case, this fortress is indeed built upon a plain. To confuse matters further the keep in itself is almost impenetrable, it is crafted from three sets of two foot thick Inpur rock staggered so that no seam is at the same point as another, lending it tremendous strength. The only entrance is via a stone door measuring wide enough for only two abreast to enter. The keep in itself may only house a maximum of one hundred men. Once inside it is doubtful any could enter against the occupants will. So we now ask the question. Why?

Why are the walls easier in turn than the last to penetrate?

Why at each wall does the killing ground reduce in length?

Why was the keep designed to house so few?

Many historians have talked of poor design, they have spoken of the chancellor's lack of understanding of military tactics. Some have even maligned the King and his judgement in building what has been described by some as nothing more than a death-trap.

I however refute those views. I have studied this building carefully over time, working closely with my learned friends the archaeologists and I have come to a rather different explanation. The King and his Chancellor did not intend to build an impenetrable fortress nor did they misunderstand or lack the understanding for their task. Quite the opposite, they knew exactly what they were doing. Simply said it is this: Bannermane is not a fortress – it is a test of courage and loyalty.

'Descriptions & Schematics Of Vedian Structures Pre-600' - Bray Curak (Historian) – Ved985

The first afternoon of their journey passed peacefully, the party had taken the south road until they had reached the towns' outskirts. A heavy rock was planted at the path junction as it joined with its east-west counterpart, stone markings were chiseled into it. One pointed to the south road and was etched with a symbol of a ship. The road wound its way southeast to Kanegon the largest seaport in Vedian, the east road was marked with a crown. The road, if followed would take a traveller all the way to Pluris the capital of Vedian and the home of the Crown Prince himself.

Arn pointed to the east road and led the others down its path. The sun was beginning to fall from its zenith and dusk would be on them before they reached the point where they would leave the Pluris road and turn north-east.

"We will carry on until dusk falls then camp to the side of the road. We may meet a few traders delivering from Pluris but I suspect not. It should be another fine night." Arn breathed in the hot afternoon air, he felt as if a great weight had been lifted from his shoulders and the further they walked from the Luff's borders the lighter the burden became.

Speck walked side by side with Joseph, the girl trailed behind, slightly dragging her feet on occasions through the dusty stones, which irritated Speck. He was enjoying his trek on the whole, the weather was fine as it mainly was in this part of Vedian, an arid if not unpleasant heat was matched by a light breeze which began to dissipate as they moved in an easterly direction. Speck rarely had reason to journey beyond the Luff and the whole experience was quite enlightening to him. He would pause in conversation with Joseph and slowly take in the full extent of the surrounding scenery, occasionally nodding to himself before venturing forward once more.

The area they walked in was, considering the lack of rain, extremely green and lush. Long grasses topped small undulating hills as they stretched as far around as the eye could see. A few small rocks lined the well-trodden path but few of the great stones that the Brillmon Plains were known for could be seen ahead.

Joseph's voice raised above the chattering of Speck as he preceded to inform his friend of another interesting fact he had read, "Arn, this road leads to Pluris, that is correct?"

The hunter did not stop walking to answer, "That's right Joseph, many leagues to the south and east."

Joseph continued, "And we wish to follow the Pluris road that is what you said earlier. So why are we leaving the road to head over the Brillmon Plains, if only to rejoin it later?"

"First, it is not the same road. This path takes you from Pluris to Kanegon, the road we will join is the Pluris to Asten road.

Secondly the road travels considerably further south east before it meets the Asten road and offers us more northward travel. Admittedly the terrain will be a little harder under foot through Brillmon but I think we will save perhaps a day for the shortcut." Arn pushed on down the path, the reasons he had sighted to the lad were correct, at least as far as his understanding went, he had never actually trodden either path that far.

His main consideration though was not distance and time but more concerned the meeting of unwanted parties. The tales he had heard from the safety of the Mariners' Arms had told of thieving and plundering centring around the main crossroads. It made sense to Arn, three of Vedian's largest towns connected via the roads and there was no other obvious route a merchant could take a cart over. The heavy stone plains would be hazardous to any caravan or wagon, bandits paid it little attention, so Arn had decided earlier that the Brillmon Plains would be a safer route, if a little harder to travel.

He had not informed the others of his fears for the crossing, in many ways he was much like them, his age had not set him apart from them in the Luff, as he rarely acted it. Yet now, out in the wilderness he felt a certain responsibility to them all. He did not feel the need to shy away from the leadership role, in fact he wondered why it came to him so naturally. Perhaps it was simply his trade as Hunts master's son, he was the obvious choice after all. Something nagged at him though, an underlying suspicion that this is how it should always have been. Arn shook his head and smiled to himself, behind him the Luff disappeared into the light of the setting sun.

As the sky bathed in its final rays of the day Arn called a welcome halt to the party. He searched the nearby area for a nice hilly outcrop that surrounded them on all sides. The air was still hot and the breeze had almost been left behind as they journeyed further down the road. They unpacked their rucksacks, laying out bedding and food. They ate meat purchased from the butcher's stall, washing down the tasty animal with some water from their skins. When the evening meal was finished Febra proceeded to light a long wooden pipe.

Speck shuffled about, eyeing the girl and wishing he had thought to bring some weed. He had never seen a wooden barrelled pipe, mostly the Luff pipers settled for the hard clay ones. The girl had grown in his eyes, it was few youngsters who took to the pipe, mostly it was the elder folk but Speck had asked Old Man Talon on many occasions to show how him how to smoke one properly and finally he had conceded to the boy.

Speck would often light his warden, as the clay pipes were referred to, and slowly puff on the weed as he sat reading one of his books, much to the annoyance of his mother who considered it a filthy habit.

Joseph nudged him and spoke in a whisper that was clearly audible to all, "If you ask her nicely, she might let you borrow it." Febra smiled at Joseph and fished deep into her sack, "I have a spare, if you would like some, and plenty weed to go round." From her pack she pulled a second wooden pipe, ornately carved around the stem.

Speck's eyes nearly dropped from his sockets, "A second! How did you purchase such pricey items. Not even Old Man Talon has two woods." Febra's face changed to a scowl and her hand holding the pipe dropped down to the ground, "So you call me a thief now do you. Why does it matter where they come from, they are here and you have need of one, is that not enough?"

Speck softened his tone, "Yes, perhaps it is, now anyway. I would enjoy a smoke and a wooden barrel would be a treat indeed." He held his hand out to the girl, "Sorry Febra and thank you for the offer. Where you obtained them is none of my business." She smiled in a strange way which left Speck unsure if his apology was taken in full spirit. Nonetheless the girl handed over the pipe and a small binding of weed to go with it. The two leaned back against the sloping hill side and puffed coils of thick smoke into the night sky.

"Joseph." Arn addressed the young lad who was still chewing on the last remnants of his meal. "I think we should hunt for some extra food at first light. We have plenty now but I am unsure what distance we may need to travel before we next encounter rich pastures. There are many wild animals in these parts and none beyond our skill to track. Let us take the pickings while they are still easy."

They chose to not light a fire, there was no need for extra heat as the night rarely dropped in temperature and Arn assured them any wildlife that came this close to the road would not trouble them. Neither did they post a watch, although Arn resisted a heavy slumber and was quickly awake to many sounds that were alien to him at first hearing.

The second day from the Luff passed without incident, they left the main path at Arn's instruction as soon as the surrounding terrain changed to a more stony appearance. From there the party began to travel in a north-easterly direction, hoping to rejoin the Asten road by the close of the third or beginning of the fourth day. The second nights camp was similar, except this time Arn suggested a rotating watch which Speck took as an opportunity to complain about sore feet and broken sleep. Generally the mood was good and even Febra seemed buoyant and friendly with each of them, taking time to walk next to Speck and talk with him further about his books. The third day was harder on all of them, the heavy stones seemed to be everywhere, sprouting up from the plains, blocking the way at every turn. By the afternoon they were forced to scramble over some to ensure they did not stray further from their core destination.

They ate meat from the second morning's hunt which had gone successfully. The beast was raw and was not to any of their tastes in particular but they agreed the wood they had collected from Old man Talon should be saved in case the weather turned as they strayed farther north. They had seen little in the way of foliage on their journey to date and as they moved northwards only the occasional scrub land bush with it's pretty, if thorny, white blossoms was prevalent.

Joseph thought that the rock would swallow him into the ground, its jagged edges nicked at his cotton shirt and would easily rend the soft material. The scrambling almost turned to climbing as the rocky hills became more like small mountain passes, none of it was helped by the heat of the midday sun, which burned down on them and was reflected by the rocks, the lack of wind served to make conditions even more uncomfortable.

Joseph's skin was browned from his days at sea and he didn't notice the sun's impact but Speck was feeling the effects quickly. His face was a red colour and his breathing became sharper as he sought to cross the rough environment. Febra on the other hand seemed to glide over the rocks, she was nimble and quick and often would have to stop to allow the others to catch up. Arn kept fair pace but by the fourth day Speck was beginning to slow. Joseph never left his side, even though he easily out paced Speck. At times Joseph would trip or stumble to ensure he did not get in front of his friend, if any of them noticed these actions, none had cause to mention them. By the afternoon of the fourth day Speck was exhausted, "Hold up hunter," he wheezed, "Enough for today, these accursed rocks go on for ever. The road may have been long but at least it was flat! Let us camp early today."

Before Arn could reply Joseph interjected, "I agree Arn, I am tiring as well. It will not hurt to finish early today, after all there is no real rush."

The hunter stopped clambering over a large outcrop that barred his way to the head of the hill they were climbing. "Perhaps it is for the best. I guess we still have one more full day before we clear Brillmon and rejoin the road. Let us rest longer now and refresh ourselves for the final push tomorrow. " Febra nodded in agreement and turned to Speck.

"Lets just get to the top of this hill, perhaps we will see the road from its hilt." The girl lifted herself effortlessly up the final plateau leaving Speck and Joseph to struggle over its final heights.

As Speck crawled up, ranting about his aching limbs, a hand clamped over his mouth. His eyes looked straight ahead to see the girl face-to-face with an enormous animal.

It was over ten feet in height, a dark matted fur about its torso and bald limbs protruding outward. Its mussel was black and wet looking and two small beady eyes were enough for Speck to take an almost fatal step backwards.

Arn held the lad firm, carefully sliding his hand away from Specks mouth, "Keep silent, all of you. I have heard of these creatures, they are like the bears that roam the Luff plains but larger and considerably more dangerous.

The creature seemed puzzled by the girl and cocked its head slightly to study her further. From its paws, long thick claws extended, scratching on the hard rock on either side of the beast.

"Stay perfectly quiet Febra," Arn hissed at the girl, "Do not move suddenly, It may lose interest."

The animal shifted its limbs outwards and dropped onto its front legs, moving slowly towards the girl, its naked muzzle sniffing at her scent.

Arn carefully released the net he wore from a belt hook on his back. The thick strands dropping silently into the hunters hands. As he reached for his spear, trying to loosen it from its resting place, Joseph stepped forward to stand alongside the girl. In his hand was a pile of the meat they had hunted. The animal snorted at the fresh scent and changed course slightly to approach him.

"Everyone walk around and climb over the next height of rock." Joseph's voice was steady and carried enough authority for them all to follow his command.

One by one they carefully stepped around the animal as Joseph placed a few strands of the sinewy meat on the ground. Once they had all traversed the next hill Joseph turned to Arn, "I thought you had a way with animals hunter. You do not have to kill everything we meet. The poor thing was half starved."

Speck interjected, "I'm not surprised ,there's nothing but rock and stone for miles."

Arn smiled at Joseph, "I wasn't going to kill it, just try and net it so we could slip away. But there is merit in what you say Joseph and I bow to your wisdom on the matter. Now let us put a little distance between him and us before his hunger returns."

They began to scramble over the hills to the sounds of Speck's voice suggesting that at least if the beast had been slain he would now be looking forward to some sleep.

As the fifth dawn broke and the party moved on once again, they began to feel the terrain thinning out. The rocks became more spread out and they were able to walk more evenly. The heat though had not let up, the temperature was soaring and sweat ran freely from their bodies, soaking their clothes.

Rain water was scarce, they had collected small amounts into their skins from pockets of shade in the rocks that had not yet evaporated.

Febra's keen eyes were the first to spot signs of the path ahead. The trail was perhaps one short march away, its long route sloping north into the lower hills and south back through the edges of the Brillmon Plains.

The party breathed a sigh of relief at the thought of rejoining the road and the hope of an easier journey ahead.

They walked quicker now, the sight of their goal buoying their pace, all hopeful of reaching the main path and camping near its borders. The conversation turned lighter within the group and even Speck began to laugh with Arn as he poked fun at his reaction to the recent encounter.

The ground began to turn from barren and dusty rock into patches of green tufts and then finally plains of grass, not as lush as the Luff but welcome sights nonetheless.

As they came within a hundred paces of the pathway, Arn motioned them to stop and quickly the hunter squatted down into the grassy hill. He turned pressing his finger to his lips and then signalled for them to do the same.

From the north voices could be heard, two men or perhaps three, Arn crawled forward in the grass, attempting to get closer to the sounds.

Confirming the head count, Arn turned to lift three fingers to the others who now all lay flat to the hillside. The speech became louder now and they could all hear men arguing between themselves. The first that drifted into view, was a thin stoic faced man who wore the garb of a tradesman. The two that followed were larger more burly men and the voices they had heard seemed to be coming from them.

"You heard rubbish, is what you heard." The burly man with the thick beard shouted at his compatriot.

"And what would you know bout's it Karan. When's did you last pay attention to any matter that didn't have ale or wenches present? I tell you, they say a curfew will be on Pluris before the harvest. I heard from the blacksmith, now his stall is near the centre of the market, right next the old Pulpit. You know where the people with the books go to talk. He says that they talked for hours about the thieving and killing going on in the town and in all Vedian so they say. Coming up from Kanegon no doubt."

The second man pulled his broad shoulders high to extenuate his knowledge on the matter. The bearded man swatted his hand into the air dismissively, "The blacksmith spends more time in the ale house than I do, what does he know about the books and their words. He would do spending a site more time heating iron and little less time earwigging. There won't be no curfew on Pluris, for a start how would they enforce it. There's few enough guards in the town as there's ever been, ain't that right now sir." The last words were shouted slightly louder to attract the attention of the thin man who walked ahead.

The tradesman turned round, a bored and tedious look crossing his face, "All I know is that you are being paid to ensure no such folk cross my path. Now be quiet with the both of you and watch the trail, Ill be damned if my hard earned produce will end up as the spoils of some thieving cur."

The trio carried on down the road south until they faded from the earshot of the party. Arn climbed to his feet and turned to see the others now sitting up on the hill.

"Why did we hide? They seemed reasonable folk, they might have helped us further with directions." Speck said staring at Arn.

"We know little of anything out here Speck and I am not inclined to trust anyone, let alone merchants rich enough to travel with hired guards. Yet at least we have heard some news from abroad, albeit rumour and gossip. We must tread carefully, if the Council are seeing fit to enforce curfews then they may also be sending more guards upon the main roads." The hunter folded his broad arms, and rested his hand on his thick chin.

Joseph was puzzled by Arn's words, "Why should this worry us, we have nothing to hide. Our task is one appointed by the assembly, they are supported by the council so we are in no danger from any guards."

Arn shook his head, "Not all men are as noble as you young sir. We are in no immediate danger but my father tells me that many of the military guard are nothing more than hired mercenaries these days not like the old guards. You can bet they would see us as just a little extra to add to their coffers, we should err on the side of caution and stay clear from strangers and the roads where possible. Yet this is a party of equals so let us vote."

No one opposed the hunters decision, Speck might have done but he was tired and his only concern was finding a camp so he could rest his feet and find some shelter from the accursed heat. They ambled onto the trail and crossed it, holding a north-easterly direction.

"The terrain should be easier now," Arn offered, "we should reach the ravine by the end of tomorrow."

"Where then?" Febra enquired.

"I am not sure, perhaps we will find this hermit of Pikes, we shall see.

The lone figure of DeFache stood facing the cold waters of Vedian Bay. His long cloak was wrapped tight against the chill night air and his breath blew high into the reaching skies above. The dock was quiet, it was said Pluris never slept, yet on a dank night as late as this, that statement was far from evident.

The harbour master had assured DeFache a boat would arrive before dawn to take him on the return trip to his homeland. It was not considered a dangerous journey to able seamen, yet all shipping off Vedian's shores was not taken without risks. The seas beyond could be variable and only three areas off the shore of Vedian were designated safe to steer a vessel. The Bay that surrounded the island of his home, the Straights of Reslin that held Vedian to the Uncharted Lands and the fishing port of Kearn Luff. He had spent some considerable time at seas travelling back and forth from the main land to the island in recent years, some trips had passed without incident, others less so but more often than not he enjoyed the days travel on ship or barge.

The Sea - He never ceased to be in awe at its contrasting natures of power and placidness, few phenomenon's had drawn his heart so far from his books on so many occasions. He often stood upon the far gardens of his Sanctuary, those standing on the western tip of the island, basking in the strong wind blowing up from the south seas and tasting the early morning spray that would leap over the shoreline.

Gru-Staedak had suggested that it was this fascination and attachment to nature that set DeFache apart from the politicians and council courtiers. He had once said, as they sat together in DeFache's scribing room, that if the council truly sought balance then they must first look to nature as their template. If those basic laws could be brought to bear on society then he was in no doubt all would achieve their goals.

Questioning the old scholar further on how nature could represent society, Gru-Staedak had replied that it simply formed a pattern of birth, death and re-birth and the rest was merely dictated by the winds. DeFache had shaken his head, teasing his learned friend at the basic premises he had stooped to in his lengthening years. It was an old argument that fate and luck were responsible for all in the world, that man had no control over his destiny. DeFache had never been a believer of this school and had even written a paper on the matter that had been discussed at The Pulpit a few years back.

Gru-Staedak had smiled at DeFache, that knowing smile that had always left the younger man feeling as would a child to a parent. It was most disconcerting, even as a renowned scholar and philosopher, the old man still held a power over him that he could never see diminishing. It was perhaps that DeFache had never wished it too diminish, the smile was dear to him, more so than any other that had walked beside him or touched his life in some way.

The old man had finally spoken again after a long stare at his pupil, "Umberto", he touched the younger mans hand softly, "For all the discussions and theorising, which has a place no doubt, sometimes it is that simple. Men as do we all, live by basic laws and beyond that fate holds parley with the choices we take in life. It is not important to second guess such chance or how we may deceive it, rather it would be defter of thought to consider how we judge our success within its confines."

DeFache quickly stepped in, "By our humanity of course, that is how we may judge?"

In response Gru-Staedak had not smiled this time, " No my friend, not humanity, but the lack of it."

A heavy sound of hooves approached him from the eastern dockside, he could barely make out the shape of a tall man riding upon a handsome beast. As the rider neared, he saw no sign of any marking to distinguish either party.

"A poor night to be riding, I warrant friend." DeFache addressed the horseman as he came to a halt a few feet from the scholar.

"It would seem many nights are poor ones in these times sire. I would ask your name, if so good you would be to give it." The horseman's voice was clear and fair but tainted with a hint of collusion and secrecy.

"I would give it, if it makes the night fairer for it sir. I am Umberto DeFache, does that mean something to you?" DeFache tried to see past the riders cloak, wrapped as it was, tightly about his head.

The horse breathed hard against the cold air, the beast had clearly ridden some leagues already this night. DeFache moved closer and placed a gloved hand upon his mane, softly stroking the beast until its heavy breathing diminished.

"It does indeed my lord. For I have been sent with a message of great urgency from my liege. I have sought you out over many days and barely missed you at Imanis before you departed for the council." The rider swept aside his cloak at the side and drew from within its confines a small parchment, upon it was laid a seal that DeFache instantly recognised.

"Long has it been since this seal passed by night harbouring messages of urgency. I would ask more of its carrier, will you stay and talk awhile or perhaps hold for a reply to return with?" DeFache took the parchment from the outstretched hand of the rider. Releasing his hold on the horses wet mane.

"My orders are to return as soon as delivery is met, other tasks are before me it would seem and I would not disappoint my Lord in this hour. I leave you with these words, for while messenger I am and proud to be such, my line that goes before, may offer more in the days ahead. This passage handed down from generation to generation and bound to memory:

'When the crown and the scholar,

Languish in squalor,

When the candles of power,

Burn in the tower.

Those that walked their separate ways,

Will not abandon their code,

Their oaths bound together again,

United upon the same road.'

"I believe there is more to these words, but I know them not in full, I believe the poem also speaks of a prince and a mariner. Yet more must now wait, as I am bound to depart swiftly, I impart these words to you DeFache as my trust in my liege is unmoving and I take his belief in your character to mine own sacred truth. I fare you well and hope for your safe passage."

He pulled on the reigns and turned the great beast westwards, dropping his hood briefly to show an eminently handsome face, distinguished with eyes that spoke of honour to DeFache. The fair man's light hair blew across his forehead as he raised his hand in departure. DeFache recognised him instantly as Madistrin's Protector.

"This meeting is already of great wonderment and concern to me, yet I doubt not your urgency Commander, go and receive my wishes for good travel with you. I think somehow we will meet again, not so distantly." DeFache watched the horse and rider as they disappeared into the darkness of the docks. Faintly he could hear the whistle of the incoming boat at his side, he clutched tightly at the parchment and waited to board. Gru-Staedak, Samuel and now Madistrin, his list was growing longer by the hour. Still the boy came first, he would return to Imanis to make safe his charge and then decide if his old mentor or the Crown Prince needed his attention next.

As the midday sun rose once more over Vedian, the sound of Speck's continual complaining began to falter until it merely became a dull ache nestling at the back of Arn's head. The trail as he had promised, was now less undulating and easier footing, yet still the sun hung above them like a shining Sword of Damocles. Febra walked at the front now, side by side with Arn, she would enter into short bursts of questioning the hunter, before once again falling silent, backing off into her own thoughts.

Over their journey the girl had begun to develop a fascination with the hunts masters son. Her exterior was quirky and unsure, hiding the true nature of her person but from her bitterness a fondness had begun to emerge. It was an odd sensation, the girl thought, a warm sense inside that drew her to Arn. She would find herself walking by his side, asking about his experiences on the hunt and of growing up with his family. When others had talked of their kin before she had only resented it because of her own loss and felt disdain and dislike for the individual, but with Arn it was different. He was so care free in attitude and spirit, he could draw her into his tales until she felt as though she was there, with him. She could only liken it to an early experience she had with a travelling bard.

Castegar, he unlike most would live long in her memory, a roguish sort who had promised her information and delivered only a pain that lingered with the girl for many sun rises after his songs had departed the Luff. He had offered her a special root at the first meeting in the tavern, brought from distant lands to the south and he raved of its enriching properties. At first she had been in awe of it's sweet taste as it allowed her freedom from the anguish and hatred inside. She had spent long evenings with the

75

silver-tongued troubadour, sitting under the stars listening to his tales of far-off lands or sharing his bed at the Inn. Then one morning he was gone, in retrospect he had said as much. Yet she had not been ready for it to end that way. He had spoken of a friend that he sought, a companion of younger days that he needed to find. She had been distraught at first, then the pain began, she craved the narcotic powers of the rare herb. Firstly she noticed it at night when they had taken its pleasure but soon after, it was morning, noon and night. She thought the longing for its sweet taste would never leave her, she stole and acquired other strange herbs but none replaced the feeling. Long after the lust for it had left her body, her pain at the travellers departure still remained.

Strangely and unlike many that had entered her short life, she did not view him with bitterness or contempt, there was but left a longing deep within her. Arn had brought this out, he was not unlike the bard, younger and full of vitality but they shared that freedom of spirit and history. It was that above all the girl yearned for, a past of her own, an attachment to something other than despair and loneliness. Her resolve settled in again, her father would be made to pay for his betrayal and no traveller or huntsman would stand before her.

The trail by afternoon had narrowed somewhat and the brush had grown dense. Still the dust that drew up with the occasional breeze would claw in their throats and they would have to pause to take water from the skins. By sunset the geography of the land had once again turned undulating and hilly.

Speck's pace had slowed to an amble and Joseph's irritation at his friends' constant complaints had turned now to concern. He walked quickly forward to Arn, leaving Speck at the back with the girl.

"Arn, I'm worried, his rantings are getting worse and his face is covered with sweat. Perhaps we should stop for the day and let him rest." Joseph slowed his pace as if to carry weight to his suggestion.

"Too late for that Joseph, we must if anything quicken not slow." Arn swiped a glance at the young mariner that startled him.

"We are not bound to time in this journey and if we were, then the price would be too high." He quickened to move ahead and grasped at the hunter's arm in an attempt to halt him.

"I choose not to speak of it not earlier but your resolve is clear in this matter my friend. Our young scribe is ill, possibly terminally if we do not reach aid soon. He has, if I am correct taking on a poison of some type." Arn's eyes did not leave Joseph's. The huntsman held a finger to his lips, "Calmly Joseph, it is not the time for exclamation."

Thoughts rushed through his mind. Why? How? When?

"How can you be sure Arn? How did it happen?" Joseph found his stride now quickening, putting some distance between the trailing pair.

"The water is how, of that I'm certain," the huntsman replied, "only the one skin and I have since emptied its contents two nights back."

Joseph interrupted, "You have known for two days! Yet you have said nothing" Joseph whispering was shrill and full of anger.

"If I have erred then I hold responsibility for my action, but I do not see any change now that would have steered me to a different course. Speck has taken on a large dose of what I suspect to be Angrillim, a poisonous root that can be crushed into liquid. It can be counteracted but I have neither the means nor the skill. I wonder now if we should ever have begun this trek." Arn's voice cracked slightly as he finished and Joseph felt a tingle of fear rise within him.

"Why did we not turn back sooner Arn?" The aggression had vanished from his voice now, he could see the huntsman was in doubt of himself.

"I was not sure until yesterday in truth, at first I thought the symptoms may be heat induced. When we slept yesterday I went to drink from Speck's water skin and smelt the faint aroma within. By then it was too late to turn, I knew any salvation was in pressing forward."

 "Why? Bannermane surely is a week from here or more?" Joseph's eyes were full of confusion and worry.

"Bannermane is not our goal, the boy does not have that time. Our hope now relies on the words of Pike Yantaran. We seek the man of which he spoke, if he lives then we are but half a day from the ravine. Speck's time is diminishing quickly and I do not think we can chance turning back."

The huntsman's words struck Joseph like ice. "You saved his life then, if he had continued to drink...." he trailed off, choking on the words.

"For a short time and that only by chance, we must find Rundell, if he lives. Do not speak of this to the girl or Speck. It will not aid our plight and we need to stay in control."

Joseph stood tall, "I will carry him to this man If I have to, my friend will not fall here in the wilderness."

"No, I believe he will not, your bond if anything will pull him back to us."

"Arn, you said your skill was insufficient to heal this sickness, why do you believe this man's will be otherwise?"

The huntsman smiled ruefully, "In truth good Joseph, I do not. Nonetheless, I got to thinking as we walked from the Luff, the name Pike had bestowed upon us niggles at my mind. I was sure I had heard it before. Long ago my father had told me a tale of the Crown Prince of Vedian."

"Madistrin." Joseph interjected.

Arn kept a brisk pace as he talked, "No, before Madistrin held the office his elder brother was in line for kingship. My father said he was a great leader and he had once met him in the days that the open season hunts still occurred, it was a proud day for my father. Not long after they met the Crown Prince was killed in a tournament of arms, crushed by his own horse, a tragic accident, the people mourned for many years."

Once again Joseph interrupted, "I do not understand the relevance of this tale."

"That is because you are too quick to halt me, hold your voice and listen to what I recall." Joseph fell silent, still ensuring he kept up a swift pace and checking behind to ensure Speck and Febra had not fallen too far away. "My father told me once that rumour had reached him that it was no accident and in fact the beast had been poisoned. In his early days my father had known many men of arms, so my mother said. He then told me that it was believed by some that the King had been assassinated by

78

poisoning his horse, so it fell lame at the tournament. As you rightly say, what links this to that event in Vedian history. Well nothing but a name. Rundell.

Joseph face was startled, "Rundell was the assassin? Then you propose we take our friend into the arms of a murderer! There can be no salvation at the hands of such a man." Arn placed his hand on Joseph's shoulder, gripping tightly the soft jerkin he wore.

"Do you trust Pike, Joseph?"

"Of course, with my life. He is an impeccable man."

"Exactly. I think it was no matter of chance that Pike met with us prior to our exit, or knew where we would be. Least of all that he would offer us a name, that he knew would lead us to danger. I do not understand all affairs that have taken place, but I too place my trust in his words. And in truth Joseph, what other choices are open to us." Joseph turned and looked back at Speck, he was mumbling now, his feet stumbling on after each other, propelling him forward. No choice Arn, Joseph thought, no choice at all.

"Attack!" The ferocity of the cry brought the whole group to an immediate halt. First to react was neither Joseph or the wily huntsman but the girl.

From the tall brush at their right side, two figures leapt from the dark.

Joseph could see the line of their shadows against the rising moon. Febra who previously had seemed content to wander forward at Speck's side now came alight at the sound of the assault. She drew forth the slim dagger from within her thick leather boot and ran directly to intercept the nearest attacker. The assailant could be viewed by the girl now, he was hard faced and his eyes were cold. He towered well above the girl and grinned as he swung forth a hefty club at her head. Easily the girl slipped under the unwieldy weapon and drew up tightly inside the man's defences. Her first cut drew blood from the burly man's cheek, the second tore deep into his blackened tunic, piercing the flesh below. He winced at the hurt and swung out again at the girl but her size made it difficult for him to strike with the large club and realising the problem, he tossed the weapon aside and made a direct grab for the girls throat. By now the second

79

attacker was upon Joseph, a short sword held aloft by a skinny, wiry figure threatening to strike the young man as he stood startled. The sharp twang of a loosed arrow dropped the tall man to his knees, a shaft buried deep in his side. Joseph looked to his left to see Arn poised with his ash bow in hand, another arrow being strung. The hunter and the girl had already proven their natural instincts, oddly Joseph did not find Febra's actions strange, in his eyes she was a strong free spirit, he did not see the anger or hatred that lurked within her, only a sense of loss. The words formed on Joseph's lips but they did not have time to spring forth as a third assailant jumped upon the huntsman from behind. He had waited behind a small hillock further up the trail, observing, watching the throws of early battle before engaging.

It seemed to Nerl, they had underestimated their opponents, not for the first time he surmised. He had hunted with many thieves, bandits and curs but rarely few as ignorant as this latest crop. He had told them earlier as they followed the party up the trail, taking care to wait until dusk before assaulting, "I tell you we should attack as one! Why take risks?"

"You'll do as we say, we lead this band, not ye! They are but children, foolish youths and a girl. We will down them without me raising my blade or Rabnerash." The huge leader motioned to his grinning colleague. The second bandit grabbed at Nerl's tunic.

"Now you'll quiet down and wait as we say, or I'll gut yer myself. If your scared of that rabble you got one way out of this little band of ours." Rabnerash smiled as best as he could manage, a long hard grimace reached out towards Nerl. The clarity of the option, had always been clear to him. You never left a group you joined, unless you died or they did. He had parted ways with a number of groups in his time, usually at night, while they had slept and the blood still ran warm from their throats. This would be his last sortie with this bunch he thought, one way or another.

Rushing swiftly from his hiding place, he drew forth his long bone handled dagger. The knife plunged into Arn's shoulder and he fell forward to the ground, his bow snapping with the impact. Nerl raised the dagger again to finish the helpless hunter, his back at the mercy of the man, there was no remorse or quarter given. Nerl knew Arn had been the danger all along, he had seen it in his actions, the way he held himself and how quickly he had strung that bow. What speed! He trained his eyes upon the huntsman's centre point where his shoulder blades met and began to bring down the blade. It was the last thing he saw, Joseph sprung to life finally, the site of Arn pushing him into action. He grabbed at the makeshift pike Arn had given him in the market, it had stayed strapped to his belt since them, he had never thought to use it. The adrenaline pumping through him and his stomach retching it was all he could do to lurch forward and plunge the point into the man's defenceless belly, the force of the attack pushing Nerl clean off Arn and leaving him supine on the floor, clutching at the long makeshift weapon with one hand and the dagger still tightly held in the other.

What happened next Joseph would find it difficult to clearly recollect, a fourth and fifth man emerged from the opposite side the first bandits had attacked from.

They were larger men and they were kitted in leather jerkins and carried long swords. They did not run but strode towards Joseph, who now stood defenceless over the fallen huntsman. As they neared his position another set of boots could be heard approaching from the trail the party had earlier walked up. Quickly the trudging sound broke into a quick step, then a run and while the mariner could see the two men heading closer and closer, all he could hear were the hard footsteps closing in on him. The sword bearing duo paused and turned to face the sound of the approaching footsteps, neither seemed to regard Joseph as a threat and in that at least, they were correct.

The mariner was shivering uncontrollably and his vision was becoming unclear but even through his panic he thought to shield himself over the body of his fallen comrade. Joseph heard an authoritative voice resound towards the men but he could not clearly make out the figure approaching.

"Let these imps alone, they are unworthy of great men such as yourselves. Would you not parley, I could offer supplies and a copper for their safety?"

Rabnaresh the larger of the two, long sword held with both hands, took a step forward, "We not 'ere to share spoils with beggars, but if you stand there long enough we'll add you to em!"

A strange calm had emerged over the scene that seconds ago had seen blood spilled on the trail. Febra stood, her chest puffing to catch breath, the slight knife still grasped tightly in her small hand. At her feet the body of the first raider was slumped over, blood ran freely, not absorbed by the hard, dry ground. The man had thought to wring the girls tiny throat, yet he had underestimated her strength. She had brought the knife up, even as a dark mist had reached over her eyes and plunged the blade through the ugly man's left eye. He had writhed with pain, dropping her to the floor, unable to focus she had stabbed three times more at the body and them rose once more to stand, oblivious it seemed to all else around her.

Febra was slightly further down the trail and could only just now make out the new figure in full view. How she viewed him at that first meeting would undoubtedly differ to Joseph's description. To her, she saw a warrior, pure and simple. She saw it in his thick set body, in his wide open stance, a slight bend in the knees and a weapon that could never be the choice of one who was not trained in its art. The man stood as tall as Arn, and his girth was as big as Pike, if not larger, while a long robe covered his whole body, covering all but the tips of his black leather boots, filthy from years of rambling the trails. His face was uncovered by the hood of the robe and while the girl would always see him as fair compared to the man that lay now at her feet, in reality it was not so.

His face was scarred both under the left eye, a deep burning wound at least two inches in length running parallel with his brow and from the cleft of his chin, a thin purple lesion that ran down along his neck, disappearing into the folds of his gown. Even as a younger man, before the ravishes of battle had washed over him, it would not of been said he was a handsome man, his hair was unkempt in a natural way, wavy and tangled. Much of what was there had now gone the way of all things that once were young. Waves hung to shoulder length but on top he was as shiny as a pin, untouched by growth in many a year.

His eyes were a dark brown, steady and a little unnerving to the girl as she looked upon this effortless soldier. A short beard mingled with the remnants of his hair, streaked with colour but now primarily devoid of it. His right arm was cocked to one side, his large hand resting on his chest and in the other which was held steady, a great ball and chain was held. While the air was still and his arm the same, the huge iron ball still managed to maintain a pendulous effect, hanging a full two foot below its handle, which was wrapped around the mans hand.

"I believe," the man began again in response to Rabnerash, Joseph could hear a strange accent in his voice that he did not recognise, "that I am a fair man. I do not condemn those I do not know and times are not what they were, that is true. Yet I ask you know, leave now and I will furnish you with food and four coppers on your way. One for each of your prey. It is my final offer."

The words were not threatening or harshly spoken, neither did they expound hidden meaning, they were steady and true. The response was quick, they had already lost two men today and curs and lackeys were hard to find with so many groups operating, this man and the other four would reimburse their hardships. Rabnerash was slightly ahead of his compatriot, they flanked the robed man looking to attack both sides in unison. By the time they had made it within three strides, the great weapon began to rotate, quickly spinning around his hand in a wide circle. While his wide stance did not shift, he dropped his knees a little further in anticipation.

As Rabnerash reached him, he brought the long sword round in an arc from left to right, trying to cut across the midriff of his opponent. Yet instead of fending or attempting to ward the blow, the robed man shifted the weight onto his right leg and spun a half circle bringing the full weight of the smooth iron down upon the head of the second attacker who had looked to move in close for an easy back attack.

The crunching sound of metal on bone, was enough to still Rabnerash from a second swift attack, while his slash had nicked the robed man as he spun, the opportunity was there now to do what his compatriot had planned. Yet the slightest pause in reaction was enough for his opponent, who now was shifted onto the opposite leg from his spin, to kick out and land a thick boot directly in Rabnerash's collar bone. While the blow in itself was not enough to knock him over, it created enough time for the ball to again begin its spinning cycle, this time landing firmly down on his leg, smashing the knee and collapsing the leader to the floor.

It would be Joseph's recollection, that he offered mercy to the defenceless bandit, a chance once more to leave the trail with his life. Febra though would only remember the sound of the ball spinning and the impact as the death blow struck him, cracking his chest, collapsing the breast bone and expunging the air within. It was the last sight she remembered as the mist took her, the deep purple finger marks around her neck finally taking their toll. The robed man stayed his weapon and moved up the trail to where Joseph lay defending the wounded huntsman. Placing the ball within his thick leather belt he knelt down and reached his large hand out to the boy. "I will not harm you, my name is Rundell. Lift yourself from thy compatriot, I will see if I may tend to his hurt." Again the voice was not in itself compassionate but consistent and rang with a sound of honesty.

By the time darkness had engulfed the plains, Rundell had tended to the huntsman and the girl. Binding the formers wound and applying salve to the mark's on the latter's bruised neck. He also took time to inspect Speck, who had seemed oblivious to all that had gone before. Joseph talked quietly with his fallen friends, offering words of hope and tidings of fairer times to come.

The warrior approached Joseph once more, "Come we must bring your party to my home quickly, your small friend will not last much longer without proper treatment and I do not have the herbs upon me. I will bear the hunter and lead the small one, can you carry the female?"

Joseph nodded quickly, "Aye...yes of course. How far must we journey?"

"Tis only a short way now, I have been aware of your presence on the trail as I am of all that walk in these parts. Yet it is hard to track without cover, so I could not approach earlier to see what manner of folk you were. I am sorry now I did not come to you sooner openly and declare myself, I offer my apologies for that error, it has paid a high price with the wounds to your party."

Rundell seemed to wait for some acknowledgment from Joseph that his apology had been accepted. The boy just nodded unsure of what to say to the imposing warrior. The journey took time even though the distance was short, Speck often stopped, caught in a distant gaze and Rundell eventually was forced to lead him by the hand with the huntsman slung over his other shoulder. Finally they entered a hollow, the land sliding down on all sides, and faintly Joseph could hear the sound of rushing water. At the base of the cut away, stood a small flat roofed house, crafted entirely from wood. He was astonished, a wealthy man he thought to himself, to have a home crafted in such a way.

The home was designed in a corner shape with two symmetrical parts, a main doorway led into a living area, incorporating tables and chairs all in wood and even a fireplace at one end, a small rock hearth, plain and undecorated. The second half appeared to be sleeping quarters and was made up of six beds, each atop another making three pairs. All seemed to be as new and as if they had never been used, the woven blankets neatly folded back on each. Rundell placed the huntsman down on one of the lower beds and instructed Joseph to do the same with Febra.

"They will sleep now and you should do the same, I will tend as best I am able to the small one."

Joseph spoke carefully, not wishing to anger the warrior, "No, I will not sleep, If it pleases you sir, I must stay with my friend. I would not abandon him to my own selfish needs."

The warrior smiled, "I hope that in my care he is not entirely abandoned. Yet have it as you wish." Rundell led Speck into the living area and sat him on a chair, spending a few moments to light the fire all ready prepared on the hearth. He then left for a time and Joseph knelt by his friend, talking softly about the Luff and their childhood. Moments later Rundell returned with a vial and a small pack. He began to tip the boys head back and pour the contents of the vial into his throat.

"What is that?" Joseph enquired, a crack of fear entering his voice.

"You do not trust me, do you lad." Rundell continued to focus on Speck. Joseph opened his mouth to speak, "Stay your words, it does not matter. I doubt that you have reason enough and much of it probably well founded. Nonetheless, believe that I will offer Speck here, all care that I am trained to give."

Joseph was still not entirely satisfied, "How do you know to treat his ailment?" Rundell turned his head to face Joseph, placing the empty vial in the pack.

"Now lad, this is my house your in and I think there is more knowledge in that question than you care to make clear. Do not ask what you do not wish to hear. I am not your enemy and I may not be your friend, although perhaps I would have it otherwise, If you would consider taking as you find. Now I will place blankets over the boy and he will sleep, we will know better by morning if his recovery is beginning. Nothing more can be done. Stay here by his side if you will, I suspect I would not pry you away at any cost." Rundell picked himself up from his kneeling position, tucked the pack in his belt and walked towards the door.

Joseph stood up, "Where are you going?"

"These are not the times they once were laddie, I shall return to the site of confrontation and cleanse the land of the signs of battle. It will be safer to do such. Those bandits are not the only dangers to walk in these parts." He turned to face Joseph, gave a smile and left. Joseph sat resting his head on the chair and holding his friends hand tight, determined to see him through.

By the time Rundell had reached the scene of their encounter sleep had taken him. On the morning that DeFache's ship took him back to his home at the Sanctuary of Bridges, Joseph awoke to the site of Speck standing in front of the now burnt out fire. He rubbed his eyes and scrambled to his feet, pushing off the blanket that had been placed over him. "Speck! How are you? You look better, I am so glad to see you my friend!" He hugged the boy tightly, a small tear escaping his eye.

"Steady now sailor. I am fine and I have been made aware of those things that transpired by our host." The mention of that had Joseph looking about conspiratorially. "I remember little of the past day until I awoke early this morning, but Rundell tells me we had quite a time by all accounts. I did have a strange dream mind, seemed to last forever, about a tower or something such...it fades now and you stood atop a battlement with..with..no. I'm sure the fever had me well to conjure such images."

Joseph suddenly remembered the others, "What of Febra and Arn?"

"They are fine Joseph, Arn has already risen in his usual humour, accused me of slacking off would you believe! He went out with Rundell to examine the area. The girl still sleeps and Rundell said not to wake her, as her wound was a bad one."

Joseph looked at Speck "She fought like a warrior Speck, she probably saved our lives and Arn too."

86

"I doubt it not Joseph, I seems to me this morning that things have changed, for the first time in my life I feel that the Luff is not what I am but now what I was. My part in what befell us was of little consequence and yet I awake changed nonetheless" The boy smiled at Speck and in it, Joseph saw a maturity that he had not previously been aware of. The friends sat and talked, Speck providing a morning broth that Rundell had prepared prior to his departure.

By mid morning the wanderers returned, Arn burst though the door, shouting and smiling. Taking time to greet Joseph before taunting Speck further on his poor performance the night before. Joseph saw a difference in the small boy, he no longer seemed to bite at the comments but took them in a jovial manner, even making a few back at the hunter.

Arn turned to Joseph, "This is an incredible place, beyond here lies the ravine of which we spoke and below it a waterfall the like of which I have never seen. You must see it Joseph, it is a wonderment indeed!" As they talked they failed to notice Febra walk in from the quarters, the dark marks still prominent around her neck.

"We must away soon from here," she said addressing Arn, "we still have a task to perform."

Rundell looked over his shoulder, "What task of such importance would that be lady?"

Febra barked at the warrior, "It is not for your ears. That is unless you would aid us further?" She checked herself and said again, "I am sorry good warrior, I did not get your name as yet. I thank thee for they aid and would ask for any further you would give."

"The only aid, I would give now to you, is more rest. You are guests here and your journey has taken a toll on you all. Take rehabilitation and enjoy my home for as long as you are able. When the time comes that you depart, I will accompany you to the ravine but I will not take you further." Rundell nodded to them and motioned to Arn, "Let us look at your skills hunter, perhaps an old dog can still teach the whippet a thing or two!" The huntsman laughed, "I doubt it! For my talents are great indeed but it would be rude not to observe as you have been such gracious a host. Let us track."

The two men walked outside and Rundell shouted back, "Mine is yours, take rest, and relax in comfort." What first was meant to be a sun rise turned quickly into seven suns and moons. Even Febra who had campaigned for them to leave as soon as possible and continue the task, quickly faltered. Life with Rundell was both relaxing and most informative. Days were filled with walking for Joseph and Speck, visits to the nearby waterfall and marvelling at its splendour.

Arn and Febra would journey with Rundell listening to sage advice on travelling and tracking and always Febra would ask about weapons and battle that the old man seemed happy to impart. The evenings though were the highlight for Joseph and Speck, they would sit by the fire or on a clear night outside on the hollow and Rundell would tell tales of days far gone.

By all account he had been a soldier for many years and he had travelled to many parts of Vedian and fought in a number of uprisings and skirmishes in main for the Pluris duchy. There was mention of other activities before, but he would not be drawn into detail and was deft at quickly moving conversation where he wished it to go. By the end of week, Arn was in awe of the man and Febra was infatuated by his tales and knowledge of war. Joseph did not revel in such stories but quickly felt his trust grow in the warrior, in truth that had been cast the morning Speck had awoke. Yet in all the time neither himself or Arn had raised the tale of the King or raised the question of the knowledge that cured Speck. So on the eve of their departure which they had finally and reluctantly agreed, Joseph took a breath and approached Rundell as he stood outside splitting wood with a double handed axe.

"Where do you come by such a supply of raw tree wood? This material would fetch a fortune at the Luff."

"Ah, I have not told you of all my talents young Joseph. I am not a wealthy man but a soldier and I do not crave riches, yet I would travel where others would not at times, so I receive this bounty as reward."

Joseph snorted, "At times Rundell you say much but tell me nothing, it would seem."

"You would rather I said nothing but told you much then?" the old warrior laughed. He changed the subject as often he did," A fine girl that one, a little feisty and oddly troubled. The Huskian's to the south have a breed of warrior females, she has such qualities. Keep her close Joseph and you will live longer at least!" the old man laughed so hard he completely missed the log he was aiming at, landing the axe deep into the ground.

The slight teasing was enough to push Joseph into action," I would ask you a question directly, would you answer?"

Rundell shrugged, "How would I know without hearing it first? You may ask and I may answer..."

Joseph interjected, "But I may not like what I hear. That is what you said when we first met. Well now I would hear it anyway." Rundell sighed a little and sat down on the log he had just left intact.

"We heard, well Arn did from his father, of a story of a King. Not the Crown Prince of today but a brother before that who died. The tale was told that his death was not natural." Rundell did not look at Joseph but continued to gaze at the floor for a time until finally he broke his silence.

"It seems that disgrace does not die with a generation, I thought once, that atonement could be obtained by isolation but it seems that will be denied me. Perhaps it is just. Why should one man's conscience be cleared by the passing of time, when he has condemned so many to disparity and chaos." The old warrior stood to his feet, the leathers he wore seemed to bear heavy upon him now, he looked aged in the evening light and Joseph felt a sense of guilt pass over him.

"I will explain myself in some way Joseph, though perhaps I will leave it to others to impose opinion of rights and wrongs upon you. I was based in Pluris in those days, a second lieutenant under the command of Captain Dre'Guist, a formidable leader of the home guard. I had learned quickly as a youngster and taken well to the teachings of arms and battle. I had been keen to please my seniors and rise through the ranks. It was not then as it is now, the guard was a respected force, employed to serve Vedian and its people, it was an honour to be chosen. The council still held a check on numbers and rights but they fell silent under the sway of Laferious the Crown Prince. All knew he would be accepted into Kingship within the year, he was popular with all subjects and had the backing of most of the Duchy's. He was a fair man and a true warrior, I never met him personally but those that did he touched in some way.

Tournaments held then were days of celebration and enjoyment, the greatest warriors from each regiment would be called on to compete in a test of arms and people would travel from far and wide to partake in the festivities. I recall the city of Pluris that day as clear in mind as you are now, a magnificent city, thriving and opulent, its subjects clear in the understanding of the rules and customs they lived under. It was a fair time, there was a place for everyone, the Scholatic would debate in the Pulpit while the Captains lanced at tournament.

The city had a feel of balance and serenity that has not been known since. I had taken seat next to the stable area, with a few of my comrades, the opening rounds had already begun and our Captain was due up next in the flail and mace category. I rose to gather ale for all and moved towards the back of the stable to make for the stalls to the rear. A hand tapped my shoulder from behind the stables and I turned to see a tall man, garbed in a long robe smiling at me.

"Good day to you soldier, do you enjoy the games so far?" the robed man had said.

"Aye," I responded, "Tis good to see so many warriors together, one day I hope to compete at the Captain class." Rundell's hands clasped around his own face, "Even then Joseph the dye was cast, my ambition would be my undoing." The man had placed a long arm around my shoulder, "No doubt you will, perhaps I could ask a favour of such a loyal warrior. The Crown Prince is due to compete later in the mounted class, I must see to his steed but I have been called on to undertake pressing duties at his side. Could you perhaps see to it the beast is fed with his herbs and watered, my friend."

"Of course," I had replied, "Would that task be better fitted to the stable hands? I have known little of mounted steeds in my occupation to date."

I remember the briefest uncertainty crossing my mind and fading away just as quickly. The man led me towards the front of the stable, "It is a busy time and I would entrust this task to a reputable friend." I had smiled and nodded taking from him a pouch of food and a skin of water, he had thanked me again and ambled off towards the royal tent. I had not thought to wait and see if he entered or question the items he bestowed upon me.

Instead I had moved into the stable nodding at one of my compatriots who had enquired on the location of their brew. It had not been a hard task to find the steed, for he was as a fair a beast as I could have imagined. I took no heed to the lack of stable boys and instead, poured the contents of the pouch in my hand and held it out for the gallant steed to taste. There was already water in the drinking trough yet I added the skins contents as well. The beast nuzzled up to my neck and I placed the pouch inside my tunic, its contents emptied. I thought no more of the action and proceeded with the rest of the tournament, shouting and cheering on Dre'Guist to a valiant first place in his category.

The day wore on happily, until the trumpets sounded for the final class, the tournament of champions. As in all Pluris tournaments the last encounter was held for previous class champions and always on horseback. Laferious had long been a valiant and able fighter and enjoyed the opportunity to share his skills with the other warriors. The early stages went well, with the Crown Prince unhorsing two opponents until only five men were left upon the field. Then as he was about to charge for his third victim the fair beast that bore him reared up and fell, Laferious was pushed from his saddle and the huge beast landed down upon him. A horrible crunching sound reverberated around the galleys and his personal guard swiftly ran out to his aid.

It was to be too late, the weight of the lame animal crushed his chest and the last breath he had was shared with his brother Madistrin who knelt upon the field holding the lifeless corpse of his beloved brother. Rundell turned to face Joseph, "So the tale is told, I hide nothing that I do not know and I ask nothing from you in the way of opinion or thought, suffice to say I realised soon after what had been done and went to my Captain to admit my actions. It was he, who saved me from a certain death, instead agreeing a banishment from the regiment against the wishes of the council.

Pass through no town and reside in the walls of no village, he had said to me. I had thought it was part of my punishment yet not long after, word reached me that he had been slain in a skirmish with curs outside Pluris while on duty. That anyone would believe a tale of such an accomplished warrior I truly doubt. So I surmise that certain individuals did not agree with his actions. Yet that is another tale."

Joseph looked long and hard at the proud warrior, he hoped to find remorse in his eyes and yet could not sense it. Rundell shook his head at the mariner, "No lad, I allow myself no regret or remorse and where possible little feeling. My actions were wrong and there is no way that I can pay for my misconduct. Therefore I can end my life, which is an affront to Laferious name and Dre'Guist's or I can live with it the best way I know how. That is why I live out here in seclusion, your coming has been a reminder that memories live long in this world."

"So you know nothing of poison then? How was it that you healed Speck?" Joseph asked confused at all he had heard.

"Oh I know much of herb, root and liquid for I studied hard in my years straight after my banishment, searching for an understanding of the events that had unfolded and moulded my destiny.

I learned exactly how the beast had turned lame and why, the herb settled, slowly reacting with the liquid to take its time in rendering the horse's pain. Well the day has worn on Joseph perhaps we should retire, our last eve together I would hope for happier tales." A smile begun to return to his lips and he held out his hand to Joseph to help him up.

The young mariner grasped his outstretched palm, "It is difficult to know if any tale is happy or sad until it is at its end Rundell. Perhaps your tale is yet to reach its finale." The old warrior nodded and walked side by side with Joseph back to his home.

The next morning they rose early, Arn and Febra busied with packing and preparation, Rundell restocked all their provisions and gave them ample firewood for the journey. Finally the four stood outside the door, dressed as they had arrived, packs slung across shoulders and weapons resting at their sides.

It had been an hour or so since they had last seen Rundell but he had promised to see them off and none of them wished to leave until he had done so. More time passed until finally he emerged from the rear of the cabin, all dressed with leather tunic and furs, his mighty bald mace hanging at his side, over one shoulder a huge pack that looked to weigh as much as Speck.

He beamed a smile at them all, "I have decided to journey with you to your destination, too long has it been since I crossed the border of a town, even one as remote as Bannermane." A huge sigh of relief crossed the faces of the party and they were quickly followed by smiles and handshakes.

"Also," Rundell continued, "I fear you getting lost on the way ahead, as even with my directions I doubt that hunter of yours could find his own feet!" The warrior roared in laughter and Speck took the opportunity to join in, he always liked a joke at Arn's expense. They reached the ravine by mid morning, a huge pass that measured at least one hundred feet across, at the far side a waterfall ran through the side of the pass.

Rundell had explained that the only way to cross was in climbing down entering through the cavern that the water ran through. He had told them that about a half a league onwards the passage rose up and met with a small river that fed the falls. The descent in itself was not an arduous task, the bank was not as steep on the close side and in places it was more like a large hill amble. By the time they had reached the base they were all wet with the spray coming from the gushing falls. Rundell led them across the water via a network of large stones that protruded thankfully from the depths below. It was slow going as was the climb into the face of the cavern, the rocks were slippery and steeper and the rush of the water over head was both exhilarating and worrying at times. Rundell led the climb, calling back instructions to the others, letting them know which rocks were good for holds and where the moss grew heavy. Arn picked up the rear and scolded Speck merrily on his way up, jeering up at him to stop loosening stones and mind where his feet were treading.

Speck did not take it badly, he had seemed different somehow since his experience with the poison. He no longer held that air of reservation and anger about him, Joseph liked him even more for it, his friend had finally grown up he thought, as they climbed higher towards the cavern. Rundell pulled them all to their feet as they scaled the final stage of the climb. The cavern within was deafening, the noise of the water bouncing off its thick walls and filling their heads to the point that it became hard to concentrate on one another speaking.

Rundell's voice shouted out to them, "Stay close to the right side, the water will rise as the path narrows, be cautious and concentrate on the journey. I suggest we keep quiet now until we begin to climb again if you are lost into the water the current will take you quickly before any here has the chance to save you. Be mindful, Speck you walk in front of me, Joseph then Febra and Arn at the rear."

They followed his instructions carefully, no one uttering a word as they looked down at the wet cavern floor, their eyes peering for jagged rock or moss that could throw them from their course. Concentration made the journey seem longer than it truly was, Speck's eyes began to ache staring at the damp floor and his thoughts began to wander to their quest. Rundell had told them a little of their destination, it was by all rights once a fortress of great note and even today the ruins were a site to behold. Mainly though he had become intrigued by the item that they were to collect, what remnant could they be transporting to Asten, an heirloom or weapon of the old days perhaps?

Something dug at the back of his head, he quickened his pace slightly, the anticipation driving him on. They had begun to climb now and the pathway had widened finally so the trek became less hazardous, the light shone brighter from the opening and sunlight sprayed across the water, lightening it to a bewildering effect. Rundell passed Speck and led them from the mouth of the opening out into the wilderness. They stood looking out across an expansive plain, the river running its way north and west towards Asten. Rundell turned to Arn, "Your eyes are keen huntsman, do you see it?" Arn walked ahead of the group and peered northward into the distance, "It is far, yet I see it on the horizon, perhaps a further ten leagues? Maybe more?" He turned to check Rundell's reaction.

"A fair estimation, we will push on until mid afternoon then camp down, my body yearns for a pipe and some stew, the head and heart are willing but my legs are not what they once were."

Speck wandered forwards, "At least we are safe out here."

Rundell smiled towards Speck and thought to himself, perhaps for now my little friend but Bannermane has been the doom of greater warriors than you I fear. He smiled inwardly, but perhaps no greater thinkers.

Chapter 5 – Bannermane

"Day 36: The clay is harder than we expected, a whole day digging and we are no further than a few foot under topsoil. The soft overground has been deceptive, we expected to uncover more by now, I will have to write to Asten again to seek extended funding.

Day 45:   Will these rains never cease? Another wash out, with our site now filled with standing water, further progress is once again hampered. Heard back from the Scholatic in Asten, not happy about having to raise more copper. We need a find soon.

Day 51: Using stratification I have pieced together a likely trench site for foreign properties. Finally a few days clear weather has seen us peer below the hard clay levels and into the depth I hoped to achieve. Only time now surely before we strike a real discovery.

Day 60: Progress demands from Asten received, I am loathed to write in return with our first discovery. It is not I suspect what they hoped for, an axe larger than any modern Vedian weapon painstakingly uncovered from the southern trenches. An amazing find in historical terms but not the type of artifact to impress the Scholatic. However if we continue to follow the laws of supposition I can only believe soon more will follow.

Day 62: Wonder upon us. We have discovered a book!"

Diary of Karl – Archaeologist of Bannermane – Vedian 997

They crested the hill without realising how close they were to the town, the landscape spread out dramatically below them and Bannermane itself was visible a quarter days walk away despite the grey overcast day. Still the sky refused to drop any rain on them but the strange pressure in the air made Joseph sure that at sometime that day the drought would break.

Rundell slowly crouched down to sit next to Arn on an outcrop of rock, his knees crackling as he did so. The others dropped their packs and lay down on the hillside. The old soldier fixed Febra with a grey stare.

"It's not too late to go back and hand over the mandate to some other fools missy."

Febra and the rest of the group couldn't believe their ears.

"How can you you even joke about it? Look how far we've come. If you have to keep suggesting things try not to make them so ridiculous."

"Always consider the ridiculous."

"More sage wisdom eh?"

"Not my words to be fair, heard some yarn spinner repeat them years ago. Those words stuck with me though, forgot the rest of the story. Shame really, I seem to remember enjoying it quite a lot."

Febra was ready to give the old man some more of her mind when a strange lilting note caught her ears. Arn had been fumbling through the pockets of his hunter's garb but now he had found something and was holding it to his mouth, a look of concentration wreathed his features and it seemed that he was unaware that his activity was being studied by everyone else. A second oddly haunting note floated from the tiny instrument that was cradled in his hands. It was remarkably different from the first, broader with a touching sentiment. If Febra hadn't been watching Arn make the noises she would have sworn that they came from completely different instruments. The hunter managed to produce a run of eight enchanting notes each with a unique feel, spelling out an octave not only of pitch but also emotion. He shook his head unhappily and pocketed the diminutive thing, only then realising all eyes were on him.

"What kind of instrument was that Arn?", Joseph asked innocently.

"Tshh... I wish I knew, I've had it since I can remember. My father says it was left to me by my great uncle, shame the old sod didn't leave some instructions with it too! I often pull it out during the lulls in hunting and give it a try."

"How long have you been trying?", asked Speck.

"Ooo.. Let me see. Around twenty years now I suppose. What you heard is the miserable sum of two decades testing."

Rundell rose slowly to his feet and paced off slowly down the hill.

"Not waiting for us then?" Called Febra after him. Arn chuckled slightly and made to follow the soldier's lead. He looked over his shoulder at Febra and grinned.

"He said he needs the head start." By dusk they were nearing the broken wall of Bannermane, parts of which stood almost unchanged since the day they were built. It was clear that the town was never meant to be siege proof but merely defensible against attacks, the fortified walls weren't tall enough and had far too many gates. Large sections were no more than rubble, mostly due to freebooters stealing the high grade stone work over decades and the wooden gates would have earned someone a pretty penny at market. The group trudged through a gap and got their first look at the buildings within, though grand by the standards of the Luff they were made for utility purposes and lacked any form of ornamentation. Once the middle wall was visible it was clear that a great deal of the modern buildings were constructed out of it's stones, often utilising the wall itself as a ready-built fourth wall. Just visible beyond the middle wall were sections of the far more complete inner ring, the upper half of the keep visible above, occluded occasionally by the misty figures of sentries. The grey stone work and the low clouds gave the town a grim and broody feeling. Joseph looked at the clouds and suggested they double-time it to the nearest inn as he felt the storm would break in a matter of minutes.

"Read the clouds can you boy?", asked Rundell.

"A sailor needs to know the weather.", said Joseph, repeating his captain's old maxim.

Sure enough, by the time they reached the only hostelry in Bannermane, the thunder rolled and the mountain of water above them began to pelt down.

With no name and only the traditional jug and cup sign outside the inn, the place promised to be as dower as the rest of Bannermane. A few quiet patrons supped beer at the benches and the innkeeper didn't even look up to see who had entered his establishment. Above the bar was hung an enormous halberd, probably fabricated as an ornament, thought Arn, the shaft being a full six feet long and the single flared blade looking like it probably weighed the same as Speck. Around the room less extraordinary weapons and armour hung from the walls, many pieces being only partially complete and almost all beyond any form of use.

"Hot ale perhaps?", a voice chimed from one side of the party. A large, busty woman with blooming red cheeks stood waiting with a tray which could have doubled as an Inpur nomad's battle shield dangling idly in one hand. While all about her the rest of the tavern appeared as dull as the clouds, this woman exuded jocularity.

"Hot ale?", questioned Speck.

"Oh yes, speciality of the house my handsome young man.", she tilted her head in a fashion Speck had never seen before, it suggested all kinds of things and each one happily given to keep a customer satisfied. "Seat yourselves at this fine bench and I'll bring it out to you. If you're not a convert to hot ale by the time you're through then it's on me." They sat where she had directed them and realised the shelter and promise of hot ale had quickly altered the group's mood. They were glad to have arrived.

By the third round of hot ale all of them had a new rosy glow to their cheeks, even Febra appeared to be enjoying herself in a quiet kind of way. Annabella turned out to be the owner of the establishment and despite their protests, let them have the first round of hot ale on the house. The drink, like Annabella, seemed a curative for the mundane and grey nature of Bannermane, bringing new life and heat to tired limbs and minds. The other patrons kept to themselves and seemed to be made up entirely of off-duty guards.

"Praise the Duke for leaving a garrison here!", touted Bella, "Otherwise this meagre establishment would have been shut years ago." At that moment a middle aged man wearing a filthy sacking tabard enter the inn, he was short but stockily built with remarkably blond and spiky hair, his self-interested look changed to one of annoyance as he spotted the group.

"So you've arrived at last eh? And seem to have wasted no time getting drunk I notice." He pulled the sack tabard over his head and dumped it by the door. His clothes beneath were well kept and foreign looking.

"Now then Karl, these fine people arrived only an hour ago, don't be spoiling their well needed rest." Annabella chastised.

"Karl of Frydbern? Would that be you?" Febra asked keenly.

"Indeed, and a motley lot you look to transport anything precious. Hot ales was it? 'Tish I expected better, I really did."

"Now sir," interceded Joseph in a conciliatory tone, "we arrived late and had planned to seek you out in the early morning. It has been a long foot march here. I hope you will find that your first impression of us does not betoken our true worth. Why not sit and we'll get to know each other better?"

The others of the group were somewhat taken aback at this fluid display of diplomacy, Arn himself had been planning to say just some such thing, he would not have expected to be pipped at the post by Joseph's simple tone. The archaeologist seemed pacified easily and pulled up a stool. He chuckled to himself for a moment.

"I think I'll have one of those hot ales myself Anna. It is pretty nasty weather." Once he had checked their warrant paper, Karl seemed keen to expound upon his work at Bannermane, stressing the honour of the commission directly from the council to do so. He explained how some of the greatest points of interest were to be found outside the town itself at the locations of the forces command encampments. "I believe that weapon", he said pointing to the enormous halberd over the bar, "was found at such a site. It should incidentally be at a university for study but the locals will not part with it."

Arn raised an eyebrow, "Surely no man could wield such a thing, I thought it was a mere ornament."

Karl sighed at the misconceptions of the lay man. "No man ever wielded it. Bannermane was invaded by a completely different race from across the oceans I believe. Other, less fine examples, are in my possession. But the size is not untypical for an invaders polearm. Sketchy accounts from the university archives tell us that Bannermane was the scene of a secondary invasion, the bulk of the invaders fighting from the east. This second front was over with relatively swiftly although there seems to be a lot of controversy over how exactly, a lot of the texts on the subject were destroyed or lost over the years, we know of them by references made but the fine details of what exactly happened here are unknown. Hence I am here, learning little by little about that time from the traces that still survive."

Karl looked them each over carefully and looked quizzically at them.

"Which of you is the scribe?"

"I am.", answered Speck, his tone telling the man that he had expected that to be self evident.

"Good I will meet with you in the morning. The rest of you can stay here or have a look about Bannermane if you like. And tell me young scholar, have you the tools of your trade with you, a quill and ink perhaps?" Speck's red cheeks told him all that he needed to know.

"No worry then, I shall entrust with the use of some of my own. There are a few notes I'd like you to take along with the book itself." "Book?", asked Speck. "Yes the artifact is a book, not what you were expecting I'll warrant. A shield or sword or some such would have been your guess eh? Never under estimate the power of ideas and knowledge, learned friend. Once translated I very much hope that this work will be the crowning achievement in historical study for the next hundred years. Who knows, perhaps longer? So whilst not of any specific military or monetary value, a scholarly burden is upon you all to succeed in this mission, not to mention my own historical immortality!" The last seemed to cause him great amusement. He chuckled to himself and took a long draught from his tankard.

The next morning Arn, Joseph and Febra trudged through the streets of Bannermane, which were turning into a dirty quagmire of earth, rain and horse manure, the only section of the town not to suffer this problem was the flag stoned area between the middle wall and the keep. They had thought once around the middle wall would be a short walk but the filth and the rag tag way the buildings had been reconstructed meant that it was becoming longer and far less pleasurable than anticipated. Arn suggested that they duck into the next merchants building so that they could shelter from the incessant drizzle for a short while. When they found one it had a circular wooden sign hanging outside without any inscription or emblem upon it, seeing no other likely candidates around they decided to go in anyway.

Once inside they knew immediately what nature of shop they were in – weapons in various states of repair hanging from every available section of wall space, there were even short swords hanging from the ceiling. At the back of the long but narrow structure an extremely portly man laboured over a sharpening wheel, periodically plying a dagger to the spinning stone cylinder and then examining it carefully. After a few moments he seemed happy with his handy work and laid it aside on a workbench along with half a dozen identical knives, only then did he appear to notice his new clientele.

"Good day sirs and to you too little lady. See anything you like here?"

"Much that I like smith, your work seems handsome and...", Arn cast an eye about the place, "abundant too."

The fat smithy roared with laughter, his midriff rolling along with the sound.

"I love to work dear hunter, yes for that is surely what you must be in those woodland clothes and such a fine quiver – do you know I tried my hand at bows once but I guess my touch is only for forging things. This 'abundance' is the sad state that the garrison is leaving me in, half of them were transferred out to other duties and the couple that came in were all old campaigners looking to trade weapons in for retirement to the farm or some such. Any road up, what can I interest you in or perhaps you just came in to get out of the rain, eh?"

"We've been rumbled.", noted Febra.

"I think you have our little scheme Master Smith, but I would gladly pay to have my knife sharpened and to look around for, say, until the rain stops."

The smith gyrated in laughter again and then held his hand out to the girl for her blade. A look of ill-concealed disgust crossed his face as he took it to the back of the shop, he gradually slowed as he approached the sharpening stone and then turned about face and marched back up to Febra.

"Exactly where might you have been swindled into buying this item? Hmmm? One of those little pig-iron merchants that sells nothing but kitchen knives and ladles? Look, look here.", he pointed to the centre of the blade and drew his little finger across a slight discolouration that crossed the metal. "It will snap at the first strong twist it gets, no I won't touch such a thing to my fine wheel. But I can't rightly give it back to you now lovey can I? One day your life may depend up it and this thing will let you down and embarrass you at the same time. I have no choice but to make you a replacement."

Joseph protested that they couldn't afford a replacement while Febra tried to shush him, the smithy was already beckoning them over to his wheel.

"They'll be no charge, it is the job of every honest and proud smith to see that things are as they should be, consider this a refund but if you ever see that fowl charlatan that sold you this again, tell him Ian of Bannermane wants a few words with him."

The smith expounded the intricacies of each step of the forging process, carefully examining Febra's hands and judging her strength. The three students stood in rapt attention to him for Ian was not only passionate but eloquent and knowledgeable. Soon the display of his art was over and Ian selected some hard wood and leather to form the blades grip, once again inspecting his client's hand carefully. Febra bounced and flipped the dagger in her hand and without warning threw it the length of the workshop into the upright of the door post.

"Incredible.", she said simply.

"Your appreciation is reward enough for me. But if I could tender a word of advice: throw only as a last resort, daggers are relatively slow and have low penetration, besides you would now be weapon less. Such fighters as I have known that throw the blades tend to have a set such as the one you see here." His plump hand waved at the six knives on the work top, they were slender and with almost no guard between handle and blade.

"If you don't mind me saying so you two look a little green for guard duty and you", he said looking straight at Arn, "might be good in a scrap but carry no armour so I'd guess you weren't long out of some woodland." Febra proudly explained that they had a charter from the council and would soon be leaving Bannermane to complete the work.

"I see...", grinned Ian, "Some form of delivery for Karl is it? Don't look so shocked, I've been here a long time and there's only two people who get the privilege of council chartered goods and your looking at one." "The council charters for you?", asked Joseph in disbelief.

"That they do lad. I may live in the murkiest backwater but even the toffs in Pluris and Asten know where to order their stuff for special occasions and the like. Ah, the last one was the previous spring, what a priceless blade that was. Shame it'll probably stay in the scabbard until it rusts. A wonder in silver and steel it was, a few touches of jet and gold on the pummel and the guard, nothing like some of those tasteless gem encrusted jobs. Besides every good smith knows that jewels make a weapon impossible to balance." Ian looked at them as if he expected them to confirm what he took as only common sense, instead Febra gave him a particularly wide-eyed look. He reddened a little at what he thought must have appeared to be a lack of modesty on his part and tried to move the conversation onto another topic.

"So, Karl eh? Guess you'll be moving some crumbling old bone, or bits and pieces of one those hefty axes. Here, can I let you lot in on a bit of a running joke?"

They all nodded and came closer to the smith in a conspiratorial huddle.

"The polearm above the bar in the inn, it's a fake." "But Karl, he's a man of lore, he would know wouldn't he?" "Would he now? Karl let me look through some of the bits and pieces of weapons he's collected from the battle field, wanted to know my thought on some of it. Well I was deeply interested in some of the workmanship and tried my hand at recreating it, took me a while mind you, once it was finished I struck upon the idea of having little Marky claimed he'd pulled it out of one of the peat cuttings and give it to the bar. Karl has never suspected it was a forgery and gets right steamed up about it occasionally." Ian tittered for a moment in a childlike fashion.

"I knew no one could have ever really wielded such a thing!", scoffed Arn.

"Lad,", said Ian, fixing the hunter with a gleaming eye, "somebody once did. The only reason Karl is so easily fooled by the little bit of buffoonery is because it's an exact replica."

Speck glanced sidelong at the book resting on a sideboard in Karl's office. He had been taking some extensive dictation from the archaeologist for almost a whole hour now, mostly to people he assumed were nobles or academics, stressing the importance of his work and the need for more funding. Karl noticed his wavering attention and placed his hand gently on the cover of the tome, treating it with all the reverence that a monk might afford a sacred relic. "Intriguing isn't it?", he said at last, "Secrets locked in a cryptic manuscript from the past. It's truly the stuff of legend, not heroic sword wielding legends I grant you but a far more encompassing tale: that of our own origins, the birth of this civilisation and it's people."

Speck nodded thoughtfully in response, he didn't take the archaeologists words lightly, almost as exciting as the mystery itself was the mere discovery that mysteries were here, in front of him, for the solving. Karl gently lifted the book, which was as thick as all four of his fingers and moved to the writing desk in front of the scribe. "See how much intrigue there is in the mere outward appearance of this manuscript." Speck nodded and leaned closely in to inspect the work.

"Twin clasps", muttered Speck, "with a locking slide, presumably made of brass, this book was made to travel not sit in a library. The cover is made of tooled leather, I wonder if Arn could identify the hide? The design seems to be geometric but not repeating, have you found any meaning in it?" The archaeologist shook is head in a sorry fashion. "If there is some numerological meaning then I would be a poor analyst, that is part of the reason I am sending it away and not trying to independently study it – as would normally be my right. However the council have placed orders on all written findings from the site as a priority.

What else catches your attention about the book?"

"The page edges have been sectioned by some kind of colour coding, my experience of books is limited but I have never heard of such a thing." Speck noticed Karl nodding with an intently interested look on his face, the boy was glad that he wasn't making a fool of himself at least. "The spine seems the most ordinary part of the book, these few glyphs above the first stitch may suggest a volume number or perhaps a title – it is beyond me to tell which, if it is a number, I would hazard that it comes from a very large series. Something tells me that these characters are more pictographic than script, could it be an authors signature or mark such as the stone workers use?"

Karl looked astonished at the final comments, "I had always considered it the title, your fresh outlook has given me much to think about." Speck made to undo the latch holding the two clasps but Karl stayed his hand.

"The parchment appears to be of the thinnest rice paper so could be dangerously fragile. I am under clear instruction for this to only be opened once in the hands of the Scholatic."

Speck made a noise of agreement but inside he longed to just see the writing held within, Karl had admitted himself that he only deeply understood his own field perhaps Speck could find some clues that he was unable to penetrate, and if he could then it might help him forge a name for himself. Better to save his investigations until he was sure that he could study undisturbed. Karl packed the book into a sturdy leather satchel and fastened all the buckles with care, examining it to see if there was any way he could further ensure it's safe passage. Finally he sealed the missives that he had dictated to Speck with wax and placed them in a wooden tube which in turn fitted into the side pocket of the satchel.

Hooking it over the boys head and shoulder he looked deep into the others eyes, "You darn well stay surrounded by the rest of that motley gang of yours, you'll make a fine scribe but you're no fighter, use your head while they use their sword arms and you'll do the best thing for all concerned. Good luck Speck of the Luff, I want to see you again someday, perhaps we'll get to mull over some of the puzzles from in here." He motioned at the book that was now swaddled in it's travelling clothes.

"I truly hope so Karl. We won't let you down."

"Look, if your lot aren't keen to get away today then come see me at the dig site south of town. You can't miss it, I've got it all staked out. If you or your friends are interested I'll fill you in on some of the details of what happened here."

They shook hands and wished each other well, Speck promising he would get to the site if he could. The young scribe emerged from the archaeologist office with a feeling akin to a sailor leaving port, his adventure had really begun. The reservations that had dogged him since they had left the Luff were snuffed out, here was the bigger, more fulfilling life that he had been seeking. By the gods, it was like somebody had injected fire into his blood! He set off back to the inn at a lively pace, swinging his arms like a soldier.

Arn grinned at the old guard as he handed over one copper coin, normally it would have been real pleasure on his face but now it just seemed a bad habit, after all in a way he had swindled the man out of his money. Still, he mused, the stones were just a game and if a fellow chose to wager without properly judging his adversary what concern was that of his? Some strange spirit of fair play rose up inside him and before he knew it he was buying the man an ale to make up for the loss. He'd never done that before but seeing the good cheer it brought back to the weathered guards face made him forget his qualms and push the man a bit further about detail of the keep.

"It's the only fine bit of stone left for leagues around here, the walls of old Banny may be rotting but from what I hear they weren't up to much anyway. Now the keep, there's a different tale altogether. Seen some of the bloodiest fighting in Vedian and truth to tell there ain't a sodding scratch on the thing. Goes down a way too into the ground I mean, some of the lads told me that there's at least two or three levels below. Nice little hoarding spot for supplies, arrows and what have you."

"So it's all stocked up for siege then is it? I shouldn't have thought the politicians cared that much about Bannermane, you yourself said it was only half-manned and the town get little or no trade."

"Stocked? Well I shouldn't think so. None that I know are let down there, standing orders of the garrison, they say that it's got dead water down there."

"Dead water?"

"Aye scurvy stuff likes the sailors sometimes get on the ships, makes you real sick if you get a snoot full. So we just keep to the upper stairs, that's no so bad you see cos' the place was made by them that know how to build and it's mighty good living for a regular like meself. You should have seen the ditch they call the Kanegon barracks, we had to pack down there for a few weeks during some o' them high and mighty chin wagging's they had years back. I'd have rather had a barn any day o' the week."

"The army life never drew me, my father was in the guards once, so he said. He never pushed me to join up just, he wanted me to take over as the hunts master at the Luff. Guess he didn't think I was suited for it either."

"Ain't much of a profession now-a-days. Even I can remember it being better in the force, council's too tight with the purse strings to keep it up you see. Robbers and thieves on the road are thicker than a tart's breath but there ain't enough man power to put 'em down, Banny doesn't even patrol nowadays, we just sit round the keep and twiddle our thumbs. I'm thinking it's time to hang up my arms and ask Ian what price he'll give me for this old sword!"

The soldier laughed in a way that told Arn it was only half a lie and it was all he could do to stop himself buying the man another drink. Just then Speck strode in looking for all the world like someone had voted him Crown Prince, around his shoulder there was a large leather satchel looking like it had just come out of the tanner's shop. He got to the table that Joseph, Rundell and Febra were idling away the day at as Speck drew up a chair.

"I've got the goods.", chirped Speck with a satisfied look on his face.

"Well then it just remains to get ourselves all packed up and out of here." Joseph saw his friends face darken at those words. He'd said something to disappoint him.

"Look, is it really wise to leave with half the day already spent? Don't any of you remember how miserable it was on the way here? Let's get good and rested before we plod back into the muck again."

"Inns cost money and that eats out of what each of us is going to earn on this job. I say get out now and pay day is that much closer." Febra dabbed her finger pointedly into the table as she made her case, it was apparent that she was uncomfortable sitting around when they had what they'd come for.

"Whether he knows it or not, the lad is right." Rumbled the reclining figure of Rundell from a bench, his words slipping from pursed lips that held a clay pipe. "If you break out of here half through a day you're gonna spend an extra half day on the road at the very least. It's sod's law, or Rundell's whichever way you choose to see it. Start fresh and get the best first day's travel in that you can while you're all fat from the inn food." The note of aged wisdom in his voice seemed to close the argument even

107

though he never so much as lifted his head, now it seemed he considered the matter resolved and was dozing back into whatever dream of lost glory he had emerged from.

"Well,", Speck added, "That's handy. Because Karl invited me out to the battle site south of town and I wouldn't want to let the duffer down, what with him being a patron and all."

Arn chuckled, "Patron is it? Guess you took a liking to him did you? Book worms together I suppose."

"I'll come along with you." Joseph said, "But you'd better leave that", he pointed to the satchel, "with these three here. It stands out a bit and we don't want it swiped on our first day."

Speck ruefully handed over the satchel to Arn, who tucked it under Rundell's grey head as a pillow. "You couldn't get a copper out from under that old bugger.", he noted.

The site wasn't difficult to spot from the southerly Bannermane road, a pair of ruts indicated the direction was used regularly by wagons. As the road began curving to the west they found the archaeologists place of interest, marked out by a great number of staves planted firmly into the ground with different coloured strips of cloth tied at the tops. For a while they saw little of interest but as they headed over to the furthest reaches of the diggings they came upon the scholar kneeling down in a recently excavated section, his sackcloth surcoat protecting his everyday clothes and trouser knees from the soil. In his hands he held a y-shaped stick, gently balancing the divining rod with index fingers and thumbs, eyes intent on the wobbling tip of the device. The practice of divining was familiar to the two boys as it was a common enough practice for finding fresh-water wells in most villages but neither of them had heard of divining for artifacts. Karl looked up at the patiently waiting pair and treated them to a rueful smile.

"It would seem that I've made a bad choice of excavation site this time around. Not a sniff of metal in the whole twenty rods square. It could be that I'm not using this darned thing right,", he indicated the divining stick, "but so far it's increased my success at finding relics a hundred fold."

"You divine for metal?"

"Yes, indeed. I see that sceptical look in your eye Speck but some of my finest finds here at Bannermane are directly attributable to the use of this rod. I make no mention of it in my monologues because a good deal of the Scholatic consider divining to be a peasant practice or worse. But let me show the proof, my field office is just over here and besides", he grimaced up at the sky, "I think it's going to rain again." They followed Karl over a wide segment of the moor like ground that surrounded Bannermane. Joseph wondered at where the hardy scholars hide out might actually be since there seemed no cover for miles around, it was difficult to move across the moor at anything more than a quick walk because of the tricky ground, one could easily twist an ankle. He hated to think of the problems that a charging army might encounter. Just as he was musing over these facts he found that he was standing on the edge of a small depression in the moorland, it dipped below the line of the surrounding ground by twice his own height and at the centre there was a stone doorway leading to what must be a partially underground structure.

Karl explained that these shake-holes were located in many spots across the moor and that they occurred completely naturally. This one had been used centuries ago by a recluse who constructed the stone hideaway, it was virtually impossible to find without being intimately familiar with the sparse terrain and offered excellent protection from the elements. Inside the retreat there was almost as much room as Karl's office in Bannermane, the archaeologist had installed an iron stove and somehow constructed a tough looking set of storage cupboards each with a padlock holding them closed.

Struggling under his sackcloth to get some keys out of his pocket, the proud resident finally unlocked two of the doors and swung them out wide so that he could inspect the contents. The first was perfectly ordinary and contained a lot of the items the boys would expect at such a locale, jars of preserved food, hard bread, tinder boxes, blankets and a host of well thought out essentials from which Karl selected a kettle and a tinder box and went to work on the stove. The second contained a bizarre array of relics carefully arranged for display, much as might have been seen at an exhibition.

The central piece was a magnificent helm, it's surface covered in mother-of-pearl and edges trimmed with gold, the shape was entirely wrong for any normal head, vastly too wide and seemingly made for someone with no forehead but with eyes very far apart, the nose guard was extremely wide and the opalescent surface seemed to make the eye holes stare vacantly.

It didn't take long for Karl to get a kettle boiling and make three bowls of tea, using some of the local herbs. He settled himself in a chair by the stove while Speck and Joseph shared a crude dirt wood bench.

"Imagine the town of Bannermane stripped of it's civilian buildings and manned by a proper complement of soldiers.", he began, "it seems clear that the invaders landed on the coastline in large numbers to the north and since Bannermane is set some miles from the coast they were able to formalise the army before marching on the stronghold. It would appear that they assaulted Bannermane as a second wave attack, with their larger force first taking Kanegon. An invasion force attacked what appears an indefensible fortress. Whilst Vedian forces held for many days there appears to have been some great military blunders that made the battle cost the kingdom vastly, one point I have noted is that there was some attempt at cavalry charges at the attacking forces early on. No doubt these mounted attacks would be dismal failures, for as you have seen the terrain surrounding the town is terribly pitted and many of the horses would have been lost even before the charge arrived at the enemy. The battle was eventually won by the Vedian's at a terrible loss but it can not be explained how, it is almost as if the enemy just stopped fighting. The final historical outcome of this battle is clear, that despite winning the Vedian forces were crippled and the opposing forces never seen again on these shores. This is what we know, but the why's and how's remain a mystery."

Speck remained lost in the description of the conflict for some time after it's narrator had finished while Joseph went back to the cabinet of relics and looked at them in the light of this new information. One question burned bright in the young man's mind and he finally asked it out loud.

"Where did they come from?"

"I wish I could tell you the answer to that one Joseph but there has been no work on the battle sites in the south and any artifacts that I have unearthed here only tell me that they were strange and exotic but match none of the very limited information we have about places outside Vedian." Finishing their tea both boys thanked the academic for his hospitality and wished him luck in his endeavours but as they trudged back toward the town in the fading light his story returned to them again and again, they were walking the very path that the invaders took to storm the town, a town which they snuffed the life from in fleeting days, a horror rushing in from the sea and bringing sure death with it. The subdued mood followed them into the common room of the tavern and they retired without taking part in the happy banter that both Febra and Arn seemed dedicated to.

Speck retrieved their precious cargo from Rundell who was sipping ale by the fireplace and grumbled slightly at the boy removing the item. Now the little scholar had his chance, it seemed that the book was almost asking him to read it, promising him insight and knowledge that was unavailable to others. Taking the book into their room he bade goodnight to Joseph who slumped on a bed and fell into a heavy sleep. Drawing a tattered blanket that served as a modesty curtain he lit a fat tallow candle and rested it on the shelf by the bed. Carefully he unstrapped the leather bag and unwrapped the protective layers around the book whose clasp shone invitingly in the flickering light. With reverence Speck unbarred the clasps and pulled them open, waiting just a few moments before he swung the heavy cover open and looked at the first page. There appeared to be no title and the author seemed to have launched into tightly packed clear writing without any of the usual pleasantries such as a preface or notes.

For a while Speck stared at different pages in despair, their was no place from which to gain any intellectual leverage in the book, no illustrations with captions, no tables and the text itself was formed from characters that seemed to have almost infinite variance. He closed his eyes tightly in a moment of frustration and cursed himself for being so egotistical as to think that he could solve what a fine scholar could not. With his eyes closed he could still remember the form of the lines he had just read but it faded away uncomprehending and tantalising. Only once his thoughts lapsed into silence did the memory distort and somehow become other. Speck did not immediately notice the effect and dolefully flicked through the pages only when a irksome sense of missing something came over him did he close his eyes and concentrate again on the passage before him.

He urged his mind to keep the remembrance clear in his mind's eye but such is the devil of memory that he couldn't retain it for long without any understanding of it and besides nothing was being revealed by this form of mental inspection. Just as he ceased the thought experiment the passage became full of mental texture, such as when one remembers the taste of an orange or recalls the feel of a horses coat. This experience was like a sudden recall of many such textures but the sensation passed in fleeting moments.

If he could simply quiet his mind from interfering in the process then Speck believed he could unlock a great deal more. He chose another page at random and stared at the first passage for forty heartbeats, all the while calming himself down and trying to surmise nothing from what he was seeing, simply to be an open mind. His eyelids gently shut and immediately the passage gained the mental dimensions he had briefly experienced before but now his observance was engulfed in the fragmented perceptions of shape, taste, light, sound and smell.

He could still hear his heart beating but the sound became fainter along with all other senses and as it did so his perception of the real world and the descriptive joined. Linking to each other as life links every coexistent thing until suddenly he was observing a road that pierced the heart of a forest without himself having any given standpoint. He was simply there, knowing every angle of the scene, every fragrance and sound at once – embracing a giddy feeling of omniscience.

Chapter 6 – Nights End

"Am I not King in waiting? Do I not deserve the crown as is my birthright? Does my lineage not give proof enough of what is rightfully mine? And yet five long years I have waited while these Scholatic observe and tinker, assessing my fitness to rule!

Well let the waiting be at an end, for after the tournament this year, the five year clock shall toll on their lethargy and let them hear the cries of the people ring out.

Let Vedian call for their Crown Prince to be King!"

Crown Prince Laferious speech to the Royal Court – Vedian 965

"Commander!", the shout was somewhere between a bark and a roar and Dior turned slowly to watch the hulking colour sergeant bounding up the steps to the command building.

"Report, Pinkerton.", Dior said in a low tone and it seemed to the sergeant that his commander had an eerie talent for being heard no matter how softly he spoke. Pinky had learned from first hand experience that when Dior was his most hushed it meant that his deadly tactical mind was closing the net on another victim.

"Captain Tress wishes you to know that the mobile armoury, triage and mess facilities are standing by and ready to move. He also needs to know if you require any of the war engines loaded?"

Dior shook his head while looking out across Nimsberg, the secret training camp of the Sabre Regiment, "They'll be no use to us, Pinky." Was all he said and then turned to continue up the steps into the command building.

Pinky didn't let the dulcet mood of the commander worry him, very little worried the colour sergeant of the Sabre Regiment. Under normal circumstances a regimental colour sergeant has to be tough, holding the men in order through brute force of body and will so that officers could exercise their authority without being sullied by facing men down. It had been said all through the Vedian Forces that sergeants define and keep the body of a regiment in check while the officers make the head. If one individual could define its regiment it was Pinky, he was strong, covered in scars and with an almost mythical status for surviving. Tress would no doubt be glad to hear that he didn't have to arrange any of the cumbersome war engines to be loaded on wagons, the logistics officer had been awake for the last thirty-six hours making preparations for departure from Nimsberg.

Though Tress was technically superior to Pinkerton, he made the wise decision of treating him as an equal; believing that a sergeant and captain should work toward a common goal. Besides Pinkerton was at the pinnacle of non-command rank, colour sergeant of the Sabres, finest known regiment of men, there was never any chance of him entering the officers ranks with no noble patron or notable family member to sponsor him. His ascendancy had been by the sweat of his own brow and if he was honest with himself then he might admit that the gentle, controlled command of an officer was not his style.

From the corner of his eye Pinkerton noticed a familiar trio huddled into the recess behind the briefing rooms. Known throughout the regiment and further as the 'Three corporals', these men were as quick with the sword as they were with their unique brand of humour.

"What's going on here ladies?", Pinkerton bellowed from just a few feet behind them. The three snapped round as if pulled to attention by unseen hands.

The usual complement of corporals to a unit in the Vedian Army was one, but Dior had increased it to three for his own tactical reasons. Whatever those reasons were, the results spoke for themselves, Sabre was the most feared Vedian regiment anyone could remember.

"Nothing is going on Colour Sergeant!", barked Paddy, a veteran of two campaigns and hero of several dubious mess hall tales.

"Then what do you have on the water barrel behind you laddie?", Pinkerton's stare could boil a man in his boots.

"It's... ahem... Pipe Major Brown's musical apparatus Colour Sergeant.", Paddy answered in a deadpan fashion. He knew the other two would agree that evasion at this juncture was itself pointless, being caught red-handed if you will.

"Well let me have a good look at them then, ah, I see. With the aid of a few balle reeds inserted into the sack here you hope to start our departure for Bannermane with something like my backside after two weeks of iron rations. That's the idea is it my beauties?" Pinky grinned in a twisted way which defied comprehension by the three men who stood motionless before him. He let them stew for just the right number of heartbeats and then tossed the pipes to Jones who caught them deftly while never appearing to lose his stance of 'at-attention'.

"I haven't seen you here lads, if Pipe Major Brown catches you though I'll have you hauling logs from the swamp to the parade ground for a full day. Away lads but I do love a good joke." From his grinning face it was difficult to imagine what kind of joke might be Pinkerton's style of humour but the three relaxed noticeably.

The colour sergeant marched off like a beast from the pit that had been taught military posture, his vast torso braced and his bovine neck holding his head straight and proud. He entered the main training ground where the sound of practice weapons filled the air. Sergeant Roust observed grimly from the sidelines, a short stocky man he was a full eight inches shorter than Pinky but was built from stern stuff. "Our little jaunt to Bannermane may be sooner than we thought Roust, don't wear 'em too thin."

"News from them upstairs Pinky?"

"Dior's getting all quiet." Growled Pinky.

"We know what happens just after that. Play times over. Torbit, Royd, Lovell. Get yourselves and these black hides back to barracks. Pack and inspection in a ten-sun!'

"See you on the road Roust. Keep 'em eager. Gotta check in with my gentleman.'

"Cheers Pinky, see you in the bar if we don't leave by sun-down.' With that Roust quick marched after his departing unit and Pinky headed to the supply building, Tress's headquarter for the regiments logistics.

Once inside the low building Pinky stood in a formal at-ease while Tress was talking to a battle-mage, one of four assigned directly to the sabres.

"I'll be with you shortly colour sergeant.' Tress said over one shoulder, never taking Pinky's presence for granted, not like some of the toff officers that Pinky could think of. The demi-warrior talking to Tress looked oddly out of place in his jerkin and trousers, his boots were those of a fighter but the candle-men, as they were affectionately known, never wore more than a light leather armour.

"...must be in tight bunches of eight to get the full effect.' Finished the battle-mage.

"That's going to be mighty tricky Fystal. I'll have a word with Pinky and the three corporals and see if they think they can make it happen. We mustn't forget that our men, however well trained, would need to pull this off in action.'

"Just an idea, Captain. Bear it in mind."

"A good one too, you chaps are darn bright. If you get any more flashes of inspiration let me hear them." The battle mage was fairly young for his profession, about forty and seemed encouraged by the officers attitude. He gave a sloppy salute, where his hand should have been sharp and horizontal, stopping short of the left of his chest it was actually a rather weak slap on the torso. Unpracticed, noted Pinky.

"Sir, the commander orders to pack no war engines."

"How did he seem to you colour sergeant?"

"Quiet sir."

"Alright Pinky old chap I'll get my shaving kit all packed up. Got the men resting have you?"

"Aye all on light duties sir, too light for some it seems."

"How's that then?"

"Wait till the Pipe Major try's to move us all out sir. I wouldn't want to spoil it for you."

"Those three been up to no good eh? I leave that at your discretion Pinky, though a good laugh might set us out on the right foot."

"We going straight to the problem then sir?"

"Not quite. We'll be joining with the Royal Cavalry on the Asten eastern border."

"Baby sitting is it sir?" Cackled Pinky. "Not quite sergeant, the Royal horses have been bolstered and should pack a pretty punch, they are more than three times our number."

"So it's a case of no-horse-without-foot is it Captain?"

"Let's hope so Pinky. Let us hope so indeed."

Dior rode onto the hilltop that was serving as a command post with two of his captains following behind. Tress, sharp as a new razor and evenly tempered. Junas, noble fighter through and through, with almost preternatural skills and the undying loyalty of his men. Dior took time to watch Junas duel with other sabre swordsmen when he could, as the captain had curtailed these challenges to but one a year due to the demand. It was only by using the heirloom his uncle the counsellor to the Duke of Lough had bequeathed him in his will that he could truly appreciate the perfection of Junas's fighting form. He had no idea how the thing worked but when he wore the copper wristlet he seemed to see events with greater clarity, almost like the passage through time was slower allowing him to perceive and perform actions quicker than others. He could observe the union of every one of Junas's actions that conformed to the elegant plan of defeating his target. It had even occurred to Dior that should he ever be killed on the field of battle he would prefer it to be done by a swordsman like Junas. There was some dignity in losing to such clarity of force.

Dior's infallible memory let his glittering mind toy with this and a dozen other topics while noting the figures of the Lord Protector and another commander standing on a low wooden platform in the failing light of dusk.

As he approached he recognised the handsome features of Danal Pluris, commander of the Royal Lancers. Tress and Junas dismounted and stood to attention while holding the reins of their animals. Dior did likewise but handed his reins to Tress. The commander climbed the half-dozen steps up the platform and saluted the Lord Protector.

"Sabre Regiment ready for duty my Lord."

The ornamental armour of the Lord Protector glinted with orange highlights of the dying day and he nodded his head to Dior, the long black and grey mane of his hair swaying with the motion. Lord Protector Estalyn was not to be judged by the foolish garb

117

of his office, he was a capable and justified marshal of the Vedian land forces.

"Take up position south of the great sea road commander. Occupy the western field and prepare any field work you find necessary." A notable look of disappointment passed across the face of Danal but he said nothing.

"Thanks to the Lancers and the Asten Swords this secondary landing has been stopped in it's tracks. I want this dealt with in short order so we can return regiments to the primary front."

Dior's face had not changed from the dutiful expression that he first wore on mounting the platform but his tone carried the barest hint of a question.

"It will be difficult to reach Bannermane's boundary in short order from the western field Lord."

"You will move in after the central charge. I hope that's clear." It was all too clear to Dior whose internal machinations showed him possible futures as others might work out the distance to a nearby tree.

The Lancers and Asten Swords were depleted to half strength by holding the march of this new landing, the Crown Infantry was situated across the central boundary in a holding pattern. With this arrangement the Protector could only be intending to use the Royal Cavalry as his hammer to smash the invaders grip on Bannermane's border. A dismally incorrect choice, with the regiment being made of two-thirds untried men across uneven territory with no run-through to break out the charge and turn on the other side. Why would the Lord Protector, a fine general make such a choice? He wouldn't.

The commander of the Cavalry was the king's second son, Prince Shartos.

Undue pressure must have been brought to bear to deliver his regiment as heroes. Since there were no easy wins on the main front the King had no doubt viewed the allegedly smaller invasion at Bannermane as a chance to shower his son with glory. Dior pictured the proud king hearing none of the Protectors warnings phrased as suggestions. Shartos would charge Bannermane and route the aliens from the shores of Vedian then take his heroes to the front and raise the courage of all around him. In his mind's eye Dior saw the dutiful Lord Protector break his composure and

118

plead with the King only to be cut down. He could almost smell the duty burning on the brow of his respected Lord. Shartos will lead the charge. Shartos will die trying and how many more will fall with him.

Breath leapt back into Speck's straining lungs and for a while all he could do was convulse in a fit of desperately ragged inhaling. Joseph tried to steady him with his hands upon Speck's shoulders and as he did so he noticed tiny ice crystals on the left side of the youngster's tunic, there was frost over the boy's heart.

"Season's preserve us!", exclaimed the shocked hunter from behind Joseph's shoulder. While still in some degree of panic the former sailor tried to piece together some plan of action, whatever had happened it was directly linked to the book and so that threat should be dealt with as soon as possible. He pried the tome from Speck's grip and shut it, fastening the catches on it and handing it to Febra. "Find some packaging to bind this thing up, don't open it or undo any of the catches.", he ordered. Speck seemed to be rapidly recovering some colour and there was almost no trace of the ice on his tunic now.

"Incredible...", the shivering boy muttered and curled up on his sleeping pallet, eyes shining with wonder.

Joseph stared into the candle flame in front of him, the common room of the inn was empty, the fires dead and not a soul stirred. Every one of his friends had changed so drastically over the few short days of their trip emerging into the characters that somehow the Luff had kept hidden deep inside them. Was he changing too? Perhaps not, he had after all spent a great deal of time away from Luff on ship. Perhaps he had discovered himself earlier than the others without the need for extraordinary circumstances to draw him out. Gods he missed the comfort of the sea and the security of the ship now, somehow the order of command on board made any trouble seem manageable – orders were given and every man bent to the task in unison.

Not so here. Febra was worryingly independently minded, she had conceived of this trek and in a lot of senses could consider the whole scheme her own so why should she listen to what the others said? Not only that, she often seemed unpredictable and with circumstances playing themselves out in such a dangerous way that could mean trouble. Arn was finding new strengths that he hadn't exercised before; leadership, will-power and responsibility. Joseph didn't doubt that he would do anything to preserve the group, as their leader and protector.

And Speck, the most changed of them all. The Luff had treated him like a child for his entire life, mocking him, underestimating him and denying him the right to prove himself in any way. Outside it's influence Speck had become more impetuous and hungry for vindication. There was no doubt that he was upon some personal quest that Joseph could only guess at, he hoped that he would like the Speck that finally evolved, his heart told him he would.

Loneliness filled the sailor far from the nearest coast and further still from the Dusk Returner, where he longed to stand and lose himself to the rhythm of the vessel as it cut through the black diamonds of the night sea. He looked vacantly at his own hands in the weak candle light, callused palms and fingers hardened by honest work, hands that had never once wielded a weapon against his fellow man.

It seemed to him then that fate had been mistaken and placed him on a journey intended for another.

"Lost in thought?", said a familiar voice from behind him.

"Wondering if I made a mistake leaving the Luff and the sea. It all seems such a good thing for the rest of you Arn but it worries me. I get the feeling I have may have left the best life for me behind." The hunter sat himself at the table and looked sympathetically at the boy.

"I'm glad you're here. Speck certainly needs you. If you do nothing else you stop us all getting beyond ourselves Joseph. At the end of this trip you might at least know that you don't want to leave the Luff, that must be worth something eh?" Something in his friend's voice reassured him, a tone suggested his concern for Joseph was paramount, Arn was developing into a real leader.

"Let us fetch a brew and sit outside, I do not care for the confines of wall and roof on a night as glorious as this" Arn left for the bar and ordered two mugs of mead from Annabella, who cast the huntsman a wry smile. Joseph followed Arn through the outer doors and the pair sat upon the ground resting their backs on the inn wall. The air was cool and the sky had begun to cloud over, leaving a translucent feel to the night that drew over Bannermane. Arn looked up, studying the sky, trying to pick out the few remaining stars that had yet been removed from sight, when he finally spoke it was with a loud and vibrant voice, "I feel I have made a friend already. Perhaps my name and reputation come before me. Arn the hunter. Arn the lover! Ah, what stories the bards would tell in times to come, dear Joseph."

Joseph smiled at his friend, "I know not of what you say, yet your passion and tone make light any concern or ill that I may bear." Arn looked down and slapped the young mariner sharply on his back, nearly knocking the broth from his grasp.

"You have been at sea too long, the cold air has numbed your wits and cooled your blood. Do you not recognise desire when you see it! The mistress of the house wants for me I surmise. To look about the scant population of this area I should be not surprised, her current selection is far from grand, yet it could be some time before I keep such company again. After all, it is a wholesome night and my need is rising, perhaps you can throw a little more light on that."

Joseph was taken aback by the hunters words and had Arn taken the time to look he would have seen it in the young man's startled face. Casual relations were by far unusual in the Luff, whether in or out of wedlock.

Yet he found it difficult to come to terms with, his experience with the opposite sex was minimal, the pinnacle elapsing in a short time at the back of the minters with the younger daughter of the inn keep. A feisty and excitable girl, whose love for all things seafaring, went a long way to smoothing Joseph's passage into her arms. More than his own shortcomings was Arn's natural confidence that left him feeling uncomfortable, or if he had been true to himself, slightly jealous. He wished he had a quart of his friends confidence and bravado. His thoughts turned to Febra and he could not hide the reason why, even to himself.

Still he felt a deep longing for the girl and although he was sure his passion was derived from love, the tension inside gave more to passion than any traits of purity. There was something about her, he could not rationalise it to himself, let alone anyone else and certainly did not care to share it with Arn.

They finished their mead in quiet contemplation, Joseph announced he was heading to bed and picked himself up from the ground. "Don't wait up", Arn said as they ambled back into the common room. Joseph shook his head and proceeded to mount the steps up to the second floor.

Febra was crouched behind the stable area, set off slightly to the south of the main entrance to the Inn. She had not come out to talk with the others, rather listening intently to their discussions. She sat contemplating her own personnel quest and the notion that what she had set out to accomplish no longer seemed to hold the same significance as it had in the long nights under cover in the market of the Luff. It was not the party that had steered her from the course but rather the old warrior. His gruff manner and short patience had only sought to endear him to the girl. To her he had been all that she had hoped to find in Kanegon, when all the hate and loathing of a lifetime had been swept away. A father figure, perhaps truer than any bloodline she could have dreamed of discovering. He had eased the lust inside her that burned for vengeance and the demons that had tormented her for so long seemed quiet and distant.

Ian sat in a large wooden chair, warming his feet from the cooling forge.

The blue pipe smoke he blew into the air drifted slowly in shifting clouds about the items of his trade that hung from the workshops beams. The weed was a gift from an old friend and its shortening supply made him realise how long it had been since he had stretched himself from Bannermane's borders. It had been a graveyard all those years ago, to warriors and fighters and still as a ghost of its former greatness it had the same effect on those that dwelled within its crumbling walls now. He found watching the billowing smoke a form of meditation, allowing his mind to turn to new projects he could undertake. He still had the gift of thought and the rigidity of self purpose, that could not be taken away as easily as status.

His first clue that he had visitors came when the cobalt clouds were thrown into chaos by a sharp gust from the smithies door. Six garrison men entered, stamping their boots and poking around his shop in a way that made Ian take an immediate dislike to them, his work was too personal for people to just prod and heft; that was just downright rude.

"It's too late – come back in the morning", he shouted. The obvious leader came around the bench that separated the shop from the work area and leant one hand on the hilt of his broad weapon strapped to his belt.

"Were not here to buy smithy, but to ask questions."

"Then go to the inn, a few ales well get you all the tall tales you can carry." The shopkeeper shifted his weight and moved to a standing position to observe the man closer."

"We will my fat friend, we will in good time. First I'm going to ask you and answer me straight or you may regret doing otherwise. Our journey has been long and arduous and I have little patience left to bandy around." The leader was tall and unnerving to look at for any length of time, the one thing this man had, Ian thought, was patience. Nonetheless this was his shop and no one came here demanding anything, looking the soldier up and down he brought his large fists onto his hips and gestated to the door.

"Little men should be careful what they say, it might get to the Duke. My patron list is long and of a quality that should concern even the highest of officers." This was no lie, his customers though not as ample as he intimated were of good stock. His merchandise was known to many and he had dealings with both Asten and Coralis.

The leader smiled wryly and a fear began to travel down the smithies back, he suspected this was no garrison officer but no discernible marks on his cloak wrapped close about him gave indication of his position. He changed his tact quickly, "It has been a long day sir, I have been hasty in my words. Perhaps I can give you directions to the Inn, so that you can freshen yourself after your journey. The ale is not the best in the land but it serves to dull the night chill."

The soldiers eyes never left the smithy, neither did they warm to his change in tone, "Indeed you can, first though I would ask if you are aware of any strangers or travellers that have passed though of late, or anyone that stays here now?" As he spoke the tall man's fingers rotated the hilt of his sword slowly. Ian was careful not to look away for any length of time, rather coughing and carefully sneaking a glance at the weapon. It was a broadsword, of that there was little doubt, sheathed in a worn scabbard, plain and leather. The faintest glance was enough however for the smithy to notice the curious and brilliant craft work on the hilt. It was carved from a dark wood, nothing like the bark imported from across the seas. Rather a material he had only seen once before, in Pluris the capital of Vedian at the university. It was the mark of the protectorate of the council that hung in their halls of meeting. He could not remember the emblem inscribed but the darkest of wood he could not forget. He had asked and heard all the tall stories the market had to offer, casting them aside as nonsense. Until he had met with a man of great repute, a Scholatic who confirmed the materials origin, hewn from the great trees of Malevolence when they were young. The hulking beasts that spawned from the ground, hurtling into the sky, surrounding the area that few now would walk on, in the days prior to the Great War when the trees where scorched with sickness.

Ian steadied himself and tried to piece together a smile, "There are many strangers that come and go, can you offer me more of what you seek? I would of course look to aid you in any way I can."

"A party of four, young travellers, three men and a woman. You would ingratiate me if you could tell me something of them." The soldier slightly turned his head and for a moment the smithy feared he was looking right inside him. Searching for the information he sought or perhaps realising the shopkeeper had not always been so.

"Ah yes," he replied, "such a band travelled though her a few days hence but I believe they moved on."

"Did they travel with any others and what was their business?" The soldier leaned forward until his face lay within inches of Ian.

"For their business I could not say, I keep my own counsel and do not interfere with others. Yet for my knowledge they passed without further company."

The soldier held his position for a few moments, processing the information and then smiled once more. "Our thanks for your aid, now if you could point my men and I in the direction of the inn, we will leave you to your business."

Careful not to hurry them away, he recounted the directions and wished them well, falling short of asking them to return at any future time. As the last sound of boot fell on the open ground Ian slumped onto the bench and thought of the old warrior and his young charges. He was no hero and self preservation was always a high item on his agenda, yet he had done what he could, what any man would have done when faced with the Captain of the Protectorate to the High Council.

From his position, laying dozing on a common room bench nearby the hearth, Rundell could see everything that was going on in the inn. He casually stirred, grumbling about the comfort of his pack under his head but he had a good view of the latest entrants to the quiet drinking house.

Keeping his eye cracked open on the side of his face shrouded by shadow, he saw what appeared at first sight to be three garrison soldiers. What immediately worried him was all of them were in their early twenties, strongly built and just the hilts of their swords betraying fine workmanship. Bannermane was a stop posting – used to usher old soldiers into retirement or keep the truly undignified fighters safe from themselves. These new arrivals did not fit any of those patterns.

Another trio of suspiciously able men came in and tried a little too hard to make a show of being nothing to do with the first group. Rundell had seen enough already. He rose to sit up on his bench with great stiffness, rubbing his crotch and peering around as one seeking relief from the evenings drinking. Once he had got to the stairs, careful to stay out of the light of the burning fire, he dropped the sleepy posture and quickly climbed, marching down the corridor to the room they had rented on arrival. Once inside he shut the door so quickly it startled the sleeping Speck.

"Get our all stuff together quickly – we have trouble." Joseph, who had been sleeping on a blanket on the floor a few feet from Febra's bed, pulled himself up and awakened the girl. Rundell recounted events surrounding the new arrivals and his fears to them all.

Joseph realising Arn was not in the room, grabbed at the old man's shirt, "Arn is not here, I think he was with the mistress of the house.." Before he could continue, Rundell stepped in, "I

125

know exactly where he is, two doors down the corridor, get him Joseph quickly and return, we have scant time to waste."

Joseph pulled on his shirt and run out the door and into the corridor, there was no sign of anyone around but he could faintly here voices from the common room below, he thought to knock but then remembered the look on Rundell's face and proceed to march straight into Annabella's room. The huntsman slept, cradling the mistress of the house in his arms, her head resting on his full chest, he stirred as Joseph moved to the bed.

"Rundell thinks we have trouble, we have to leave now!" Arn shifted himself from the bed, careful to not awake the sleeping woman.

He grabbed his trous, flung earlier onto the floor and unable to find his shirt moved out of the room with Joseph in tow. He briefly turned back to the room and smiled at the sleeping Annabella before silently closing the door. By the time they had returned everything had been packed by Febra and Speck

Rundell went to the window of the room and peered out carefully, seeing no guards in the alley below he opened it and leaned out.

"Don't fall out will you? Febra half invited in an attempt to make light of an increasingly tense situation.

"Girl, someone in this inn is being readied for a royal gutting. Now we are the only lodgers and none of the driftwood soldiers garrisoned in Bannermane could do anything that might merit this much attention. So its us or a really big mistake and these sword notchers don't look like the type to make mistakes."

Speck by this time had his pack slung over his back, "Back stairs?" he asked.

"Still take us through the common room, look here though." He pointed out of the window and showed them where the inn abutted onto the outer wall of Bannermane. The upper storey of the building was thinner than the lower, leaving some roof on their side all the way to the wall.

"It's clear they do not know we travel together or they would have got me in the common room. Guess their working off information from when you left the Luff. So here it is then, I'll keep lookout downstairs, you get out and onto that wall, take it east and I

126

catch up to you on the road out." The old warrior held each of their eyes for a second and then turned for the doorway.

Joseph spoke the words but it could have been any of them, "We would stay here and watch with you Rundell, I know not why we are sought out by these men but I suspect it is no fault of yours. We would not have you fight our battles, it is more than we could ask." The others nodded in agreement.

"Well fortunately for you Joseph, it is not less than I will give." Rundell turned to face the young scribe, then swiftly grasped his hand and pulled him close until the old man's mouth was parallel to Specks ear, "Time is everything laddie, I more than most know that. Do not pursue that which will come to you, rather savour the moments before, they are all too fleeting." The old warrior moved away, passed a final nod to Arn, is if to confirm with the hunter the group were now under his charge.

"Be quick for love of Vedian! I don't want to be hanging around any longer than I need to." He waited just long enough to see Febra, the last of the group, exit through the window and make passage onto roof. Rundell went back out of the common room and bolted the door behind him. As the trooper was at the top of the stairs preparing to go back into his drunken act, he could hear the voices of at least three men at the base of the staircase. No way down now and a pitched fight on the stairwell was not his style, he needed room to wield his weapon of choice. He thought hard off any ruse that might delay the men, given the party precious time to make their escape. He cursed himself for not arming for all eventualities, his old corporal would not be pleased. This was a knife fight or a short sword at best, if he could not gain access to the common room this could be short lived.

Having weighed up the options he backed up a couple of feet from the top of the staircase, maximising the available space he drew his weapon. He would make them fight as they reached the top of stairs, who knows, they might fall back down and break their necks but somehow he doubted it.

They spotted him quickly enough as the three turned to climb the steps, they shouted to alert any others and drew their weapons, long swords not ideal either given the confinement of the area. There was no way to fight three abreast and even two might easily impede one another, so the last ended up skulking a few steps down, awaiting his chance.

Rundell let the handle of his ball and chain waggle in his hand, like some old warriors do when their arm goes – he even stood with his feet close together to give the impression of a novice. His opponent a well built man in his twenties, with a sharp square chin, grinned and came in with what should have been an overpowering first strike, either to remove the weapon from the old warrior's grasp or go through his defence and score a strike. Rundell side stepped and sloped the handle of his weapon to deflect the over confident blow, letting it follow through and over balance his opponent. A quick half shuffle to the left and a flick brought the heavy ball up into his adversaries groin with a crunch. While the man stumbled to the floor, Rundell used the opportunity to snatch the dropped sword and let his own weapon fall to the ground. When eventually the wounded man slumped in front of him, he cut him at the back of the neck deeply.

As the second man approached it was with a greater caution, Rundell put all trickster thoughts aside now and stood balanced, as wide a stance as he could allow, sword firmly ready, eyes gauging the way his latest attacker moved. The new assailant was left handed which proved detrimental in the narrow hallway as he had to come at the old man from the right side of the stairwell to avoid his fallen colleague below. The blood from the victim was pooling across the floor, giving little doubt he had now expired.

Rundell exchanged a few sword blows with the left handed man, little more then 'how-do-you-do's' until he was satisfied of his opponents capabilities. The second round of attacks came dazzlingly quickly and even though he had been expecting them, the old trooper defended with difficulty, it had been too long since he had parried and thrusted with a blade. In response he feigned to the right but instead of following up with a left attack he feigned again to the left and swept on the man's right side. His opponent was quick and able, normally he would have read the assault, defended and countered all of Rundell's moves but the blood on the floor made him lose traction. His back foot slipped out automatically raising his blade arm which Rundell slashed across the wrist, with the weapon out of commission he followed through piercing the breastplate and deep into the chest.

By now help had arrived on the stairs and instead of the third man standing up he stood aside for a tall, brutal looking soldier accompanied by a another bearing a loaded crossbow. With a modicum of respect, the tall swordsmen made a show of honour to the fallen men, then smiled in a crooked fashion at Rundell. It was that gesture that the warrior recognised and from it his memory unrolled like a woven rug.

"Where's that pretty Captain's uniform?" Rundell said, careful to not drop his guard.

"O, I don't like to get blood on it Rundell" The tall Captain slowly advanced, hugging the right hand of the staircase, ensuring he did not eclipse the crossbowman's target.

"I make sure you don't get a chance then shall I?" the old warrior reposted as he lunged at the Captain. The tall man was quick and agile, he smashed aside Rundell's attack and drove him back a few paces, so he was clear of the bodies on the ground.

"You have beyond that door what I seek? He gestured at the locked door that Rundell was now level with.

"You won't get in to find out, their too decent to understand a word from the likes of you anyway."

"Look how high and mighty you are now, a protector of men? Was it not so long ago you were nothing but a renegade and traitor! Do you look for redemption in the arms of babes now old horse?" Another blistering offensive put Rundell almost against the end of the corridor. The Captain swung right and a crossbow bolt ripped through the old troopers shoulder, pinning him to the rear wall. It was all the old warrior could manage to put his sword in his left hand and hold it up.

"Now, isn't this pretty?", said the Captain snidely, "Perhaps we'll get to have a little fun with you after all."

"You ain't fit to wipe a real soldier's arse, that's why only the council will have you and your ilk."

The Captains eyes seemed to burn for a few moments, then he raised his sword up to Rundell's throat level. Too weak to hold it off the pinned man just grinned and said, "Even the council think your some jumped up dog, do they reward loyalty with a juicy bone?"

"You know nothing of loyalty brigand!" The Captains fury could hardly be held at bay as his sword pressed at the old man's throat.

Arn had seen the last few moments of the fight through the hallway window, from the eastern section of the wall. He sent the others on but stopped and strung his bow, when Rundell was pinned he hurriedly notched an arrow but had to calm himself before taking on the shot. It was seventy, maybe eighty paces to the window, no wind, the brute levelling his sword was all he could see but from the attitude he knew Rundell was alive. He breathed out and held the target steady, then slowly inhaled until his expanding lungs and back seemed to thoughtlessly release the bow string, all the time his eyes and mind considered only the target.

The shaft smashed through one of the window panes and crossed the Captain's collar bone, it was made too high by the refraction of passing through the glass. The tall man roared in pain and stumbled out of the view of the window. A second quarrel pounded into Rundell's chest from the crossbow and the old soldiers head slumped forward, the sword dropping from his grip and landing at his feet.

Chapter 7 - The Long Cut

"While ordinary men succeed by whit and guile, pushing tactically to a goal that they may eventually achieve – similar results are often achieved by the truly great almost instantly. It is this brutally forthright means of success and gusto that makes lesser mortals sweat and raises the hackles of angels and demons alike, for a certain element of his formula relies on setting one against the other so that neither dares raise a hand against him.

This common quality of the hero leads us to question the safety of his technique, for while soldiers and politicians work towards less glorified goals in a more mundane fashion – an epic figure cannot help but load the environment around him with desperate potential. Hear then this wise counsel: a prudent figure uses the heroic and great figures under his power sparingly and with limitation; seeking always to carefully remove weights from the scales of conflict immediately after they have served their use."

'Maintenance of the Power Politic' - Si'an the Justified – Vedian 788

Arn was seldom within sight of the group, Joseph could only assume that he had them under surveillance most of the time, occasionally the hunter would rejoin the party whispering pieces of advice. Asking that Joseph keep his weapon to hand and that Speck should be careful to remain exactly between the leading Joseph and the trailing Febra. He offered no explanations but stalked back into the gloom.

It was all that Speck could do to keep Joseph and the huntsman in sight. His lungs were breathless and his chest felt hot and tight, but he did not stop, fear drove him on. Fear of what was and fear of what could be if the assailants caught up with them in the open. The land was desolate as far as Speck could make out, in all the time they had ran, he had touched not so much as brush or rock. The terrain was flatter here than the undulating plains to the south, it meant their chase was unhindered by surroundings.

Speck realised that the same would be true for their pursuers.

Arn still ran ahead, dropping back to ensure he led the others in the correct direction. He had not dared give time to his thoughts, rather concentrating on navigating the quickest course east. He was aware of the coastline to the north and was careful to not veer too close. It would be easier to track them near the shore than if they stayed on the plains, he knew the only saving grace they had been delivered was darkness. The night was black as any he had witnessed, the air was thick and warm, the low clouds shielding them from any light of star or moon.

He knew approximately the distance to Asten's borders as he had discussed it with Rundell. He winced at the thought of the old warriors name. How had he forsaken him! He should have stayed and fought side by side with him, perhaps then he would have stood a chance. Instead he had hidden like a child, frightened and cowardly.

The wind whipped across his face as he ran, quickly wiping away the tears that stained his cheeks, leaving them to rest briefly on the arid plain below. There was nothing else for it but to continue the race, if they stopped and rested here in the open they would certainly be discovered by morning. It was many more leagues to the City itself and even with a forced march that journey would see the rise of three new dawns.

At the first sign of dawn, on the morning after the attack, Arn finally called a halt. He had been out of sight of Joseph for a while but the mariner was not sure how much time had passed. His energy was sapped to exhaustion and at the huntsman's word to halt he dropped to the floor, grasping for the air, that while all about, seemed to be in very short supply. Looking up at Arn, he could see the athletic man breathing heavily but showing no real signs of fatigue. Febra was the last to arrive at the spot Arn had chosen to end the chase, she sat down calmly on the floor, sweat was covered about her face and her thick hair was pushed back with the moisture it created. "How far have we come?" She puffed as she addressed Arn. The huntsman turned towards the east, looking to the direction they had come from earlier that night, "It is difficult to say for sure, perhaps four leagues, at the most five. Our direction has been true as I could make it, using the tracks on foot and stars above to guide us. " Speck looked up at Arn, his bright red face was etched in pain, the journey had been punishing and yet he had never stopped to ask for quarter. Arn looked upon the young man, his respect had been renewed over the past night, he had carried himself well considering he was easily the least fit of the four.

"I know your question Speck, as I can see it in all of you. No, as far as I can surmise we are not followed. In fact I am unsure if the chase was ever truly upon us. I even begin to wonder if it was us that the assassins wanted and that makes me sadder still. If they came for Rundell and I deserted him in his hour of need, it would be surely more than I could bear." The hunter turned away, hiding the tears that welled up within him.

Joseph stood up and placed his hand on the hunters shoulder in an effort to console his grief, speaking softly "My admiration for Rundell was great, for I saw him to be an honest and noble man who had taken great pain for a wrong he once did, unbeknownst to him. Yet I would not question the manner of his end, in that it was of his own choosing. If we had stayed and fought, I doubt that we would stand here now, for those men looked more than curs and bandits and Rundell was familiar with one of their number. Maybe the old warrior knew a lot more than he felt it was safe and good to tell us. He obviously felt the sacrifice made was for a cause he believed in, if that is so, then I would honour his choice and would bid you do the same Arn."

The hunter turned to look upon the young mariner, "You are wise Joseph, of that I have never doubted, old beyond your years in the way you see the world. Yet the warrior in me has been hurt on this day and I would have vengeance upon those that brought me this pain. For now though, we will continue onto our goal, perhaps in Asten we will discover more of what has gone before." Speck stood and pulled his pack from his shoulders, it felt like a boulder had been removed from his aching back. He sorted through the jumble of items within, not having the energy to look up as he spoke. "For all the men I have met, Rundell was not the one I shared common thoughts with and no doubt I am as different to he as fire and water but he treated me as an equal and that has been a rare occurrence in my life so far. We will have our vengeance, of that I am sure. In time, justice will be served."

133

Madistrin stood in his private quarters, the room though large was not adorned as richly as would be expected of his position. He had never given much time to property and riches, rather dwelling on sentimental keepsakes. His eyes caught the helm that sat proudly on the chest of drawers next to his bed, it had been his brothers. Madistrin had carried it from the field on which his brother had fallen and often he would look upon it in times of trouble, considering what Laferious would do. In truth, he had known for some time that things in Vedian were not as they should be and certainly not as they would have been if his brother had still lived.

A knock came at the heavy door and he called out, "Come forth." The door swung upon and four men entered bowing before him, each offering their personal pledges to his name. He addressed them each in turn, a smile crossing his sullen face, "Captain, it is good to see you again. Did all go well with the message you held?"

The tall man, stood from the kneeling position, his fair hair adorning his handsome face, slim and angular his body was testament to long hard days training at the Pluris barracks. Beneath a tunic which bore the royal insignia of the house he served, a pale linked mail armour covered his torso and strapped upon his back a broadsword was sheathed.

His tone was soft but his voice commanding, "It did my liege. I delivered three nights past and then moved at speed to parley as requested with the Earl of Medwere." Madistrin clasped his hand warmly, "Your tasks as ever have been carried out with precision and loyalty, rest yourself now as you will, for the hour is nearing when I would call of your services again Parran."

After bidding farewell to all, the Captain left and traversed the halls out into the main entrance to the palace. He thought to go straight to his bed at the barracks but instead decided on a drink at the mess. It would be good to see his men again, he knew soon they would be called upon and they deserved his attention. The streets were quiet for Pluris and he ambled slowly, taking in the cooler air that sprung off from the nearby Bay of Vedian. As he neared the mess, he began to hear loud voices within, whatever circumstances or difficult times they lived in it could not be said that soldiers of Pluris did not now how to enjoy themselves. As he pushed opened the door and entered the busy room a familiar voice shouted out from the bar.

"Captain Parran Dre'Jan your men have waited long and hard for your return. It is dry as the Lough Dessert in here, would you not purchase a mug of ale for desperate men!" Parran pushed his way through the throng of bodies, a lot of new faces he thought, it disconcerted him. A broad smile crossed his lips as he met with the owner of the voice that had greeted him, "Its good to see you my friend, I hope all has been well since my departure?"

The large man at the bar, grasped his foreman in a lock and pulled him close to whisper at his side, "I would speak with you alone, soon, in private but not here." The two men parted and Parran greeted the others around him, careful to not let the words of his friend show on his face. Things were changing quickly in Pluris, too many new recruits, new units being formed under the instruction of the council, it was not like his Lieutenant to be unnerved easily, he would meet quickly with him for a debriefing and then report back to the Crown Prince before the night was over. It would seem sleep was a luxury that would have to wait.

Madistrin sat around the small rectangular table at the top of his quarters, on the other sides representatives from Coralis, Asten and Kanegon taran's waited for him to begin. These men Madistrin trusted, he had known many Earls and Dukes in his time, some honourable most indifferent, more interested in their duchy's and personal riches than Vedian as a whole. These men were different, he had long trusted their opinions and knowledge and believed they had the same goals at heart as he. Redrick of Medwere was the youngest of the three, a confident and comely individual in his late thirties, often more at home in the hills and mountains of his home than these surroundings.

Madistrin breathed deeply, it had been too long since he had stood at the shores of Lake Medwere, looking up at the vast mountain range that ran many leagues into the north. It was a sight that had left him quite heady as a young man, the early morning dew laying deep upon the rich grassland that surrounded the lake area. Coupled with the mist that ran down the mountains like an avalanche rushing towards him, only to hover wistfully over the lake. Waiting.

He had often visited Medwere in his youth, his health never being of the highest order, it was seen as a place of recuperation and convalescence. Madistrin had thought little of it at first, annoyed with the time that took him away from his brother and the capital. Yet as time went on, he met and befriended Redrick and a friendship was forged. It was strange he had thought, Redrick had been so different from his brother, uninterested in matters of state. Rather keeping to wander the mountainous region and exploring, often disappearing for days at a time tracking. He was in fact a captivating conversationalist and knew a fantastic breadth of tales and stories gleaned from travellers that he had met and was always one for the ladies. A talent Madistrin did not share.

As time had passed the two had kept in touch but pressures of state had worn heavier on Madistrin in more recent years. They had exchanged messages, occasional letters but this had been the first meeting in perhaps two years. Madistrin smiled across at his younger friend, a warm smile that told of history and experiences shared. Lost on those who had not trod the same path. For the first time in an age, Madistrin felt a warmth and confidence inside himself, he had felt so alone for so long now.

To Redrick's left, sitting uncomfortably in the slim crafted chair was a man of considerable girth and equal heart. Asten's Duke, Durgal or 'Digger Durgal' as he was less formally known in Asten. Not from any lineage, Durgal had acquired the title of Duke via a fortune made from stone mining the foothills. He had traded throughout the land and was a respected businessman in commerce as well as being head of a respected blacksmiths in Asten. It was said that he had dug the first ten weight of stone in one day with nothing more than pick and shovel to hand. A burly man in youth, fortune and fair living had softened the muscle considerably. His adequate stomach sat comfortably on the huge adorned belt that hung around his waist. He wore the clothes of office that he prized so highly. A plumed hat and frilled full coat, he was quite a sight and known well throughout the taran's. His beard was kept and full, a dark mass that combined with long sage locks of hair. A mouth of full lips and broad smile that rarely left its keeper, he was a jolly fellow indeed and always good company.

Madistrin wondered often why he kept friendly with such a scoundrel, for that is what Durgal was he had no doubt. His business dealings were dubious on occasion and his Dukedom was ineligible, purchased rather than acquired through lineage. His blacksmithing skill however was undisputed and for all his shortfalls he had heart, Madistrin never questioned he was a man that the people trusted in Asten. He had experienced where they had come from, he knew of their lives, their ways and fears. The people could respond to such a man. Aside from those factors, Madistrin liked the chubby stonemason, his laugh was like a bellowing bugle, sounding out through the walls of his home, coating them in a light heartedness they rarely had been accustomed to.

The third man was Miles Oply, Duke of the seaport Kanegon at least in name. His office had for some time now been little but a name above the door of the town. Kanegon had changed more than most over recent years and Prominence Bast'wa was the real power in the area now. He was a sincere and old fashioned man in his late sixties and had been a loyal servant of Vedian and importantly Madistrin trusted him.

Durgal's voice boomed out across the table, "Are we to sit her and stare at each other like lovers, or are we to get down to matters at hand! I would discuss rather sooner and therefore eat not so late."

Oply turned his head to Durgal, "Do not trifle Duke of Asten, the matters of which we discuss tonight are of the utmost importance to Vedian and its people. You know that."

Durgal smiled, Oply always addressed him by his title, he liked that.

"I would merely progress with matters, it has been a long journey and man can not live on gallant heart and good deeds alone."

Madistrin, smiled at Durgal, "It would seem you have survived well till now my friend."

The hearty laugh filled the house and even Oply chuckled to himself.

Madistrin motioned to speak and the men leant conspiratorially forward, hands clasped tightly together resting on the table.

"I can not thank you all enough for a long journey that has been made in such short a time. I can only apologise for the haste of my request but hope what I have to say will bear that out."

Madistrin paused, as if to consider himself, then once again turned and faced the others, "No perhaps we should approach this differently, I would be certain first before I speak. Come tell me of your tales. Durgal what events unfold in Asten, what is the mood of the people and I would hear of all, especially any talk surrounding the university at your shore."

The Duke sat back in his chair, preparing for a long speech, his eyes tight, the skin stretched in lines around them. A seriousness burrowed in his brow, "What I would tell you, is not news that you may wish to hear, I would not be the bearer of such tidings yet it seems no other is in position to do so. Asten is far removed from Pluris itself, yet our trade routes are tight, we hear many things and my words are influenced by such rumour. For some time now the trade routes have been trodden by curs and the like, yet of late it has worsened, lawlessness reigns in the wilderness, if yet it has not spilled into our city. The response has been muted from our esteemed Earl of Asten, he has sought no addition to the watch or internal militia. The trade council but ten moons past petitioned he and his followers on the benefits of a border guard to be installed. Even offering to foot the cost of such a force, it was declined! His reason given was a lack of necessity, it seems the threat is real only in certain eyes. In itself I find that strange for that is fact, what I tell next is rumour and less am I able to substantiate its content. As you would expect I have sound ties with the blacksmiths of Asten, a rowdy if usually honest bunch, the talk is of a bumper year. Orders up and their days full, extra carts arriving from the south delivering ore, of that I am sure. One said that arms were the main uplift in requests, swords and shields. Being the inquisitive fellow I am, I dug a little further. I had checks done on caravans leaving Asten for a week, a watch on every stone and drop of wheat that passed our borders. The reports gave a stark contrast to the blacksmiths words, no arms had left Asten, with the obvious exception being our chain armour which is imported throughout the land to all town barracks."

Chain armour from Asten was a prized possession for anyone joining the Vedian army. Crafted from the finest ore and smelted by Durgal's own blacksmiths, the House of Histevirrillm. A family smiths dating back an age, they had produced fine chain before the great war, it was believed that they forged the great chain worn by the Sabre Regiment, although that has never been confirmed by Bannermane archaeologists. On induction into the military a young man would be presented with his chain and trusted to care for it for many years, long serving commanders often still wore the chain of their initiation.

"So the questions were still unanswered, who was ordering the arms and how and where were they being delivered? I spoke to a friend at the House of Brillve, a smithy retired now but knowledgeable in affairs. He was unable to confirm the buyers, only saying that no pattern had emerged in large scale dealing. Most requests had been spread out and from variable sources. Yet has was able to tell me of a caravan route regularly delivering off the normal trade lines. Apparently a small camp south of Kanegon had been set up to receipt these goods but the caravan was not taking the southern road instead travelling at great distance over the foothills south-east and around Kanegon. In itself this would delay a journey by days and I would deduce can only point to ill doings. I decided to make the Earl of Asten aware of my findings, my first if not my last mistake. At best he was flippant towards the matter but as I pressed he became irritated and drew reference to my own business dealings, suggesting I would be careful to watch my own caravans and concentrate less on others. I might have put this down to his own ignorance were it not for events of the next day. Reports came through to the town of an attack on the House of Brillve, curs had broken into the grounds looking for bounty, the elder smithy had apparently tried to halt the break-in and paid with this life. Stabbed thrice through the chest with a sword, an unusual choice of weapon for those looking to steal. Normally long knifes and clubs are more your average thieves weapon of choice."

Oply interjected, "That in itself is no confirmation of wrong doing, we live in a lawless age, swords are not the blade of militia only."

"I did not claim it was proof in itself, my learned friend, yet it is but another piece in a jigsaw that puzzles me. Perhaps the arms are to travel south to the Lough for the Huskian's to war upon each other, it is not unknown for tribe to invade tribe. Yet they tend to be an honourable and direct folk, if not entirely civilised. I have little more to say at this time, only to bring to your attention the general feeling at Asten that those arms may be finding their way to a darker place. That is one of my concerns and fears, to add to it the people are seeing growth in crime and a reduction in those that could stem its tide. Yet at the head of my taran no concern or direction is given to these matters. I am a wealthy man, I count my coins and I guard my belongings, It is my experience that nobility are similar in their approach to what is theirs."

Durgal folded his arms and rested them on his ample stomach. The stone maker was worried Madistrin thought, he reads the signs well but he needed to see how far the spread was. The Crown Prince turned to Oply.

"Can you give credence to this theory Duke? Could these arms be making there way to Bast'wa?"

Oply scratched his balding scalp, "It is difficult to be certain. Kanegon is rife with thieves and villains, law and order is barely held and little of it from the militia. Copper changes hand everywhere, my experience of Bast'wa has been that he only does that which benefits himself. What could be the purpose behind stacking arms? He already benefits from the majority of trades that come through the city. It is possible I suppose but I would not guess. What I can bring as fact is that lawlessness has increased, it has been long since your liege has journeyed to our city, it has changed and not for the better. I wish I could do something but it seems respect for my post has long since passed. There was a time when a man's services could be bought for coin and now his loyalty and conscience it seems." Oply bowed his head slightly.

"I am sorry Miles, it has been long since I walked from Pluris borders, it seems now, far too long And what news to the north east Redrick. Is Medwere and its villages blessed with happier times?"

Redrick's voice was unusually tame compared to the stone makers, yet its tone carried much weight with everyone who listened.

"What news I have, I would surmount, you already suspect, yet it is clear that you seek clarification prior to deciding a course. For my own, I perhaps hope that its direction does not blow towards Medwere. Selfish I know, yet I would look for no more incident than already dwells in our valley and for myself too long has it been since I walked among the buildings and roads of the town. I will tell you what needs to be told. As you know Medwere is blessed rich in trade, even if it does not have the history of Asten

140

behind it, I would like to think those that choose to dwell there do so because they feel an affinity with what it represents."

Durgal looked puzzled, "What does it represent, it has no specialists or experts, a pretty place indeed for those that trifle with such matters, but I do not see what you drive at?"

"As well you know my ample friend, Medwere is a city of idealists not cowards or traitors as some would have it. Do not be so quick to judge or dismiss, for it takes a man much freedom of will to choose a course such as this, as committed a man as would charge a tower with but sword and shield."

Oply interrupted "What relevance is this, no war is brought on Vedian, no battle is to be waged here. I do not understand your point." The old man looked to Madistrin but the Crown Prince kept focussed on Redrick..

"As you know, the University of Coralis is now home to SanPollan a man of dubious morality but a political fox. He has risen sharply in the Scholatic and heads the learning of Perennial philosophy now. He is allied to Shel-Toro that is of no doubt to me and his word is law in Medwere. He takes with one hand from the people and gives with another, he offers trinkets while he removes liberty. The Earl is akin to Durgal's in Asten, he does nothing to counter him or put obstacles in the way. Medwere is now guarded by only the Coralis Swords under Rayan and they are reduced to two battalions, patrolling the borders of Coralis no arms are permitted in the city of Medwere. "

Madistrin nodded, he had been made aware of these developments from his Captain many months ago and had not moved to challenge them. He grimaced at his earlier errors in judgement.

Redrick continued."A conspiracy this does not make I admit, yet it is in the philosophy of SanPollan and his master that I most fear. For they believe in balance, to the finite. Medwere therefore is in great contrast to this if you would believe my earlier words, we are a thorn in the side of the new Scholatic. A city of pacifists, men that would make their own choice. I fear these scholars would have it differently and they unravel a plot to bring it to bear"

Durgal looked visibly surprised at Redrick's admonishment of the Scholatic, "These are hasty words surely! I would be party to caution although I have no love for the lore masters myself, yet you talk of plots and schemes, I would first hold us to caution."

An air of uncomfortable silence held the room for a few brief seconds before Madistrin spoke, "My friends I fear I have put the whole of Vedian at risk through my selfish actions, I believed that in living out my life as best I could, not challenging for the right of Crown Prince in earnest, I would serve Vedian well. Yet this now seems but a falsehood. A simple lie I have let myself believe over the years, I thought my dear brother to be the rightful King of Vedian and so it should have been. I never looked to fill the gaping hole he had left, rather leaving our country to the whim of the Scholatic, for a time I saw no wrong in that course, for men like DeFache are honourable and trustworthy. Years have now passed since that fateful day and I see a country full of fear and dishonour, the Scholatic are no longer men of good faith, they are politicians at best and schemers at worst!" Madistrin had stood up and was gestating graphically to the other men, "I have laid quiet and timid as the walls of oppression have closed in on our people, I have done no honour to my brother or to my name and least of all to Vedian herself." Madistrin looked at Durgal, the stone master's eyes were like huge bowls starring back at him in disbelief. "I am sorry my friend, you know little of what I could tell you and I would not alienate you here. It is true that the time for friendships of old will soon be nearing, we will rely on the deeds we have done to serve us here in the present. Let us hope we have made stronger friends than enemies."

A knock tapped on the door of the chamber, startling all within.

Madistrin calmed himself and sat before calling entry. The door opened and Parran walked slowly through, he bowed to all three individually, "I am sorry for the intrusion my liege but I would speak with you on a matter of urgency."

"Then speak here Captain, there is nothing to be told that these men can not hear. I see concern on your brow, tell me of your urgency."

Parran recounted the meeting with his Lieutenant soon after they had met at the barracks. He told of the changes to the Pluris militia, even personnel within his own company that had been signed off without his consultation. " My lieutenant also informs me that the watch has identified a crop of mercenaries moving through the town. Dangerous men usually encountered in three

142

and four's at worst, yet I am told that dozens such men have been spotted in the last two weeks. There is also talk...." Parran tailed off.

Durgal quizzed the Captain further, "Of what man, speak your mind."

Parran eyed the stonemason with suspicion, "I would not say, for I do not believe in gossip and rumour. Yet I feel I would have you informed rather than in the dark. There is talk of treason in the royal household. Talk of the Scholatic plotting to infest Pluris with mercenaries, to undermine the smooth running of the town. I would say to you that I am unnerved by these events, I can not explain it but I feel that law is breaking down at the very heart of our country. The barracks today has the stench of disorder about it. I would lay claim that the changes are not of a natural making but something that is being orchastrated."

Durgal grasped his head with both hands, "What day of dark tidings is this. I would rather walk through the forests of malevolence as a child then spend another sunset listening to these harsh tales. I came to Pluris to talk of concerns and worries, I thought that your calling was strangely timed, yet never did I think these ills would be set upon me."

Madistrin motioned to his Captain, "Draw a seat Parran, stay awhile, we have much to discuss. I will stay my hand no longer, these words of yours are the final confirmation for me. I fear the trap is already being laid and the course we are to tread had perhaps been walked upon by our enemies in advance, nonetheless, I will take us down it, to its conclusion. We must take urgent action, to tarry would be to concede defeat and I will not do that again. I would look now for two things, loyalty and courage. Parran, find me those men and those men alone. I do not wish to involve others that do not bestow those virtues. Find any you can spare and send them out to the borders of our land, we must know the scale of the opposition, mercenaries, curs and thieves perhaps but I believe there will be found organisation and planning as well. Seek it out and report to me at the Sanctuary of Bridges. I would go now with great haste to seek out DeFache, he hope he will help, he maybe the only one that can. Durgal I am deeply sorry my friend but I would ask a further task of you. Whatever connection or power you have, stall the blacksmiths work, cut off the supply to our enemies for I no longer doubt now, that is what it is. I would ask you to be careful if you take this charge, the days ahead will be hard for all of us."

Durgal's mind was whirling inside, he could not take in the chain of events at the pace they had happened, yet his respect for Madistrin was considerable and at heart the prince had known one thing, he was a good man. "I will do what I can or what I may. The charge I will take and return to Asten with haste, though I have no idea how to carry it out." A grin crossed the big mans face, "But then a man does not grow this fat and wealthy without learning the odd trick or two. I will find a way."

Madistrin smiled back, "You will go with my thanks blacksmith. To you Oply I would ask that you return to your city and do what you can to counteract the work of Bast'wa and if possible confirm or deny the weapon shipments Durgal has spoken off."

Oply nodded in agreement, "I will do what I can my lord." .

He turned finally to Redrick, "In many ways my friend your words troubled me most of all, it is because of that I would seek out DeFache. A time may come soon when the people of Coralis may be in grave danger, prepare for it and stay close to Parran, I would ask him to escort you to Medwere and meet with Rayan."

Parran interjected quickly, "But my liege, surely I must travel at your side to the Island, I am your protector."

"Yes and much more than that. For this time though, I ask you to go with Redrick. Your loyalty is unquestionable and does you honour as always, provide me a trusted man from your company to travel with me if you will. Now let us all rest and go about our deeds swiftly on the morrow. The great wars saw Vedian invaded by a foe of might and power, so it is told, but the struggle that is coming may pitch countryman against countryman. It could threaten to tear our society to pieces, stay true to ourselves and we will hold as one."

"As one with Vedian." Parran replied.

As the third dawn broke since Madistrin had met with the Dukes, a lighter mood began to fall on the party. The past two days they had marched at a swift pace, never once hearing sound of pursuit but always tense with the listening. Conversation had been limited and the bleak foothills of the north offered scant attraction to turn their thoughts from Rundell's demise. More often than not, they walked in single file, occasionally grouping to discuss distances travelled and onward directions.

At all times Arn kept them within distance of the road, always adjacent to its winding path in an effort to avoid easy detection. He knew the city of Asten was not a coastal port but he was unsure exactly how far north they had to travel, he wished now he had questioned Rundell while he had the chance. He was looking for grazing land or livestock as a sign that they were approaching the town and only then wanted to rejoin the main road.

Joseph's mind wandered to the more mundane issue of supplies, scant time had been given to organise food or water and all the packs had run dry the night before. There had been no rivers or creeks to restock from and though the weather was less heated than the Luff it was still a dry air that left a parched feeling. He wondered what waited for them in Asten, they had not discussed what to do next. Should they return to the Luff he wondered? Any thoughts were interrupted by Speck, who had ambled up to his walking pace.

"I suppose we can not go back now Joseph. The road leads to Asten and we must still deliver the book."

"How did you know, what I was thinking." Joseph replied.

"We are all thinking it my friend. I am hungry, thirsty and I would walk through the forests themselves if a hot bath were at its end. Yet we must press on, the Luff itself will be no haven if we fail to discharge our duties and I fancy Febra would be against any change in our course." The young man glanced backwards at the girl trailing behind. "She is of a mind to finish what we begun and Arn would seek to carry on for Rundell. Too many unfinished issues surround us now."

"And you Master Lucent", Joseph smiled "why would you carry on with such a task?"

"For all of those reasons I suppose, I am frightened Joseph, I would admit that to you. And yet I would see Asten for myself, Rundell said it was a city of knowledge and learning a fair place where we could find men of honour. That in itself is a reason to continue and let us not forget payment on delivery. I did not come all this way for my health!"

Joseph laughed for the first time since they had left Bannermane and although tinged with guilt, it felt good.

A whistle from their guide motioned to the others to gather, "The terrain is changing, there is grazing land to the north-west for hunting.", he pointed upwards to an area of open grassland, Joseph could just see movement of animals in the distance. "We will follow to the south and all being fair, should connect with the road in a short time. Our journey is coming to an end but this is not a time for complacency. If we enter via the road it could be watched, therefore we shall split into two pairs and stagger our arrival. They are looking for four traveling together, so lets not make it easy to spot us. If any ask we are merchants seeking to buy from the market. All towns like traders so our passage should be safe. I will go with Febra first, Joseph and Speck follow in after, we will meet up at a central point, perhaps an Inn or the market."

Febra interjected, "The instructions were from Karl at Bannermane to take the item straight to the University, let us not delay its delivery hunter."

Arn nodded, "Yes if the book is the issue then we will be safer once it is delivered, I agree. The university it is, we will take cover outside its walls and wait for you there."

By the middle of the day they were upon the road and signs of life could be seen, merchants with carts travelling up from Pluris to the south-east and farmers working crops and livestock to the north. The bustle increased in all directions as Arn drew them to a halt and motioned for Joseph and Speck to wait.

"Good luck my friends", Arn waved and smiled warmly, "Stay quiet and try not to engage anyone in conversation, if you have to exchange pleasantries do so but be cautious not to mention anything to do with our journey and on all counts do not give mention to the artifact"

The pair began the short journey north towards the town entrance, the vibrant sound of town life bustled ahead becoming increasingly audible as they walked along the dusty road.

Febra's right hand fidgeted on her belt, constantly tapping the hilt of her dagger that rested within. She wished now for this journey to be over and the quest performed, in all the happenings that had befallen them since the Luff, her original seemed to have lost purpose, Rundell's death had created a vacuum.

Arn turned to whisper in the girl's ear, "We are merchant's from Pluris, looking to purchase from market, skins and wool I think. The hunting forage looks fair as we passed the green lands."

Febra snapped back at the hunter, "You need not treat me as you do the others, I am well aware of how to lie. I am not your child to protect huntsman, just ensure you do not let slip any other snippets of our journey, you more than I possess a wandering tongue."

Arn walked on silently, the girl had a way about her that could make a man feel very small, perhaps because she was right in her summary. Arn was prone to talking and he knew what he needed now was a cautious approach, he nodded to a passing townsman, smiling genially.

They entered into the foot of Asten and looked upon the sprawling buildings that sprung up from its widening road. Arn had never experienced such a cacophony of shapes and sizes, people milling in doorways, buying and selling. To their left an inn of at least three stories towered over them threatening to block out the sun itself. A sign hung from an iron hook, revealing the name of the abode to be 'The Journeyman's'. It was crafted beautifully in bright colours and shades and depicted a sole traveller bearing a long crook standing upon the road with a hot sun upon his back. As his gaze stuck upon the picture he failed to see a man of indefinite girth wander into his line.

"Watch it fool!" The man grunted as he barged into Arn's shoulder, "This ain't no place for sightseeing, get off the road before you come to harm."

Arn moved aside and held his hands up to his chest, palms wide open, "I am sorry sir, I was just admiring the majesty of the place, I apologise for my clumsiness."

The large man was dressed in merchant garb and pulled a small handcart behind him laden with foodstuffs. "The only majesty I know of lies in Pluris but if you think there is some here then a stranger or fool you be." The man ambled further on the road, huffing and puffing as he dragged the heavy cart.

Febra looked at Arn, who stood still, slightly shocked by the event. "Well done huntsman, ten steps into the town and already you reveal yourself. The fat man was right, now watch the road and let me do the talking."

Febra strode purposefully forward towards the doorway of the Inn, checking only briefly to ensure Arn was following. She waved away tinkers and sellers that crowded outside the doorway touting for business, as she pushed open the thick door. The size of the interior left anything the Luff could offer to shame. Tall lanterns burned from every wall, lighting the rectangle shaped ceiling which stood at least three times Febra's height. Tables where strewn all over the area, small stone stools placed about them in no fashionable order. Most were taken and the place itself brimmed with activity. Febra cast her eye over the clientele, the Inn seemed to be as it name suggested mainly full of merchants and travellers, some clutching their wares to them and suspiciously eyeing those that sat within close proximity, others drinking and talking but perhaps without the light hearted feel that The Luff always had. The air seemed a little thicker here somehow, Febra made a line directly for the long bar that stood at the rear of the Inn pushing past a pair of local types, conspiratorially whispering together. Eyebrows raised as the girl followed closely by the huntsman drew up to the bar and hastened for refreshments. The keeper was a slim and wiry man of indiscernible age. From his bottom lip hung on a precipice a pipe carved after his own image, long and with a brittle look. .A tiny wisp of smoke would occasionally appear as if to confirm its fire still burned. As asked he delivered two mugs of mead to the pair and Febra parted with the little coin that still remained from their original payment.

"Market good today?" the girl enquired of the keeper.

he man eyed her for a moment, "So I believe, the talk is of ore from the south, a large load and our first for some days, there was quite a bustle this morn, with the smithies arguing over availability's and quota's."

"Why the wait, is there an issue with the mining?" Febra kept the conversation ticking along, careful not to ask her question too early and arouse any suspicion.

"No, it is the thieving robbers that leave us dry. The Pluris to Asten road is awash with the dregs of our society, looking to steal an easy wage rather than earn it. The previous two caravans were set upon, murdered would you believe, miners

148

and merchants, shameful days. A man is not safe to ply an honest trade and what do we hear from Pluris, not enough resources, fully stretched manpower, it is a joke and not one to smile at."

The keeper continued to chat and talk of the current state of order in and around Asten and of stories that came up from Pluris. Arn bent over to whisper at Febra, "We shall be here all day, if you let him carry on." Febra raised her hand for the keeper to top up the mugs, which he did and waived away request for payment, he enjoyed talking and this one clearly had not heard much of his content on offer. As he paused in between breaths Febra finally interjected, "Does the university not intervene in these issues, for I hear that Asten has a prominent hall with many learned talkers."

"In many ways that would be the problem, too much talk, action on the other hand is in short supply. There was a man, a senior body at the hall, yet he is old now and rarely seen these days. Gru-Staedak is his name, a well known and kindly respected man, he would give the locals here the time of day, more so then many that walk in those walls. He came in here more than once, talking with travellers and merchants, a quiet man, a listener but fair and paid a pretty tip, that I do remember."

"The University is near?" Febra mused careful not to imply it as too direct a question. "Oh aye, a mere amble up the north road to market centre and then just north and west past the House Of Histevirrillm. Now there is a place to visit, if one needs arms, you sir," he motioned over Febra to Arn, "you strike me as the outdoor type, take my advice and stop by the house, I have had men in here say there are no finer hunting tools in the land."

"I thank you for your sage advice keeper and I will take you up on the thought now. We appreciate your hospitality." The man looked a little disappointed as they quickly downed their remaining mead and once again thanked him for his time. They left swiftly, pushing past the crowd that had grown since their arrival, quickly they returned to the main road and walked north as directed to the market centre, the day no longer in its infancy had grown hotter and little or any breeze blew up from the north.

Speck and Joseph had waited a few minutes and made their way into Asten following the merchants, managing to pluck some general directions from a trader and ending up in the market. It was a fascinating sight, small tents and carts parked in a huge circle around the centre, many doing brisk trade. In the middle around a large fountain which pumped water from the base a statue of a man, dressed in the garb of a soldier stood many entertainers. Animal tamers, jugglers and minstrels, plied there own trades to the applause of the surrounding audience. The pair wandered up through the throng to look upon the carving on the statue.

"What does it say Speck?" Joseph asked his friend, not too loudly. While he did not doubt, reading may be looked on somewhat more friendly in a large town like Asten, he was still uncomfortable to derive any more attention from those around than was needed. The young man, pouted his lips and peered down at the writings, "It appears to be nobody and everybody," he paused a moment to ponder further, "yes, I see, it is a tribute to those whom died in battle, long ago by the looks of it. It is meant to be representative of all but not to any individual likeness."

Speck pointed his friend to look upon the face. "You see the lack of features, it is purposeful I suspect. Yet we digress from the matter at hand, perhaps once this matter is dealt we shall have a little time to inspect Asten further." Joseph nodded in agreement, "Aye, it is a fine place to look upon and many differences from the Luff. Now that old man you asked suggested we travelled the north east path, a little tight he said but much wider at the top, we should push on and meet with the others."

They moved past the crowd and as the sounds of talk and banter died away they approached the small path, it was narrow to the feel as the houses and buildings seemed to lean over to meet one another and it blocked out the natural light ahead.

"It does not appear over inviting, yet if Febra and Arn can make the journey then we shall too." Speck took the lead and the two wandered at a brisk pace down the cobbled path, a heightened smell surrounded the buildings and the pair begun to feel they were not in the most savoury parts Asten had to offer. At various points a tiny alleyway would spike off the main path and they would hardly be able to see a few paces before it was plunged into darkness. They pressed on without talking but their pace increased, as they reached another crop in the road, a figure stepped out to block the path, it was difficult to even make him out in the poor light but he was dressed raggedly and his face was heavily pot marked. As they paused to see the man's next move another figure appeared from one of the buildings, it happened so quickly they could not tell from where, a doorway or window perhaps, and then another from behind and a fourth and fifth from the alleyway where the first figure had arrived. Finally they stood surrounded by six and for all the fear that fell down on the pair at that moment, Speck's first thought was to the book.

As the last light from the day fell across the easterly windows of Asten University, a knock came at the study door. A young man entered, a youthful appearance sullied somewhat by the drab grey robes he wore about his person. He settled the tray down upon the hard wood desk, careful to not disturb any of the parchments scattered on its surface. He waited for some sign from the elder that his duty was done, the seated man scribbled furiously only pausing occasionally from his task to dab the fine writing implement into a shallow well cut into the tabletop. Eventually he seemed to notice another person in his vicinity and waved a hand casually without turning from his work.

"Good evening to you Prominence Lamentor." He spoke softly and closed the door quietly behind him. Lamentor placed the writing tool down on the edge of the table, it rolled slightly, finally coming to rest on a natural ridge. An audible sigh came from his lips as he dropped back into his chair and reached for the mug that had been delivered moments before. He drank hot water, flavoured with the grasses that grew on the banks of Medwere. It was a traditional beverage for most Scholatic, preferable to anything alcohol based or containing stimulants. It was refreshing and widely believed to aid clarity of thought. The waters in the mug ebbed and flowed toward the rim, his right hand shaking slightly as his thoughts turned to the matter at hand.

His mind flew back to all those weeks ago that the first news had come to his attention. There was no doubt in his own mind that archaeologists were of a lower station than scholars such as himself, nonetheless he was astute enough not to remove all contact from their station. Many of his brethren would have no communication with those outside the borders of the university and to all intents that would be wise council. Lamentor though had found his place in the Scholatic not through prowess or agility of mind but through cunning and guile. He had realised early on, even as far back as his original Pulpit debates, that he could not hope to join the luminaries of the Scholatic, he even feared being thrown out at inception and facing the same fate as the rabble at Bannermane.

So he had found other ways to hold his position of office, he provided favours, sought after gifts and tokens for those that needed them. His eyes turned to the bookshelf below the window, a thick wondrously bound volume titled, "The Neutrality Of Discovery". He smiled to himself, he did not have to look at the author to know it was written by DeFache. Lamentor's secret was the knowledge that the Scholatic were not neutral but competitive to the core. They sought to out do and out think within the borders of their own houses or between university's as a whole. There were a few of course, who couldn't be swayed, fools like DeFache and Gru-Staedak but most could and he had profited well in his calling.

He knew Karl, a naïve man at best and an irritant at worst, how many hours had he spent having to listen to the drivel of historical significance, waiting to gather information on items and artifacts. But this time it had paid the highest of dividends, he had received a message two months ago from the archaeologist asking him to visit Bannermane on urgent business.

He had cursed the thought of an another night spent amongst the ignorant but the letters content had intrigued him enough to set off with some haste. On arrival he had been bored rigid for an evening in the accursed drinking hole that stood for a tavern, hardly managing to get in a word as Karl raved of his finding. A book of lore dating back to the days of MonPellia himself, clearly a finding of magnitude and immediately he had set about agreeing price and package for its delivery. He took action quickly, Karl had already passed word to the council of the items existence, he needed to act in an appropriate manner. He decided to send quest to a small village for its proper delivery to Asten rather than making a hasty attempt to move the item himself. He had thought that there would be less publicity in such a small village and those taking on the task so inept that there would be few if any questions asked.

The problem that concerned him now was the length of time elapsed since agreement. Could his envoy's have been so ill equipped to have been taken on the road by thieves or so shallow of cerebral matter that they could not find their way. Worse still the council had made it to his prize first and he would miss out on huge opportunity to curry favour He cursed his original decision, bringing a fleshy fist down onto the hard wood, the writing tool dislodged from its post, rolled over the ridge and dropped to the floor.

He was not one to court with either danger or the wrath of Shel-Toro, if it was lost he would be clearly out of pocket and still there was the issue of the archaeologist reporting of his agreement and visit. He would declare he sought it out for the council as he feared for its security with all the bandits. There would at least be some favor to be courted, even at this late stage of events.

He smiled again, perhaps he would even be awarded with a seat on the council, now that was a prize worth considering.

Arn continued to pace up and down the lush grasses that bordered the university gardens. For a time they had waited at the rear of the area, cautious to stay hidden from wandering eyes but dusk had fallen on Asten and they had become concerned that there was yet no sight of their compatriots. Febra sat leaning against the metal railings that penned in the university grounds, her knees pulled tightly up to her chest, head bowed down in reverence to the darkness.

The building itself was a wondrous construction, levelling four stories and covering an area that could house the whole of the market at Kearn Luff. It was built of coarse stone, smoothed with a type of limestone they had never seen before and adorned with huge glass windows. Often figures could be seen passing in the candlelight within, shuffling from room to room, going about their daily chores. The gardens themselves were as beautiful and wholesome as any they had laid eyes upon, herbs and flowers were groomed in symmetrical patterns. Organised in beds of six and eight, creating a maze of walkways that all led to a central podium. It was set within a circle of tightly cut grass, rising up to the second level of the building and housed on a marble podium. The statue itself seemed to shine even in the darkness, a polished veneer that did not give itself to any material they had witnessed. The strange parody of a stone tree in the centre of a garden so verdant with life, it struck Arn as both strange and also thought provoking. The hunter turned again, stopping in front of the girl.

"I can not stand more of this waiting, we should go back and look for them."

Febra looked up slowly, raising her head, "And then what Arn, what if we can not find them, what if we become lost or they arrive and we are not here. We must wait, sit down and calm yourself."

Arn's brow tightened and unwittingly he became a little annoyed, "These are my friends girl, It will not stand if they are in danger. You speak with no concern in your heart, are we all to you but a means to the end? If you can not find it to think of them, then consider your precious trophy that they carry. What will become of your reward if they do not return? Think on that, if you may."

Febra's voice was surprisingly calm, softer than the hunter had heard before and tainted in melancholy "You judge that which you do not understand, your anger at the old warrior's demise is clouding your thoughts and for that I am sorry. As to my heart and soul, then I suspect you know as much as I, for lately I have felt at odds and find it more difficult to know my true feelings. We have come a long way and yes I do wish to complete this quest but I would not do so for the copper which you suggest but more because I would not have seen Rundell's death be an empty one. I look around me at this place and I see how little I know of Vedian."

Arn felt the anger vanish from him and kneeled beside the girl. "I...am sorry, I feel the burden of leadership that the old man bestowed on me in our final moments, I do not wish to let my friends down and I fear I may have made ill judgements in splitting the party. You are right Febra, we have slept in the security of the Luff for too long, the world is a bigger place."

Febra nodded and uncharacteristically placed her hand on the huntsman's forearm.

"The Luff was not my security Arn, it was my punishment."

154

The scarred figure moved closer to Joseph, allowing enough of his face to be illuminated by the little light that fell into the alleyway. He was no older than either Speck or Joseph but with harder features made worse by the marks that crossed his forehead and both cheeks. At a closer glance Joseph could make them out to be scorch marks, blistered but cold with age. The young man addressed the pair,

"We have little time as it is not safe even here, you are to come with us, we mean you no harm."

He motioned further up the passage. Joseph looked around him at the other figures and then at Speck, who was clutching at his arm, his eyes wide with fear. "It seems we have little option," Joseph said calmly, "perhaps though you would be good enough to tell us your name and where you would lead us?"

"My name is Calan, I am servant to the House of Histevirrillm and it is there we will must go, if you give me leave to lead you." There was no hint of malice in Calan's voice and he waited patiently for Joseph to reply.

"If we choose to do otherwise Calan, would your allies here stop us?"

"No. Yet I would then have failed in my task and I would not go back to my master with such news. I do not know your name, although I suspect this one", he pointed to the young scribe, "is Speck. Please trust that what I say is true, the roads of Asten are not safe for you to wander unaided. If it is for your compatriots you are concerned, then let me ensure you I will have my brethren search the city for them if you have information to where they might be. They will bring them to you at our house."

Joseph thought to himself, it was one thing to take this man at his word but another entirely to lead Arn and Febra into what could be a trap.

"Of our compatriots I cannot say, we have been parted for some time but we will follow you to your house as I have many questions for you and your master. Least of all how you come to know of us and our whereabouts." Calan, led them further into the alleyway, pausing briefly to give instructions to the others in his group. Speck stayed close to Joseph's side as they traversed the wiry paths leading north through the town. By the time Calan called a halt they had entirely lost their bearings, although the road did seem to now widen and the last evening light shone down on the houses either side of them. It seemed to the pair that they had moved out of the living area of Asten and into the trade quarter. The buildings were larger individually and flatter, mostly one storey they were also wider apart, some housing looms and spinning wheels on the large porches others had hides and dye tubs.

Calan turned to face the pair.

"We are nearly at our destination, my house is at the junction up ahead.", he pointed north to a crossroads. A large building jutted out from the right hand side, outside its entrance a horse and cart was being loaded by two men, garbed in the manner of smithies. They stopped short of the main entrance, cutting right into a side passage that led to a small door at the rear of the building. Calan knocked and waited for the metal door to be unbolted from the inside. It swung open and he ushered them inside, to what appeared to the pair as some kind of workshop. Tools and metals were haphazardly strewn over various work surfaces and shavings lined the floor mingling with a dust that infested the air. The man that had unlocked the entrance departed the room swiftly before either of them had a chance to properly look at him. Moments later heavier footsteps could be heard moving towards the workroom.

"My master comes.", Calan said smiling.

A heavy set man with huge arms and bushy dark beard turned into the room, dressed in full coat and a wide belt that held the pressure of his weighty stomach. He was sweating somewhat and held a small hammer in his right hand.

"Well done Calan, now return to your duties, prepare the quarters for our visitors."

Calan nodded to the pair and departed on his errands, winking to Speck just out of eyesight of the large man.

"I am Durgal, my young fellows and you are here at my leave. This is the House of Histevirrillm, the finest blacksmiths in the whole of Vedian. As to your names, I could surely guess and be safe in the knowledge I would get at least one right," his wide mouth grinned wholesomely at Speck, "Ian of Bannermane always was a very descriptive fellow."

Deep inside, they breathed a sigh of relief.

Chapter 8 - Lineage

"We are now left in no doubt that MonPellia was a learned scholar and forward thinker, the like of which Vedian had never seen before. I would take you to a time when he was at his zenith, the Moot of the Factions. Testament has been given by earlier scholars of the way in which he brought together all the leaders of Vedian on the Island of Bridges. Calling them in a parley of truce to end the wars that had brought our country to its knees. The land was famished, its peoples decimated by battle and lawlessness was rife. It has been said that MonPellia used his superior negotiation and debating skills to agree a way forward for Vedian. He fathered the birth of the Scholatic and the council itself to work in accordance with the Earl's to ensure a passage of stability in the land. In itself this would seem plausible, the king and his line had been lost to old age and war, the Dukes fought for the right to rule over the peoples of all taran's. To create an overseeing body to judge until a rightful heir could be found was clearly an intelligent way ahead. And yet if we look at the Dukes of the time, self centred war mongers who cared little for their people, it begins to leave doubt that any man, no matter how skilled and persuasive could have steered them from their destructive course.

So instead let us consider another more grave and dark scenario. MonPellia was a single minded individual and he believed he knew what was right, he saw a path for the future to change and make better the lives of the common man. He had no love for the Earl's, yet even if he had, I would suggest that his course of action would not have been different. He saw his charge over the people as a calling, a protector of man as a race itself. So I would put it here that MonPellia took the only action he believed would resolve the issue at hand and deliver the people from bondage. He drew the Duke's in under parlay and delivered them to their deaths. It was no moot on the Imanis Island but a carefully organised assassination for the greater good."

'Biography of The Protector' - Lasan Raltalan – Vedian 850

"A letter arrived two days hence, carried by a guardsman of the barracks. He had been instructed to deliver it into my keeping with great urgency and return forthwith with confirmation. I had the old boy stay the night, though it took some persuading, we fed and watered his mount and sent him on his way this morning. I gave the content of the letter what I attention I could, for many other matters of importance require my time at this moment."

Speck interjected. "Tell us more of the letter itself, what did Ian say?"

"I was just getting to that young master, it would seem the impudence that comes with youth carries itself beyond the borders of Asten!" Durgal scowled at Speck but with a slight smile, "I have known Ian for many years, we have a sound business arrangement and I often put certain customers his way that require an individual touch. He is a solid and likeable fellow and I have never known him to ask favours. So when the letter requested I gave aid to a travelling group who may be arriving at Asten under," Durgal paused slightly, considering his words, "difficult conditions, I trusted your need was great. Now though, let us come once again to your compatriots, my lad tells me claimed you were unaware of their whereabouts. Is this true? For I would fulfil my obligation to Ian if at all possible, although I will question him on his timing when next I we meet."

Speck looked to Joseph, checking for an acknowledgement of trust in the smithy's words. Joseph pushed himself back into the cold steel chair and breathed in slowly, much in the man's words gave confirmation to his story and certainly he felt that he was the type he wanted to trust. He tried to think as Arn would, "Could it be too much to ask to see the letter Durgal, I thank you for all your help and would not wish to put you to further trouble but our friends are dear to us and I would seek a final confirmation." Joseph bowed his head slightly to infer respect.

"Manners and wisdom is an odd couple to court at any one time, yet you carry them well in your arms Joseph. I will bring you your letter and then I hope, find your friends and deliver them to you safely. In happier days I would spend time with you, for you seem like good, honest types but your arrival is not favourable and I must return soon to other matters. For that I offer my apologies but while you stay here you are my guests and will be treated accordingly by all at the House Of Histevirrillm. I consider myself a sound judge of character my young friends. I have little more than that and a strong arm but I would say that you are more than you look to be or indeed think you are." Durgal laughed loudly and departed the room.

Speck raised himself from his chair, "What did he mean by that?"

"I do not know but I feel safer here under his roof than I have since we walked with Rundell." Joseph looked about the long room, "It is a wondrous place, I have never seen so many things cast from metals, even the walls themselves seem to be lined with some form of tin." The table at which they sat looked to be entirely moulded from iron and while not ornate was as sturdy as any Joseph had witnessed. The walls shone with the strange metal that coated them and all around great armours and weapons were mounted to view. Joseph stretched his arms out wide and yawned, "I would give anything for a nights sleep but I would first hear that Arn and Febra are safe."

"Do you think we should try to find them?"

"In honesty Speck I think Durgal's people would do a sounder job then we could but knowing Arn, he will give them less trust than I. So a token of some sort is required I think, to convince him all is well. Do you still have the pipe Febra gave you?"

"Yes. I was rather hoping to partake of it again, it has been far too long already."

"Well that will have to wait, give it to Durgal on his return and bade him present it to Arn as a token of our well being. As to what we do after that, I am unsure."

Speck leaned forward, "I know we should deliver the book as planned and that seems to have much sense to it but I would know a little more of it and its keeper before we hand it over. Perhaps I should look at it further, try to glean more of its knowledge?"

Joseph placed his hands out flat on the table, "I think we should be cautious, its effect on you previously was quite strange. If what you told me on the journey here was correct, it would seem to have awoken dreams within you. I do not attempt to understand it but I am wary of it."

Durgal returned with the letter and presented it to Joseph, he gave various instructions to men that came and went from the room, asking that beds be readied and food prepared. Joseph skimmed quickly over the content of the note, he had already decided that the smithy was a man he could trust and described to him where they had arranged to meet with their compatriots earlier that day.

"Asten, like all of Vedian is not the place it once was but they should be safe if they have stayed where you agreed, none will pass the border of the university and it is a fine area even in darkness. I will send my men out immediately to recover them, please rest and take what meal you require, I must now move on to other pressing business." Durgal gave a comical bow to the pair and smiled. Speck took the pipe from a pocket in his robe, "Please ask your people to present this to Arn, when you locate him, he will know us from this token. "

Speck paused for a moment then continued addressing Durgal, "I also wonder if there is anything we could assist you with sir, since you have been so kind to help us. On many occasion in a short time you have spoken of pressing business, perhaps there is a service we could offer?"

The large man eyed Speck for a moment, weighing up his words as he took the pipe from the lad's hand, "It would perhaps be short sighted of any man in these times to refuse aide from any source that he deems to be trustworthy. If this task were of any other nature I would tell you more of its detail, as you have placed an equal trust in me. This unfortunately is not 'any' task and therefore for now at least I would decline your offer but let it be a postponement only, I am always glad of a debt! Perhaps Master Speck I will call on it in the future, if I may."

By the time night had drawn its veil over Asten, Arn had become increasingly frantic, he had time and again discussed with Febra the option of backtracking in an attempt to find their friends. On each occasion she had calmed him down and reiterated that they should remain in place at least until dawn. The night was warm and comfortable and they had witnessed few people crossing their path as the day drew to a close.

"I will wait no longer Febra, I must seek them out." As the girl was about to stand to once again converse with the hunter, two figures approached from the northern path. The men were dressed in leather garb with chain tunics on their torso. They changed direction from the path and approached the pair.

"Do not be alarmed," the first man said, "you are Arn and Febra. We have been sent by your friends to bring you to our house in safety." Before Febra could speak Arn moved forward to the man, grabbing his tunic.

"Where are they, what have you done with them! I will gut you like a cur if any harm as befallen either of them."

The second man moved forward, placing his hand softly on Arn's, "We are not your enemy Arn and your friends are in no danger. I have here a token of their well being they have provided to guarantee our words."

He offered the wooden pipe to the hunter, who released his grip and carefully examined it for a moment before passing to Febra for confirmation. "Granted, this adds some weight but it does not confirm their health, you could have stolen this item."

"That is possible Arn but it is an odd token to choose, if we looked to lead you into a trap. This has been a long night and Barin and I both would wish to return to our beds and a warm fire, please come with us. We will deliver you to your comrades."

Febra put her hand on the hunters shoulder and looked into his eyes, "Let us follow, it seems plausible, trap or not at least we will know what fate they encountered."

They journeyed on to the House of Histevirrillm, Febra talked with Barin and Calan all the time they walked, leaving Arn to trail at the rear. All the time she was careful to ascertain extra information and snippets that confirmed their story. By the time they arrived at the house it was well past midnight and they were quickly led into a small practical room. A fire burned in the hearth and four seats were hugged around its warmth. At one end a corner table was stacked with meats and bread and a set of hands could be seen from the rear dipping in and out of the tasty meal.

"Joseph! You have led us a merry dance, what happened, why did you not meet with us? Are you safe? Where is Speck?" Arn grabbed the mariner out of his seat and hugged him tightly.

"I thought the worst, when you did not arrive. I am sorry Joseph, I should never have split us up." He stared directly into the lad's eyes, "I will not make the mistake twice." Joseph smiled at his friends and sat them down, offering food and mead. He took time to thank Barin and Calan and asked them to pass on his heartfelt regards to their master. Recounting the events of the day, the trio sat and bathed in the sanctuary of the house.

In the bedroom, situated at the front first storey of the house, Speck sat impatiently. His lithe fingers drummed the canvas of his satchel, his mind considering the rights and wrongs of his action. He had left Joseph after his earlier meal and retired to sleep but it had not come, the book played on his mind, he was sure more was to be learned from its contents and he was certain it would benefit them all to know more. He knew that it would not sit well with his friend but the possibility of knowledge pushed him on to remove the book from its resting place. Carefully unstrapping the satchel and removing the binding that protected the weighty tome, he glided his hand over the clasps a final moment before making his decision.

As soon as he opened the page and concentrated on the symbols the familiar feeling rushed through his mind.

Dior sat quietly in his tent, sipping on a mug of ale, outside the voices of his men could be heard singing and laughing. They were good men, he thought to himself, the best in all of Vedian and yet the folly of the charge endangers them all. There was no honour in this, no victory, they may yet hold Bannermane but at what cost? He felt the air brush across his face as the flap of the tent was lifted. Lord Protector Estalyn stood at the entrance, without his regimental garb of office he was still a formidable figure. Dior rose quickly to attention, addressing his liege formally.

"Lord, what orders would you have me carry out?"

"Stay your hand Dior, I have no orders for you this night, rather I would just sit with you and share a drink if you seek companionship." Dior was slightly surprised but did not show it.

"Of course, it would be an honour."

He drew up another chair and poured a second mug of ale. It was unlike the Lord Protector to mix with the troops, even someone of Dior's position, he was a cautious man who normally kept his distance to reinforce his rank. It was not a personnel issue, merely the duty of a man who may send the men under him into difficult if not fatal battles.

"I am sorry Dior. I have tried everything I could to persuade him otherwise. It is not my way to discuss matters of duty but in this task I find need for a friend. In all my years and campaigns I believed honour and duty would be enough to see me through, enough to hold my sacred oath.

Yet in this matter I am most vexed, it is madness for Shartos to take to the field, the cost will be too high, we are stretched thinly Dior, more so than you may be able to see. We can not afford a massacre to any unit, but cavalry we can least afford, they will soon be needed on the front and I wonder what steeds we will have left to send? I would not pass this burden on to you, except that I know you already feel its weight," Dior did not reply, rather bowing his head slightly in acknowledgement. "Shartos is a boy revelling in the spoils of war! He will drive us to extinction and our land into bondage, why must wars be fought by politicians. I am a warrior Dior like you, when the time came I did not have the words to persuade the King to change his stance, I was the wrong man and my ignorance will cost men dearly. I have failed and the thought is hard to bear. Is duty everything Dior? Is it enough? Will history judge us by duty or by honour?"

Dior waited for a moment before he spoke.

"I do not know the answer to these questions my liege but of one thing I am sure, the men will follow your orders, the Sabre Regiment will hold Bannermane while Shartos charges and when you require, I will lead them to battle. For when duty and honour are no more, left bloody on the field of battle by meddling dignitaries, there is always the oath of bondage. Our oath is to each other, from man to man, from soldier to officer and war and time will never diminish its power."

The ferocity of Speck's awakening seemed slightly less this time, he was still shivering and found it difficult to catch his breath but his mind was clearer. He steadied himself on the bed, dangling his legs over the edge, taking in a handful of deep breaths. His mind was considering the events that the book had revealed to him, he felt sure know there was something more to these visions or dreams. He snapped his fingers together, irritated by the feeling that he was omitting an obvious detail or message. Clearly these people he saw were historical, his knowledge of the old days lacked in detail, he had read snippets of references to Vedian of the Great War and certain things seemed to have an edge of truth to them. Perhaps the tome was a record of events and acted as a caretaker to ensure certain things were never forgotten, he was unsure, there was something more, that was all he was certain of. He thought to rush downstairs and relay the description of the vision to the group but he held himself a moment, Joseph would be annoyed that he had ignored his warning.

Speck stood up, his body temperature was beginning to warm, pacing up the long room between the bedsteads he considered his options carefully.

Stopping by the window he peered out to the dark streets outside, all was quiet and few lights could be seen shining from other buildings across the street. Pushing open the window he breathed deeply in the cool air and finalising a decision in his mind, he brushed his hair back in his hands and began to walk towards the hallway.

Arn's voice could be heard as Speck approached the lounge area at the west of the ground floor, he was deep into recounting one of his infamous hunting tales, no doubt it would culminate in the capture of the beast single handed and a night spent in the arms of a local girl. For all the huntsman's tall tales ended in a similar way and yet for all his bravado Speck's admiration had grown over the past weeks. It was different with Joseph, they were friends, they had a bond of time that had created a trust. With Arn it was more something that was demanded but not in a way that Speck did not wish to give.

As he pushed open the door, the heat of the fire swept over him, closeted within the confines of the small room. The three turned round and smiled as he sat himself in one of the chairs next to Joseph.

"I thought you had retired, you do not seem surprised to see us my young friend, had you forgotten us already in the time we were parted?" Arn grinned.

"Barin came up to the room and let me know you had been safely found and returned. I would be hard pressed to forget you hunter if I lived to see a thousand seasons! But I interrupt a tale, do not stop on my account, I know how hard it is for you not to

164

spend time talking about yourself." Speck pushed himself back in the chair as the others laughed loudly.

"I think this is yours," Febra stood up and handed Speck the wooden handled pipe he had given Durgal earlier, "I have filled it for you and it is ready to light if you would like."

"I would indeed, you have my thanks. We have come along way the four of us and my ignorance has diminished the further we have travelled." He smiled warmly at the girl and Joseph nodded in agreement. The tale went on for some time and another followed, it seemed that Speck's jest was not far from the truth, Arn did not tire from talking of his own adventures and true or not all three listened with interest.

By the time the hunter finally completed his third story Speck had decided he must recount his earlier experience. "Joseph I have an admission," he begun," I was intrigued you see and I thought it wouldn't hurt so I, well I used the book again." Speck rushed through the final few words, hoping it would sound better at pace.

All three lent forward in unison, "I thought you might," Joseph said calmly, "though I doubt its wisdom, you know more of these things than I. Well let the rights and wrongs wait for another time, what did you see?"

Speck was surprised by his friends words, he had expected to be scolded at least. "I saw a similar scene, at least two of the people I witnessed the first time. It seems they were waiting for a battle to commence, they discussed an enemy and problems with internal politics. They were both sad, I could go further into description but that is the feeling I had, a great sadness within both men but also determination. "

"What does it mean, if anything? Perhaps it is a historical reference, something created in the old days when such things were possible." Febra said. "I don't know anything about books but I do know they don't talk. What good is it to us? Although I would still feel hard giving it up now, copper or not, it was too much of a sacrifice to get it."

Speck stood up and addressed the three, "Yes. Your right it was exactly that, Rundell sacrificed his life and I think something in these visions is trying to warn us. I am finding it difficult to interpret them but I am sure they have meaning." Joseph placed his hand on Speck, "Sit down Speck and recount the tale again in detail, let us see if we can decipher a message, if such a thing exists."

Speck recounted as much of the vision as he could recall, detailing the surrounding area, colours, sights and words spoken, he tried to leave nothing out.

"Well," Joseph said leaning his chin on his clasped hands, "It seems we have a battle to come, two men concerned over the future and a belief that an oath is stronger than royalty. Do you think they took the field Arn? Would men such as Speck describes disobey a King's orders, even if they knew it would lead men to death."

Arn replied quickly, "No. Dior and Estalyn are men of considerable rank, their lives would have been one of service and loyalty. I think Dior was just trying to give courage to Estalyn to assure him that they were bonded, he was not actually suggesting they took to the field before the cavalry. Men such as they do not make light of orders, they would know more than most, that a military force stands or falls by the ability to command without question. It does not stop at one rank or another but is the same from top to bottom, as it has to be. I believe they would wait and they would have seen the cavalry charge and fall beneath the enemy as they stood on the battlements. Men that had been betrayed by the pride of a father and the arrogance of a son."

"That's it!" Speck shouted out," You have it Arn, it is a vision of betrayal and loyalty, it is warning us of just that, two paths that we must choose. If we return the book to its owner we will be loyal to our charge but will we betray Rundell's sacrifice? Or perhaps it us that will be betrayed if we deliver it to the university. I am certain it is a warning, we must not deliver the artifact!"

"I do not claim to understand it but I agree on one thing, this book is valuable." Febra looked quite serious as she spoke, her eyes fixed on Joseph.

"I am not comfortable with either scenario and so I will follow the majority. What do you say Arn, should we deliver and put an end to this journey? Or if we hold, then what next?"

Joseph turned with Febra and Speck to face Arn, the hunter did not flinch from the responsibility. "I did not walk this far to just end without understanding more and most of all I am certain somehow this book is tied to the fate of Rundell, while we have its possession there is no doubt we are all in danger. Yet it is also the mechanism which I believe will deliver the old warrior's assassin to our hands, next time we must be ready. For I will not turn tail and run like a frightened child for a second time. We hold the book."

They slept late that morning, the sun had already risen to its height over Asten and busy hands worked tirelessly over hot coals, shaping the heavy lumps of metal into a myriad of items for trade. Arn was first to wake, stirred by the heavy snoring of Speck in the bed next to him. He glanced across at the sleeping figure, a quick grin of familiarity crossed his face, it felt good to have friends around. Last night had been good for them all, they had trekked hard and travelled far, for the first time they had as a four, talked and laughed and exchanged tales. More importantly they had come to an agreement, a bond, the book held them together now, they were bound by its nature and its cost. Arn pulled himself up from his warm haven, pulling on his britches and finding a fresh cotton shirt laid out on the table opposite the window, there was one each for Speck and Joseph as well.

For Febra, a blouse of silk was laid, a fair garment in any house, certainly an unlikely one to be found at a smithies. Yet it would seem that they were not the guest of just any metal grinder, Joseph had spoke well of Durgal and the hunter was already keen to meet their host. He laughed inwardly, Febra would be most displeased to be treated any differently to the rest, she would rather four shirts of rough bark then anything that set her out from the party. The cotton was fresh against his skin and fitted well, the sleeves slightly long as he liked them to be. He was careful not to stir anyone and slowly parted the door and slipped into the hallway, the faint sound could be heard of hammering and voices but it seemed far off. He journeyed down, reversing back under the stairs at the base for a door at the rear of the house, he passed no one as he strolled along. It would seem the front of the house was not part of the workshop, the east and west rooms were lounge or dining areas and clearly the house was not unfamiliar with visitors. As he laid a hand on the iron cast handle of the rear door, a booming voice came from behind him, so loud he jumped slightly in surprise.

"Good morning to you Arn! What a fine day we are blessed with." Arn turned to see Durgal who he recognised instantly from Speck's description. He was easily identifiable from his strange mixed dress, crossing smithy and dignitary, the leather apron tied around his considerable waist and a full length coat of fine material draped around his body. He was an odd sight but a friendly one, the smiling face and pumped up cheeks harbouring a rosy glow that reflected days over fires and nights consuming ale. He seemed to Arn as a man should be, the product of hard work and good living.

"And a good morning and many thanks for your assistance sir. I am in your debt for the help you have given to us all, your house is a credit to you and the hospitality fine. My thanks for the fresh shirt, Asten is indeed all we were promised it would be, a city of honest folk." The smithy, clasped Arn's shoulder, "Aye that it is, in the most part. Let us not talk of debt anymore, you are my guests and as such you should receive the personal tour of my house. Come I see you have an eye for craftsmanship, let me show you around the workshop."

Durgal pushed open the door and wandered through a large room, many names were spoken and introductions made, Arn struggled to keep up with them all. He acknowledged the faces he had met the night before and smiled thanking them once again. Across the benches finished tools and various armours sat, shining in the late morning sun. Barrels of ore clustered around the outer door and the sound of delivery carts could be heard unloading from outside, retrieving the completed articles and carrying them to market.

Clearly this was a well run trade with capable men employed, Arn often stopped to ask questions and Durgal seemed to enjoy this, he found great enjoyment in talking of his people and the trade that was undertaken. He was proud of his workmanship and hastened to point out his merchandise travelled the whole of Vedian to be sold in all the major towns.

"Have you heard before of the House of Histevirrillm laddie?"

"I am ashamed to say not Durgal, the Luff does purchase tools but I do not know were they come from. How would I know who makes any particular piece of merchandise?"

"Ah a good question," Durgal stooped down and picked up a protective armlet, plain and smooth to fit the forearm, Arn surmised it could be a piece of a larger set, "every item that is produced from our house is carved with our mark, it confirms quality and anyone that knows to look for such a mark is one who cares for such detail."

"Are you referring to arms and armour, soldiers would need such quality?" Arn took the armlet and turned it over, in the far upper right corner that would fit nearest the wrist, a tiny scratched mark could barely be seen.

"In part but all men need quality that respect their work, be you a farmer or fighter. Our work is built to last, we mine the best ore and work from the hottest fires, our men are experienced and knowledgeable in their craft. We hand down from father to son, in the old ways."

Durgal moved to the bench at the wall and in the metal dust that had collected he made two downward strokes and one crossing them horizontally from top to bottom.

"That is the mark of my house, look for that that and you will receive the quality you seek."

As the morning stretched out they finally arrived back into the long room Durgal had sat in previously with Speck and Joseph, a meal had been set for five and the smithy motioned for the hunter to sit and take a drink.

"You have had a hard journey by all accounts Arn. What do you desire to do now? You have the hospitality of this house for as long as you wish it to be. I would have done so for Ian asked it of me but I do so now because you are of a good breed and your small friend intrigues me, he is not the type I have met before. Clearly you are a man of craft and experience, you I would drink and talk with of history, Joseph too is an honest fellow, trustworthy and friendly. Your Master Speck though I find it harder to pin down, he is of strange stock, I have lived a full life, it is not often I find things that are new and different.

"He is that and much more Durgal. No craftsman or warrior is our Master Lucent but he would be both if it meant standing by his friends. As of our plans we have decided to keep our prize, at least for now. Joseph already informed me he has told you of our tale and I seek not to hide any of its content from you. We must go to the university and meet with our employer and see what unfolds."

"That is an unfriendly place for those not of its ilk. Who do you meet with?"

The door swung open and the three others paced through the door led by Febra, wearing the beautiful silk shirt, she appeared to Arn almost womanly.

"I can answer that smithy, assuming from the others description you are our host Durgal. So if we had any secrets, they have fallen by the wayside from Jospeh's estranged tongue. We are to meet with Prominence Lamentor, who lives at the university and we are going to give him nothing that he wants."

"Well young lady, you are not from Asten that is clear. Yet if plain speak is what we have then surely we are already good friends! Come dine at my table and tell me of your home, for all my travels I have never had the honour of visiting Kearn Luff."

They ate ravenously, still hungry from the long journey, Durgal and Arn held the conversation mainly, with the others chipping in between mouthfuls. Durgal's mind often wandered to his task at hand, he wanted to share his concerns with his new found guests but felt the burden of duty was his to carry. As Madistrin had asked, he had sent his people out to the town to discover more of the shipments they had discussed. Folk had been tight lipped and there had clearly been a feeling of fear that gripped tongues.

He had discovered that almost every other smithy in Asten had been working arms to dispatch south but the destination was still unclear. Last night he had sent two of his men to track the caravans, he did not do so lightly and bade them take care in their task. He had also arranged a moot with a few learned craftsman for this evening whom he knew and trusted. He had been cautious to not raise any suspicion and offered the meeting in the guise of a presentation of new finishing techniques. Durgal was well known for his art and it was not unusual for him to share his findings with other houses for the greater good of the craft. Finally the meal was completed and Durgal pushed back his seat and raised his formidable form from his chair, "Well my friends if you are to carry out your decision then I suggest you go while the day is still fair. Few things in this life feel as comfortable in the night air, I will have Barin escort you to the university and wait for you to return. Perhaps we could dine together for supper as I have business of my own to attend to this night." They thanked their host in turn, with even Febra offering a warm smile and consideration for the food and clothes. The southern street leading towards the central market was now brimming with life, every which way Joseph looked, people roamed from house to house, some stopping to converse with friends, others trading at the side of the road. It was hive of commerce, copper changing hand, tradesmen carefully counting the dull tokens in and out of belt pouches. Barin chatted to Speck and Arn predominantly as they walked at a steady pace, he spoke of his master and the pleasure of working in such a fine and respected house. It seemed to Arn that Barin was still in the early days of his apprenticeship, mainly running errands in the day and learning from skilled elders of an evening. A full time occupation and one the young man clearly revelled in.

Joseph paused the group as the first sight of the university peered over the rising slopes of the roadway, "I think it would be best for you to speak Speck, you understand their type better than the rest of us. All of us must be on our guard, doubtlessly he will question you anyway as our scribe," Joseph motioned towards the girl, "and possibly you as well Febra, it is after all your charge that was taken." As they reached the gardens, a little more life was evident than at the previous evening Arn and Febra had spent waiting on their companions.

"There is little activity? Is that not odd?" Arn said to Barin, peering to get a good look into the upper windows.

"No, it is the norm, rarely do the Scholatic wander from their sacred walls. They fear sullying themselves with the common man's touch I would wager." There was more than a hint of disdain in the young smithies voice. Barin pointed them to a smaller entrance to the west-side of the building, smiled and sat himself down, propping his back against a small mound of grass. He pulled a ripe apple from his pocket and chomped down hard. "I will wait here for you, be safe and be careful!" Joseph and Speck were still in awe of the huge structure as they approached the doorway Barin had directed them to, Arn banged heavily on the metal and stood back a couple of paces. Seconds passed until the frame swung open, a middle aged man in full robes appeared, his cowl was pulled back to reveal a lined face with tiny eyes set below a high forehead. His hair was thin and long and streaked casually into his hood. "Yes?" he offered.

Arn raised himself up to full height in an attempt to give authority to his words, "We are here to see Prominence Lamentor, he is expecting us, we have urgent business to attend."

The man looked over Arn's shoulder at the strange group and pulled a face, "Come in be seated, I will send word. I am aware he has been expecting visitors from afar. You certainly fit the description as I would say you are not from Asten."

He led them into to a thin room, it was basic and dark, only narrow slits let in any natural light from the outside. Small stools crafted from iron were scattered against one of the walls, the floor was covered with a bare rug, thinning from wear and faded in parts where the light from without touched it. The man ushered them to the chairs and without looking back moved on through a further corridor that angled off to the right.

Febra crouched down over one of the metal seats, "No wonder they don't like visitors, it isn't too inviting. I have seen more pleasant places to take shelter at the bottom of the fish market."

Arn smiled, "Aye, it certainly lacks a sense of character, perhaps this is just a trade entrance, I should imagine the rooms and halls further in are abundant in quality and splendour. By the way Speck, I was thinking as we walked here, can these types sense things that are magical in some way. I know nothing of such matters and little of the Scholatic themselves, do your famed books tell you anything?"

Speck brushed his chin with a long forefinger, pondering a reply, "As I understand it the Scholatic are not linked or indeed have never practised any kind of enchantment. If that is what our book is. They are thinkers by nature, I do not think they have any abilities over and above that but the scripts I have poured over in my time," Speck began to ramble in a desperate effort to impress the group at large, "give little weight to any more factual evidence."

Febra cast a wry smile at Joseph, "I think he might be right at home here."

Footsteps could be heard gathering pace again from beyond the room, faint at first but they resonated against the walls to provide a rhythmic beat. From the angular corridor the robed man appeared, he motioned to Arn and then glanced at the others in confirmation for them to follow. He walked at a brisk pace, the place was like an old badgers warren Arn thought, turning left and right through narrow passageways that continually spiked in different directions. All the time Arn felt they were moving slightly downhill, he couldn't be certain at first as it was a very slight decline but as the seconds moved on, he was more conscious of the decent. Finally they came to a set of doors, four in all, each identical to the others.

Their guide turned to them and pointed towards the entrances. He nodded briefly and began to ascend back up the long corridors.

"Wait! Which door will we find him in", Joseph exclaimed.

The robed man continued to walk on, apparently disregarding Joseph's question. "It matters not," his voice echoed around the corner, "they all end in the same place." Arn shrugged his shoulders expressively and reached to the ornate handle of the second door from the left. It opened with out so much as a sound, gliding aside to reveal a hard stone floor covered by a bare woven rug. The room itself was busy, shelves laden with books and scrolls, parchments littered on desks and chairs. Arn had never seen so many books.

Light in the room came from globes fastened to the wall, small candles burning brightly within, the circular holders reflecting their light into the deep recesses of the room. The tall hunter peered round the entrance, searching for signs of life.

"Enter at your leisure. For surely that has how your journey has been taken to date!"

The irritated voice was ingrained with accusation. From behind a high shelve of tomes that almost touched the rough ceiling, a figure arrived, robed as their earlier guide had been, save for a slightly more ornamental belt.

The man was old, at least that is how it seemed to them all, in truth he was far from his twilight years but a hard lined face and lazy stooped pose gave weight to the thought. His hair was a murky brown, cut short at the sides and back, in one hand, held tightly in a fist was a set of parchments, in the other a clay cup, hazy smoke rising erratically from its surface. His hard soled shoes scraped on the floor as he dragged himself closer.

"I have waited weeks for your arrival. What incompetence is this that greets me now? I was promised a swift delivery." Arn was about to speak when the man interjected, "Do not suppose to sully my mind with your foolish banter and excuses, bring forth my goods and be gone from my sight. I have tarried too long with you already." His face was turning red in the cheeks and his throat tightening, his obvious displeasure plain for all to see.

Speck motioned a hand forwards, "Prominence Lamentor, for that is I assume whom you are. My followers and I," Arn's eyebrows pricked up in surprise, "have most distressing news. Please let us sit, for our journey has not been delayed through bad judgement or leisure but through ill deeds of others."

Lamentor, eyed the smaller boy, he spoke with some authority, more than he would have anticipated, "Sit then," he pointed to a group of chairs huddled around a hardwood table near the far wall, "but do not try my patience, for I have little enough to spare on commoners."

The group sat and Speck began to recount a version of their journey, careful to miss out any reference to Rundell or Durgal, "So we collected the book as planned from Ian of Bannermane and slept for one night at the Inn. Upon the night it was set upon by bandits and vagrants, they plundered the quarters, we were lucky to escape with our lives. The book was lost to us, I fear we have failed in our quest, I humbly apologise for us all and ask for your forgiveness. Perhaps there is another task we can do for you in the meantime to atone for your loss?"

Lamentor's eyes never left Speck through the whole speech, he was hunting the boy out, checking for inaccuracies or pauses misplaced in his story.

It seemed to add up, this group looked an unlikely band to manage any betrayal and not clever enough to warrant the value of the item in question. His mind was awash, on news of their arrival he had been ecstatic, the book was in his hands, he would use it as planned to heighten his reputation with Shel-Toro. Perhaps even a place in Pluris itself would be forthcoming, now matters had turned for the worse. Caution pushed him to not take anything for granted yet and he decided to verify the travellers story first hand.

"This is ill news, you will understand of course that your story must be confirmed with my contacts at Bannermane. You will in the meantime wait at the Inn, you can not as commoners stay within the university walls, until we can discuss matters again."

Joseph piped up, "We already have quarters at..." Arn interjected swiftly but in a calm tone, "At The Journeyman's. A fine abode for any traveller, Asten should be proud of such hospitality."

"Yes, yes," Lamentor waved his hand dismissively, "I will send word when I have confirmation, perhaps there are other tasks you can perform in compensation." The group stood to depart, casting careful glances at one another. At the door stood their guide again, ushering them away, Febra looked surprised, she had not heard him called for and no sound of his arrival.

"Oh, one more thing," Lamentor smiled, his mouth crooked and head shifting to one side, "do not consider leaving Asten before we speak again, it would be unprofessional, you understand I am sure. It would not sit well with your council and rest assured I would be most displeased."

The ascent seemed quicker and they all felt more comfortable when the light from the main door could be seen glistening through the gaps. As they exited the University, the guide turned back and whispered conspiratorially, "His Prominence is not a man to displease."

Chapter 9 – Opportunism

"There were in total built six universities, each individually crafted by the greatest stonemason of an age. They were constructed at the end of the last great war, as change came to Vedian. Exactly where the first Scholatic came from is questionable but their first true university was built in the capital Pluris. Next followed Asten then Kanegon, Lough and Coralis. All a mirror in design but of differing sizes. The smallest in the Lough furthest south.

The sixth university is structurally different in design, it was erected on the Imanis Island at great cost and time to his Prominence MonPellia. It is not understood why he choose to build his 'own' university, but it was clearly not to the liking of the wider council. He named it 'The Sanctuary of Bridges' and he passed from the world in its halls, buried in the gardens, marked by a simple stone which reads 'Let knowledge guide you'.

I offer one final commentary which my colleagues suggest is pure myth, however I have found that often history is built from a mixture myth, legend and somewhere in between a dash of truth. I refer to a seventh university, conceived by a man called Pionor Saban who it is said, was cast down from the Scholatic. The university was rumoured to have been built at the border of the Inpur desert and at some point destroyed. It is difficult to confirm anything from the ruins, as it is south beyond the Huskian border and no historian or archaeologists have made that trip to date.

However be it six or seven, the most stunning must be Pluris, with its huge glazed windows and marble floors, so polished you can see your reflection in them. If you look to make one trip, then let it be to lay eyes upon the marvels of Pluris University."

'Post Modern Vedian' - Bary Curak III (Structural Historian) - Vedian 945

Asten was bathed in hazy sunshine on the third day since the meeting with Prominence Lamentor had unfolded. Joseph had spent the time familiarising himself with his surroundings. Years as the Luff as his home had increased his appetite to embrace new surroundings. He had taken in the vibrancy of the market square, where traders dealt in many types silk and leathers, tanners from Vedian over seemed to have produced the product on offer and women and young girls hunted for the best prices and most fashionable stock.

The second day he had visited the renowned Stone Pillars of Asten, a raised marble area from which erupted six marvellous towers of stone. Each plinth travelled over twenty feet high and while chipped and embedded with a deep moss cover, a majesty held sway over Joseph as he climbed to their base. He knew little of their significance historically but was vaguely aware they had some military poignancy. He had consulted with Speck that night, who revealed they had been a meeting place for the Sabre Regiment in the wars and it was rumoured they had held against a superior force under the shadows of the pillars as the enemy had flooded from the western shores into Asten.

He walked without company in the daytime, leaving Speck to spend time at the House of Histevirrillm where he troubled Durgal's smiths with question after question around the ancestry of the blacksmith's house. Arn chose to frequent the local tavern, spending more time with a local barmaid than Speck thought was appropriate. The hunter opting to ignore his critique and spoke at length in the evenings on his return of his blossoming relations, adding considerable detail to embarrass the reserved lad. Joseph had little concept of what Febra did over the three days since they had met with Lamentor at the University, she seemed to depart their lodgings each morning but where she went he had little idea and he felt comfortable to wander the streets of Asten alone.

On the third morning, he had caught site of Febra, skulking around the marketplace, she seemed to be watching the other young girls as they went about their lives, ever watchful, Joseph could not decide if it was jealousy of what she had not had, or a lingering sadness for what she could still not bring herself to have that troubled her. He did not however feel the need today to enquire, Febra had intrigued him greatly in the Luff but he felt less drawn to her as their journey had matured and his world had opened wider. At present he was enjoying the freedom of Asten and wished to once again visit the university gardens under less pressing and uncomfortable circumstances. He had never before seen such a richness of greenery that surrounded the buildings walls and the flint structure with stone foundations was an impressive design. He was forbidden access to the building as only Scholatic could wander its walls if not on invited business, the outlying areas however, oddly for such a closed group, were open to all. Joseph wondered if this was true of all universities in Vedian or if Asten had a different policy. He breezed through the tall bush that lined the gravel path, heading towards the fountain that was recessed at the rear of the gardens.

Sitting at the side of the water, he closed his eyes and listened to the flow of the water fall, surely the embodiment of serenity he thought. Joseph had no real concept of how long he sat in that spot, only that the calmness was broken by the scraping of something on stone. He opened his wide eyes to see a venerable man crouched at his side, he was drawing patterns in the gravel underfoot with a stick crafted from what appeared to be ivory. The smooth cane itself was etched with a strange pattern of circles that turned dramatically around the shaft. The man did not look up, rather he continued to draw an odd symbol that Joseph did not recognise.

"Good day, sir," Joseph offered, expecting a curt reply, "this is a wondrous place."

The old man did not stir from his task but his voice came to Joseph, cracked with the venerability of years that disguised at first a confidence of tone and resolute defiance.

"I have sat in these grounds for many days, searching for the answer to one question, if this place was truly wondrous as you suggest, would I not have found the answer by now?"

Joseph bent down to try and get a look at the man's face, his hessian robes rolled over his arms and below his feet and his long bedraggled hair swept across his face making it difficult to get a clear picture of his identity.

Joseph instinctively thought of his mother, "When I was young, I was told if you are not sure of the right answer, you should try thinking of a different question."

The man paused, his cane finally coming to rest and he rose slowly, as he did Joseph got a first look at his face. His skin was stretched tightly about his cheeks, drawn and pallid, his eyes dark blue, narrow and overshadowed by two riotous brows of grey.

He nodded vigorously, "I do not miss youth, it was a dull time and I lacked the understanding or intelligence to fathom even the most basic of truths. If age has robbed me of strength and sanity, it has at least provided me with patience!" He was pressed quite close to Joseph now, not in a aggressive manner but with an eager disposition.

"Anyway, let us pray it has not robbed me of courtesy, I am Gru-Staedak, I live within these walls and I am Scholatic. To what name do you travel with my boy?"

"Joseph, I am visiting Asten on business with my.....um associates." Joseph scrunched his nose, as he often did when he was unsure of himself.

"Well let us hope they are as insightful and challenging as yourself or the day may truly drag," Gru-Staedak's voice was playful and dry in tone now and Joseph felt himself smile.

"However, maybe you are right, to some questions there are perhaps no answers but the ones we already know. Let us try another question as you suggest. What do you know of the Scholatic?"

Joseph knew little of them in honesty, Speck had mentioned a few things but he had paid little attention, "I think they are the ones that rule over us."

The man shook his head, "I would say you are wrong, I would say the Scholatic are not here to interfere or instruct but merely to guide you first and then most importantly, themselves. Yet in current times, I fear you may be right, my order has changed and we have become like the Dukes of old, more interested in our own stability and continuity of power than the continuity of balance." Gru-Staedak continued to talk about the Scholatic, he spoke of his beliefs, his place in the order, the fact that he had been sent from Vedian's capital to Asten in disgrace by his order and now lived a restricted and quiet life. Some things Joseph could barely understand but he was mesmerised by the man. He came across so openly, no secrets, no flaws in his character hidden, everything laid bare for another to judge.

A week passed in Asten and on each day Joseph walked directly to the gardens and spoke at length with Gru-Staedak. The charismatic man seemed happy to talk constantly and his breadth of information and detail was stunning. He spoke of the history of the Scholatic, of his desire to walk a line of support and trust with his brethren and the men of Vedian. Yet over time if had become more and more complex, differing views, new voices, the Scholatic became a debating forum, gossip and niche groups became the themes.

"I was once a noteworthy voice, although that was a long time ago." Turning away he said "They say beware those closest to you.....", he begun to mumble to himself, "..never learn...ego is nothing.....".

Joseph moved to look at him in the eye, "I am sorry, I did not hear."

"And if you did would you understand", Gru-Staedak was for the first time looking tired to Joseph, he had carried so much energy in his discussion these past days.

"Have I kept you too long sir?", Joseph offered tentatively.

"I think young Joseph, it is time you returned to your companions. You have business to attend to and today he will call for you again."

Joseph stepped back immediately his mind was whirring, what could he know, how had he found out about the others and Lamentor. He tripped over his words in denial but as he did he begun to run over the conversations the past few days. He had been so careful, spending time listening and just asking questions on the subjects Gru-Staedak had offered. He had revealed nothing of his own journey or the others. Or had he. Small comments here and there,perhaps he had mentioned Arn once just in terms of hunting and they had discussed books naturally, the old man had been fond of talking about those things he had read and written but he had not mentioned Speck's book. Joseph was no longer certain what he had revealed, he panicked and turned to leave the gardens. Gru-Staedak's hand grasped his right arm but the grip was not tight and Joseph easily tore himself away.

"Joseph please. I am not your enemy.", he shouted but Joseph had already ran back through the path and left the grounds of the university. His one thought was to get to Arn, he would know what to do. He chastised himself, why had he been so careless.

On the night after Joseph's departure from the university, Madistrin boarded a small vessel bound for the Imanis Isle. It was a supply boat, he had waited until a regular dock was available so as not to draw any attention to himself. Against all Parran's protest's he travelled with just one protector, an experienced and trusted member of his guard, who had fought in many campaigns in the south. He was a squat fellow, thick set and clad in light leathers which he wore concealed under his fabric shirt.

"I would like to thank you Lint for accompanying me on this trip", Madistrin put his hand on the warriors shoulder.

"My liege it is an honour.", Lint bowed slightly.

"Please Lint, do not address me by title or bow. The captain is with us but the crew are unaware of our presence, I needed this trip to be as normal as usual, so as to draw no attention to my journey. I may be getting paranoid over recent events but I have made too many mistakes already to not be a little cautious."

Madistrin sat on the hardwood floor. This was one of two small ships in dock, barges carrying wood supplies it looked like. Apparently it was how Prominence Bast'wa had made his fortune in Kanegon. He provided the ship and would pay men to sail across and back through the Straights of Reslin. The ones that returned easily made up for any losses. Much of that booty found its way to the capital Pluris for trade.

The Captain of the ship was known to Parran and he believed him to be a trustworthy man, he had immediately agreed to take the passengers and say nothing to his crew. The vessel was a Trade-Cog, designed specifically to carry loads shore to shore, its flat bottom making it easy to harbour. Crewed by two men in addition to the Captain, they had been told nothing of the passengers. It was not unusual to ferry the odd person from mainland to island, as this was the only way to get across.

"I suggest you get your heads down," the Captain shouted, "be almost a day until we arrive at dock."

Lint turned to Madistrin, "Get some sleep, I will keep watch."

"Oh I think we are both alright to get some hours here, we are in no danger."

Lint whispered "Perhaps not sir but Parran will have my arms if anything happens to you, so If you don't mind I will keep one eye open."

The Crown Prince smiled and nodded to Lint, pulling a hardy blanket made from horsehair over himself and laid down to sleep.

Madistrin awoke, he heard shouting and he felt himself fall off the seat onto the deck. He turned to see one man grappling with Lint, another to his right was on the floor, blood streaming from his mouth. Lint had hold of the man's throat with one hand and the other was gripping the arm which brandished a long thick bladed knife.

The second man began to get to his feet, groping around for a short cudgel which had rolled under the seat when Lint had staved off the opening assault.

Madistrin pulled himself up, his chest tightening with the effort, he lunged at the man in an effort to try and stop him obtaining the weapon. He grabbed at his back, putting his weight on the man, in an instant he was turned over, the attacker quickly gaining leverage on the weaker man. For the next few seconds all he felt was pain, a succession of blows to the face and chest, in desperation he raised his hands in protection, they were just slapped aside and the torrent continued. Then when he felt consciousness slipping away it stopped. A sudden silence, he felt the blood on his face slipping down his throat, turning on his side he coughed and instantly passed out.

Arn half opened his eyes, next to him he could feel the soft skin of Murie nestling into his chest. She was not the first barmaid he had been successful with but no doubt she was the one he had been happiest spending more than one night alongside. She was funny and enthusiastic towards life, always laughing and joking with the customers. She lived with her aunt in the poorer end of the town but nothing seemed to dull her spirits. The events of the past few weeks had almost been forgotten to Arn, as he lay, his mind empty of thought or purpose. The peace was swiftly broken by the banging on his door and then without invitation it burst open.

"Arn! Arn!", Joseph almost fell over the small slate table that was in front of the bed.

The hunter rose from his bed grabbing his britches, "Joseph a minute please, whatever it is can surely wait until I am less vulnerable!"

"Arn I think I have made a terrible mistake, I think I have put us in danger." Joseph had not even registered the presence of another person in the room. The older man grabbed Joseph by the shoulders and pushed him to sit on the table, he squatted down to his eye level and spoke slowly in an effort to calm him.

"I am listening, now one step at a time, tell me what has happened."

The boy recounted his last few days, his time spent with Gru-Staedak, their discussions and what the old man had said at the end.

"I think he knows what we are doing, I think he may be with them!"

Arn raised an eyebrow, "Well, I have no idea who 'they' are but it does concern me nonetheless. Let us return swiftly to Speck and Febra and see if all is good with them" Arn gathered up the rest of his clothes and gestured to Murie. For the first time Joseph became aware of her presence, startled he stood and turned to face her, his mouth was wide open.

Arn turned to look at his young friend, "Now I know you have seen a woman before Joseph, stop staring." As his gaze joined Murie as well, he noticed she had risen from the bed and as Arn had been earlier, was in a state of undress.

"Oh." He smiled at Murie, "For god sake get something on, or the poor boy is likely to die of shock." Arn exclaimed.

He bustled Joseph out of the room and they walked quickly out of the tavern still pulling on his shirt. As they turned the corner to the road the House of Histevirrillm was located on, they ran directly into Speck and Febra coming the other way. They all started talking at once, trying tell each other their news that little could be understood.

"Quiet!", It was Febra's voice that made them all stop and look at her, "one at a time."

Joseph relayed his tale and then Speck told of a message they had received at the house.

"Just a short time ago, a man came on a horse, he declared he must speak to Joseph for some reason. He bore the insignia of the university, I explained he was not here and he left the message with me to hand over. Of course I immediately opened it being the only one here who can actually read properly."

"For god sake, stop blowing your trumpet and tell us what it said", Arn exclaimed with a streak of annoyance.

"I was coming to that.", Speck scowled at the hunter, "It was a message from Lamentor, he demands our attendance at dusk."

"What does that mean? Is it good or bad?", Joseph wondered if the old man had spoken with Lamentor, where they in it together, did they know the book was still in their possession?

Joseph shared his account of the conversation with Gru-Staedak as they walked back towards the house. Febra's opinion was clear, suggesting they ran and looked for passage south to Kanegon, as far away from Lamentor as possible.

Arn disagreed, concerned that they would be hunted down by the university and could never go home, as they would have broken their pact with the town. They entered the house, there was little activity and no sign of Durgal, Barin or Calan.

"Where is everyone?" Arn asked inquisitively of one of the smithies working.

Speck sat down by the hearth, grabbing a leg of chicken now cold from lunch, "Durgal was called away this morning, some sort of meeting he said, seemed a bit upset to me. Barin and Calan rode with him, so it must have been important. He seemed a bit agitated the last couple of days, of course none of you lot would know, as you're never here."

He sounded like a child, is if he had been abandoned.

"I am sorry Speck but we have matters we must attend to now! I will go and see Lamentor, you should all stay here." Arn was adamant and argued with all of them but they he would not back down. Febra even threatened to cut his legs off if he went without her.

"Speck, get the book and keep it close." Arn instructed.

As the sun began its descent behind the town of Asten, they opened the door of the smithies house. They could see horses riding up the winding road from the south. The party waited for them to come into view and pass. As they came closer into view they could make out the figure of Durgal emerging with another rider behind.

Arn ran out and caught the horses reign, the large man almost slid off his saddle and Arn could barely ease him to the ground without losing his own footing.

A voice rang out behind, "His wounds are grave, please help me get him inside." It was Barin, sweat running down his face and blood running freely down his hand from a wound in his forearm. He dismounted and ran towards Durgal's heavily breathing body, together they raised the hefty figure inside and laid him on the huge dining room table. Speck ran to stoke the fire, while Febra and Joseph gathered bandages and water at Barin's instruction.

Durgal's face was white and Arn immediately feared for him. "What the hell happened to you both and where is Calin?"

"Dead." Barin barked back "I would be as well if not for the man laying here. He was betrayed, I fear we all were."

Barin called up for the servants to gather an apothecary from the town, while Arn held pressure on the wound on his stomach.

Speck turned to Barin, the boy was frightened but his natural hunger for knowledge took over. "Barin, please tell us what happened."

"I have been sworn to secrecy by the man laying before you but things have changed. He trusted you, of that I do not doubt," he looked directly at Speck. "A moot was called, of smithies. Not an irregular occurrence, often they would meet to discuss trade. However Durgal was looking for information, he is not just any blacksmith you know. Not a common trader or barterer, for he is friends with the Crown Prince Madistrin of Vedian!"

Febra sparked, "That makes no sense, what would royalty want with a smithy, a new set of armour aside."

Barin cut the girl a glare, which even she took to be quiet.

"The Prince was of the belief there is trouble brewing in the country and he tasked my master with finding out about shipments that have been travelling south with armour and weapons. We had arrived at midday and a number of the others were already there. Durgal went to meet with the other house leaders, while we broke bread with other junior smiths. There was one man not present, a tradesman from Kanegon, Haverman of Otenhof. He works for Prominence Bast'wa of Kanegon, an unpleasant and cruel man if Durgal be any judge. He was always at these meets, always looking for a deal."

"What drew you to his absence?", enquired Joseph.

"Well he dresses like a peacock for one thing and he also travels with some unsavoury men. They normally sit with us while the talks are taken. I was pleased with their lack of appearance and mentioned it to Calin."

Barin stopped for a moment, the name sticking in his throat.

"About half way through the talks, we were sitting on our backs debating about which house had the best armour, the moot was in a small valley surrounded by a rock face six feet high to the south. They must have been waiting there out of sight. They rushed straight for the leaders, a rabble twenty strong stripping them down like animals, swords and maces everywhere it seemed, by the time we had got to our feet, over two thirds of them were dead.

We rushed to the defence of our masters, there were a dozen of us of us but we carried only knives and most had seen little combat. These mercenaries went to work, I fought back to back with Calin, we managed to get to the horses and grab a short sword each. By then there were a handful of us left and they came towards us in numbers, I could no longer see Durgal but I heard his roaring voice taunting the enemy.

I parried two blows from the front and cut a man down who approached from the side up the hill. I have used swords before, Calin and I were brought up with them. Durgal always said, 'Love everyone, trust a few and always be ready to kill the one', he trained us in swordplay, I never knew where he learned how to.

One moment Calin was there, the heat on my back and the sound of his breath. Then gone and I turned to face a secondary attacker. I thought it was the end, it is impossible to fight from the front and rear. Then as the blade came down in front I raised my sword and blocked, waiting for the blade to hit my back from behind, yet it never did. There was Durgal, he carried two long knives, both crafted from marble, both bloodied from the enemy. He plunged one blade into the eye socket of my front attacker and pushed me back towards the horses. He told me it was now or never, the last few smithies were falling under the mercenaries swords and they began to focus on us. I grabbed two horses but Durgal had gone back and was confronting them. He was like a bear, bellowing and hauling up a corpse in front of himself for defence. I grabbed the reigns of his steed and rode towards him but they were too close, I could never get to him and mount before we were cut down. Anticipating we needed time, he raised the corpse up and over his head, the old muscles that once broke stone flexed again, he threw the body and the mercenaries fell back. He mounted and we rode, only later did I realise how badly injured he was."

"He was incredible. But I guess a boy always loves his father." Barin's eyes were full with tears.

For a while there was a silence, the medicine specialist had arrived and was treating the old man's wounds. The four of them shocked by the revelation that Calin must have been Barin's brother and they feared for him to lose two members of his family in one day.

Barin had sat quiet for a while as the man worked to save his father's life.

"One more thing," he rose his head, "I think the Crown Prince was right, there is something happening in the south, some army is being built and these men came to keep that secret quiet. Durgal was almost sure Bast'wa was behind it"

Arn pensively put his finger to his lips, "Then if they know you got away, surely they will look to finish the job."

Febra,"That may include anyone you may have told!".

"Christ girl! Do you have no heart, The man is lying in front of you fighting for his life, where is your compassion. We will stand here and we will defend his house and its incumbents." Arn looked to the other two for reassurance. Joseph nodded and Speck took the time to grimace at Febra before moving to the table and taking a damp cloth to Durgal's brow. He had been kind to Speck and that was not something he experienced a lot of from strangers. Looking up he saw the medicine man cleaning his hands in a bowl of red water.

"I have done all I can," he spoke clinically. Addressing Barin he said, "He will live, if he survives the night and the fever does not take him."

As the house calmed, Speck approached them with a new option. "I will go and see Lamentor, Arn is needed here more than me. I will not take the book, just try to throw him off the scent. I would stay as I have grown fond of the old man, however lets be honest, I will be no use if an attack does come. No doubt you will spend more time worrying about me than is helpful."

Joseph was not convinced, he was sure it was at least as dangerous at the university than it was waiting here. Speck sensed his concern, "Do not worry my friend, I can tell a lie with the best of them. I am learned as you know.", he winked in an attempt to reassure him.

"Get in and get out Speck, I do not trust him", Arn walked up to the boy towering over him.

"If he has found out we do have the book, you may be in real trouble."

Only minutes after Speck had left the house, they could hear shouting from down the south of Asten road, it was muffled and still distant but Arn could just about make out a bright light.

"What is it Arn?" Joseph enquired a slight crack in his voice revealed a fear of their current predicament.

"I am not sure," Arn peered forward, his sight was generally strong from all the days out tracking deer. He wished for a moment he was back there on the plains, a fire cracking at night as he lay on the hard ground looking up into the sky.

A revelation broke his wandering thoughts, "Fires. The town is burning!"

Barin came running to the door, "Could it be connected to what happened to us?"

"Seems possible, either way we need to be cautious. Barin, Joseph take Durgal into the cellar." Arn directed.

"We were told not to move him until morning, we could kill him" protested Barin desperately.

"Would you rather wait for them to finish him off! Take him now." Arn was commanding Joseph thought, stripped of his gaudy nature he was a real leader.

Barin and Joseph hauled Durgal down the cellar steps as carefully as possible, he was huge weight and the mariner strained and puffed, desperate not to break his hold. The cellar was ten feet across and almost twenty long, packed with a mixture of fermented ales at one end and stacks of various ores and marble at the other.

"Will you stay with him Joseph, I beg of you." Barin pleaded with the boy.

"I could help up there."

"Perhaps but I am a trained swordsmen, I would defend this house but only If I know my father is safe. Please." Barin looked directly at Joseph.

There was no getting away with it, he would be less use in a fight, at least he could help them in this way. He sat beside the old man and rubbed his hand, I hope this night is not the last for both of us, he thought.

There was no doubt in Arn's mind now, they were heading this way and by all accounts burning everything in their path. He looked to Barin, "There must be fifty men, we can not hold this house if they come, yet it seems they are warring on all of Asten. Why do this if they are just looking for you?

"I am not sure it is us they have come from, look some have moved away to the east and west, only a handful are moving north." Barin pointed towards the south road.

"Well my smith, fifty is a depressing number to any man but a handful, well that is always welcome." Together the men drew their blades.

Shel-Toro looked out over the walls of his house, standing atop a purpose build rampart so he could survey the lands beyond Vedian itself. He was concerned, events to date had been executed exactly as planned. Aside from the location of the artifact, which had been a surprise even to him, the uprisings were all too easy to arrange. An army was building to the south and DeFache was locked away where he could do no further damage. Gru-Staedak ostracised and neutralised, his opponents, banished to the walls of their universities.

He had played Madistrin like a flute. It was difficult even for a man as efficacious and calculating as he was not to feel a sense of pleasure. From their universities they would rebuild a balanced society and they would watch over it from within. For years he had seen the country decay: murder, adultery and thievery were rife, bastard children had no discipline.

The Scholatic above all sought balance: to the east Medwere and those pious fools with their history of non-aggression was at odds with that aspiration. There had to be an equal amount of everything, the world must be in balance for its own prosperity and the health of its people. Certain areas of the country had broken the balance, the city of Kanegon and Medwere were disruptions and that would lead to man's downfall. For Shel-Toro could see only one thing clearly in the future: a devastating civil war that would devastate the country and bring the men that lived it, to the edge extinction.

He was forced to take control. It was not a choice it was a calling.

To separate himself from the ones that said it would be alright or that mankind would regulate himself. Madness, thought Shel-Toro, you only had to look to see that wouldn't happen. His plan had taken years to come to this point and the key had been his advice to Madistrin, his encouragement to take more and more of a back seat, allowing him time to destabilise the economy and infiltrate Vedian's militia.

Durgal the blacksmith had been a thorn in his side. Shel-Toro counted himself lucky he had the alliance with Prominence Bast'wa in Kanegon. It was Bast'wa who knew everything that moved from one part of Vedian to another and controlled almost all of it. The Scholatic had arranged for Haverham of Otenhof to put an end to Durgal's interference, there could be no turning back now, regardless of how difficult the decisions.

He had instructed Bast'wa to raise an army. Mercenaries had been paid for to take control of Asten, by the end of the night it should be in flames and Durgal would be a corpse. That would be the catalyst and the dawn of a brighter future. Lough,

Kanegon and Coralis would swiftly follow and finally when nothing else stood, Pluris.

The road running up to and past the house was five foot wide, beyond it opposite, was a row of shops, the tailors and haberdashery. It was too open to hold eight men, they would soon be overrun. Arn could see them now, shouting and bellowing, three brandished torches and they were dropping behind as they stopped to set fire to anything they could find. The other five had a selection of short swords and were dressed in leather tunics, they wore hoods to cover their faces and just one long slit revealed their eyes. These did not seem like the men Barin had talked about, these men were enjoying themselves, more akin to common bandits.

Two pointed towards Arn and Barin, "Well lads, we got ourselves some smithy boys, lets get them to shine our boots." The man had a short sword in one hand and a hunting knife in the other, around his left wrist a red scarf hung, flapping wildly as he motioned towards them.

Arn & Barin backed into the entrance to reduce the circumference of attack.

"Go on Macca, show em your skills!", the red scarfed man sat down a few feet away, watching.

"Not on me own, there's two of them." A broad chested vagabond was brandishing a torch in one hand and held a long bladed knife aloft. A second man came forward next to Macca and in tandem they approached the two defenders.

Arn turned to Barin and whispered, "Can you hold them?"

The surprise in Brain's face was obvious, "What?"

"Can you hold them for a few seconds"

"I will hold them until my death." Barin stated sternly.

"Well lets hope that's enough." Arn shouted as he disappeared back into the house. It had only just occurred to him he had the bow Durgal had given him to replace his broken one upstairs and there was a window overlooking the road, he just needed a few seconds.

191

The first man thrust straight at Barin's chest, he turned swiftly and kicked him in the shin, clipping his leg, the attacker toppled over backwards. His purpose was to delay, he knew he could not take them all on his own. He trusted Arn, he knew this intrinsically, time was a factor, whatever he was going to do it needed to happen now. The red scarfed man had taken the opportunity to swipe at his left, as he fended off the first attacker, he caught Barin at the lower back, cutting through his tunic and into the skin. A flesh wound but it stung and the smithy winced. He retaliated with a cross slash with his longer sword but the man was fast, he dodged back and pressed forward with a stab to the leg with his knife. The floored man was now rising and the others were beginning to close the gap, clearly wanting to finish him and move on. Barin did not recognise any of the men from the earlier incident that had almost killed his father.

A sharp shrill rang in the air and the man that had been sitting down shouted in pain, a long feathered arrow stuck in his stomach. There were shouts and pointing above, Barin used the distraction to thrust his sword directly at the man who just got back to his feet. He fell. From behind a second man dropped to his knees and his attacker looked around and decided enough was enough. He ran and the other five in the area followed. Only two made it down the hill and back to the pack, Arn struck two in the back and one in the leg, who slowly tried to crawled out of sight.

Arn came back down the stairs, "Can't believed I missed two."

Barin grasped his hand, "Thank you my friend, I am indebted, you have great skill with that bow, it was a prize well given."

"We need to get out, they will be back in larger numbers.", Arn called downstairs to Joseph, "We are departing, get him ready to carry out."

When Balin spoke it was steady and certain, "I will not leave this house to pillagers and thieves, this is the House of Histevirrillm. Take whatever you need and leave with our thanks."

Arn smiled, "We can not leave without you Balin. Not on your own."

A voice gravelly and wholesome came forth, "He will not be on his own in my house."

Up the stairs came Durgal, with Joseph under one arm, desperately trying to prop the huge man up.

"Father! You must not get up, let them take you to safety." Barin pleaded, tears filling his eyes. Durgal was white as a ghost, his bandages becoming blood stained with each movement.

"This is the house of my father and yours, neither one of us will dishonour the other by suggesting anything but staying. Arn take your friends to safety, I will not have you die here with us, you have already risked too much. I will not tell you again but ask your respect my word. Quickly get your things, get to safety."

Barin embraced them all and suggested they take flight to Speck, the walls of the university could not be burned and he did not believe they would dare try to enter.

Arn told Febra to collect the belongings from their bedrooms and within two minutes they were ready.

"I do not like walking away Durgal and I am not sure our friend Speck will forgive me." Arn looked at Durgal and realised there was no arguing. The old smithy took a leather satchel off the wall and quickly filled it with some items from his working room, "Take these lad, they may help you on whatever journey you go on."

Arn approached the big smithy, "We will never forget your kindness."

The old man chuckled heartily, "Trust me, not half as much as those coming up the road will."

They left through the back door and raced towards the university, each corner they turned there was screaming and fighting, as they reached the university walls they could see the gates had been shut and locked.

Febra moved so quickly they barely saw her jump up grabbing a hand hold to scramble over the wall. A minute later from ahead they heard a voice cry out and the next thing was the sound of the gate unlocking. The girl stood in front of them, flecks of blood were on her face but she seemed oblivious.

"Quick inside there are more in the gardens." She ushered them through to the grounds of the university. As they entered the bellowing cries of 'Histevirrillm' sung out and then all was silent.

The last line of the House of Histevirrillm had fallen.

Chapter 10 - The Defence of Asten

The 'Great War' was described as such because it was a time in which Vedian was united against a common enemy. This was not Huskian against human, or man fighting man but a whole land defending against a foreign invader. From across the western sea they came, a species for which we have no name, they stood eight feet tall and their bodies were carved in a natural armour. The invaders swarmed Kanegon taking the seaport in a day so it is said. Of the early skirmishes and battles on the western front so little is known, as few survived the initial onslaught.

The King and his Chancellor pulled together every man in the land to defend Pluris and thousands died for the cause, alongside many Huskian's. It is told the final defence that threw back the offenders from Vedian took place at Bannermane. A battle of true glory and chivalry that every boy in our land should be told of. Led by the Lord Protectorate with the Candlemen at his flanks and Sabre Regiment at his helm, they stood firm under the mighty walls of the castles protection. Wave after wave came crashing down upon Bannermane and was beaten and broken on its harsh stone. If there is ever a reason to celebrate the glory of Vedian and the true freedom we have today, then the debt is to those that served and died in The Great War. For let it be clear, there is no richer and more noble fate, than to die serving the greater cause of Vedian."

'The Great War O Rejoice' - Pulpit Speech from High Protector Twill -- Vedian 815

Speck had sat in the corridor of the university for a few scant minutes but it felt like forever. He had been greeted coldly by the same man, instructed to sit on a stone bench nestled in the same damp alcove. The university walls where a mixture of flint and dark sandstone, the lamps that adorned the ceilings reflected off the cut stone, sparkling in the gloom. It was quite mesmerizing and any other time Speck would have been enthralled but right now all he could concentrate on was the clamour coming from building outside the building. He was startled by the man returning, his cowl no longer shading his face, long thin hair scattered wistfully about his shoulders. He peered down to the seated boy, Speck quickly realised something was not right.

He looked scared, his eyes wide and alive, he motioned almost pulling Speck to his feet, "Quick we must make haste."

Speck walked swiftly down the corridor past the room they had met with Lamentor, just a week past. They turned left and then right and finally up a small set of stairs, leading to a hall at the back of the building. A huge glass window was set in the wall, looking out over the gardens at the rear. A number of aged men congregated around a large set of tables at the centre, they were hunched over and voices raised in a mixture of fear and anger.

"These walls will hold against a thousand brigands and thieves, no commoner will enter by force."

"You're mad Alver't, look at the window before our eyes, what small boy with a large stone could not enter at will. We must evacuate now, before it is too late, let them waste time on the common folk, while we make haste!"

"They will not dare to enter the home of the Scholatic. We will post the guards to the door to send anyone who dares knock away with haste," the old Scholatic rose up pushing his hands onto the table, frustration shaking through his arms, "how dare they!"

Speck was struggling to identify who was saying what. Then from the rear of the room a figure emerged and for the first time Speck laid his eyes on Gru-Staedak, he had no reason to be sure but somehow he knew it from what Joseph had said. He was enchanting and persuasive as he spoke.

"Calm, is needed my brethren. Let us wait to see what presents itself. This is our home, our only home, we can not run from our only true sanctity. Let us hear the mantra of the house to bring us comfort."

Together the men held their hands across their body's and chanted, "Knowledge will protect us, knowledge will guide us." Again and again they chanted, Speck thought it quite haunting.

Gru-Staedak walked towards the young lad, "Something tells me you may be of assistance to us?"

"No brother." from the table on the right Lamentor rose and hustled in his long gowns towards them, "No, he is but a messenger and a fairly useless one at that!" He glared at Speck. The young man felt a sigh of relief wash through him, Lamentor had believed their tale, whatever Karl had fed back to him, it had not betrayed them.

"Perhaps my brother of intellect but I believe he has friends and they may be of help to, if we are to remain as masters of our home." Gru-Staedak smiled at Speck, it was a warm gesture and he felt no distrust.

A voice rose up from the tables, "Unacceptable, we will not rely on commoners. What will we be left with, even if they do help."

"Our lives." Gru-Staedak replied, "I for one will be thankful to anyone who can spare that."

Lamentor sneered, "Of course we know of your belief in the 'common man'",he spoke those last words with real spite. "we know why you came back here."

"As do I Lamentor", the older man's voice quickly changed, it was forceful and intimidating now in equal measure, "I am here because the council wills it, I am here because I lack the cruelty that Shel-Toro has developed," a gasp came up from the hall, "and I am here because I choose to be."

Gru-Staedak turned to Speck, "I am sorry you have to listen to our squabbling. Speck isn't it?"

Crafty old man, he got more from Joseph that his friend could have guessed but to Speck's mind he was not threatening to them.

"Yes, it is."

"Well Master Speck, outside Asten is under attack and my colleagues and I fear it will be us next. Will you help us? We have only two guards and they are not in their prime."

"If the town is under attack, my friends will be in danger and I must go to them!" Speck begun to run back down the stairs. He collided so fast and hard with Febra that they both bounced backwards. By the time he had shaken his head and looked up, he double checked himself fearing a concussion of some sort. Above him stood Arn and Joseph both looking worried with Febra who staring at him as if he was an idiot. They sat down in

196

the hall and Arn recounted the attack on the town, the description of fifty men was received with a lot of bowed heads and even the more officious of the Scholatic had gone quiet.

Joseph had sat at the back, carefully eyeing Gru-Staedak. Speck noticed his friend and edged over whispering while Arn continued, "I think all is fine Joseph, there is something about him I like, trust even." Joseph was not sure still but he was relieved to hear Speck's thoughts and decided to leave it for now.

Speck tuned back into Arn's speech, "We were told this was the safest place in Asten but I am looking at a twenty foot glass window?"

The aged Alver't piped up once more, "It is safe, for no commoners dare enter it's boundaries!"

Arn stared at the man, "Well then, we will leave you all and try to find our own way out of this town." A number of the men had been quite impressed by Arn's speech and were beginning to think he may be their best bet. Voice's shouted down Alver't and Lamentor turned to Arn.

"We agree to give you the honour of defending our university. To assist the Scholatic will be your greatest achievement."

Febra stood and walked straight up to Arn, "Why would we lay down our lives for him hunter? What world do we live in that makes this fair?"

Arn bent over and whispered in the girls ear, "I can not offer you fairness, riches or their humility but inside you girl you have a demon and tonight we are going to let it loose!"

One of the Guards had come up to the hall to speak to Gru-Staedak, "My Prominence, word comes that Asten burns and many are marching on the university. They will be here in minutes, What would you have us do?" He was at least 60 years old, a veteran of the Asten guard, retired to work his days for the Scholatic. A good post and he was paid a fair wage. They addressed him as simply 'guard' but his name was Oron, only Gru-Staedak used it.

"It is not mine to say Oron, we are in the care of new minds now. Speak with Arn here", he pointed at the hunter, "he will give you your tasks and you may choose to follow it, or I give you leave to follow your own course."

"I have served all my life sire, my wife has passed on, I wish for nothing else but to complete my duties." He turned to Arn. "What would you have me do?" For all his confidence Arn was worried, how could they hold the window against thirty men. The front door was cast of iron, almost impenetrable, the only other way in was the huge elevated window, that would be a completely different matter to defend.

"Hold with us, this is where they will come. Although seven men is not enough to hold thirty or forty." He paced along the hall thinking to himself, finally he addressed the Scholatic. "We need more hands, which of you will stand to save yourselves?"

Lamentor exclaimed angrily, "We are not warriors, we are men of intellect, we will not sully ourselves to fight!"

"Then you will likely die unsullied, but die you will. If you will not help, then go to your rooms and pray to whatever it is you believe in."

Slowly they walked from the hall and returned to their rooms of luxury, only one remained. "I am not sure what help I will be, yet I will stay," Gru-Staedak looked at Joseph, "I will stand with you all, if I may." Joseph nodded at the old man. They could hear voices now, from below and at the front of the building. Speck was scared but he kept it to himself, not wanting to be the only one. Arn gave one of his hunting knifes to Joseph and told him to stand at the back with Speck. Nearest the window was Oron, Febra and the old man. The guard with his long sword, Febra her twin daggers and Gru-Staedak with a short sword provided by Oron.

The noise grew louder and they could see torches reflecting through the window. Arn stood on the central table, arrow notched, he thought of Murie and hoped she was safe. The iron door was taking the strain of shoulders, he could hear the thudding from the corridor at the front of the university. No way through there, he was certain.

The window was elevated above floor level in the sizeable hall, about four foot off the ground Speck estimated, it would at least slow them and he smiled as he thought of another way that may hamper the attackers.

"Arn, shoot the glass."

The huntsman looked at him with a shrug,"Why? It might hold a few blows."

"You may be skilled with a bow and a natural leader but when it comes to intellect....", Speck trialed off, "Did they have bows the ones you encountered?"

Arn shook his head, "No. They were all carrying hand-to-hand weapons. Get to the point, they will be round here in moments."

Speck accelerated his delivery, he could feel the panic rising and threatening to take hold, "They will have to climb in with their hands."

Immediately the huntsman understood and from a smooth leather quiver strapped around his waist, he pulled a single arrow. Its feathers pure white, plucked from the ducks in Kearn Luff. He notched the bow and drew the string to the side of his face, resting the shaft slightly so it pushed into his cheek. The distinct shrill of the string sang out and struck the window dead centre, a small hole was made and the cracks all around it begun to grow, expanding up to two feet from the source.

He cried out, "The chair!"

Oron moved quickly for a man his age and was first to grab the small stone chair and hurl it towards the centre of the window, striking almost two feet above him. The window shattered, hundreds of thick shards falling to the hall floor, some into the gardens outside. The ground was a river of glass. Torch light could now be seen as it rounded the side of the university and voices were shouting. They could hear clearly instructions being given to set the university ablaze. This is no coincidence,Joseph thought, no marauding band, they have purpose, were he and the others the objective or the university itself? Who would be fool enough to attack the Scholatic, even Joseph knew their influence reached throughout the whole of Vedian, shore to shore.

The first action was revealed as two torches landed in the hall, thrown from outside. There was little to burn in the room, the chairs and tables crafted from stone and just a few rugs adorning the walls and floor in places.

Almost thirty men had now amassed in the gardens and most were viewable from the window, they goaded the defenders and swore a variety of expletives, seemingly in no rush, they appeared to enjoy the attack of words. Gru-Staedak had been silent, standing in his robes of office, the short sword held limply in his hand. He looked right through the men outside, unaware of their jibes, almost as if he knew something no one else was aware of, a calm serenity consumed him as he turned to Arn.

"I think now is the time huntsman, if you will."

Notching a second arrow the hunter began to draw back the bow. The men focussed on Arn, they ceased talking and ran purposefully towards the window ledge. Clambering up their hands were cut by the shards, glass cracked and splintered, quickly mottled with the blood of the aggressors. As the men gained traction on the ledge they were met with either the svelte arrows of Arn or the longsword of Oron, the guard attacked with sharp stabbing motions, looking for quick wounds to push the raiders back. By the time the second line of men had assaulted the window ledge four laid on the floor below with mortal wounds and five were already lifeless. Oron was now hand to hand with two men, a lanky figure bearing a dull long sword and a short rough looking rogue, he weilded two fish knives tightly in each gnarled hand.

From between them pulling himself to view came a man, Joseph first thought might be a giant, he had broken through the front line, pushing Gru-Staedak to the floor. Heading directly for Speck who was locked in startled surprise, he closed the fifteen foot gap that separated them across the marble floor in a second. Arn had been forced down from the table and the bow swung back across his left shoulder, he now defended himself with his short hunting knife. Their numbers were growing and as he attempted to fight off multiple enemies, he was being backed further and further towards the wall. Joseph fleetingly looked for Febra but could not see the girl, he started to move to intercept the giant man but instantly knew he would never clear the few feet to Speck in time. The man was sinewy and his muscles defined, a short stubbly beard and hair cut tight to his forehead. He wore no armour, preferring to display the assets that his trade demanded. He was no soldier Joseph thought, a brigand from Kanegon possibly or one of the mercenaries from the Huskian skirmishes down south. His booted foot planted in front of him and he swung a club three foot in length is if he was casting a rod. Speck never moved, his eyes widening but not flinching as the blow grew closer to impact. Joseph shouted out as if the sound of his voice could repel the attack but to his amazement the club did not swing forward, rather it dropped to the floor and with it the mercenaries huge body fell like a sail cut from the wind.

As the corpse fell, Joseph could see her wrapped about his neck.

Feral and wild looking, her dagger still held tightly in the back of his neck. She sprung up as the body struck the ground, in one motion extracting the dagger from its tight crevice. Like a geyser unplugged, the release of pressure produced a river of red. Febra did not look up, neither did she acknowledge either of her compatriots, rather she spun on her heels and threw herself back into the fray. The floor had become unsteady underfoot, the blood of eight men was now lining the stone and Arn was struggling to keep his footing. He ducked under one desperate lunge while feigning to his right and jumping up to bring his knife sharply down into the chest of his stocky assailant. The attacker fell to the floor, he could see nothing of the others from the far corner of the room and prayed they were still safe.

They were undermined, not by any lack of skill on the guardsman's part but by the misery of luck and the blindness for justice that nature offered. Oron had held his attackers, striking one a killing wound to the chest, a second he cut deep into the thigh, as he had turned, adroitly for his age, an arrow swept into the hall. Fired from a short bow in the gardens it had ricochet off the glass remnants, hanging from what was left of the window and buried itself in his back. He fell to one knee, longsword still raised, as the darkness overtook him, he plunged the weapon into the torso of the man in front of them. They died together, the embrace of death as their corpses leant against each other a reminder to Joseph, that which ever side you are on, the fates may deal the same hand. What difference in men's lives, good, bad, right or wrong and at the end, the reward was parity. It was an empty thought.

As Arn dispatched his last mercenary, he finally could see the room clearly. Joseph and Speck remained at the back left, almost where they had begun, he saw no injury upon either but memory and fear. Near the window three men still stood side by side, in front of them only five paces away was Febra, the girl crouched, her knife held sideways so the blade protruded out of

201

her left hand pointing away from her body. She was covered in blood, her head lowered, facing the last three. He immediately saw Oron's lifeless body, propped up against his enemy and finally on the far side the old man lay, only viewable from his robes which covered him totally. He knew there were still a few outside but they did not seem as keen now to maintain the attack. Arn moved forward slowly, one eye on the men and the other on Febra, waiting to see what the girl would do next.

"This is not your fight I suspect. You have already lost many tonight, is gold worth the cost of your own lives? I offer you the chance to stand down.", Arn's voice was steady as he purposefully calmed his breathing.

The men looked at each other and the dark haired man, clad in leather tunic and black slacks shouted, "Now we will go but I promise you this hunter ,I personally will ensure this devil child", he pointed to Febra, "is gutted and hung once the boys are finished with her. This is just the beginning you fools,you have won nothing here, where ever you go the same fate awaits you!"

The three climbed slowly down from the ledge and retreated from the university grounds but all around fires burned and the smell of decay was hanging in the air.

Arn had never taken his eyes from Febra, the huntsman was certain she would attack, sure she would not let them leave. He slowly and carefully placed his hand on her shoulder. She did not jump or move, just stood fixated, looking at the space where the window had previously taken.

He whispered in her right ear, his breath moving her hair slightly where it was not clotted from the blood, "If there is a demon inside you, then it is one that gives life. For I am certain that those who stand here tonight do so because of you and your actions. Not all of us are given the gifts of purity and morality but that does not mean our deeds can not be good."

Joseph had noticed the absence of Gru-Staedak and surveyed the floor, seeing the robes he rushed forwards sliding down at the old man's side. He pushed back the cloth and turned him carefully over, so his head was resting in Joseph's hand.

In his left side, just below the rib cage a short sword was lodged about three inches deep, a pool of blood had gathered below and only stemmed by the blade not being withdrawn.

His face was white and his eyes barely open enough to see but the mariner could feel him breathing. He shouted for Arn and the hunter came quickly over, he looked at the wound and kneeled to help Joseph support the weight of his head. The huntsman shook his head.

"We can not remove it Joseph, he will lose too much blood too quickly."

Gru-Staedak's eyes opened slightly and his mouth quivered, "Your friend is right my boy, I have all my life at the mercy of intellect and I am to die by the polar opposite. An irony I suppose not entirely lost on me." The old man did not seem to be addressing anyone now, he continued mumbling to himself, then stopped and moved his head slightly to face the young man.

Joseph tried to smile but tears filled his eyes, "I am sorry I ran away, I am sorry I doubted you. Why could I not be like Arn? Why could I not have fought? I could have saved you but for my cowardice!"

The old man's voice was clearer now, "Perhaps you could but I did not look to you as a blunt instrument of violence. Had you done that, I could have been saved and perhaps all would be lost."

Joseph looked at Arn confused, he wondered if the old man was becoming delirious.

"All my life I have looked for one thing, purity of knowledge. In that understanding I learned a truth lost on my brethren, that sometimes the greatest wisdom can come from the unlikeliest source. One who stands not for his own gain but only to pass on the reality of life, to be a voice, when other voices go silent. That was passed to me by my own mentor, a man as intellectually powerful as he was ruthless. I tried to conduct myself without those aggressive traits but it seems he knew better than I.

For it seems I have fallen foul to a man who had all that with cunning and I fear I have endangered Vedian with my ignorance. I always believed my student would take up the mantle but he was either not ready, not able or perhaps simply not willing. I give it you Joseph and ask only you accept it."

Joseph was confused, "What is it you would give Gru-Staedak?" his hand slipped into the grasp of the old man and it felt cold.

"No crown, or jewels I am afraid, neither sword nor shield. Only the truth but look at me now Joseph and know when the time is right you will now find no greater or more devastating a weapon.

"Will you accept?" His voice was becoming weaker.

Joseph nodded, still unsure of what he was agreeing to.

Arn began to lift the old man, "We should move him to one of the bedrooms, try to make him comfortable."

Gru-Staedak coughed and blood trickled from his mouth, "No huntsman, no. I have two more things before I am done here. Joseph there is a book, it will be in Lamentor's library, it is called The History of Vedian - Vol VI, inside you'll find a poem, 'The Order of Change', it will help in the days to come."

"I...I cannot read....", Joseph stumbled over his words.

"No. Yet you travel with one who can. Young Speck come to me." It was clear to all, the old man had little time left, his body was slumped and his voice was a whisper.

Speck leaned so his face was almost touching the Scholatic's, carefully turning his head so he could hear.

"Go to the Tower, ignite the flame that once burned, for you will only truly be able to help your friend if you are brave enough to leave him."

He died and a part of Vedian that was true and good, passed away with him.

As a calm finally came over the university the other Scholatic began to emerge from their rooms. On seeing the lifeless body of Gru-Staedak they stood silent, heads bowed and chanted.

"Knowledge will protect us. Knowledge will guide us."

Lamentor moved to the front and addressed the group.

"You have served the Scholatic well. One of our own has fallen and we will tend to his burial in the gardens as would have been his wish. For now you must leave these walls as this place is not for the likes of you." He held his head high, oblivious to the carnage that surround them. Arn had moved to Febra and his hand was firmly on her shoulder. She glared at the Scholatic with genuine repulsion.

"We will leave with your thanks. Our service though has a cost and we would see ourselves paid before we leave." Arn smiled slightly.

Lamentor was furious, who were these commoners to ask him for anything.

"Save your fury Prominence, it is not your gold I ask for. Simply a book from your library. The History of Vedian, Volume VI if you will fetch it." Arn rubbed his hand up and down his now sheathed hunting knife.

"What possible need would any of you have for one of our texts! Ridiculous," as he spoke he looked around the room, moving from Arn's gaze, the impact of the battle quickly took hold of him and as ever he thought of himself, "nonetheless, you have been of some service as I said. The text is of no value and I warn you there are few drawings inside for you to look at."

Arn bowed, "You are too gracious but I am sure my friend here", he motioned to Speck, "can make some sense of it."

Lamentor looked at Speck with some disdain, "I doubt it."

By the time they left the university it was early morning and the night was black, they considered making their way back to the House of Histevirrillm but Arn was not sure of their safety and did not want Durgal's sacrifice to end in their capture. They sat behind the walls of the garden, voices still all around the town at such a late hour. They debated the next course of action, what had Gru-Staedak given them this new text? What was this tower which the old man had referred to? Arn was sure of one thing, he did not feel safe, the mercenaries would report back to whomever their employers were and they could send trackers.

Joseph felt his mind drifting to home and an idea formed, "If we are to be tracked, lets go to the one place we can not be. The sea! Boats can moor just up the coast here, perhaps only three hours on foot. There is a cove where the tides are less rough, I remember Calan talking about it, saying they sometimes got deliveries from Kanegon."

Speck looked less convinced, "Even if there is a boat there, I doubt that and we could persuade them to take us aboard, the seas are perilous around here. You know this Joseph."

"I know exactly what these waters are like - but Pike said you sail anything with enough skill and luck." Joseph looked pleadingly at his small friend.

Speck shook his head, "Unfortunately we have not been forthcoming with the latter to date. However I trust you as a sailor, if you say it can be done, I will follow you. And once we are aboard perhaps a look at the book could further our knowledge..."

Speck panicked, where was the book?

"I left it at the house. In all the commotion! We must go back. Now." he had already got to his feet.

Febra laughed, Joseph for the first time, felt slightly unnerved by the contrast of her behavior.

"The satchels on your back you fool. At least one of us knows its whereabouts, even if we no longer have someone to deliver it to." Speck reached back and felt the reassuring feel of the packs contents.

Joseph knew a small amount about the seas to the west of Asten, it had been here that his father had met his fate. There were pools of water that could drag a boat under once caught in its downward spin. The weather out to the west according to Pike was also treacherous, storms were continuous, with sheeting rain and winds so ferocious they could break a mast. The reason Vedian was so barren in wood was due to these waters. Across to the west was a continent rich in maple and oak. Boats would run the gauntlet from Kanegon to the west coast through the Straights of Reslin to harvest on barges but only a small number would make the return trip. At its central most point between the two continents it was said waves would form higher than a hundred feet and could break a hull or smash the barge and envelop it in the waters below. There was only one reason to sail these waters and it was coin. Wood sold for a lot of copper due to its shortage and men would risk their lives in its pursuit. Pike had always said there were only two types of men that sailed the western waters, the greedy and the desperate. There was no question which of those they fell into. They could take a boat east but that was risky with its underwater rocks that lined the coastal journey. Alternatively

206

they headed south west and tried to make Kanegon but that, without doubt, was not going to be an easy journey.

"Arn, where are we heading?", Joseph looked to the huntsman for direction.

"I do not know the western coast lands and Kanegon even less. We could take could hope to make our way back home but my mind turns to Rundell. We agreed we would help clear his name and my heart tells me that course will be the hardest. Lets get to the cove and first see if an option presents itself. More than anything my head tells me to get clear of Asten and quickly." The hunter stood and the others followed.

The slipped out of the town keeping to the dark shadows avoiding any noise they heard, Arn wished he could check on the Inn and ensure Murie was unharmed but he knew that would put them in danger. As they made their way north, keeping away from the road into Asten, the sun had began to rise from the east and the warmth that came with it felt refreshing and cleansing. Joseph felt for the first time in hours a sense of comfort and while his thoughts never strayed far from the old man, his senses were lifted by the heat of the sun around him. He walked side by side with Febra, who was as talkative as she had been since they left the Luff, she seemed almost jovial and at ease, a pale imitation of the girl that had fought so fiercely the night before.

"Would you take a wife Joseph.", she asked with a curtailed grin.

Speck butted in and pulled on his friends arm, "No one will have him! He is destined to sail the seas a lonely nomad."

Febra looked sharply at Speck, her gaze changing from wistful to determined and stoic in a second, "And you would fare better?." Speck stopped and stared at Joseph, shrugging his shoulders as the girl slipped to the back of the group.

The trail was not hard and they made good time, passing only a few travellers on the road. By nightfall Arn could make out the coastline and demanded to the group they push on under cover of darkness. "We can observe our options best at night, then decide on the course of action to take."

The first sign of activity was from a light emanating from a small building at the waters edge. The dock was barely the size of the Luff and no more than one frigate and two small barges would have had room to dock at one time.

Arn pointed to the larger of the two ships and whispered, "That has enough capacity for us all, we need to engage its captain and see its course. Too many of us to all wander in, I will go with Febra, a friendly female face may prove useful." Specks eyes rose at the description but he said nothing, as the pair headed off to the dock.

The young scribe tucked into the hillock they crouched behind with Joseph and they unpacked their sacks to produce some wool blankets. As Speck pulled out the cloth, he tugged on the book they had procured from Lamentor. With a glance at Joseph to confirm agreement, he opened the cloth bound tome. The title was embroiled from a green hued thread and the pages a thick papyrus, used by the university for most of its writings and produced by the men of Medwere from the reeds that grew all around the lake town in abundance. There was no contents table, so Speck flicked through, scanning the pages for a title or phrase that matched the last words of Gru-Staedak.

"Here! I have it, 'The Order of Change', shall I read it out loud?"

Joseph nodded and listened intently as Speck slowly read the poem.

Arn counselled Febra as they approached the building with the light they could see from the road. The girl nodded, she seemed agreeable to the suggestions he gave. As they approached the door they could hear a number of voices reverberating from the walls. The hunter knocked on the door and stepped back, one hand cautiously at the hilt of his weapon. A young man opened the door, dressed in cloth trousers and an open necked shirt, once white but muddied and sullen now. He winked at Arn, his long chin protruding out of the building, "What's your business?" he enquired factually.

Arn spoke in a friendly tone, "We were hoping to secure some passage and meet with the captain of the ship out there." Arn gestured to the dock.

The young man glanced at Febra, who was trying hard to smile, "Come on in, I'll see if he will talk to you. Its a bit crowded, got all the boys and a few other merchants stopping over from Kanegon."

The boy was not joking, the main room was barely twenty paces in a square and over twenty five men were packed in drinking ale and exchanging banter. There was only one table and the young lad beckoned for Arn to follow as he made his way through the crowd. Around the table sat five men, two each side and at the head a lithe bearded individual, he wore a fur lined jacket bound with heavy leather, his grey tinted beard platted into five even strands. Weary eyes, heavily bagged and testament to many late nights and early mornings. The boy knelt close to the sailor and whispered in his ear, so only he could hear.

He pointed at two of the men seated to his left and they immediately rose and pushed through the crowd to a serving hatch. "Sit." He gestured to the bench and Arn sat closest with Febra to his side.

Arn began, "It is with thanks you see us at this late hour, my colleagues and I are looking for passage and would know your destination?"

The man leant forward and spread his hands wide, "To the point but let us exchange names and drink before we get to business." He gestured to the boy, who had stood at his rear and he whisked off to a backroom, darting through the crowd once more.

"I am Arn and this is Febra, we travel from Asten and are on business." He smiled looking to keep all discussions on a good footing.

"Well Arn, I am Captain Bolt and these fellows," he pointed to the men on his right, "are my First Mate Fillesne and Seaman Fyle.

The second man was built like a bull, thick necked and arms wider than Arn's legs. Arn noted the bruises on his knuckles and the ink marking each of them with a letter. Fyle reached forward and grabbed Arn's hand in a lock, "Well met laddie."

Bolt continued, "We have just towed from the west and delivered, a long and arduous journey. We have some merchants here that look for return journey to Kanegon. Can we interest you in that trip?" He was making efforts to be courteous, the extra coin alongside the four merchants they already had would make the trip a real success.

Arn checked a look to Febra, "How much do you ask?" The boy had now returned and delivered two mugs of ale in front of Arn and Febra, refilling the others drinks from a huge jug.

Bolt smiled, "We can accommodate a fair rate, as the journey is already planned. Let us say two coppers each?"

Febra's eyes widened, "That's rich for a trip you're already taking."

"Perhaps girly but I am guessing you are keen to move, word says Asten has troubles at present." Bolt tapped his fingers on the table, drumming out a popular sea shanty.

Arn thought to himself, it was not the journey he wanted but east was too risky and he wanted to put distance between them and Asten now, "We will pay you the four copper but for four passengers."

Bolt looked bemused, "Then my friends you have passage, we sail at dawn. I suggest you find two others quickly!" He roared out loud and begun singing the shanty he had been drumming out, the other men quickly joined in and the place shook with the sound.

Speck cleared his voice and read:

> *Did you wake upon the hearth once heated,*
> *Did I see you in the forest without trees.*
> *If I dreamt of the promise that you gave me,*
> *Was the answer in the fields of reeds.*
>
> *Did your son shine in the gardens,*
> *Did I leave you alone in the tower.*
> *If mine actions caused you pain,*
> *It was only to give you power.*
>
> *Wake now Spring, Summer and Fall,*
> *For Winter sleeps at the break of dawn.*
>
> *Find the blood that wakes the dead,*
> *Find the forgotten in the sands.*
> *Find the mages that knew how to fight,*
> *And unite them by Kings hands.*
>
> *Not every book tells a story of truth,*
> *The tale is written by the survivor.*
> *On the Isle where the factions stood,*
> *Lays the lies of MonPellia the philosophiser.*

Wake now Spring, Summer and Fall,
For Winter sleeps at the break of dawn.

Speck looked at Joseph, his face a puzzle of questions, "What does it mean?"

"I do not know Joseph but everything I have seen since we left the Luff tells me, we will soon find out."

Chapter 11 - The Drain

'The west and north-west coast of Vedian provide the most interesting and dangerous marine geography available to us. Unlike the Pluris coast, depth readings become impossible to take after only a mile or two from the shore and weather conditions are of a far grander and formidable scale than it's more moderate eastern counterpart. This increase in risk is not without it's corollary benefits; whales and other large sea creatures can be found in the sea of these coasts, better wind patterns make sailing faster and there is something far more appealing to the lover of the sea about this deep, awesome ocean. From the peninsular of Asten you look out into one of the greatest mysteries of Vedian and it stares impassioned back at you.'

'Marine History Of Vedian' - Sea Lord Grenton - Vedian 799

The Coral Mariner sliced through the water under full sail on its westward reach with the mainland visible to the south. The ship and crew had strained to push north with the mild changing winds from the coast but once around the headland the prevailing westerlies let it spread its wings and fly. A pair of dolphins kept apace with the Mariner leaping out of the bow wake and then falling back to repeat the trick. While most of the deck hands were busy keeping a ship under full sail in order, the non-seafaring passengers lined the bow rail to watch the Mariner's playful blue-gray companions. Joseph came forward to check on his friends.

"They're said to be good luck." He indicated the dolphins with a nod. "But I suspect that we see so much of them because Fyle throws them kitchen scraps when no one's looking. I hear he can also tell one from another and has names for them."

Arn nodded with interest while Febra made it clear she thought anyone naming fish was positive evidence of insanity. Joseph had twice his normal presence once he boarded the Mariner; he walked differently and responded to questions with a note of certainty and finality in his voice. Whether this was caused by a true seaman taking back to the waves or just that he had returned to familiar surroundings none of the others could quite be sure.

The ship itself was some one hundred paces long, a gaff-rigged schooner designed for whaling in deep sea conditions. She first put to sea over half a century ago and her infrastructure was of a fine wood that had not been indigenous to Vedian, repairs had been made out of the same fine material and wherever possible dirt wood replacements had been used. These were crude and had a short lifespan of only a few years. Many of the original fine brass components had been replaced with iron fittings, a cheaper metal in the Luff.

Occasionally the Mariner would pass within hailing distance of smaller fishing craft, not designed for the deep sea journeys that the Mariner required to hunt down larger prey. Two days after they had boarded the ship, they passed within a few thousand paces of a fishing smack, the crew of the little boat waved wildly to the Mariner. Bolt appeared and strode onto the stern deck.

"Close haul!" He bellowed and came alongside the ship's mate at the wheel. The crew jumped to their duty but there was no disguising the fact they were surprised by this turn of events. Rope tore through blocks at a frightening rate. The mate changed his course toward the shore and the small fishing craft. The Mariner suddenly put on a turn of pace and cut through the water like a predator, heeling over slightly on its new bearing.

"Hunter! Get your bow and get over here!" Bolt pointed at Arn, who for some reason to date seemed to be the snub of his crude humour. When the woodsman got up to the stern deck with his bow and quiver the captain passed him a piece of paper and some twine.

"See to it that that message arrives on that boat when we pass it by. If I have to come about to deliver it myself I'll have you scrubbing these decks for the next week." Arn grinned. He knew that Bolt would do no such thing but if he couldn't hit the side of that boat, then he was no hunter at all. He notched an arrow and began to judge the rate at which they were approaching the other vessel. The Mariner undulated slightly as it cut through the waves making the task at hand slightly more difficult. Arn relaxed his knees to absorb the rolling motion as much as possible. When they seemed to be at the zenith of their passage past the boat Arn loosed the arrow at a path less than thirty-five paces.

He judged that he needed little arc to cover the distance. The crew of the fishing boat realised at the last minute what the Mariner's captains intention was and dropped to the deck moments before the missile was sent over.

"Bullseye my boy! By god, it's sticking out of the mast! You'll be the stuff of sailors' stories for months on this caper my lad!" Bolt issued orders to the mate to resume course and put his arm around the hunters' shoulders.

"You know I should thank you for that, stories of the Mariners prowess have reduced trouble at sea and ashore for us. That little display will bolster our reputation for a while."

"I don't suppose that means you are going to tell me what the message said then?"

"Just an order for more tobacco for myself and a few others at Kanegon. I make a modest profit running odds and ends around. In truth without the side business there may not be enough cash in the strong box for our winter overhaul. You've got to stay flexible to stay alive, you see? It's true in everything: morals, business, goodness even marriage I've been told, though presiding over a marriage is probably the closest I'm ever likely to get to it."

"Amazing how sound doesn't carry all at sea though isn't it?" Arn scorned.

"Have you lost your mind boy? It travel leagues further at sea than on land!"

"Then why not shout an order to the boat rather than risk skewering one of them?"

"Brains will take you a long way Arn but you've got to learn when to use them and when to keep quiet about using them."

Speck had not fared well once the ship set out to sea, his stomach churned constantly and just as he thought the sensation was passing a fresh wave of nausea flooded over him. The embarrassment of sea sickness was made all the worse as neither Febra nor Arn seemed troubled by it and the sailors were overjoyed that they were having exceptionally smooth weather which they claimed wouldn't last once they rounded the cape. At first he suspected that he had a genuine disease but soon it was all too obvious that he was just not a natural sailor.

Fyle the steward tried to comfort him by mentioning that he had been sick for his first week at sea and even now he found it queasy the first day aboard after a long shore leave. Speck listened politely, he appreciated the cook's attempt to console him but all he could really think about was getting back to the ship's rail as quickly as possible.

During a lull in his nausea Speck wondered if he could divorce his mind from his body during this distressing period then perhaps he could spend his time usefully while his physical self got on with the business of being sick. His idle speculation turned from mental dawdling into deep thought when he recalled the effect that the book had on him. His physical self had become suspended while his mind was elsewhere and he didn't remember being aware of his body or the conditions around it. As Speck ruminated further he also managed to suppress the niggling question of whether it was safe to use the book again. Nestled in the folds of a hammock he cradled the tome in his arms, he hoped this gave him two benefits: that he could not fall over onto the floor while under the influence of the book and that to any passing sailor he was mostly hidden by the hammock. Running his fingers around the edge of the familiar artifact he found the clasp. He took a moment to utter a short benediction on his own soul and then opened its pages.

"Let them work their way back to us." Said Pinkerton to the concerned soldier on his right. All along the line men were peering over their shields to see how the renegade corporals were doing in the thick of the enemy. Their view was impeded by the growling row of enemies, most of them at least six inches taller than anyone in the Sabre regiment, they were a fearsome opponent. Somewhere behind that line of over-sized men the three corporals were in a fight for their lives.

"Pick up my dagger Roz?" Pleaded Fiddler. The three soldiers each faced a different direction to hold off the circle of wary enemies. One of the corporals glimpsed quickly at the floor.

"Why the hell did you drop it?" Roz didn't feel inclined to lose attention from the robust looking attackers in front of her.

"I didn't mean to did I? But now that I have - I'd really appreciate if you could pick it up for me." Fiddler saw that Roz had no intention of stooping for his dagger. "Milli got that for me when we were last in Pluris - come on - be a sport."

215

"Leave it there Roz," said Peaks, "We'll all roll round one to the right and see if he fancies picking it up himself." Nimbly the three each skipped to the right and took the place where the last man had stood. It was so quick that their assailants didn't have time to try and take advantage of the move, one of the enemy howled in anger and clashed his spear against his buckler.

"I think they're getting frustrated Fiddler. This one looks ready to pop: sure you won't swap back?" Roz said.

"You keep an eye on that one. I'll just see if we can get a step closer to the lines." Fiddler looked quickly down at the dagger that was now between his feet, the two attackers watching him noticed the glance and when he gestured as if to take a knee to retrieve it they launched into him. Unfortunately for both the opposing soldiers this was exactly what Fiddler wanted. The first had an axe and the other carried a short spear and shield. The axeman had to build a back swing while the spear man jabbed hard at Fiddler's torso. Coming up from his lowered position Fiddler closed the gap between them with a lunge, clipping the spear upward with his sabre and brought the point across the spearman's wrist then onward toward the axeman who had expected cover from his compatriot: now he was left exposed with his weapon dragging behind him. Fiddler brought his blade across the man's neck and chest. At the same time Peaks took advantage of his enemies distraction and distress at seeing his two fellows cut down. The stocky soldier beat the weapon out of the enemies hand in an instant and drove his sword four or five inches into his adversary's chest.

Out on the line the rest of the Sabre Regiment could hear the corporals were getting closer. Pinkerton strained his ears to judge the direction and distance. From a way behind him he heard the calm voice of General Dior speaking from horseback.

"Thirty yards dead ahead Sergeant Pinkerton."

"That's very useful information sir. With your permission I'll retrieve our lost property."

"In your own time Sergeant Pinkerton." Dior spurred the horse away down the line.

"Twenty either side of me - ready to rush - second line fall in to cover the ground made. Nobody goes ahead. Nobody leaves the line." He waited for confirmation from either side. "Silent count

216

from ten boys - starting now." The Sabre struck hard and with momentum. Pinkerton crashed into the soldier in front of him, driving him to the floor and striking a fatal blow. Either side the line was coming up with him too. He flashed blows left and right to assist the men on either side, buying them the distraction they needed to win the fight. The second row didn't expect to have to face the enemy so quickly and tried to back up into the lines behind them, some of whom were unsure which way the threat of the enemy was most dangerous, the Sabre line or the corporals. Caught in indecision the brave attackers in the ranks tried to improvise skirmish groups but the Sabre had punctured their line in a broad wedge with Pinkerton at the head.

"Did you hear that?" Peaks asked the large warrior in front of him. "Sounds bad to me. Sounds like the general has ordered that motherless killer Pinkerton to come and fetch us. I'd make yourself scarce if I were you."

The huge assailant, wearing a colourful tabard over chain armour, clearly couldn't understand Vedian but knew when he was being goaded. He muttered a few bitter sentences in rebuttal and held his ground.

"I'll give you this: I've never seen one of yours turn tail and run. Not once. But if what was coming up behind you was coming up behind me - I'd be off for the Inpur desert quicker than you could say absent-without-leave."

The attacker muttered to himself, setting his balance and tutting his contempt. Peaks was generally accepted as the statesman of the corporals which simply meant he had better manners than the other two. Fiddler was a cunning slip of a man from the wrong side of Kanegon. Roz, the daughter of an ore trader, signed up in Pluris to see the world. Peaks was generally considered to be the charm contingent of the three corporals.

"Do you know I think this weed-eater just told me to shut up? Well I'll be. You deserve everything that's coming to you."

At that moment the fighters immediately behind the enemy began to mill about, the din of pitched battle came to them in a ebb and flow of screams, metal clashes, shouted orders, cries for help and the unique smell of fear. All three of the corporals made a run straight at the line in front of Peaks, their blades cutting through a tunnel toward the milieu. Their opponent didn't

217

last long with all three swordsmen coming at him, but he didn't turn and run. The corporals did everything possible to stop the enemy ranks closing in on either side of them but they didn't have to wait too long.

"What in Vedian do you three think you are doing?" Bellowed a familiar voice.

"Harrying the enemy at all costs Sergeant." Roz shouted while chopping at a phalanx of spears and axes.

"Fall in you useless toerags!" Pinkerton roared. The corporals darted back into their line where gaps had opened up to accept them and closed as soon as they had passed through. The battle settled back to a stand off, the enemy fell back twenty paces and formed a robust shield and spear wall. Pinkerton called for the second rank of the Sabre to come forward and relieve the first. The corporals lay exhausted on the ground behind the line, sweating like animals while laughing at each other, lost in the euphoria of having cheated death. It was only a minute later that they noticed the figure on horseback standing still as a statue nearby, a giant figure, staff held aloft and a dripping broadsword in the other.

"You three will clean up and report to the command post in ten minutes." The sergeant ordered, his fiery gaze lifting the spent trio back to their feet and marching them in the direction of the stock wagons. As they past Dior on his horse the general spared them just a moments unreadable glance before he turned his attention back to the battlefield.

In the command tent Dior traced his finger along a map which covered a trellis table. A candleman stood beside him following the line carefully and muttering a series of numbers over and over while his eyes twitched in their sockets. As soon as the generals hand left the map the candleman stopped his litany, slumped and then held the edge of the tabletop while he recovered himself.

"Take a moment Fystal." Said the general.

"No need sir, I'll be fine. Besides, you have guests." The candleman indicated the three corporals standing nervously beyond the tent door.

"Indeed. Be kind enough to call them in would you?" Dior drew a piece of cloth across the centre of the map and sat himself down in a chair. He closed his eyes for a minute to set his frame of mind for the corporals, how they had had time to collude their answers, who would have led their real decisions and which of them was slippery enough to suggest enhancements to their story. When he opened his eyes again he took in the details of the three corporals, the state of their armour and weapons, the look on each of their faces, slight cuts and bruises that were visible, the remnants of the quick splash of water each had been treated to. The corporals intrigued him greatly, they could be analysed equally validly as a single being that happened to be split into three bodies. They stood at attention in silence as he assessed them.

"Ranks in the Sabre have a certain flexibility. Not all ranks are command ranks - not all pay is equal to the brass on a soldier's shoulder. This freedom entails a degree of risk and with that risk we expect every man to bear a responsibility to the regiment and to me, yes me personally. Who will be forced to explain to the King, the Council Superintendent, the Prince," he counted the names out on his hand, "and the Marshall General who let us not forget is opposed to the idea of a single regiment not directly commanded by his good self? Who will explain to them why tactical decisions appear to being made by corporals? Corporals, who in any other regiment, be expected to lead out ten men a piece and die nobly for their country." Roz was biting her bottom lip while Peaks seemed to be suffering a terrible case of nervous blinking.

"I sense that Corporal Fiddler has something you want to put forward." Said Dior.

"Actually yes sir. If I could..."

"Remain silent Fiddler. I'd be far more interested in hearing the turn of events from Corporal Rozillich."

Roz stood as tall as Peaks, she moved in full battle armour with veteran ease but any bravado she might have summoned vaporized under the mounting pressure of Dior's attention. The general was famed for his faultless memory and tactical prowess, he was not an ideal opponent for a lack-lustre liar.

"We were covering the fall back of the third regiment you see sir, to the east of Bannermane where the Manefont houses are." She paused to collect herself.

"Just as it happened Rozillich, there is no need to form any fine words or sense of drama for me." Dior pressured.

"So the third were falling back to the cross hills and we were giving them support by harrying the enemy, as ordered sir, but with their numbers we needed to find some cover and Manefont has some good dry stone walls. Bannermane cut off from us and the first - well you know there's nothing left of the first. We see the enemy have managed to send out some sapper groups and one of them is heading right into Bannermane to the main wall."

"That is completely correct. Carry on Rozillich, you're doing very well."

"Corporal Peaks then observes that if we were particularly quick, and as the battle on the east is pretty rag tag, we could likely get to the wall before them. " Rozillich took a deep breath. "So we skirted the wall and made our way - rapidly - along the farm edge, onto the approaching path and came out where we had to clear several stray attackers from the area."

"And where was the rest of your group at this point?" Dior asked.

"They were ordered to continue covering the third back to the muster point and to inform Sergeant Pinkerton that we had headed into Bannermane to harry the enemy."

It was all Dior could do not to let out the smallest hint of a smirk, "Excellent. Do carry on."

Arn watched Fyle dance around on his toes, suddenly the big man looked far more nimble and deadly than he had thought possible. Shaking his arms out and hanging his head down so that his chin touched his massive chest the cook appeared to go through some kind of psychological metamorphosis. When he raised his head there was no jolly glint in his eye; no suggestion of the compassionate, thoughtful man that Arn thought he was. One word seemed to describe this new man's expression: purposeful. Tanwell the challenger was throwing air punches in his corner, he seemed to be attempting a similar mental preparation himself but if he had succeeded the outward effect was far less obvious than it had been for Fyle.

The ship's mate rang the bell and both men circled the centre of the roped off deck. Tanwell threw out some experimental jabs which Fyle dodged, blocked or simply ignored, Fyle didn't seem to need to weigh up his opponent in the same way, perhaps simply defending the initial blows told him all he needed to know because on the next jab from Tanwell, Fyle dropped and hammered a swinging left fist into his opponents exposed ribs. Tanwell leapt back and covered his side, obviously shocked by the blow while Fyle seemed happy not to press his attack.

"Just saying hello there." Noted Bolt.

Tanwell circled again and probed with cautious jabs, actually landing a reasonable blow on the cook's left cheek but not seeming to phase the man. Arn's instincts told him that Fyle had let the blow through his defences for some reason but couldn't fathom why until he saw the result. In committing to the successful blow Fyle's opponent and come nearer and circled, leaving him far closer to the corner of the ring than before. Fyle launched a blistering combination of punches that put his target completely on the back foot and further into the corner of the ring. From then on it seemed as if the fight was surgically finished. The rocking, twisting Tanwell tried desperately to escape a tirade of body blows by lowering his guard to his mid-drift when the focus of the attack suddenly changed with a lightning left jab to his face, stunning him with his hands down.

"...and there's the goodnight kiss." Smirked Bolt as a brutal right cross lifted Tanwell off his feet and dumped him onto the ropes, bouncing off to arrive in an unconscious heap, face-down on the deck. Arn watched the cook back away from the motionless Tanwell, still ready should the recumbent boxer actually rise up again. It didn't happen. When the other man was finally counted out Fyle was again shaking out his arms with his chin down on his chest, moments later when the mate held the man's hand in the air he was the same jovial human being that Arn had experienced previously How elastic the soul of man must be, thought the hunter, to use personality like a weapon in that way. To change psyches with just the goad of a perceived need, as simply as a workman changes his clothes.

"The wind has risen but we are getting no more traction. I've put more sail up but she makes no more headway." The bosun kept his voice low as if he still might be overhead in the captain's quarters. Bolt and Joseph looked at each other grimly. The captain had quickly spotted the boys seafaring skills on the first day of boarding The Mariner. He took a liking to him instantly and for Joseph it felt like being back with Pike again. For the last three days sailing they had kept close quarter.

"There can be no mistaking it then we are either dragging some kind of crap from the coast or..."

"We are snared by something else."

"You know what that would mean around these shores then lad?"

Joseph nodded and hung his head, he knew only too well what this meant. His father knew all too well.

"Well this is the hero hour and damn it I don't want to go down with the ship but you know the choices, let loose some boats with the crew, someone leads it away in the main vessel. We can't stop for anything, if we do the thing will be upon us and you're in fifty shades more trouble than we were before. No one will get out. Not the life ships. Nothing."

Joseph waited and thought, he was aware this was a critical moment and he knew the wrong decision here could be the death of everyone on board. There was no place for extravagant emotion, Pike had taught him you either are adding information to the situation and producing new solutions or you are a poor commanding officer. His father had tried to save the Dusk Returner from the serpent or 'Drain' as it was often referred to but lost both the ship and almost all the crew in an attempt to sever the creatures ties from the hull of the ship. They had no idea even if it was a single creature or a breed that lived in that area but they knew that no solution had been found to the fatal slowing of a vessel. Stop - you're dead. Push on - you're dead eventually. Let loose the majority of the crew and you can save lives but lose the ship and the skeleton crew on board. In this case Bolt was suggesting he could pilot the ship alone for enough time to get a everyone else clear in the the two launches. It was time to think like a man. Bolt was asking for suggestions that wouldn't involve him sacrificing himself for his crew.

All sailors knew that this was a captain's job if the time came. His father had believed both ship and crew could be saved and lost both in the attempt according to Pike. The sea had no time for the heart, only factual determination. There were less than

222

minutes in which to decide the fate of lives, it was simply a matter of calculating chances.

Joseph held himself aloft and spoke calmly, "Take to the boats. I will hold the windward course, you can ship the launches back and lee to coast. I am a fast swimmer and younger then you captain, my survival chance is greater. I'll light the foilers fuse before the ship goes down and that will give me the opportunity I need." Bolt and Fillesne the first mate, gave the statement the time it deserved for digestion. There weren't going to be any rash decisions at this, the most critical of moments a sailor could make, but inside they were both calculating alternatives. By their expressions Joseph could tell his proposal was not going to meet with approval.

Bolt spoke first.

"You haven't served on this ship as I. You've clearly been around and I respect you lad but this is a job for the crew. I have twenty years on you at sea, I can do this. She's one of the last Vedian ships and they'll be no more like it I warrant, I can move faster single handed than you might imagine and that'll make sure that the rest of you are clear and safe."

In that moment Joseph damned all the experience gained at sea in his youth, when Pike had taught him about ship and command. All seemingly functional at it's time but now compelling him to react accordingly to the words he was about to hear. His soul rolled within him and fought against everything he knew, that the best decision was just that, not to think about the individual.

"You know it's my job lads. Lets not mess about."

And that was it: a loss that hurt everyone as deeply as a family bereavement was about to happen but they were expected to act swiftly and without question. Not to do so would be a disrespect to the very man that they would honour later.

Joseph turned to Arn and whispered in a guilty tone, "It seems my family name is cursed, have I brought this on us, father to son?"

"Nonsense boy!" Said Bolt overhearing. "You are talking as if I were already dead. Grak! I'll drag the thing on shore myself next Tuesday and make a fortune on the fisher's market. You'll get none of the profits you understand."

223

As if to emphasise the point, the decks of the ship groaned under the strain of making headway and holding the unseen tethers of the sea leviathan that would eventually pull the vessel down to the bottom.

"I'll pull the ship in as many directions as I possibly can." The captain looked up the rigging. "But I'll need storm halyards put out for me, if I am to change sail without a crew. Even then there's no guarantee that the Drain won't get hold of the skiffs."

"We should dump as much cargo and barrel's into the water as possible just before we launch, with any luck the thing grabs at so much of that it won't pay any attention when the real hulls hit the water."

"Should we load the whaling harpoons do you think?"

"It can't do any harm lad - if there's a chance that I can use them to free a boat from a single tendril then give it a go."

"Who gets which oarsmen?" Bolt asked his first mate.

Fillesne looked about him, replying to his captain. "There's some that won't go in the skiff with the girl. They have the right. Tanwell won't, nor any of the crew from further south, bad luck you see a woman"

"Fyle will - let the other two be split evenly for speed, Mister Fillesne you're to see it's done right."

They changed tack back toward land and as the coast on the horizon came into far sight the sails became alive with men jury rigging the ship so that a single hand could keep it close to full pace. The long whaling skiff's were arranged for launch from the port side of the vessel so that as Bolt turned the ship into a long reach away to starboard they could make as much distance in the opposite direction. Water and food barrels, ammunition casks and cloth bundles - anything that could be made into a decoy - had all been brought up onto the deck. The sun poured down on them from a clean blue sky as if nothing were wrong, as if they weren't about to sacrifice a captain to the sea.

"It's a fine day." Bolt mused. "The wind is up. I'll bet you could see ships rounding the headland from the crow's nest. By Vedian I have loved the sea all these years."

"We could tie the wheel and jump for the last long boat as soon as the others are off." Joseph's mind was still looking for methods of escape without losing Bolt. "Or make for the headland rocks and scupper her."

"All good ideas but my boy, time is against us, very soon if we make no change of tack the ship will be at a standstill and the Drain will tether it to the bottom, it'll run a thousand poison threads up and down, then the hull will start to split and she'll be taken down for the thing to suck whatever it wants out of the wreck - god knows it probably thinks we're a whale. The only way to delay is to be like a fish trying to stop the fisherman reeling you in - pull against and change, hold and change, don't let your nose get turned into the nets."

Fillesne came to stand by them. It meant the preparations were ready, it meant that it was time to man the boats and leave Bolt.

"Wait for us to be closer to the shore?" Asked Fillesne.

"No, there's not the time. You'll have to put your backs into the oars for the rest of the day." Bolt said. Fillesne shook the captain by the hand and then emotion took over and he embraced the tall sailor. He turned to get the crews ready to drop boats into the water in an attempt to hide his eyes. Joseph wasn't able to look straight at Bolt now. The dry calm of old sailors under pressure can run right to the verges of their lives but the young suffer far more. Bolt put his hand on the young man's shoulder and gave him a little help walking to the steps of the mid-deck. The crew turned silent as Bolt remained above looking at them.

He addressed the crew, "You're all kin to me, even those that just joined us. Old hands know that things like this happen when you live with the sea, no one can stop it. I want some volunteers to take oars on the mates boat." He pointed at the long boat that Febra would be taking, the one, if the crew was left unchanged would be rowed by Joseph, Arn, Speck, Fyle and the girl.

"Consider it a last request."

The captain didn't wait to see who stepped forward. Sailors are a superstitious bunch but none of them wanted to overrule the captains last wish. They crowded around the mates boat.

"Equal rowers is best boys." Fillesne bellowed while beaming with pride at the crew. "Marlone grab your harpoon and pull alongside Fyle, Tanwell you can pull at the back with Banworthy.

Girl, you'll take the bow and Speck you're on the tiller. Tick your in skiff one command and Oldman skiff two."

They begun to climb into the rowers, Fyle stayed aboard to help lower the launchers into the water with Bolt. His sinewy muscles pulling hard on the ropes to ensure the heavy vessels remained balanced on their descent to the waters below. Bolt addressed his cook. "No time for one last bite then. I could murder a slice of rare cooked boar with those dandy herbs you soak it in. You're gonna get wet now Fyle, climb down half way before you dive in." He motioned to the big man and winked conspiratorially.

Fyle leaned over the bow, "On your way boys! Nothing more to see here!" He turned to Bolt, "Not gonna happen Captain. Not this day. There's enough bodies to get them to shore. You can not do it alone and don't bother arguing or Ill beat you down to the brig and leave you there while I take all the glory for myself!"

Bolt smiled, he did not bother beginning to argue or protest, he knew a man's decision when it was taken. "Then you offload the cargo to distract the creature and man the gunnel, I will sail us free. Don't worry Fyle you'll get a mention in my tale!" As the burly cook moved to the bulwark to begin to offload the cargo, a huge crack came from beneath the Mariner and the boat lurched to one side.

"Its now or never Captain, shes giving!" He turned his weight to the barrels first, hurling them individually in one movement from deck to waters.

The lithe Captain moved quickly and purposefully, tacking the ship starboard swiftly turning against the pull below. The skiffs below were hurled up and down against the waves created by the Mariners movement. The force of the waves pushing them in the direction of land as Bolt had planned and the incumbents begun to take up the oars and row.

Fillesne roared above the crashing waves, "Row lubbards, row for your lives!" His boat was ahead, already two ships distance away from the Mariner, the other two had fared slower and were still close to the ship.

Then, for the first time, Joseph caught sight of what had been in his dreams for a lifetime. A huge tentacle broke from the water, grey and thick, as wide as six feet at its broadest point. It flailed aimlessly in the air and then seemed to find its sense. Pausing it flicked back on it itself striking the water nearest the boats closest to the Mariner. The strike upon the waters created a huge wave, enveloping the first ship, crashing against the second. For all their experience and time at sea, none had seen anything like this and panic came over some of the crew. They lost the rhythm to row together and Tick was struggling to shout orders to the other men, desperate to stay in control. He looked frantically for the boat that was led by Oldman but he could see nothing of it. Fillesne's boat seemed to be getting further and further away from them, the floor was half filled with water now and they were still in range of the huge tentacle.

"We have to go back!" Joseph shouted at Fillesne. "They will not make it."

"There's no going back boy. Only forward, together. Now row, two, row, one." He pounded out the command again and again as the Mariner began to become smaller and the other skiff disappeared from view.

Bolt changed the sail for the third time, he had seen the skiff go under from the mast position and desperately looked to move again to shift position. Anything to distract the beast away from the tiny boats below. All the cargo was now overboard, most drifting around the Mariner, some locked with smaller tendrils wrapped around it. Fyle was on the gunnel, he aimed carefully for the large tentacle still above waterline. Time, time he softly thought to himself, only got three shots, must make them count. The first harpoon was away, cutting through the air, its metal shaft piercing the air, hurtling towards its target. At the last moment the tentacle lurched upwards and the harpoon splashed down into the waters below, sinking without trace.

Fyle was quickly onto the second loaded gunnel, steadying himself against the bucking ship. He could see the tentacle rising again, ready to crash down near the skiff. They would not survive another impact so close.

Bolt saw it and shouted with urgency, "Now god dammit! Now!"

Fyle crooked his head to one side, closed his left eye and released the second harpoon, it tore into action, the rope it was attached to whistling as it loosed. It struck the creature full in the tentacle, half way above waterline, the boat shuddered as the grip on the hull all of a sudden seemed to pull down on the

Mariner. They had succeeded in refocusing the attention on the boat itself and Bolt could see the skiff begin to clear the Mariner. He tacked twice more but the pull was greater now and it was becoming harder to move the old girl. She had begun to leak water to the stern and he was certain below decks were filling up already.

"Its directly under us. Not sure how much more she can take. The hull is breached I am sure, one more try. He pulled on the lanyard to fasten the sail back and tacked the ship for a final time, towards the west and the harshest waters. The second skiff was now out of reach, two saved, he could live with that and the boy made it, that felt good. Perhaps it was his time, it was always going to happen at sea, he knew that, in truth, he hoped for that.

The ship had hardly moved this time, the pull was too strong and the creature seemed to now be focussed on dragging the Mariner down from the hull, its distractions of skiffs and cargo forgotten, now its one goal was to suck down its prey into the waters below where it was safe. Bolt knew there was no escape, it was too late for that but perhaps they could achieve what others had not. "Fyle can you demount the harpoon? Can you aim it directly below, fire it into the hull by hand?" It was a desperate request, the mounted gunnel would weigh a tonne. It normally took four men to set into place when the ship was rigged.

Fyle looked first surprised and then a huge grin crossed the massive man's face. "Aye Captain, I'll pick it up and wave it like a kiddies rattle! He removed the pins holding the gun, balanced and quickly rotated the fixing screws. Bracing his legs he took the weight onto his chest and heaved the harpoon aloft, seven foot it rose in the air, step by step he carried it to the middle of the Mariners great deck and carefully lowered it downwards. The sweat was running freely now and the metal cut into his rough flesh but he did not feel it, only a sense of exhilaration coursed within.

Bolt had climbed halfway up the main mast, looking down on the Mariner, he took in her final majesty. "Through the amidships Fyle, into the belly of the beast." he shouted against the crashing waves, the cracking of wood could be heard everywhere now.

He looked up one last time at his Captain and they exchanged the briefest of exchanges, a moment that conveyed a lifetime of shared experience and respect.

Fyle held the huge gunnel firm and pressed hard against the trigger, an explosion of splintering wood as the harpoon took flight down into the lower decks, through into the hull and finally and definitively into the centre of the Drain itself. Fyle's huge frame followed swiftly down into the broken deck, crashing against the splintered planks jutting out at every angle.

Bolt saw his old friend fall and thought he could hear a shrill cry of pain from the beast below, he hoped so. It would be good to think that was the last thing he heard as the Mariner tipped over onto its stern, he was thrown into the waters below, his aqua filled grave, his destiny, his one true love.

Chapter 12 – The Merchant of Vedian

'There is said in the whole of Vedian to be no finer jewel craft than you will find in Kanegon. Stones from all over Vedian are mined and brought for shaping and sale in its market. The finest commissioned by Prominence Bast'wa from the Lough stocks. The rough diamonds are mined deep below the Inpur Desert which provides both their rarity and magnificence. The Huskian owned Desert can not be crossed by any Vedian and only a singular trade route through Lough and into the Desert provides the Huskian's with product they require in return for the precious minerals. The trade route only recently re-established by Bast'wa has been a marvellous benefit to the mineral trade in Vedian and is testament to his negotiation skills, that he has been able to bring the historically reclusive and backward Huskian's to the table once more.

The Crown Prince Scepter holds the 'Moonstone of Scholars', considered the finest cut of diamond ever created, as heavy as a lodestone and bright as its namesake. I however have it on authority that recently a larger uncut diamond was aquired by Prominence Bast'wa and is to be presented as a gift to His Prominence Shel-Toro. The diamond was shaped by the famed jeweler Trine of Pluris and encased in a cacophony of rubies mounted in a magnificent pearl brooch. The commissioned piece has been entitled 'The Adamas Truth'. We can only hope the trade route holds and more of these incredible stones continue to be purchased from our Huskian neighbours. An arrangement that is clearly benefiting all parties.'

'The Trade Keepers Journal' – Scribe Mollen - Vedian 997

SanPollan flipped a coin between his fingers, manoeuvring the metal between each knuckle with ease. The night had not gone to plan and he was caught between anger at the fools he sent to complete the task and irritation that it should have been him to arrange it.

This was work for the Protectorate not Scholatic, why had Shel-Toro insisted he see to this task. Important, yes, he acknowledged that but still, it was an unpleasant feeling to get his own hands dirty. He did not like to interact with the common man on any level, even at its point of elevation that involved the Crown Prince. The attack should have been simple and quick, the captain and small crew had been paid handsomely for their part.

Rising, he threw his hands in the air and shouted at no one in particular, "One old cripple and a single guard! Idiots! I am surrounded by the incompetent and unwashed!"

He kicked out at a goblet, that had earlier been placed on the floor, missing it by some distance, he instead completed a rather comedic air kick, which, had the servant not feared for her life, she would have howled out loud. She settled with a laugh inside and quickly left the room with a good tale her husband would enjoy later.

The ships captain had reported back in through SanPollan's guard at dawns light. All had gone well, they had boarded as planned and set sail for the Island, they waited as instructed until they were well into sea before attacking. The Crown Prince had put up a fight but he was quickly dealt with, his protector on the other hand had fought like a cornered rat. Three men had been kept at bay, he had cut, stabbed, tore and finally kicked and bit his way to a skiff. Two men were dead on his crew, one would never walk again, SanPollan could see by the blood still rife on the captains clothing and the missing ear, his words were true.

He had protested violently, complained of lack of ability, immaturity of execution and anything he could think of but the fact remained the Crown Prince was gone, escaped on a small skiff, launched by his guard. "I tell you," the Captain had reported, "no way that man can still be alive, he was more blood than flesh. He fought like a wounded animal protecting its nest, I need recompense for my men."

That had been enough to instruct his guard to send the man from his sight. He would get nothing for his troubles and was lucky he was not executed for his failure. SanPollan considered that poor form, he did not like to sully himself. His mind turned to Shel-Toro, this would not go well for him, he needed a way to spin this news, to turn it to his advantage. He flopped back onto his blanketed chair and rubbed his pointy chin, his lavish rings of office chinked together. He fought against the urge to rise and stamp his feet, the sullen child within him threatening to rise up. He wished his nonny was here to soothe the pain.

No, he was Scholatic, he was in charge here, think, think.

When the skiff launched they were nearer the island than mainland, and it is was a questionable doubt they had even made shore, it could only be on Imanis Island if they had. There was nothing for them there. DeFache had not been seen for days and he was definitely no longer at home in Imanis, Shel-Toro had ensured his days of university living were over. It did not pay to converse with savages, DeFache was a fool and his error opened the way for SanPollan's rising. There was minimal guard on the island as he understood it and only one way to return to the mainland, which could be easily intercepted.

There had been no failure, the plan had worked, all was well and the blow had been struck to the uprising fool of a Prince. He was the victor, the true Scholatic. He gestured to a servant who waited stoically at the doorway.

The man bent double to greet him, "Yes Prominence?"

"A message Fredric, to Shel-Toro forthwith and with much haste. The best carrier you understand." He raised an eyebrow, wanting to ensure the servant understood the gravity of the request.

"Of course, as you wish." He took out a quill from the marble table drawer and a thick papyrus and paused awaiting the sound of SanPollan's voice.

"The task has been completed successfully. I SanPollan can confirm the death of Crown Prince Madistrin on the night of the 12th day of the eighth month of Vedian 998."

At the mention of his name, Fredric halted writing, his quill frozen on the C in Crown. The air had been sucked from his lungs, he felt light headed. Quickly his wits returned and he continued scribing the note as instructed.

"Right on with the task and send me in the guardsman, I need to arrange another matter. Oh and Fredric, utter a word of that and it will go ill for your family"

"Yes my lord." The frightened servant skittered away.

SanPollan felt happier inside now, contented, there was no way out for Madistrin, he would send assassins to Imanis Island and if by some miracle they had made it alive, their respite would be short lived. To be sure there was no way off Imanis, he would mount a blockade off the island coast, nothing would leave dock from Imanis.

He knew he was gifted, he had always been a clever child but right now he felt lofty, untouchable, a seat by Shel-Toro's side awaited now. Made vacant by DeFache's ignorance and made possible by his own brilliance. Oh nonny how proud you would be if you could see me now, in my splendour, my pomp!. My light shines just a little brighter than most, the way Scholatic do when surrounded by men.

They rowed for three straight hours, the sun had climbed down from its peak and was dropping from the sky into the sea. Twilight, the magic hour some called it. The seven oarsman that steered the skiff to dock did not feel magical. They felt tired beyond imagine, Speck had ceased trying to row over an hour ago, his arms just had nothing more in them, his limbs ached and he slouched into Fillesne's back, drained of all energy. The others fared marginally better, Arn and Joseph had rowed on and off in the latter stages, taking turns on the port side, while Barnworthy and Marlone did the same on the starboard. Fillesne and Febra were the only two to crew the full journey, the girls stamina was incredible and even an old hand who had seen women all over Vedian like Fillesne, checked more than once that she was still rowing. He had seen Huskian women with less endurance and they at least were built like men, she was small framed, it made little sense but the First Mate did not want to look a gift horse in the mouth. She was making his job easier as she kept pace with his stroke.

Two of the Kanegon dock hands pulled the rope in they threw ashore, burly men, they were clearly surprised to see a skiff arriving. It was not the first time a ship had found peril at sea but it was unusual to see a skiff make the journey to shore intact. Normally they just got remnants and occasionally some lucky bounty cast along with driftwood. Fillesne talked to the men once they were safely tied off and on dry ground, explaining the chain of events that had befallen them.

Arn dropped to the floor, arms and legs spread out wide like a huge starfish. "I have never been so happy to be on Vedian's grounds. Not for me Joseph the way of the mariner, give me the dry hunt any day."

"You barely paddled half the way ranger, what are you complaining about?", Febra taunted him with a grin."Now how about you get off your bony backside and find us somewhere to sleep." She stretched herself tall, pleased to be have been freed from the confinement of the tiny boat.

Speck acknowledged the banter without being entirely comfortable with it. He cradled his pack in his hands, his mind turning back to the book and keen to find the warmth of an Inn and a good meal. Fillesne explained that the Kanegon dock workers would watch for the second boat and send word further up shore in case they arrived in the dark and drifted off target.

"Well I am sorry our journey was not as planned but we did get you to your destination, no?

Joseph at first thought it an odd comment, then realised what was behind it. "Arn," he called over to the hunter, "we need to pay for our passage."

Arn was about to argue, then looked at the men. They had lost much and a few copper would hardly be recompense for what they had suffered. "Of course." He slipped a hand into his leather pouch on his belt and pulled forth the copper owed, handing it Fillesne. "I am sorry things went sour, they were good men."

"Not all hunter, not all. However thanks for staying honest with us. You'll be looking for rooms, try 'The Sleeping Whore' just up Dock Street and left, he pointed towards the track leading into the town. And a word to the wise, keep your hands on your coin and your wits about you, this place will eat you alive as soon as look at you."

They all shook hands and the men went on their way, quietly drifting up the track and parting company at the crossroads.

Joseph looked around for the first time, acknowledging his new surroundings, the towns dock was far larger than the Luff, buildings were strewn everywhere, tracks led up alleyways, some lit above, some not. He could see stalls, now empty, scattered around the dock, fishmongers trade posts he thought, this must be quite the sight in the day. There was a noise from the town that they had never hear in the Luff, a grumbling of sound, that suggested activity. He turned to Arn, always his first point of reference when he was unsure.

"Well my friend, we have arrived, planned or not, in a town famous for thieves and bandits. We do not know where we are, where we are headed or anyone to call for assistance. He glanced at Speck, we have a treasure we do not wish to use and a poem I do not understand. To top it all we have a debt to settle and we have no idea where to start. What say you."

The hunter beamed a smile that crossed his whole handsome face, "In my experience, we should start with an ale. Most of the best answers have presented themselves to me there."

Joseph turned to Speck and then Febra, looking for support or someone more rational to speak. The girl shrugged and begun heading towards the road.

Speck put his arm around Joseph shoulders, "I will take a soft bed and a good nights sleep."

Arn clapped his hands, "Then onto The Sleeping Whore' my friends and let us hope she is welcoming."

It had been just a few short days days since the council had met at Coralis in secret and DeFache could not believe how much had changed in the world. He had, as he intended, made straight for the Isle of Imanis, the short trip across the south eastern waves that unbeknownst to him Madistrin would make only a few days later. He had reached the serenity of his home in the University of Imanis and found all unchanged, the gardens had blossomed well this year, perhaps as fair as they had ever been, a testament to the boys skills with flower and seed. He had met men of herbology before, a distant and reclusive lot, only happy in the depths of their botanical creations. Samuel was not of that ilk. He was a happy and carefree individual, a spirit of nature, fair in face with hair of golden blonde. DeFache had never yearned for a child, it was not the way of the Scholatic but if he had, then he would have liked a son like the small gardener.

He could never quite make out if he had asked the boy to stay or if the boy had let him, either way it had been two years since

Samuel come to the island. Alone in a small boat, he had rowed to dock without a word of where he had come from. He had set himself to work in the gardens until discovered by one of DeFache's people. It had been suggested he was sent back to the mainland or given to a family in the small village that had grown up next to the university. Yet DeFache saw something in the boy, either his petulance or his warmth, probably and on reflection, some of each. He challenged DeFache in a way others did not, he just made him think differently, for a Scholatic like he, that gift was priceless.

He kept a very small guard at the university, there was little need, few made the journey to the island unless on professional business and the local populace was respectful of the grounds. However he maintained three men to keep order in both the grounds and would often lend them to the village if events needed supervision or assistance.

He smiled and greeted each of the men individually and took time to speak to all his university staff. Quickly and efficiently but enough time for each person to feel valued as an individual. His manner was disarming, it was personal enough to catch a man off guard while poignant enough to drive the key questions home. Raleigh his longest serving protector had some news however that troubled him further.

"It is not just a couple of idle gossips now my lord, I have heard it from a number of sources from the mainland. They are saying Asten was attacked by mercenaries, that the city had been usurped by brigands under the cover of night. Some are even saying it is not a random event, that martial law has been put in place in the name of Vedian. I think that last piece to be misleading as you my lord would know such news if that decision was taken." Raleigh looked at DeFache, trying to read what impact his story had.

DeFache looked up into the rafters of his hall, a one room structure with a lofted ceiling, three great torches hung on each wall and light reflected through the window of the southern side, which accounted for half the wall. A banner dropped from the ceiling displaying the insignia of Imanis, a five pointed star and a sword driven through it. At the entrance door to the north of the room a stone laver was filled with water, DeFache moved towards it and cupped the liquid, throwing it lightly into his face for refreshment. It was not the most ornate hall a university of Vedian had to offer, that prize would go to Pluris, where true magnificence could be viewed but it was home and DeFache had completed some of his greatest texts under its roof.

"Too much coincidence Raleigh, means no coincidence at all. I had planned to seek out Gru-Staedak at Asten university in the next few days, now you share this grave news. That the two events are not linked seems improbable. I will travel tomorrow and see for myself what fate has befallen Asten and my mentor."

Raleigh raised his hand. "My lord that is inadvisable, the roads may be laden with brigands and thieves and who can even say what state the town is in. Even if we hire men to make the journey with us, I could not assure your protection. Please reconsider, rather let me take word in your stead to the university."

DeFache bit his top lip, considering different paths. "No I must go myself, Gru-Staedak is an old man, with a tongue befitting a fool at times but he is also the wisest and greatest man I have met in this world. Make whatever arrangements that can be made to grant us passage, we can seek out the smithy Durgal in Asten, he and his house will assist. Go."

Raleigh, bowed and moved swiftly from the room, he knew better than to protest further. He would speak to his brothers in arms and see what support they could buy on the mainland for the journey. The crossing a day or two and on horse a further two weeks on the Pluris to Asten highway. Much could befall them in that time, they would need to be cautious and take coin to buy their way out of trouble.

As he opened the door adjoining the hall to the kitchen, a feeling of cold came over him, then a sharp pain in his neck, his left hand came up to press at the sensation. As his fingers wrapped around the shaft of the tiny dart, he fell to the floor, as he pulled to release it, sense drifted from his body. He lay motionless on the cool stone slabs.

The scene that greeted Joseph on entering the Inn was one he could only have imagined. The journey to the establishment had been fairly uneventful, they had passed a few men going about their own business, the buildings grew closer together as they walked farther up the main road, like oak trees in a forest they seemed to draw closer the deeper you ventured in and they all marvelled at the number of two storey buildings that were housed in the sprawling town The sheer noise as it reverberated off the walls attacked their senses as they neared the inn. There was no problem identifying their destination, outside men sat on the floor wielding huge jugs of ale, women dressed in bright ruddy fabrics hung off their shoulders and cackled at their attempts at humour. Light was thrown down onto the throng from two tall standing wrought iron coal lamps. They were never thrown as much as a glance as they pressed through the single doorway underneath the swinging sign of the Inn.

Inside was more of the same on a grander scale, tables where everywhere and around each of them men and women cavorted, playing drunk and amorous games that Joseph was certain were not in anyway gambling related. In the far corner an area had been cleared and a group was gathered around a bare knuckle match. They could not see the combatants but the cheers went up each time a blow was landed. Along the right side of the inn a long bar stretched the whole wall and stools were set into the ground in stone. Arn pushed his way through to the bar with the others behind. A middle aged woman, sporting all the constituent attributes Joseph expected in a place such as this served them.

"What it be lovely?" She enquired with an up and down look at the hunter.

"Four ales and a table if you have one?" Arn replied. It was customary in the Luff to request space at a table.

Her response suggested the custom had not caught on in Kanegon. "We got loads of em, good luck getting one." She placed four jugs of Ale on the counter and took Arn's coin.

"We're looking for rooms too?" Speck called out to her, pushing forward to the bar.

"Just rooms?", she asked enquiringly.

Speck looked at Arn and shrugged his shoulders.

"Just rooms thanks love", he winked at Speck, "A large and a small if you have them."

"Yeah should be able," she turned towards the back entrance adjoining to another room, "Oy! Jack you lazy blighter get in here." A young man barely Joseph's age came in from the back holding a large flagon.

"These folk want one large one small, show em where and get them keys lad." she turned back to Arn, "Money upfront love, you understand, some wrong uns about. Mind you," she licked her lips staring at Arn, which made Joseph feel a little queasy, "we could negotiate on price."

Febra stepped forward and addressed the woman, "Just the rooms, were not buying or selling anything else tonight."

After they had finished their ales the young man showed the party up the stairs to the second floor and to their sparse if functional rooms, Febra took the small single room and the three of them the large. Speck stood outside on the balcony looking into the inn floor below, he could see the bare knuckle fighting which seemed to go on forever, scuffles would break out on occasion over gambling accusations but generally it was a raucous if happy mood in the place.

Speck watched Arn go back downstairs and buy another ale, he began to mingle into the crowd, it was fascinating to Speck to see the hunter move from one group to the next, social and friendly as if he had known them all for years. Arn was blessed with a confidence Speck could only dream of. He made people laugh as he moved around and got as many propositions from men as he did women, a little less rough than most around, his looks could no doubt get him far in a place like this.

By midnight Joseph and Febra were asleep in their beds but the noise in the inn had not diminished, Arn came up and sat next too Speck who had his legs dangled out over the platform fascinated by the scenes that coloured his eyes.

"Well I thought that might prove useful. There's a lot of talk about Asten, its being said martial law has been called after bandits swarmed on the town. A curfew is down and the militia now have hold of the town in an effort to bring things under control. Makes sense right?"

Speck nodded.

"Except that they are also saying martial law has been declared in other smaller villages for their protection and rumour has it that a large force is moving south to Kanegon. Now why would Vedian's military need to stretch its grip all the way south when the only attack has been to the northwest? Something odd is happening. Not that this lot seem to care. However I somehow cannot see the type of people who live here caring much for martial law or the militia that enforce it. One chap said there are only three types of people that are in Kanegon, those that live here are desperate, those that journey here are fools and those that were born here are truly amongst the most unfortunate."

"What does it mean for us though Arn?" Speck asked with a hint of concern in his voice.

"It means that we have to be ready to move quickly. I am going to go back down and see if I can find out anymore, plus I am keen to see if any have ever heard of Rundell's tale in these quarters. You go to bed Speck it has been a long few days." He patted the young man on the back and departed back down the stairs.

Speck wandered into the room, Joseph was face down, a familiar loud snore coming from his bunk. He was tired, Arn was right but one more look before he got some sleep wouldn't hurt. It was a shock to the system but it also felt good, it felt like he was attached to something bigger. He pulled out the book and opened it once more.

Speck could feel the sensation before his consciousness became aware that Arn was physically shaking him awake.

"Up, up. We have to leave."

Speck looked around, the book still in his hands, Joseph was dressed and peering through the doorway to the balcony area. "What is going on?"

"The town is under attack I think, a whole army has marched on it, people are fleeing." Arn looked on earnestly, "We will have to make for safety to the south road and double back later, I begin to wonder if we should consider heading towards home? Something is happening in Vedian and we are not safe on the road, we perhaps should return and speak with my father?"

Speck pulled up his belongings into his leather pack and went to stand with Joseph, "It is madness Speck. I can see fires through the windows and there are shouts from everywhere. We will have to be swift are you ready to run?"

"I feel like that's all I have done since we left the Luff, walked and run. However if it means a chance to get back home, I would happily run the three weeks at a canter!" The young man smiled and amidst the disorder and chaos that surrounded him Joseph felt glad his friend was with him. Arn had slipped downstairs and grabbed hasty words with the young man that had showed them their rooms the evening before. His hands were full of various trinkets and he was being constantly instructed by the woman behind the bar. They swiftly slipped down the stairs, Febra appearing from her room to make the quorum. "Right there is fighting in the central square, they are moving in from the main Pluris to Kanegon road. We need to head south through the market district and he suggests there is a road that takes us past Castle Bast'wa. He says that is heavily fortified with local guards and they will meet with resistance. A good opportunity for us to slip away unnoticed."

Arn led from the front his natural leadership instincts alive once more, he checked the entrance, cautiously looking at all exit options. On the streets there were people rushing in all directions. Some to their homes and some away from them, others headed to the docks looking for a passage to safety. They moved south at the junction that had previously led them to the inn, Arn took them at a forced march, not wanting to run until they needed to, "Conserve our strength." He had reinforced.

They could hear shouting from the east and torchlight was bright and hazy in the night air, a large congregation was heading towards them from that direction. The buildings around them begun to thin out and they entered a sizable square, desolate but for empty stalls and countless woven tubs and carts, ready to hold the mornings wares for sale. They would lie empty tomorrow, Arn thought. The track through the centre wove left and right and eventually forked in two directions to the south east and south west. Arn instinctively picked the option that took them away from the commotion, turning in a westerly direction as they joined a southern fork down a narrow pathway that moved them into a more built up area of the town. For a few minutes they walked, scarcely seeing any others, most it seemed had barred their homes in the area and were waiting it out.

"No this is not right!" Arn exclaimed, the path had looped back east and was directing them towards the lights.

"Do we go back?" The sounds seemed to be closer and Joseph was sure the lights were as well. "The other path took us in the same direction, they may join up anyway." He did not like the idea of retracing their steps, rather to push on.

The hunter nodded, "I am unsure, lets move cautiously forward, stay close to the buildings, use cover as best we can."

They moved forward at a slower pace, the noises coming closer and the lights burning steadily more intense. Voices were now coming through clearer and the road was widening.

"Its leading us into the town centre, stay quiet and on the edge, we will hold the southeastern side and hope they are not interested in a small party." Arn moved forward a little quicker, picking them up to a full walking pace.

It took a few seconds to realise just how many men were in the square, his eyes adjusting to their bright lamps some held aloft, others placed on the ground in burners. Over a hundred men stood formed into ranks in the town centre, dressed in various armour, they were not a rabble, this was clearly Vedian militia. Some were herding locals into homes, others were not as accommodating and beatings were being handed out to those who were less inclined to follow instructions. Men were being sent down different paths in troops of around twenty. There was no way they were getting through the town unnoticed.

Febra, "I can maybe slip through alone but no way we can all get past that many eyes. We need to double back and find another way."

"There may be an alternative but you are not going to like it." Speck looked at Arn.

"Well spit it out. We have to choose quickly," The hunter gestated with his hands to encourage the young man.

"I may have learned something last night, a trick lets call it. A way to give people cover of darkness for a short time." They all just stared at him, as if he had gone quite mad. "You just need to trust me, now gather together." He motioned for them to stand tight in a group.

Arn wanted to protest and argue but something in Speck's voice made him follow the instruction and they tightened together.

All he recall of the moment, was Speck's eyes closing and a low mumble of words that meant nothing to him. He felt no sensation but when he looked at Joseph, his form was hazy, like he was peering at him through drowsy eyes.

"Right I'm as surprised as you all are but it seems to have worked however I am unsure it will last. We must move now." Speck led them into the town centre, they kept as close to the outskirts as they could but so many men filled the area, it was hard not to move within a few feet of someone.

Arn could see their banners now, they were Vedian Scholatic, he did not know the houses but there seemed like various insignia's. Why would the militia be trying to take the towns? It was like Asten all over again but less mercenary types and more organised this time. He froze as a guard dressed in full leather armour turned quickly towards him, the hunter held his breath as the man seemed to stare right at him. At least right through him. The soldier turned, shook his head and gnawed down on an apple. They reached the turning that took them south and branched off, moving for a further five minutes until Speck stopped and turned.

"Its gone", he stared at them each in turn, "faded at least, we no longer have cover."

"When we get out of here, you need to tell us what the hell that was Speck. But right now, lets push on south and get out of this town. I don't understand whats happening here but I have a horrible feeling it may involve us." Arn took the lead again and they headed further down the path that led out of town, the noises and lights however still seemed to be following them.

"Looks like troops have been sent to check through this area, we need to keep moving." Arn directed them forward as the area sprayed out into tracks, ahead of them they could clearly see the land was becoming greener, an entrance to grounds of some sort and beyond that a few hundred feet in the distance a large building rose above them. The darkness stopped them from making out the full structure but it looked like the castle that Joseph had been told of, Castle Bast'wa.

The voices behind were now gaining and the marching troop could be heard closing the gap behind them.

"Into the grounds lets hide in there, while they pass on." Speck suggested.

They pushed through some border bushes and fern, the gardens were large fanning out into a centre piece adorned with marble figures. Climbing over a three foot tall set of conifers they lay flat on the ground, cool grass on their hands and faces was refreshing to the touch. They waited as the marching boots came closer and heard a voice shout, "Split left and right, ten men each, Tam you lead the right."

"Yes sir, men with me."

Two minutes later the boots had marched on and the voices diminished into the westerly wind. Joseph looked up and climbed onto his knees, looking carefully over the brush. He felt the blade press at the back of his head at the same time as the others.

"Don't move!" An authoritative voice instructed. They lifted their arms slowly, there was no getting out of this, they had been so focussed on the troops ahead, they had been oblivious of anyone approaching from the rear. They were all dragged to their feet. Five men stood in front of them, they were armoured but not like the troops in the town, this was more regalia like, Arn thought. Dress armour that was often worn at jousts and meetings. A plume of purple adorned the metal helm of the man that addressed them. "You are trespassing. That carries a penalty, turn out your packs."

Speck tried to plead, "The town is under attack, we were just trying to get away. Please we have done no wrong."

The men turned to each other and laughed, "Kanegon is not under attack boy," The helmed man retorted, "they are here for its protection. We are now all under the watchful gaze of his Prominence Shel-Toro, these are his militia and by all accounts a number of other universities." He grinned and it did not fill any of them with confidence, "There are outlaws and thieves in the city, it grows more lawless by the day, about time someone put that right."

"So you do not fear them?" Arn enquired.

"No. We knew of their arrival, our Lord Bast'wa has informed us. He is well connected to these things." Right I think on seconds thoughts we should get you inside, keep you safe. Our Lord always has use for idle hands. Ain't that right lads?"

The others laughed and pushed the four towards the main entrance, blades still pointed in their backs.

Febra whispered to Speck, "I hope you have another trick for this situation Master Caedron."

Speck mulled over the thought to himself, If I could read the book again, perhaps it would give us another way out. It was too much of a coincidence it showed him the exact incantation he had needed to get them past the troops. It had been used at Bannermane, he had seen the Candlemen use it on Pinkerton to slip into the opposition forces under cover all those years ago. Somehow the words how stayed in his head and he just seemed to know how to use them but as soon as he had uttered them they seemed to leave his mind as quickly. He must get time with the book again, salvation may well lie in the pages of the past.

Once inside, they could see the scale of the building, almost castle like without a drawbridge, rather two large doors opened to receive them, its entrance hall was at least as big as the one in Asten University. They were led through the hall and past a long corridor adorned with rich tapestries depicting various scenes of pomp. Whomever owned this place had a certain eclectic taste. Down a set of winding stone steps and down again until the air became musty and damp. The corridor was narrow now and they were stopped short of a thick door with a tiny window slit.

"In here until we speak to the lord of this manor. I am betting he has just the job for you lot, we will relieve you of those belongings though, won't need those were your going." The man laughed and pulled the packs off their backs." Speck momentarily pulled his back but the blade was pushed into his side, enough to break the skin, He winced and released his prize possession. They sat down on a stone bench the only seating in what was clearly a cell, no more than five foot by four and obviously meant for one detainee not four. Speck recounted what the book had revealed the night before and how he had learned the cantrip he used in the town.

"So my learned friend. Can you weave that magic again to whisk us from this place?" Arn said with a hint of hope in this voice.

"Its not magic. At least I don't think so. Its just knowledge. Knowing things others do not, makes it look and feel like magic but its just a trick really and no, I have no recollection of how I preformed the words. If I could just get the book, maybe it would give us something." Speck slumped his arms into his lap. "I do not really want to see what this Bast'wa has in store for us, I am guessing it will not be anything we will like."

Arn spoke softly, "What we need is a thief. Or perhaps the next best thing", he looked directly at Febra, "Bait."

Joseph keep looking down at the floor, away from the conversation being held just a few feet from him. He could hear her voice, quietly whispering to their jailor. The breath of the man getting slightly heavier, as she teased and promised more. Then the clink of the keys being released from his belt, the bolt retracted and the door opened and closed. When his head rose, she was gone. He had told Arn they should just rush the guard but the hunter had assured him that would not work, any kind of confrontation would bring more guards and they knew from their arrival, there was only one way in and out.

Febra never argued, never asked for more instruction, she just went about her task like she had been asked to pick up some stock from the market and bring it home. It did not seem right, that they would ask, or right that she would agree. It did not match Joseph's view of the world. When this journey had begun, his life and the way he saw it was so established and ordered. Now he was miles from home, he had seen things and met people he never knew existed. One part of him yearned for more and another part, the cut of him that was tied so firmly to the Luff begged to go home.

An hour past, Joseph kept looking at Arn, at times with an accusation, at others simply concerned. Then footsteps were heard and once more the rattle of keys led to the door being opened.

She breezed in, no smile but a sense of control surrounded her. Joseph was quick to her side, "Are you alright?" He spoke but in truth did not want to hear an answer.

"Fine. More importantly, I have our prize." In her hand she held the book, which she passed over to Speck.

"How did you..." Joseph started and then thought better of it.

"Surprisingly easily, I just asked for it. You may be shocked to hear it but men like that have no interest in books. They wanted our coin and kit, the books they had already discarded. He gave it to me as my....reward...he called it. I would like it to be his undoing. That is assuming our Master Sorcerer here can pull a rabbit out of it."

"I am sorry Febra..I...I...we should not have..." Joseph trailed off again, lost for the right words.

"Its done. I will not speak of it again." The girls voice was curt and cold.

Arn wanted to explain, to rationalise his part in the decision, "It is just a tool in the arsenal of wits Joseph, sometimes a blade at other times virtue, one as potent as the other in the right situation."

"Perhaps..." Joseph wanted to challenge the hunter but lacked the words to express himself.

Speck broke the awkward atmosphere by opening the book and begun to read.

The Lord Protector Estalyn surveyed the scene from the the inner first wall of Bannermane. On the deep hill front to the west, he could see only a litter of corpses adorning the grassland. Beasts and their riders lay side by side, many brought to their end by the long spears used in the attack. They rose upward from the once proud soldiers, like tall reeds in the Coralis waters. So many dead in a single rout. He knew it was the wrong decision, by all of Vedian he knew it! Why did he not insist, change the order, that is all it was after all, just an order. An instruction from a man that knew less than he. Words that were tainted with pride and emotion towards a son.

He could have saved him all the pain to come by just disobeying that order. Yet he had not, he had sent forward the Lancers in a flanking movement from around the forts edge, under the disguise of the hills, they would not be seen until the attackers were on top of Bannermane's first wall. They would fall between defenders blade and attackers lance. Yet they did not, as they moved to attack the fort, at the last moment they turned and faced the hillside, charging the riders with their long spears dug into the ground. He had told the King, the weapons they use are most prevalent against our mounted divisions, imagine a whole army of pike wearers, a horseman's nemesis in battle. They went down so quick! The beasts neutered by the heavy trodden soft ground, there had been no escape.

By the time he could mount the Sabre Regiment to open the gates in an effort to press back the attackers, the damage was done, over seventy percent of the Lancers were dead or would never ride again. The last time the Asten Lancers would ever ride under a Vedian flag. They knew they were coming. They knew. Estalyn feared what is worst in war, he feared it was one of his own men. Someone had passed word to the enemy, they had a spy in Bannermane. He would send the Candleman to interrogate the prisoner, he had to know where the information was coming from.

Fystal looked down at the long winding steps, damp and cold, it chilled him to his bones. How many more tasks would their be in this endless war. Estalyn had given him so many already and he did it for his love for the Protector, for he had known him since he was but a child. He was old now, older than any living thing on the land had right to be and so very tired.

His hips ached as he slowly walked down the stone passageway, age was so debilitating, he could remember all the things he did as a young man, sharply and defined like crystal but his body could not replicate any such experience.

He knew the Shaman would offer him nothing but lies and half truths, he would not try to play wordsmith with him. He needed one simple truth and he only needed to be close enough to get it. Acknowledging the guards outside the cell door, they greeted him in the way that men always did, respect with a dose of fear and a sprinkle of disgust. They needed him and his followers but they did not truly want them. It was simple - men could not understand or embrace from where they came.

He placed a hand on the wall and begun to recite an incantation, the cell stone begun to shimmer where his outstretched fingers were placed and images flooded into his mind. He just needed to find the right path, concentrate. Then in a moment, a face flickered in and was gone.

A voice came from within the cell, "You have nothing I would not have given you. The deed is done, we care not. Do with him now as you will. He is yours not ours."

Speck awoke peacefully this time, he did not have much sweat on him and he felt more in control of the experience.

"Well did you see anything?" Joseph asked quickly.

"Yes, I am not sure what It can do for us but I think I have a way to extract a thought from the mind."

It was next morning, probably dawn, they could not be sure in the absence of light, that they came for them. No words, just pushing and shoving back through the corridor and up the stairs. The guard Febra had acquired the book from offered coarse words in her ear as they were steered up, it appeared to have no effect on the girl, if she felt anything she certainly did not show it.

This time they were taken to the back of the castle into an oddly furnished room. Arn would have imagined this to be how circus folk would decorate a castle if they had one. The colours were in bright pinks and reds, tapestries depicting various sexual scenes with men, women and animals left the huntsman rather uneasy. There were vases of all sizes and gems were crusted into every cushion and fabric that adorned the plush seating. A huge chaise lounge sat on a raised platform at the end of the rectangle room. Behind it was a roaring fire that gave off an amazing amount of heat into the large room.

The guards pushed them down to the floor and announced, "Take a knee for the great Prominence Bast'wa."

Through a second double doorway to the opposite side of the room came four lightly dressed men in effeminate garb, feathers of light orange hanging around their cloth tunics. They held aloft a lectica which appeared to made almost entirely of gold minerals. Adorned on each plinth were the brightest red rubies they had ever laid eyes on. Atop this priceless marvel, lay a man of considerable proportions. Dressed in nothing but the smallest linen cloth, dyed the now familiar red, he propped himself up with one arm, lazily wafting the other in the air, as if he was orchestrating musicians.

249

The four man walked the lectica up to the platform and carefully placed it down to rest.

"I am Prominence Bast'wa." His voice was unusually high for a man of his girth. His hair almost eroded, just a few strands remaining pulled forward. "You have trespassed on my property and must be punished." He eyed each of them slowly, stopping for longer than was comfortable to view Arn. "Do you know who I am?" he pointed at the hunter.

"No my Lord, we were just sheltering from the soldiers, we...."

"Enough prattle. You look like pheasant but you sound like brisket! You offend me. I am the greatest importer and exporter of jewels in Vedian. I am known by all."

Speck suspected that last bit was more than true.

"I walk with Kings and Princes. However I am a merciful Lord. I would protect you from these brutish soldiers. No harm will befall you, Shel-Toro is known to me and these are men sent to quell the lands not harm them. Too much lawlessness in Vedian, it has to be brought under control, for the peoples sake you understand. We need order."

Joseph spoke before thinking, "We need justice."

"Oh you are a snappy one. We will have to work you hard boy. I think some time in the mines will rehabilitate you. I can always do with some extra bodies there. That one," he pointed to Speck, "doesn't look like he will last long but its all free hands I suppose. One month hard labour and then you are free to go."

Joseph shouted, "We will not. You have no right!"

"Now my lad, that is not strictly true, I have rights of offence committed on my own property, given to me by Scholatic. I can show you the documents if you wish?" He shook his head. "No? Oh well. Lets get to it. Away now, I had thought to keep the rough but pleasant one for some amusement but my tastes have drifted. Take them all away!"

With a wave of a hand he was aloft and carried out of the room.

Arn whispered to Speck, "Did you get anything?"

"Yes and you're not going to like it. Not one bit."

Chapter 13 - Mines of the Inpur Desert

'In appearance the differences of race are more than subtle and less than obvious. A typical Huskian stands on average a foot taller than a common man, slightly larger in frame and their hair is always dark. Their eyes are wider and often hazel in colour and hair flaxen with a cordial dark hue. As a species it is suggested they fare well in manual tasks, specifically mining and desert farming. There is no example of any Huskian being a member of the Scholatic, the latter always having been bred from men.

There are those that would refer to the Huskian populace as savage or barbaric, I believe these comments are broadly ill informed. I have spent time with these people in an effort to understand their way of life and be best able to compare the species, to find differences and similarities. It is true they are more locally managed, small tribes will run their own system of law but the governing principles remain the same across most of the small clans.

An interesting difference is the seniority of women or 'Huskean'. They hold a much stronger sense of responsibility and command in the working structure of a tribe. They are revered by their life partners and are the ones to choose a partner or husband as we would know it. I have found them to be a people of great conscience and heart and would recommend to anyone who gets the chance to interact with them, as it is a rewarding experience.

Of recent times their lands suffered from arid weather, driving them to rely more and more on foodstuffs from import. The trade developed with Kanegon in exchange for the gems they mine appears to be a good and positive connection and prominence Bast'wa has been an important link in placing our great species closer together. Not since they fought in the Vedian Wars have we had so many relations with them and long may the kinship continue.'

'Voice of the Forgotten People' - Bray Curak (Historian & Amateur Anthropologist) - Vedian 991

It was two days march south through the tracks that led into the plains of the Lough, green hills that stretched further than their eyes could see. On the second day they had camped and Bast'wa's men had handed them over to a new set of guards. They exchanged a few words mainly about affairs in Kanegon and the arrival of the soldiers. The men coming up from the Lough looked less impressed at this event than the others. They handed some letters over and Joseph heard them talk about mines and a single hand cart was provided, laden with leather bags. Bast'wa's guards argued about who was going to take the first shift and they ended up playing cards for the chore. Joseph did not wait to the see the outcome, he lay down between Arn and Febra and did his best to keep warm. His wrists ached from the tight bonds that attached them all together and his mind drifted and wandered as far as the Luff, Pike and his mother standing at the market, Rundell was there too and another man, in robes of black, he did not recognise him. Sleep took him and he slipped further into dream. The dreams changing swiftly from pleasant thoughts to more nebulous images.

He was back at Bannermane, the clash of blades, the fall of Rundell. Onto the high seas and the demise of Captain Bolt and finally resting on the face of Gru-Staedak in the walls of Asten University. Death filled his dreams and the final image left him cold, yet he awoke resolute. Sacrifice for a greater good, the world being more about the whole than a single individual, he felt connected and smiled at Speck.

"Well that's an odd look for our current predicament." His friend spoke quietly.

"I think it will be alright Speck, for the first time in a long while I really do. It would be good to understand where they are taking us." Joseph's optimistic tone spurred the young scribe into recounting what he had learned from Bast'wa.

"It is grave Joseph, he is raising an army to march, I could not get a clear sense of where they were headed but in his mind I could you the shipments arriving of armaments and mercenaries being bought."

Joseph looked to Arn who shook his head, "I know it doesn't make any sense the Scholatic have militia at their disposal, why would Bast'wa need an army? He clearly is working with the council not against them. Where is the opponent?"

Speck interjected, "I have been watching this new group for a few hours, the one at the back they call Shun would be a favourable target I think, if we are to perhaps learn more. He had lost every hand of Ral's coin they played last night and his wits do not appear to be the sharpest. For some reason when I learned Bast'wa's thoughts the knowledge of how I did it has not left me." Speck concentrated and murmured at a barely audible level the incantation he had seen in the books vision. Joseph and the others stayed quiet but they could see his body tensing and his left hand seemed to glow slightly. He tossed Specks pack over his hands to obscure it from view. The young mans body relaxed, the tension visibly draining from it as they watched.

"Well?" Febra said.

"We are going to somewhere in the Inpur Desert, a workhouse of some sort underground. It was difficult to get a clear picture, he mind is so crowded with imagery of everything and nothing. "

The guards begun to pack up their camp and one motioned them to their feet. As they got up Speck whispered to Arn, "Watch him hunter, he has desires on Febra and we must keep her from more torment." Speck resented the way he had treated the girl in the Luff now. He had thought about it many times since they departed. She had done nothing but try to protect their group since they left. He had been hurtful and scornful of the lonely scully and he knew that had to be put right. He turned to face her and with as purposeful expression as she had seen from him spoke, "I will try to protect you Febra, as you have done me on this journey. Once I would not have known how but I have something these men do not, I have intellect and only, now for the first time am I beginning to understand its power."

They walked for a further day through the greenest hills, constantly up and down into dales and across fields of the brightest flowers and radiant grass. It was as pleasant a journey as you could make, tied up and bound as they were. On the next day the ground begun to change, the grass became sparse and flower turned to brush. Ahead of them they could make out a yellow paradise. Desert stretching for miles to the south, the sun bearing down on its dunes, absorbing the air around it, leaving it dry and tasteless. Arn made a further attempt to demand their release and know why they were being taken there but the guards did not even bother to respond. Just a shout and a swift kick to keep them moving. At dusk of the fourth night since they left Kanegon, they arrived at a stone structure, a shelter at least from the constant sun that had beat down on them ever since they arrived at the shore of the Inpur desert. They were led inside and rudely thrown down to sit on the refreshing cold rock below. Inside two men sat, both in light cloth, no armour but they both wore scabbards at their belts.

"A package from his Lord Bast'wa and a message. Three deliveries this month, not including the one we sent off at the meeting point"

The two men shook their heads, "Even with these extra hands, we will never make three. Its getting harder and deeper, we lost two this week and many of the old hands are weakened." The taller of the two stood and inspected the group, "These two look able, pointing to Arn and Joseph, this one won't last a week and this one would be better refreshment for the boys. However we need all hands on, so for now they all go in. Take a message back with the next delivery that we need more time."

The other man spoke, his face was tanned like an old leather and weathered by months in the hot sun's desert. ""He ain't gonna take well to that. An I can do with out his lot crawling down our necks. We can press them all a bit harder, put these new four down deep and see who makes it."

Arn protested, " We have done nothing wrong and were told we would be released after a month."

The tanned man turned to face the the hunter, "I'll do you deal, if after a month you can walk across the desert out of here, you be my guest." They laughed to each other, cruel and disdainful. These men would see them die here, their suffering would have no impact, it would not weigh on them. Joseph wondered what type of life one had to live, when the fate of their fellow man left no scar on the soul.

They were left in the stone hut for the night. They slept from sheer exertion of the journey and were fed the next morning well. It seemed starvation was not to be their end, their strength was needed in the mine. A further two hour march supervised by the tanned man and his compatriot, through nothing but sand and dust. It tore into their throats, leaving them instantly parched and their eyes were sore and reddened, constantly squinting against the wind. They could see the mouth of the mine about an hour before they arrived, as the wind finally dropped the distance they could see ahead was enormous. The mine entrance was cut into a huge dune, stone crafted with wood used to cut support plinths. Arn could only imagine how they could get wood supplies down here, so far to the south of Vedian. The cave opening was a welcoming shelter from the burning heat and Speck collapsed into a heap on the floor under its gloomy protection.

The chamber fed into three main tunnels, one large causeway which seemed to quickly slope down, the left widened into what appeared to be a living quarters for the guards. Beds and sacks were strewn about the place and they could make out about half a dozen men sitting around talking. The right passage was blocked by a door with steel bars, either to keep somebody from getting in or stop them from getting out. As they emerged deeper into the chamber Arn could see the barred room was filled with bags like they had seen transferred onto the cart. The tanned guard caught him peering into the room, "Have a good look at what your hard work is going to fetch for us. You see this mine is home to some of the most precious gemstones that have been found in Vedian. Diamonds above all his Prominence seeks down here and every month he gets a little more greedy for them. So you're here to ensure we deliver this months orders. You will live down there, eat sleep and above all work. Good company you'll have." He laughed and the other guards some of who had come through from the quarters joined him. They exchanged details about the hand over and the increased quantities required for the month, there was a lot of shouting and cursing.

"We sweat down here every day with these dirty folk and for what a few copper a week, while he hauls in thousands!" One guard exclaimed.

"That's the way it is Ran. That's the way it's always been. You get your head down and work for your earn, one way or another. You steal from this one, you end up dead and so do your family, remember Old Cooty?." There was a lot of nods in the room.

"What happened to him?" Speck asked inquisitively.

The tanned guard lurched down to the young man, "He stole a bag of those gems for his own and fled. His Prominence hired some of the finest hunters in Vedian to track him, find him and bring him back. In the meantime they caught every family member ever linked to Old Cooty and once he was caught, he watched each of them lose each hand and foot before being hung from the castle as a warning. Then once he and his special aides had finished pleasuring themselves with Cooty they sent him back here to work the mines. Bast'wa referred to it as his penance. So there's hope for you all yet, redemption awaits you." He chuckled with the other men and they begun to point the four captives towards the main passage.

"On your way. You sleep below tonight and start at first light. Well not that you'll know it but I can assure you, that's when you will start work." The tanned guard walked in front of them and led them down a wide causeway, the main path raised up from the cave, it felt cool and damp as they trudged further down and down. They continued downhill until the causeway which had begun to level out just stopped in front of them. The tanned man shouted and grabbed a mechanism near the floor, it was a pump of some sort and he pushed down on the long handle, below them they could hear a clicking and whirring.

The noise became louder and in front of the back wall emerging from the floor below came a meshed steel cage. Big enough for four, they were ordered to enter through the gate. The cage swung and knocked into the recess as they entered, the weight pulled at the chains that held it, as the last of them, Febra, got in. The tanned man smiled at them from the other side of the cage.

"Not making the trip with you, not so keen on it down there. Sure you'll be happy though. Seems a shame to be putting Vedian folk in with those dogs, their not the sharpest tools but they don't half move some stone. Pleasant dreams wont be seeing you again." The last thing they saw as they entered the earth below, was his sneering leather face beaming from above them.

The chains rattled and the whirring and clicking echoed off the harsh cave walls, down and down they dropped into the depths of the world.

Shel-Toro paced the rooms of his office. It was not adorned in majesty as with some university masters. He believed in a certain restraint, knowledge has no need for opulence only growth he believed. Two of his senior advisor's were trying to get his attention, like two desperate lap dogs yearning for their masters goodwill. They had been discussing a matter of history in regards to the King's intentions in the great war. One of his aides had suggested that the King's good intentions should be a factor in their character assessment. Shel-Toro in a blink came back to the matter at hand and turned to address the men.

"Intention is simply a word of excuse or failure. If a man steals is his intention not clear and his failing to be punished. If he argument is that he steals to feed his family, is his intention good and acceptable? No. It is not. For Scholatic law forbids thievery in Vedian. We forbid man from stealing as we know the path that can place them on. So his intention is not a factor in our assessment of his character and is a King not a man? So as such we treat his assessment no differently. Do not ply me with intention, give me decision and I will judge so."

The men nodded and fawned slightly in reverence at his words. A knock came at the office door and a voice called out, "His Prominence SanPollan awaits your presence my lord."

With a wave of hand Shel-Toro dismissed the advisor's and beckoned his visitor in. He bowed as the guest entered the room and the gesture was replicated. They sat on two heavily bound leather chairs, a small carved table between them at an angle. Shel-Toro crossed his long legs and threw his robes over them. He moved an open hand towards the ornate wine pitcher that rested on the table, SanPollan smiled and nodded and two goblets were filled.

Shel-Toro moved the wine around his well versed palette, taking in the vineyards from Coralis and the warmth of its dawning sun. "So my friend, what news do you have for me?" SanPollan relayed the tale of the attack on Madistrin, this time ending with his death at the hands of the mercenaries at sea.

"This is rich news. This will not go unnoticed at the council, even if we can not formally detail your role yet. I will ensure it is not omitted."

SanPollan smiled knowingly. He was so close now to the second seat and his next words would secure it.

"I have another piece of news, one that perhaps my Lord Prominence is not aware of."

Shel-Toro looked inquisitively at him, eyebrows crinkled in expectation, "Then do not keep me waiting."

"I had men in the vicinity of Imanis post the mission ordered, I thought it prudent to ensure a final piece of the puzzle was nullified. We have taken control of Imanis university under the rules of old. For no 'man' shall live under its roof."

"You have evidence the boy was living at Imanis? It has to be clear." Shel-Toro voice was authoritative and without emotion."

"Yes we have it validated from those living in the nearby village. We have the university under lock down. No one in or out while further," He paused. "considerations of future arrangements are made."

"What is the count at the University? How many are bound to its walls?"

"Ten living, one dead, an unfortunate instance."

Shel-Toro eyes flashed at the news.

Seeing the reaction he spoke quickly, "No, no just a guard who became aggressive. We hold six servants, three guards and Umberto DeFache." He could not help but smile at the mention of his name. What a stroke of luck, the assassins had not found Madistrin yet but they had returned news of DeFache's attendance at the university. He had them interrogate a few local villagers it had not taken much for a couple to spill the news they needed and a few copper always helped push things along. It was so opportunistic and no doubt Madistrin's body had washed to sea. This could not have turned out better.

"Grave news you bring of the falling of one of our greatest sons. I hold myself responsible for everything but the act itself. It shames the Scholatic and that can not and will not be accepted. The timing however is fortunate. As you are aware I have raised the militia to take control of Asten, Kanegon and Coralis that leaves us only Pluris, which we could not move on while Madistrin was in still in governance. With him gone, we can advance plans on bringing the city to order, however this will

258

prove more of a struggle. His guard will not give up the city to the militia easily but they will give eventually. We then bring Vedian under tight rule and once Madistrin is pronounced dead, the Scholatic will be formally placed to rule.

I will do so firstly with a harsh hand to cleanse the land and then in time with a soothing touch.

"You will be a great leader my Lord, the common man is very lucky to have you looking out for their well being." SanPollan bowed his head slightly.

"Kind words and righteous, however there is further work to be done. I need to raise more men if we are going to take Pluris into our bosom quickly and with minimum fuss. Two weeks and we should be in a position to bring the militia law to Vedian and then at the Pulpit I can announce the terrible demise of Madistrin and betrayal of DeFache and then I will simply await for the people to call us."

Shel-Toro looked wistfully, "The day feels fairer does it not old friend?"

"It does indeed my Lord." He replied with a smile.

Their first night had actually been a welcome respite, out of the elements they had slept well in the cavern which they had been directed to. They were given cloth to sleep on and while the ground was hard, it was cool and removed from the harsh winds. The first Joseph knew it was morning was a swift kick to his ribs.

"Get up!" A voice came cutting through his sleep.

He opened his eyes, as the guard used his torch to ignite the one held in wall mounted brackets. Light danced across the cavern, resting on faces he did not recognise. He counted at least twenty people not including the four of them. Most looked old and tired, weary faces and bent backs, some of them were oddly different, tall and burly looking with piercing hazel eyes.

He motioned to Arn, "Those people look odd? Different."

"I believe they may be Huskian's, native to these parts of Vedian." The hunter scoured the cavern to reinforce his words.

Joseph had heard tales of the desert people but had never laid eyes on them, until now. To him they were nomad tribes who lived off the sands, beasts as much as men according to the stories told. There were three guards ushering the detainees into the work area, each guard took a group of seven, all were bound together by chains. The links could be taken off one set of manacles and slid easily to another, to join up new groups and allow total control of movement. The four had arrived together and were already grouped so probably out of sheer laziness, Joseph thought, they were just added to another three. The nomad people, which he thought was compromised of two men and women, although Joseph was not sure, the third seemed smaller in stature and build more like their size and she had longer hair, draped down to her back in brown locks. Joseph was closest too her at the rear, the last in their line and she was the first in hers. He looked around, his eyes trying to adapt to the constantly variable light as they passed a well lit area, then quickly as they moved, plunged back into near darkness.

Her face was fierce, sharp and angled in the cheek bones as well as strong and committed in the eyes. She was almost completely coated in a dark dust, likely from the working conditions and with her naturally dark skin, her eyes were beacons in the gloom.

"Hello I am Joseph." He offered rather timidly, turning as they continued to walk forwards.

"I am Dance." Her reply was was coarse and raspy but enough to assure Joseph this was a female. "You should be quiet."

"Why?" Joseph begun to ask until he felt the crack of a whip flick across his waist.

"Into line you scum. This is not social, its work. March!" The guard had moved from the front, the dark leather whip brandished in his left hand, threatening Joseph. He was quite short, no taller than Joseph, he wore a light leather tunic and belt with a sheathed short sword. He was a plain looking man, brown short locks, hairline receding under the helmet he wore. Eyes tired and squinting tight from the ever changing light in the caverns.

The walk had all been downhill, the cavern passage was narrowing as they went, they could see the cutaway was fresh and small rocks were littered everywhere. Large pails topped with silt and stone stood stoically on the floor. The passageway was now barely wide enough to walk two abreast. "Right we need to widen again so I want two pushing forwards and two each side cutting out. You and him," he pointed to Arn and the larger of the two Huskian men, "forwards. Huskian show him what to do and no chatting or the whip will find you." The two moved further up the tunnel, the Huskian had to stoop and eventually both were on their knees.

Joseph had been paired with Dance and Speck with the other male Huskian.

The guard turned to Febra, "Right my lovely I think you should stay with me for a while, we will go and make fire and ready water for later." He motioned for them to backtrack up the passageway. If I hear any sound there will be trouble. Work hard, work fast and it will go better on all of you." Febra walked next to the guard, she was engaging him in conversation and seemed to have no concern for her own safety. They disappeared from eyesight almost immediately in the poorly lit environment. Joseph thought to protest but the image of the whip bounced back at him.

"I am Arn, a hunter from the Luff." He offered to his large compatriot as he picked up the metal pickaxe that hung on a peg hammered tightly into the shaft wall.

"Chan-Re, of the Dusk Sands Tribe. You strike axe, I will fill rock and remove." The pickaxe work was gruelling, striking at times into thick rock and digging out the hard walls to fill into large containers or pails. They would then be carried further up the tunnel and left for removal Arn assumed. After an hour, the hunter was freely sweating and his arm ached.

Chan-Re looked at him, "We will change over, you are tiring quickly." He took the gnarled tool from Arn and directed him to start loading the waste.

Joseph had begun with loading the pails and Dance had dug the first hour, she was at least as strong as him and her stamina, it quickly became apparent, outstripped his own.

"When do we get water?" His mouth was parched from the dust kicking up and his eyes were burning.

"A while yet. That is if he doesn't forget. Your friend is tough yes?"

Joseph thought briefly, "Yes. Yes she is."

"Good, then she will be survive. She is tiny like a child but I can see in her face, she is a survivor. She would make a good Huskean'

"Will you tell me about where you come from? To at least take my mind off this building thirst."

"Yes but we must speak quietly. I am from the Dusk Sands Tribe,as is Chan-Re and Kin-Re", she gestured towards the other two Huskian's. Over two score moons ago we came to a decision with other tribal leaders that the food from our farms would not last. We had previously been visited by men from the north offering exchange of goods for access to our land to mine. The days are harsh in the desert, even around areas we have irrigated from the mountains, to keep crops is difficult. We had lost too many, so we made a deal with the trickster to provide us food from the north in exchange for access to this land. So it begun but then demands came for workers into the mines, the men they bought from the city knew little, he needed our craft as well as our land. So he held back the food and as he said 'renegotiated' our deal. Now we are forced to provide hands, each tribe in rotation, for twelve moons to labour. It was just supposed to be short term, we knew we could farm our way back, it just needed a little time. Three moons ago, our crops died on mass, a red beetle plague, arrived overnight. We will never be rid of the trickster, we are damned to his toil now and our children after us."

"That is terrible, I am sorry. Have your people appealed to a Vedian governing body, to the Crown Prince even? "

"We are Huskian, we have had no contact with men since the Great War. Our first time has ended in bonds of service, my peoples will have nothing more to do with men. We should have remained to our own, many think we are being punished for entering into any parlee with the men of Vedian. It is our punishment for this transgression."

"I do think you are being punished for anything. You have been unfortunate to broker a deal with a man who has no moral or law but his own. I have met your persecutor, your trickster and he is nothing but a fat man in poorly chosen clothes. We will help you. I will help you, If I can."

"Even if we could get out of this place, my people will not ask for help. They fear the consequence of our actions"

"You said your people did fight alongside men in the Great War? Correct?"

"Yes. It is written and the tales are still told. The Huskian's marched at the final hour to come to the King of Vedian's aide. A personal debt owed by the Huskian Prince of old, when we as a people were united. Since then the tribes have splintered, we agree of little in this time." Dance had stopped cutting the rock and was engrossed in the conversation.

"What was this debt?"

"It has never been revealed. It is not present in any of the tales, only that it was personal between the two men. It is lost forever unless you know someone who fought in the Great War?"

She laughed to herself. Joseph turned to look at Speck.

Slowly and sluggishly his eyes begun to open. His hands grabbed at wet mud, he could feel it on his face, lifting his head in front of him the waters flowed, splashing against his cheeks. Slowly his mind begun to piece together the events of the previous night, the attack of the boat, the immense bravery of his protector. Lint! Madistrin pulled himself up on his arms and looked around desperately seeking for a sign of his guard. Further along the wash, he could make out a body, half in and half out of the waters. He pulled himself to his feet, his face throbbed and his chest was tight with pain. He dragged himself across the waters edge and grabbed at the body, flipping him over he confirmed it was his protector. Kneeling close he could make out a shallow breathing, Lint's arms were soaked in blood, the cloth tunic, muddy and bloodied. He cupped water in his hands and cleaned the mud from Lint's pale face, sitting down he nursed his head into his lap.

His eyes scanned the area again, this was Imanis, he was sure of it, one of the coastal bays, not a landing point, there was only one dock as far as he remembered. He could see a row boat floating a short distance out from shore. Lint must have fought off their attackers long enough to get them away and too shore but at what price?

263

He needed to get help but would never have the strength to carry his guard to safety. Standing he grabbed under Lint's arms, slowly and carefully pulling him further into land. He nestled the man onto a slope of grass and whispered words of reassurance into his ear. There was little movement, only the slow shallow breath.

Madistrin needed to find help and quickly. The Isle could be no more than half a days walk across, he needed to get to the university or the village. If he cut straight across, he should be able to see the building, given its size on the landscape. Resting Lint against a mound, he rubbed his shoulder softly before beginning the journey westwards. Patting at the blood on his forehead in an attempt to soothe the wound he could feel his strength ebbing after a few minutes. He was in no condition for a trek at the best of times and these were far from those.

Why had the attack taken place? How had they known? And most troubling, who were they?

The thoughts scattered around his mind, helping to take the pain away. He saw the university from a good distance, its main hall roof, peering above the hills as he climbed. Doubts crept into his mind, should he just walk into the university. What if they had already got here, waiting for him. He needed to be cautious, what would Parran's counsel be in his place? Take the road less watched, that is what he would say, if it has to be done, then let it be done with stealth. The university was the obvious choice, but he decided he should try to veer off south and enter the village first, look for help there and see if he could get the lay of the land before deciding next what to do.

He dragged himself up the hill and begun to traverse his way down the other side, wishing he had his stick with him, his leg was aching nearly as much as his face and chest now. Crouching he could hear voices as he entered the borders of the small village, it was almost midday and the sun was risen high in the skies above. He took cover behind a large barn and crept around, looking for signs of aid or danger.

From his hiding place he could make out a small smithy working with his fire and a fishmonger's stall next to a butcher, perhaps no more than fifty people lived in the village but he was sure they would have someone skilled in herb. Then he saw a small structure with a hanging sign above for an apothecary. He edged round building by building, trying to stay in the cover of shade as much as possible. A few villagers were milling around the market stalls, some chatting others going about chores and duties, oblivious to the Crown Prince's peril. Madistrin paused to catch his breath before moving around the building and onto the raised platform that led up to the entrance.

The woman standing behind the counter was about to greet the stranger, when she became aware of his injuries, blood was smeared across his face coated with mud from the river bed. He looked shattered, limping on his strong leg and a look of sheer desperation in his face.

"I , I need help. Please, you must come." He stretched out an arm, to steady himself on the counter. "My friend is hurt, near the wash to the east. He needs urgent help, I can take you to him."

The woman was shocked, she could see some of his injuries were not accidental, defensive wounds about the face for certain.

"We will need help, I will call for the smithy. Wait one moment, I shall fetch him." She flicked up the latch that held the hatchway in place moving towards the doorway.

"No please. Nobody else, it is not safe for me. You do not understand." Madistrin thought about announcing his name but the nagging voice of Parran was at the back of his head, whispering words of warning, "Please I mean you no harm but I need your help and I fear my friend will die if he does not get aid soon. I will explain everything but I would just ask this one favour. Please bring your herbs and follow me."

It was madness to go with him, the island rarely got strangers from the mainland, when they did it was often soldiers. She knew going off alone with this man was a bad idea but there was something about him. For one, he looked nothing like a soldier, more like a victim. His nails were manicured and his belly too big for a militia's rations. He spoke with a soft tongue, the men she had met were rougher toned and more aggressive, demanding and pushy. There was no law in the village, the university guards helped keep the peace but mostly the villagers looked after their own affairs via a community council. The smithy Walen was a man often brought into solve disputes and help deal with drunkards and scuffles. He had a good mix of common sense and muscle. She wanted to call out to him but the look of desperation in the man's eyes held her course.

"Alright. Tell me of his injuries. So I can prepare what herb I will need."

"He had cuts, some deep. He bleeds from the legs and arms. I am not sure he is conscious and he was hot."

She turned and walked behind the counter, gathered a belt of pouches from beneath it and linked it round her svelte waist.

Her attention turned to the many jars stacked on shelves on the back wall. "We will need plantain leaves and speedwell. If he has a fever I would need to mix an elderberry and yarrow tonic but it must be heated. We will need to bring him here, is that possible?"

"I am not strong enough to carry him, it is on the eastern coast, I walked almost an hour."

"Then we need to make the fire there, grab that tinder with flint and a small pot." She pointed to a crate in the corner of the room.

"I would give you my name but I have too many fears, would it be too rude to ask for yours?" Madistrin was comforted by the woman's precise organisational approach. He liked order, he was happiest when plans were clear.

"I am Mistress Vale. You can address me as such, until the time you are prepared to identify yourself. Now pack these things into this bag, while I prepare the pony." She handed him a grey backpack and moved towards the door.

Madistrin reached out a hand is if to stop her but realised he could not and he would simply have to trust her. The situation was outside of his control now. After a few minutes had passed Vale returned. "I have told the Smithy I have herb gathering errands, he was not surprised, I often go out in the dusk. Come stay this side of me, once we are clear of the village, you can mount the pony."

Madistrin thought to protest, then swiftly realised he would likely not make the return journey on foot. The pain in his chest was tighter than ever, his leg was agony, he needed to stay awake long enough to direct her to Lint. Vale moved the pony carefully around the outskirts of the buildings before moving out towards

266

the eastern grasslands. She directed Madistrin to mount the beast, a dirty brown friendly pack pony. He snorted at the weight of the Crown Prince, Vale led him by a reign towards the wash. As soon as he was astride the beast, he felt himself lean forwards and nestle into its soft mane.

He was awoken by the soft feeling of a hand on his cheek, Vale's face looking up at him, "You fell asleep, which way? We are nearly at the coastline."

Madistrin looked around, trying to take in any landmarks that were familiar. "south a bit I think, yes look where the land pushes in making a bay, it was just down from there I think. Should be a rowing boat about, off shore maybe, drifting."

The sun was beginning to fall in the sky by the time they found the row boat, drifting offshore as a marker. Madistrin had gotten down from the pony and was muttering to himself, recounting his movements from earlier. "There!" he pointed to the grassy hill. "There he is."

Vale was quickly to the guards side, touching his head, examining his wounds, making that critical first assessment that would impact the outcome of his survival.

"He is alive but barely. Get a fire going and heat up the water. Salt water is fine." Vale removed a small pestle and mortar from the backpack and begun crushing herbs from her pouch mixing it with what looked like honey. She spread the mixture across cuts on Lints hands and legs.

"The cut on his abdomen is deep. I need to stitch it first and pad it with cherry plum and rock rose. Stupid woman! Why did I not bring my five flower remedy. We will have to make do." Vale begun to pull the needle and thread from her pouch and prepared the wound for stitching.

Madistrin did not have the heart to tell her that he had never been asked to make a fire before. He stacked the kindling together, a small piece of lint at the top as his ignition. He then begun to strike the flint hard onto the 'C' shaped piece of steel. Again and again he forced the flint against the hard metal but he could not make the tiny sparks appear that would light the fire.

Vale caught his eye after a multitude of efforts. "Don't bang down on it, strike it across the steel."

"I can not seem to make it spark."

"Its not the sparks that start the fire. Its a tiny strip of steel heated that you tear away with the flint. The sparks are just a show for men. Think of it like stripping an apple peel."

Madistrin took an angle and looked to carve a light shaving off the steel. Once, twice....a light! He was quick to get down and softly blow at the base, now glowing a hazy red and yellow hue. Wisps of flame began to dance from the lint and onto the kindling. He placed the water filled jug on the fire over holding strips and looked on to Vale and Lint, "How is he?"

"I have stitched and padded the wound. Once we have the hot water I can make the compound to bring down his fever. Then it is only rest that will tell. In the meantime we will patch you up. I would suggest returning to the village for assistance, failing that, have I done enough to prove my worth, to hear the truth of things?" She sat cross legged, her leather trouser and jerkin tight about her frame, for the first time Madistrin saw an attractive women in front of him in her early forties. His instinct told him Parran would disapprove but he felt she deserved at least the truth after what she had done.

"I am Madistrin. Crown Prince of Vedian. This man is my protector and we were attacked on our way to visit Prominence DeFache of the Isle. I was saved by Lint and we washed up here. I wish urgently to seek out DeFache but I was concerned if the men that attacked us had made it to the island in advance or got word to others of our escape. I am can only apologise for asking so much and offering so little."

Vale started to stand and bow, clearly surprised by this turn of events "My liege, I did not know it was you."

"And yet, you aided us anyway." Madistrin motioned for her to sit.

"I believe however you made the right decision. Yesterday Walen told us of men arriving at the university, apparently there has been an issue and Prominence DeFache has been removed from his office. He is held at Imanis awaiting trial by the Scholatic."

Madistrin was shocked, a part of him afraid of the news and another part gladdened that DeFache was here on the Island.

"Their plans have clearly accelerated if they have moved on him as well. I have to get to DeFache, I must enter Imanis tonight."

Chapter 14 - Uprising

'There has been talk, idle whispering, in the halls of men who should know better. To my even greater disappointment, I hear of discussions rearing up in the university walls from the mouths of my own brethren. Of course I understand the path that many walk in times of peace, in times of idleness, where wandering minds have less to focus on. Men need a sense of business, a sense of purpose, a challenge to be overcome or enemy to be dominated. The toil against something is a need and men are only truly happy when oppression and fate is near to their door.

I have however, only over time realised this reality, I have fought against it, truly I have.

Yet when I hear my own dear learned scholars talking of change, muttering of what is fair and equal, I can no longer treat this as frivolous. Perhaps Vedian does need something greater, something more challenging, it seems man was only truly happy when on the brink of destruction. Ages on, he still sits by the fireside and recounts the tales of those long since passed, a distant dream, kept alive by a willingness to suffer.

It is a burden, true, but I am Scholatic, I am born to bear such a load. If that means delivering man from its age of insignificance than so be it. I fear, if I do not take action soon, in a controlled and thoughtful way, then man's fallow years shall end in the worst manner possible.

I will not allow it, I am their senior and their protector. And thus I will deliver them from their self-inflicted bondage.'

'Man's Hollow Irrelevance & The Indisputable Path Of Their Own Making' - Shel-Toro - Vedian 991

Five long days had passed, there was no obvious way to tell if it was night or day, with one exception. They worked all day, a gruelling shift of axe work and cutting or the brief respite of rubble shifting. Either way it was proving too much for Speck, his body ached like it had never done before, his lungs full of the dry dust that sprayed up into the air with every swing. He coughed and spluttered his way through sleep and in the day, shuffled up and down the passage dragging the large pail behind him. Chan-Re had abandoned offering him the pick-axe two days previously, the Huskian had not complained. He slowly went about his toil but he too was tiring from the incessant workload.

They had been surprisingly free to talk, the guards seemed fairly uninterested in them, only shepherding them from workspace to sleeping area twice a day. They kept them to the same groups and their supervision was with the same guard. On an occasion he would come storming down the passageway brandishing his whip, lashing out at the nearest of them. Joseph had received two harsh slashes across the back, one had broken the skin and it was raw and biting from the dust that irritated it. There was no plan to their incarceration, no order, the guards just lashed out at random, believing that show of aggression would keep them all in line. For Arn it was just stoking a fire, prodding away bit by bit, anger swelled within him.

On the night of their fourth day in the mines, they had sat as they had every night, with bowls of oats and a piece of bread. They were fed plenty, the guards knew their strength had to be kept as healthy as possible, there was water stored in leather skin bottles, handed out four times a day. Dance had said they would have plenty of supply, the land deep below the mines had many streams.

Joseph turned to Speck, "No luck again last night?"

His friend stretched his legs out and coughed a little, "It is so hard to see in the little light, I am struggling to get a focus, a few images but nothing like before. I am so tired Joseph, If I could rest and restore perhaps it would be easier."

Char-Re looked up from his oats, "Nothing here is easy little man, the sands do not offer help, you get what you take. These ones know that. They take our freedom, they get their jewels. The spirits will only honour the strong."

Speck mumbled quietly, "Then I fear there may be no hope. For I am not strong and in truth never have been. I am no longer even sure why I am here."

Joseph placed his hand on his friends shoulder in a conciliatory fashion. "We will find a way out Speck, I know we will. For us and for these people. Their suffering can not go on at the hands of this man for ever. There must be something we can do. I have been thinking, two tales we have heard on this journey, both have ended badly and both with poison."

Arn swung round, "You think the Huskian's crop failing was not chance occurrence then?"

"I think that in itself is clear, someone poisoned their crops for Bast'wa's gain, just like the Princes horse was poisoned all those years ago."

Dance looked up from her bowl, "Yes Joseph I think you are right it was poison but the tribe elders will not move on Bast'wa without proof. They believe it is us that have wronged the spirits and Bast'wa is simply a means of punishment."

Arn asked hopefully, "Do the Huskian's have enough warriors to attack Bast'wa?"

Kin-Re, the older of the two Huskian's replied, "No. We could easily lay waste to his men but he is protected by Vedian guards, the elders will not risk a war with man."

"Better we fight, than lay like cattle awaiting slaughter. We should fight." Chan-Re looked fleetingly at the older Huskian as he spoke.

Kin-Re half smiled, "Spoken as only a young warrior truly can. You are strong my brother and your time will surely come as the spirits demand."

Febra had maintained minimal conversation for most of the days and nights since their arrival. Each day she had spent time with their guard, taken off for an hour or two and then returned to work. She spoke no detail of what had happened and they eventually stopped asking, Joseph felt ashamed and wanted her to cry or shout but she was stoic and just seemed numb to everything and everyone around her.

"What proof would your elders need?" She addressed the question to Dance.

"Testimony from one in his service, better still the perpetrator."

"I think they know what happened. I think they all do. If I get him to tell me, will that be enough for you?" Febra was held Dance's gaze as she spoke, searching out confirmation.

"It may be enough but he would have to come with us and be presented to the leaders."

272

Arn felt motivated and energised for the first time in days, "How do we get out then? Overpowering one guard is fine and even if the other two come we can handle them but on the surface they are better armed and will no doubt be ready."

"I will get word to the other groups, we will take down our own captors in tandem and make our way to the surface as quickly as the lift can take us. Perhaps six at a time in our groups. However the first group may encounter the brunt of their defence, they would need to buy time for the others to use the lift and reinforce. If the way up is lost, it will be quickly over." Chan-Re's voice was determined and resolute but with a hint of sadness. He knew who ever went up first would likely not make it out.

Arn looked at Speck, "The incantation you used to hide us in Kanegon?"

Speck shook his head, "I do not know how, as soon as the words are spoken they seem to leave me. I was able to complete the thought reading twice but then it left me to. I am of little use to you Arn."

"Enough little sorcerer," Febra's eyes were wild and her words spat out of her mouth at Speck, "enough of your self-pity and weakness. These men would leave you here to rot, you are nothing to them, a toy to be used and thrown out. Take their malice, indifference and hate and throw it back at them. Take what they have given you and return it, in a reckoning."

The whole group was silent for a moment.

"You are right Febra. I have failed to do what I promised butt tonight I will read the book and I will find a way to help us get out. I will prove myself useful to this group, to you. This place will not be our grave."

Dance looked at them one by one, "Then we are the first group, it is decided. Chan-Re get word to the others, we attack tomorrow when the first waters are served. May the spirits of the sand guide and protect us."

As they laid down to sleep that night, Speck drew out the book. They had not bothered to take this trinket from him. None of the guards could read, it was worthless to them, just another point of amusement. The weakling, the tiny man with the reading book.

He squinted as the torch light bounced over the pages, his anger focussed him.

"Pinky!" Get clear of the walls dammit man." Tress shouted up.

"I would Captain but they these corpses keep blocking me in. They just keep mounting up sir."

"Yes Sergeant because you keep killing them. Now get clear of the damn wall or I will put an arrow in you myself."

The second wall had fallen, Tress knew it and he was not about to lose any more of the Sabre Regiment for a lost cause. Pinkerton would sit up there all day, as the enemy piled over the battlements, the corpses would indeed be high but sooner or later they would overwhelm him and the others. They had to fallback to the last wall, use the killing ground between them again. Since the routing of the Asten Lancers on that first day, there had been little to go right in this battle. The first wall had gone over almost immediately, the defeat of Prince Shartos had hit the troops hard, for a time they had lost order in ranks, only the methodical defiance of the Sabre Regiment on that first day had saved them. Organising the retreat to the second wall, defending the ground systematically to ensure they held the enemy push in waves. Slowly they had regrouped and held the second tier for a further three days and nights.

Dior had called the release of the second wall, it was a decision based on losses and time. They had begun to lose holds and more and more of the enemy swept forward onto the ramparts. It was a crucial call of when to stand back and accept the wall to be lost and when to hold. He trusted Dior like no other man he had ever met, he was not his friend. In truth he was not sure Dior had any friends but he was respected by everyone and in the military that stood for everything. The last night had hit Pinkerton hard he knew it, the loss of his long time compatriot Piper Major Tom Brown. The spearmen had buckled in the middle of the battlement, the hoarding had been set alight and they had lost focus trying to dampen the fire. A swarm of invaders had quickly mounted the rampart and cut off Brown and a few others from the main defence. He had fought to chisel through the enemy, to regroup and hold a line but their enemy had seen an opportunity and threw themselves to take a corner of the battlements.

Pinkerton had seen it from the other side and ran, cutting his way through, one after another, his longsword swinging swiftly through the air. There was just too many, Brown had died from a crushing blow to the back from a heavy mace, he fell as did many others. Pinkerton carried him that night from the battlements under their own flag. Not the first man to fall under his command and looking out across the stormy skies, it would not be the last.

From his rear he heard the soft booted steps of Fystal, he knew instantly it was the mage. They just didn't walk like soldiers. He greeted him with a nod and continued looking out towards the skies.

"I think I may have something for tomorrow, maybe no more than a distraction." his voice unusually lacked certainty.

Tress smiled inwardly, He had learned over the years, that anything this lot came up with was worth listening to. They had never been many, twenty to thirty in their pomp, now a couple of years into the war only a dozen remained. They did not mix with the men, which was for the best, they could impact a sense of enjoyment. None of them drunk for a start and that was more than odd. As Pinky always said, 'If you can't see the bright side of life in a flagon of Vedian Pure Mead, then where can you.' However in all the time he had served alongside them, he had never seen one of them run. Men flee, it is just the way of things, sooner or later even the toughest and most experienced soldier comes to a situation where the fear of battle is just overwhelming. They turn when they should hold, their indecision preys on them, its inevitable. Those are the days you die, unless you're lucky enough to have someone watching your back. He looked across the wall and could just make out the figure of Junas his oldest friend, sitting sharpening those beautiful blades. Sometimes you need someone, who is just a little more than you are.

The Candlemen however, seemed to have no such fear. Mainly they would take a stand from a distance, chanting incantations but if the battle went against them, they thought nothing of moving to the front line. In the front line wearing a jerkin, in all his days Tress would not understand it. A warrior without armour. He had seen two Battle-mages hold a line when a platoon of swordsmen had fallen back, their movements so fluid, so perfect. If they had something to say he would listen.

"We are going to set up some incendiary fire in their rear guard, to be honest it is little more than elaborate fireworks, it will not do much damage but it will be noisy and bright, should give them quite the jolt. Just as they hit the wall, hopefully enough for a counter?"

"I have never seen you complete anything that far? Normally its all within ten or twenty metres, their back line will fall over a hundred from us." Tress questioned, he had watched them over the years and learned.

"You are very aware Captain. More than most men. You are correct our incantations are normally short in range, it takes a lot of effort to project further distances. It will have a price but if it buys the time we need, then it will be worth paying."

Tress shuffled uncomfortably, "Time for what I wonder? Dior has spoken of time, needing more time. There are no more reinforcements, every other swordsmen is fighting to retake the front at Kanegon, the Lancers are no more, only a few remain from the attack. Even if recruits are found, they are not hardened to last. I can not see what it is we are buying time for?" In his voice Faslyn noted a hint of desperation, something he had not heard before, it was the fear of failure that held him now.

"Do you ever wonder why this fortress was built so Captain?" The mage tapped his staff along the hard floor.

"Of course, it is one of the greatest topics of conjecture amongst the military, the most popular view is that Bannermane is a test of courage. Its reduced elevation built at the base of a set of hills, rather on top of one. It is the ultimate test an an armies organisation and one we are unfortunately not up to the challenge it would seen." Tress was frustrated at the line of questioning, this was nothing new, what was the point of it.

"Perhaps it is. There can be little doubt the design is intentional but sometimes puzzles are better unlocked when reversed. You are a soldier Captain, so you look at everything from a singular viewpoint, honour, courage, hold. You are aware of the inner keep of course but are you aware of the cells that sit far below its belly? In which we hold one of the enemy, a powerful shaman,

276

one of the most powerful wielders of the faith I have ever encountered. You were at Kanegon when it fell, yes?"

Tress nodded, his interest piqued, why was he being told this?

"The speed the landing boats cut through the waters that we have found so difficult to navigate all these years. High seas that have claimed so many venerable sailors. Not by chance. Weather controlled by the enemies most powerful enchanter. We suspected it early on and when our forces splintered so quickly we knew there was more behind it. The King and his Lord Protector immediately commanded us to find him and to be truthful it was luck that delivered him, not skill or planning. We were scouting their camps when we found him gathering herb off the borders of Kanegon, he seemed so unaware of a reason to travel alone. He had no consternation, because he simply did not believe anyone in Vedian could harm him. We lost five of our number that day, that was the price of his capture. Be clear Captain, these men will never be replaced, our order is dwindling, the Scholatic grow, their thinking and new order outstrips our faith, you will not see our like again once this war is done." Faslyn stopped and sat down on the rampart steps, the cold stone close to his skin was refreshing, he liked the cold, the feeling of being outdoors. So many years spent in the Tower he imagined.

"So what has come of this Shaman?"

"He is held prisoner in the Keep, we question him each day. That's is to say I do, as even now he is exceedingly dangerous. The King believes he holds the key to ending the war. I am not sure why he believes this. So each day we spar, sometimes I gather information and others, well, other days are less successful. The time of which you speak is for me, to wrest this thing out, this memory, idea, plan whatever he may hold. Your men die in the field and on the battlements to give me time Captain."

"And Bannermane? It does not explain why it is....Ah I see. It is so simple, I can't believe it has never been suggested. We have always been so focussed on the fortress from our perspective. Why now? This information is surely protected by the King? Why would you tell me when Dior, who no doubt knows, does not tell me himself?"

"Dior is like yourself, a soldier. He follows orders and would never move against the King's will. If you needed evidence of that, you only needed to see the folly of the Asten Lancers on our first day here."

Tress looked to interject to protect his Commanders name.

"I am not criticising Dior Captain, he is a fine man and a great leader of men but at his end he will always be a soldier. He is bound to the life and to its shackles. When a man's free-will to act is held fast by his bondage of service, who does that protect or serve?"

"It has served me well and saved many lives. Without order and duty, my life would have been lost many years ago on a battlefield." Tress was looking sharply at the mage now.

"Yes, there is of course a need for that order among men and soldiers more than most. That however only works when men have hope and as we look out into the lands of Vedian before us, I see in you that is failing. I offer you this information, to, when the time is right, make the hard decision. A choice that others more senior or even able, have not and will not. Even if that damns your regiment with you for an age, I believe you will do what is right, even when the soldier within tells you it is wrong."

"I could never hurt my men or the name of the Sabre Regiment, it is too dear to me. You have put your trust in the wrong man I fear"

"That's is the thing with trust Captain, it is given with faith and mine will not waiver in you. You now know why they fight, why they storm the fortress night after night. You know they will never stop before they take this place and every man in their way is laid to their end. We call them invaders but why do they invade our land Captain? When for all these hundreds of years they have never sought to cross the divide. Is it perhaps they are not who we think they are? Perhaps before they ever took to their ships, someone from these shores made it to theirs. It is possible, we know that, it has been done many times for wood gathering but that is just the closest inland point. If one ventures further east, they would set upon their nation. Perhaps if ones greed were great enough, they would steal from such an honest and venerable race and bring that prize back to Vedian as a trophy. And now in our deepest pits, in the mouth of this beast we hold not just their spiritual leader but something valuable enough to go to war over. A great relic perhaps."

Tress breathed heavily, "Bannermane was never a fortress it was built as a prison. We are not keeping them out, we are holding him and it in."

Faslyn slowly nodded, "So Captain are we the defender or aggressor?"

Dispatching the guards at the mining level had been a simple task. They were easily outnumbered and a whip strike was far from enough to hold off the six of them. Arn's group had no fight at undertake all, by the time the mornings water break was on them Febra had already been gone an hour. They walked up to find her standing over the guard, his arms bound behind his back, an old rag pushed into his mouth and his whip one end wrapped tightly around his neck, while the other she held firmly in her hand. She dragged the guard to his feet as she approached Dance.

"He has admitted the attack on your people. They know Bast'wa arranged to have your crops poisoned, to enable his cheap labour for the mines. They all know, it is nothing more than a joke to them."

Dance nodded, "Thank you, if we can make it to the surface alive, I hope the elders will listen."

The three groups huddles at the base of the lift, Arn pushed his finger tightly to his mouth, "From here on silence."

He ushered the five others into the lift and forced in the guard behind. It was tight. Arn put his hand on Speck's arm to signal him. One of the Huskian's begun to pull on the winch and hoist the lift though its cog system. It felt like an age, all the while they could hear Specks soft voice repeating words over and over. The chant was fixating as they journeyed up the long dark shaft, it seemed to be taking an age to get to the top, longer than their original decent a few days earlier.

Above them a flicker of light could be seen emerging from the vapid gloominess and then it begun. Huge banging and crashing from the distance followed swiftly by shouting and panicked voices. It had worked. Speck had told them of his vision he had seen the mages of old perform, of the plan to project a distraction into the desert at the entrance to the mine. When they finally reached the top, there were the sounds of bedlam, like a huge town festival had run out of control. They took no time to send the lift back down and gather the second group up, they would wait as long as they could to increase numbers before moving forwards.

All of a sudden Speck dropped to the floor. He lay on the rock in his robes unmoving. Joseph was first to his side, looking up at Arn for help. "What happened?"

"I don't know but his distraction has ended, we need to be ready, they will come back to guard soon."

The lift had reached the cave below and they could hear the stretch and pull as it begun to ascend for the second time.

The first two came noisily around the corner, talking furiously about what had just happened, conjecture flowing between them. The guard on the left was dead before he knew they were there, a large rock slammed into his face by Kin-Re. As the huge Huskian moved towards his second target, Arn grabbed for his throat but not quickly enough to stop him letting out a shrill cry. Behind them the sound of the winch turned and scraped at the metal cable, slowly offering them the hope of reinforcements. The men that turned the corner next were ready, they bore small round shields outstretched and short swords slightly behind. Arn grabbed at one of the dead guards swords, looking to engage on the left hand side. Kin-Re did not contemplate looking for the blade, he hurled himself at the guard on the right with his full weight behind him, pushing the smaller man to the floor. Other voices begun to sound, they could hear weapons being picked up, the rest would come now.

The passageway was opening as they pushed the guards back and it was not to their benefit, they would be better served without flanking space. The floor was slippery with mold but Joseph held his footing as he scrambled for the second discarded blade. The other guards had arrived, five more to make seven. The new arrivals saw the Huskian mounted on top of the floored guard, pummeling down, his helmet knocked clean off. They ran now, swords cleaving down at the defenceless warrior. Dance slipped forward, she intercepted one, striking blows to his lower abdomen just behind the protection of his leather breastplate. He winced and dropped his shield guard, she followed with a knee up and into the chin area, blood spluttered out as his teeth bit down on his tongue.

Chan-Re slower than his younger consort had now arrived from the rear and pushed back at two of the men looking to engage the kneeling Huskian. Arn had dispatched his opponent, drawing him close with a dip of the shoulder, the lunge had left him wide open for a reversed stab into the lower back as his jerkin rode up. The hunter desperately tried to defend Kin-Re but it was too late, a flurry of cuts and a final blow to the skull ended his life.

Febra was still at the rear looking down at the darkness where the lift would be, she held a tight grip on the leash that secured her captive. Speck laid motionless at her feet. For a moment it looked as if she might dart forward but she glanced again at her prisoner and held her ground, she knew if he died this would be for nothing.

Chan-Re, Dance and Arn stood across the wider passageway, the five guards remaining had regrouped and were now more cautious, moving as a group towards their prey. Chan-Re cried out loudly and charged the middle of the five, looking to drive through their ordered advance. He toppled one and two either side were thrown off balance. Dance ran forward and slid gracefully on the ground, using the moisture to her advantage, she passed the guard on the furthest right, sweeping his legs from beneath him. His head cracked on the hard floor, only saved death by the iron helmet he wore. Arn engaged the left side first and then as the second guard regained his form from the charge he faced two opponents. The hunter was deft with a blade but he had no protection, he longed for a bit of distance and his longbow, he knew this could not end well for him. He drew the left guard on to him, allowing the lunge, he backed his body away while contemporaneously sweeping his blade forward towards the exposed neck. The distance was too far for the shorter blade and he missed. The second guard was on him now, he took a cut to the right forearm, the pain stung but he shook it off. His defence however was impacted and he did not react to the second attack from the other soldier, his blade driving into Arn's extended left thigh, the pain was incredible but it had pulled the guard into range and he thrust his blade up and into his exposed neck. Blood flowed freely, Arn sank to one knee, the air was misty now, he could make out a body moving towards him but try as he might he could not refocus, consciousness quickly left him.

Dance was engaging the two on the right, one guard slowly rising back from the floor, dazed and lacking in coordination. She could not afford to go for a finish and expose herself to the other, she backed off slightly, moving towards Chan-Re's back who was under assault, his forearms covered in slashes, the old man was struggling to fend off his assailant. She had seen the hunter drop down, he was brave, she liked him but he was as good as dead now. Joseph was a spirited lad but he did not have the hunters skill and he could not protect himself or the fallen man for long against an armoured guard. In her head she could hear the grinding of the gears and whirring as the lift extended upwards, a salvation that seemed ever out of reach, precious seconds, more time!

Speck passed out at her feet, Arn bleeding out on the floor, Febra had waited long enough, she quickly tethered her captive to the pulley and rushed forward to help Joseph. They just needed a few more seconds until the second group would emerge and they would have reinforcements.

She leapt forward, running full pace past Joseph's aggressor and turning on her heels, she jumped onto his back. The leather faced guard had seen the girl but was so surprised by the manner of the attack he was unsure how to defend himself. She pushed at the back of his helm, slipping it forward and leant tight into the man's neck, pushing her face into his cheek and biting down hard onto his ear. The flesh tore as he cried out and pulled away, throwing the girl from him, he dropped his shield as his gloved hand came up to grasp at the pain.

Joseph looked at Febra, her mouth covered in his blood her eyes were wide as she seemed to look right through him. "Joseph!" she cried out. As he spun he could see the captive guard at his back, his feet kicking at the pulley, the shaft snapped and a spinning sound came, as the weight went into free fall, down and down into the earth. A huge crash followed, as the casket and its passengers, struck the rocks below. There would be no reinforcements.

The guards had retreated slightly and begun to regroup, four remained, two were injured and they looked back and forth at each other, considering themselves and assessing their enemies. Joseph and Febra had formed a pair as had Chan-Re and Dance. The older Huskian addressed them, "You may yet kill us but you will pay a price for that victory. Is it worth the coin you are being paid?"

The tanned faced guard that Febra had bitten was spitting as he spoke, "You will all die and that bitch devil at my hand."

"There will always be death but not today for these." Chan-Re moved forward pulling two large rocks from the floor below, he stretched out his arms wide and drove the rubble into the guards, dust perpetrating the air around them. It was an attack of folly a mere distraction and Dance knew it. She looked at the others, "Now!"

They flanked the distracted guards as their blood craze reigned blows down on the shoulders of the venerable Huskian. Dance drove her weapon between the shoulder blades from above as she jumped up and behind one, Joseph pushed his short sword into the side of another. The Huskian lay silent on the floor, mortal wounds etched over his back, the final two guards turned too late, Febra's fingers drove into the wounded guards eyes, pushing hard and quick down into the sockets. She gripped like a vice as the eyes popped and his body fell to the ground heavily. The leather faced man begun to back away, seeing the battle was lost, he threw down his shield and sword and ran for the tunnel entrance.

"Stop him, he will send word," Febra motioned to follow him.

Dance put out her arm, "It is days to help, if even he makes it across the desert without provision. Let us tend to the wounded."

Joseph and Febra treated Arn as best they could, patching up his leg with long strips of cloth from the guards bedding, enough to stem the bleeding in the short term. Speck was breathing steadily but they could not seem to wake him. Dance called down to the depths below but there were no voices, she knew in her heart the group below would have been caught up in the falling debris.

Chan-Re and Kin-Re she did not move or look to bury, she spoke a few words and kissed their foreheads. "The spirits will guide them now, they have no more use of these vessels. Their death was honourable."

"They saved us." Joseph said, looked mournfully at the old Huskian.

"Do not dishonour their actions, it will be time to rejoice in their passing soon. First we have to gather provisions and make for my tribal village. The elders will have to call a gathering to hear the murderers words." She gestured to the tied up guard. "I will return with others and we will drop ropes and search below for survivors."

"We can not get two bodies out of here with just three of us, we must try to wake them." Dance pulled a water canteen from the guards resting area and begun to wash the cool liquid across Arn's handsome features, "Come back to us hunter." She poured a tiny amount on his lips and he begun to cough. "What....where.." Arn was confused and his leg was cold.

"You have survived my friend. Yet we have another task, we can not carry you." Dance looked into Arn's eyes, he had almost a Huskian look about him, strong and determined. "Come lean upon me, your wound will be tender but we must test it."

Joseph in the meantime had managed to slowly wake Speck the young man seemed dazed but otherwise unharmed.

"What happened? One second you were speaking then you dropped out like a light."

"I do not know. But it was a huge strain to project the incantation, I could feel it pulling at my head, like a tort muscle that just snapped. I have never felt anything like it."

"Well you did enough but it was not without further cost." Joseph explained what had befallen them and the others below. Speck shook his head, "If I had lasted longer, this would not have happened, this is on me Joseph. They are dead and I could have stopped it, I was not strong enough. I wish someone could help me understand this...what ever this is."

Dance who had got Arn to his feet, looked across and addressed Speck, "It is not your fault my friend and you played your part as did they. Your destinies were simply on a different path. There is a man in our village that may be able to help you. He is not everyone's choice but he is respected amongst my people and it is said his knowledge is old."

There were ample supplies in the quarters and they gathered enough for a couple of days travel, Dance assured them they would be be at her village by nightfall of the second day. Joseph and Speck had made a long crutch for Arn to help support him but mostly Dance walked alongside him, the two softly conversing. Joseph and Speck walked together at the rear and in between Febra and her captive, still led by his whip not a word passed between them. As Febra walked in silence, Joseph and Speck talked constantly about what had happened since they left the Luff, how much they both would like to see home again but mainly about the people they had met and the feeling that something was occurring in Vedian that they had become part of.

Speck slid his feet through the shifting sands, "I just want to learn more and quickly, I think I could do so much for us, if I could just harness it. Its incredible Joseph the feeling as it begins to well up within you, the energy. I have never felt anything like it. There were men in the Great War that could wield this, they called themselves Battle Mages, they were known throughout Vedian."

"So you will be our mighty Battle Mage! And the enemy will bow down at the sound of your name, O mighty Speck!" Joseph poked at his friend.

Due to Dances perfect knowledge of the desert, they encountered little issues with the trek, when the sun rose at its peak she always found them shelter and they walked mainly in the evening, resting at the midday sun. By dusk of the following day they arrived at the village as she promised, every Huskian just stared at them, stopping to look, children pointing and gasping at their entrance. She took them directly to a large tent with a grand canopied area reaching out towards the centre of the village. She asked them to wait as she entered, emerging a few minutes later with a Huskian who wore a number of ornate bone chains around his neck, a leather skirt with a long handled knife at his belt and little else. He was of a venerable age, grey long straight hair, small eyes with large bushy eyebrows and his body which once muscular, now hung loose.

"This is the Elder Orn leader of the Re tribe, he has agreed to hear our story and consider if he feels this is enough to call a moot of the others."

Orn invited them to sit on the floor in the canopied area, it was shady and seemed pleasantly cool as the sun dipped down in the east. Dance explained their escape, their suspicions of the crop poisoning and then turned to the guard.

"Tell him what you told the girl." Dance instructed.

The guard looked around him, "I will tell you for all it will do you, if you promise to let me go free."

The elder seemed to ponder for a moment and then waved his hand, "If you speak the truth you are free. No Huskian will harm you and we will give you provision to cross back to the land of men."

The guard recounted what he had heard. He did not see what they could do with the information and it if they let him go he would just deny it ever came from him, rather blame it on one of the others. Maybe he could even make some coin from old Bast'wa by being the one to get back and tell the tale. One where he fought back the captors, yes this could turn still in his favour.

"You have done us a great deed, " the elder addressed Arn and the others "but if we are to engage Bast'wa and his personal army then we will need all of the tribes together. "I will call a moot three days hence to hear the testimony."

Joseph spoke up, "Are there enough of you to defeat him?"

Orn smiled, "Perhaps not. But I will look to do one better, I will ask for permission to petition the Crown Prince in the matter. Look for support from Vedian itself, we do not trust men and Bast'wa is testament to that but I have always understood your Madistrin to be a good man, I met him once long ago and his brother. Huskian's once did a great favour to men perhaps it is time that was called in return."

They slept well for the first time in days, the village healer tended to Arn's wound with Dance never far from his side. It was sore but the mix of herb used had an amazing impact over the first night on its recovery. Dance also introduced Speck to the village Shaman, she did not give him a name only that he was very old and that he read the fortues for the village. He was a difficult one to engage in discussion, speaking in short sentences, much of which made little sense to Speck.

"How long have you been the village Shaman then?" he asked.

"Always."

"I see and what do you do with these Ashes?"

"See, now and then."

"Right. Dance says you might be able to help me understand these incantations I can do? Do you know of this?"

"Seek the Tower."

Speck shook his head, then his mind took him back, he had heard that before. The poem they had been instructed by Gru-Staedak to take on his death. That had talked about being 'alone in the tower'. Was this connected? He tried to press for more but the Shaman offered little sense in return.

Joseph enjoyed the village life, in many ways it was like the Luff, simple, its concerns food and farming. The Huskian's and they were much alike, it made no sense for them to be so removed from their Vedian counterparts, he thought that Pike would have liked it here, although the lack of water might be a factor for the old sailor. Only Febra kept to herself over the seven days, choosing to watch her captive day and night. Tied up, it was difficult to see what he could do and Joseph thought it was just an excuse for Febra to remain aloof from the others, she had seemed to go back into her shell, more like the girl he first met in the Luff. More than once he thought about attempting to talk with her but then dismissed it, she made him feel uncomfortable somehow, he no longer felt the attraction to her he once did.

The Elders begun to arrive on the eight day of their stay, some in the morning, others from greater distances in the afternoon. By the evening a great fire was lit in the centre of the village and seven of the tribal leaders gathered in a crescent, seated on the ground as was their way. The whole village was gathered, food prepared for a great feast in honour of the visitors. Dance explained how rare this event was and that relations had been strained through numerous small disagreements over the past years. This however effected them all, the farmlands crops were a shared resource by all tribes, worked by each tribe in a cycle of seasons and the bounty divided, when the harvest had failed it had struck them all hard. They had needed Bast'wa's help what ever the cost.

The captive was brought outside by Febra, still tied by his own whip and secured against a tall carved rock that stood at the centre. When they were ready, he Orn asked him to tell his story once again to all present.

"...and so it was that Prominence Bast'wa hired a man, a very skilled man to enter your lands and lay a poison on your crops, it was the concoction that caused the failing not your deal with us. Bast'wa just made it look like that, he knew you would turn to him for help."

There was a murmuring around the Elders.

Orn rose his hand, "We will now deliberate. He is free to go as I promised." Orn motioned to a Huskian beside him, "Give him provision and set him on a true path to the Lough border."

The Huskian moved towards the rock, as he did Febra raised her hand to speak. Orn looked at the girl, inviting her to talk.

"You promised him no Huskian would harm him."

"I did. My word counts for everything I hold dear. He will go free."

"I would not disrespect your words, I have listened carefully to them." From her belt she pulled a long knife, in a singular motion she stood face to face with the guard and spoke calmly.

"I give you in return the love you showed me." The knife reversed in her hand, she swept it across his neck, as the artery opened the life quickly left him, his head hung loosely against his body.

Chapter 15 - Malevolence

Away you go little boy of mine,
Over the hills and beyond the vales.
Morning of high sun softly shines,
In the brightest lavender dales.

And when it darkens, when you feel unease,
Look all around you quick.
Stare up, stare down, look all around,
See the wood plays a trick.

Its cold now, wrap your wool tight,
Eyes down, eyes down, resist the flight,
Its old now, in your dreams light,
Eyes closed, eyes closed, out of sight.

Fear not my dear, be good and brave
And mothers benevolence,
Will protect you little one
From the forests malevolence.

Children's Rhyme from the Luff - Anonymous

The mood was uncomfortable the next morning. It had taken a number of pleas from Dance to calm everyone down, Febra's actions had not played out well to the Huskian elders. She had explained what the guard had done, or what they suspected as Febra has never spoken of it and Orn eventually conceded she was granted a debt that she effectively claimed with the guards life. Orn asked to see Febra alone, the others tribal leaders having left at first light, their moot had continued on through the night and decisions were completed. Not everyone was in agreement, some of the older tribes still favouring the spirits intervention but most agreed they had been betrayed by Bast'wa. Eventually two key actions had been passed. Firstly for Orn to send a messenger directly to Vedian to request the Crown Prince to intervene, if a response was not received within one full moon then they would raise the Huskian arms together, in the meantime they would begin preparations for war and be mindful of any attack in response to the mines.

Orn had sent a small group out on the first day to look for survivors, Dance had begged to go but he had stayed her hand, the news they returned with was painful if unsurprising. No survivors, the falling vessel had crushed against the rocks, ending the life of everyone in it. Dance knew better than to cry in front of the Elder but the tears welled up as the search party relayed its ill news, she walked to where Arn was practicing with his bow.

"I can see by your face the news is not good." He shook his head, "I am sorry. Truly."

"Just hold me please hunter. " They embraced tightly.

"I will always protect you Dance. I am sorry I could not do more for the others." He whispered softly in her ear.

Joseph had been astonished at the events of last night, he understood her pain but to kill a man like that, in cold blood. He could not face her, he just did not know what to say anymore. However he was mindful that an audience with the Elder could get her in even more trouble, so reluctantly he went to her tent.

Febra sat carving a small stick with her knife, he recognised it straight away, the same blade that had cut the throat of their captive yesterday. If he had hoped for signs of remorse, he was disappointed.

"Please Febra be courteous with the Elder. You need to be careful, we are his guests." Joseph pleaded.

"I do, do I. I need to and why is that Joseph? I do not fear any action he may take, I fear nothing."

Joseph tried a conciliatory approach, "I do understand Febra, I do."

The girls face instantly changed, "Oh you understand do you. You understand the feel of his hands, the hot breath and sweat staining me. You see my friend Joseph, I can deal with the beatings and the rapes and the hate but its the ones who think they are giving you love, them I truly despise. The ones who want to hold you close after they have you. You understand nothing and you can not understand me because you will never endure what I do."

290

She began to settle back and her breathing calmed. "Let Orn do as he sees fit but I wish only the worst fate for men that think they can control and manipulate others."

They remained at the camp for a few more days, although they spent much of the time apart, Speck with the Shaman, Arn with Dance, Joseph on the market stalls, helping with chores and village business. Oddly after the meeting with Orn, Febra could often be seen outside his tent, she did not speak again to Joseph but Dance brought word to them on the tenth day of their stay.

"This is a strange news, I have heard from Orn that he has placed Febra under debt. A curious outcome it has to be said, I expected her to be banished or similar. I do not recall this happening with an outsider before."

Joseph queried the words, "What does that mean for her?"

"Effectively she is in the Elder's service. She has to serve her debt until she he gives her leave to be free once more. It could be a day or years, depending on when Orn decides it. She has accepted it apparently."

Arn pushed his leg out, stretching the healing wound, "I too have an announcement of sorts. I intend to stay with Dance to help the Huskian's in their fight against Bast'wa. I feel I owe it to those who died."

Dance looked at the hunter pointedly and he spoke as he looked into her eyes, "And....I would stay regardless, with her."

Joseph smiled, "Our hunter is in love Speck!" he patted Arn on the back, good for you. "Of course we will help. Won't we Speck."

"No. I am afraid there seems to be a different road for me." Speck's tone was sombre as he spoke, "I have spent many hours with the Shaman and I have once again looked in the book, it all seems to be pointing me to this tower. I have never felt such a pull but I know it is where I must head. I am sorry to leave and..," he turned to Dance, "I hope you can understand, I do want to help your people. Yet I feel I must move on, perhaps I will return, I am unsure. I think Gru-Staedak's poem and the Shaman guide me to the same purpose."

Dance tenderly spoke, "I think your journey is elsewhere little conjurer. I knew when we first met you were different and the shaman knows it too. It has been a long time since he spoke so much in a persons company. If he guides you then trust the spirits will join you in that journey."

Joseph was confused, he could not leave his friend to travel alone but he wanted to help the Huskian's. "Speck I....I can not leave you but I too feel a debt to these people."

Dance looked at Arn, she could see the love the the two friends had for each other and wanted to ease their pain. In the end she knew Joseph would not leave Speck to travel alone.

"I know a way you can help us and your friend. Orn needs a messenger to leave for Vedian as soon as possible, they need to travel in secrecy and men on the road undercover of merchants moving to Vedian would be a lot less obvious than a Huskian from the south. Speck what road do you mean to take?"

"It is not clear but I think the Tower lies between the border of Asten and Coralis, we could follow the Vedian road all the way to the north and then as it moved east I can split off through the forest."

Arn's eyebrows shot up, "Through Malevolence! That's a pleasant journey to be had indeed. However you are right it would save you days going around it and that would mean moving back into one of the towns which I assume you would want to avoid."

Joseph looked at Speck, "I will do as Dance suggests and go with you to the forest and then we will break company and I will deliver the Huskian's message to Vedian."

They sat together that night for a final meal, Dance recounted to Febra their decisions and even the girl sat down to eat, although she remained silent throughout. Arn spouted stories and as ever lifted the spirits of those around him, he was becoming popular in the village and the local Huskian's had really taken to his demeanour.

"Mind yourself now lads, word has reached here of more trouble in the towns to the north, we do not know how much more militia is on the road. When we started this little journey I would have bet against you getting out of your own front doors intact but now. Well, events changes men and my little fellow," he slapped Specks back so hard he nearly fell forward, "you are quite the surprise package! I am travelling with a patrol to scout the Lough borders for activity from Bast'wa tomorrow, so we will leave together and you get a Huskian escort through the desert, which I think we can be appreciate is a must. What about you Febra? " Arn turned to look at the girl, picking at her food, "What does tomorrow deliver you?"

Febra looked up, "I remain with Orn," she stopped and then begun again, "I am sorry to see you both go. I wish you well on your journey. I would ask just one thing. Will you keep an ear for Rundell's name in Vedian Joseph?"

They all started at his name, so much had happened since Bannermane they had planned to find out more in Kanegon but events had overtaken them.

"Yes Febra, yes I will. I thank you for reminding me, he was too good a man and we remain in his debt"

Arn picked up his wine cup, "A toast then to Rundell."

"Rundell," the others from the Luff spoke repeated together. They slept outside as the fire burned down to leave only the simmering embers, Joseph took one last look at the night sky of the Inpur desert and wondered if he would ever return to see it again.

The day after Lint had been treated on the shores of Imanis they arrived back at the village. Vale had persuaded Madistrin to hold on his venture to the university, first returning to collect a horse and cart so they could transport Lint back to her house. His guardian was desperately ill, the fever had failed to break and Vale feared he would not last unless it did.

"I can treat him better at home with my other provisions." Madistrin was not about to give up on the man that had saved his life and they lifted him carefully onto the cart. Once they were at the border of the village they covered Lint with leather skins and the Crown Prince pulled on a large hood to cover his face. There were a couple of waves from other villagers Vale knew but no one looked to intercept them, they pulled up to her house and carefully carried the pale body of Lint inside. Vale was stronger than her figure suggested and she took most of the weight as Madistrin continued to struggle on his weaker leg.

293

The apothecary placed the warrior in her own bed, she had made up a wash to clean his body, unbuttoning his jerkin and removing his clothes so as she could properly cleanse his body from the sweat that permeated it. Madistrin happy in the knowledge Lint was in the best care let her know he was going to scout out the university. She explained the entrance locations and the best way in under cover. Instructing him to take some herbs from the shop and a basket and if challenged to say he was delivering to the University on her behalf. Madistrin was determined, he knew this was not his skill but he had to get to DeFache. He gathered the items as instructed and walked out of the village on the track, keeping his head down and avoiding direct eye contact. He initially took the path that led out to the university and then veered north to the tree line that surrounded its grounds. The huge oak surround provided good cover as he circled past, he could hear an occasional voice but activity outside the university seemed limited. From the trees he could make out the trades entrance down a flight of steps at the rear of the building, two men stood outside, neither bore the Imanis crest on their uniform, so he assumed they were not university guards. He paused unsure what to do, Parran would have him flee, run with his tail between his legs back to the mainland. By then it could be too late for DeFache or worse still, Vedian. He had to act. He placed the herbs from Vale's shop into the basket he had brought and carried them at his side, took a sharp intake of breath and walked down the steps.

The guards discussion was interrupted by his arrival, "Well its better than the bloody city duty this. At least.......you, what's your business?"

Madistrin was careful not to look at them directly, "I am delivering for the kitchens, herbs for the pot."

"Well give em here and we'll take em in." One of the guards put out a hand to take the basket.

"No, no. I have to get the cook to choose what she wants. They are fussy here, only fresh and best herb for Scholatic."

"That's about right mate, bloody snobs, sitting in their towers talking gibberish. Go on, go through but be quick about it." The guards waved him inside and carried on their attack at the class system of Vedian.

294

Madistrin was sweating, he was also trying hard to manage his weaker leg. It was agony walking for this long without his stick but he did not want anything to give him away, to reveal his true identity. These might be city guards for all he knew and they could well have served in or around his own house, although he suspected not, Parran was very cautious who served close to the Crown Prince. They were more likely mercenaries or Scholatic militia, either way not friendly to the name of Madistrin.

The flight of steps from the rear entrance led straight to the kitchens at the base of the university. He could hear a bustling as people went about their business, carrying pots of stew and chopping various vegetables.

He was here, now what on earth did he do? He would never find his way round, in an impetuous moment the Crown Prince of Vedian took a gamble.

"You boy where is his Prominence? I have leave to see him with special herbs for his thinking."

That last bit had not come out quite as he intended, he half smiled at the lad, he was slender with bright yellow hair cut in a circular bowl.

"I imagine DeFache is longing for some," he cast his eyes into the basket, "parsley and lavender. I am not convinced by its thinking properties by they both hold a lovely aroma." The young lad grinned and gestured for him to follow. They walked through the kitchens and into a recess under a large staircase.

"One chance for the truth, just one. Who are you? As you are no herb dealer, at least not one whose lore extends beyond the most basic principles."

He did not think, he just spoke, looking into the boys eyes and inherently knowing that he could trust him, "I am Crown Prince Madistrin and I need to find DeFache for the sake of Vedian, please take me to him."

"Thank you. I am Samuel, I tend to his Prominence's gardens, I know who you are, assuming you are of who you speak. His lord is held in his main library under guard, he is forbidden to leave the area, held captive by Scholatic guard from SanPollan.

Suddenly Madistrin understood, "You. You are the boy who DeFache has had residing in the university walls. It is you that

295

Shel-Toro uses to weaken DeFache and hold him against his will. For it is clear SanPollan is just a tool of the councils will and that will is bound solely to Shel-Toro himself."

Samuel bowed his head, the shame was apparent, "Yes, I am to blame and I begged my master for a different outcome. I wanted to leave and never return to save him from this. Yet he insisted this was my home, this was where I belong and he told me you should never be parted from where you belong." The boys voice was welling up as he spoke in such a heartfelt manner.

"Well right now, that is not of consequence. You have to get me to him."

"I might be able to get you in the library but beyond that they will never let you speak with him. He is completely locked down from communicating with anyone."

"Communication has a way of usurping the greatest chains lad. Just get me to him, please."

Samuel led him up the main staircase and through a long hallway the balcony of which looked down below at the entrance area to the university. They moved past a run of endless doors until finally they turned a corner to reveal a circular dead end. A guard stood idly at the only doorway, slumped against the wall and gnawing down on an old pig leg. He threw it onto the plate on the floor as they approached.

"What business?"

"We bring herb for his Prominence, it is for his knees, they are lame." Samuel spoke with a great confidence.

"I have no orders for herb. Get away with you boy and you go on." He waved them away.

"I do not think your lord SanPollan will be pleased to hear his Prominence has fallen to the gout due to your order. For the knees are swollen with the bloods, he needs Sarsaparilla and Parsley to reduce the swelling."

The guard peered into the basket. "Looks like lavender."

"Well of course it does. Have you ever seen Sarsaparilla?" Samuel looked incredulously at the man.

"Nope."

"There we are then. Now please let us just get these herbs applied and we can be on our way."

"Get on with it then and no talking." The guard grasped the door using a bronze long handle and proceeded to kick it open.

Inside the room was piled high with books in every direction, some of the shelves rose as high as the ceiling, others housed singular huge volumes behind glass windows. In the centre a large rug lay, stitched into it the crest of Imanis. A small plain desk in the centre, carved from a wood Madistrin was not familiar with and on an upright chair, bent over a papyrus and quill sat DeFache. He looked older somehow, bent, his tiny spectacles resting on top of his long nose.

As he turned, he caught the eyes of Madistrin for a moment, a pure moment of intensity and understanding. The guard from the corridor emerged and shouted at his two colleagues, one standing near the window, the other coming out from behind the maze of book shelves.

"They have to give medicine, get them in and out." He retreated and slammed the door tight.

Samuel who had not seen his lord for days started to speak, "My Lord..."

The guard by the window was quick to intercede, "Shut up boy. No speaking, do your medicine in silence or not at all."

Samuel pulled out straight DeFache's leg, indicating the area they would treat by rubbing just under his knee.

"Fair enough Wilam, could you be as good as to fetch that stool I use to collect the high books so I can rest my leg on it. I could ask them but of course that would be conversing, which I know you are very much against." DeFache smiled at the guard as he walked round the back of the tallest bookshelf tutting and swearing to himself.

DeFache's mind was swimming with possibilities, why was Madistrin here? How was he here and why was he alone? Where was Parran? Something dire must have happened. He picked up the parchment and wrote quickly, three questions that's all there would be time for. Scribbling his words down he turned the paper to face Madistrin.

Are you alone?

297

How wide is Shel-Toro's influence?

Is Vedian in danger?

Madistrin thought quickly as the guard handed him the leather stool. DeFache turned over the paper, he was pretty certain the man could not read but he was not going to take any chances.

Madistrin lifted up DeFache's leg onto the stool, "Come on boy I feel like I am alone here! Now keep the application wide on the knee, That's it, no wider. For god sake boy I have travelled from Kanegon to Pluris and I have never since such incompetence. If we do not treat this right, immediately, it is in danger of infection and then who knows what. We have to fight it now." Madistrin looked up to DeFache and if it had not been clear from his words, it was plain from his face. Shel-Toro and the council had reached out far and removing DeFache was just part of a wider plot. He wished upon everything that he had been quicker to travel to Asten, to seek out Gru-Staedak. Why had he ever let a wedge be driven between them, he had thought Shel-Toro's words to have been right, that the old man was causing trouble in the council for no reason. He had treated him poorly and given no will to his words, he was ashamed of his behaviour and his actions. Now the time had come to put things right, to start to balance the scales before Vedian paid the price for his mistake.

"That does feel better already but I think it would improve faster if bound." He looked back to Wilam who had returned to the window area, "Could they be given leave to return tonight with bindings, once the ointment has worked into the area. That would be a great relief." DeFache groaned slightly, as if to accentuate the pain he was in.

"Yes what ever. Back tonight. Now both of you out of my sight."

Madistrin afforded himself one more glance at the scholar before they departed the room, he just needed a sign, some idea of what DeFache intended him to do. As he begun to turn the door opened and the guard outside stepped through and grabbed him by the hood, "On your way, both of you. Get out." He pushed Samuel and Madistrin from the room and slammed the heavy door shut, then went about attending to the remaining carcass that was left on his plate.

As they walked side by side down the long corridor Samuel whispered, "What are we to do? What does he bid us do?"

"Tonight we must return and somehow we are going to reclaim Imanis."

They left the village in the early morning, everyone travelled apart from Febra, she never strayed far from Elder Orn's side now. She nodded as they left, Joseph thought to give her a hug, while he no longer seemed to feel affection towards he still felt a sense of responsibility and wanted to give her comfort but he did think she would thank him for it. So instead he smiled and waved goodbye, it felt odd leaving without her. Dance and Arn accompanied them with two other Huskian's for the first days march, they made the borders of the desert by nightfall taking the quickest route north in an effort to meet up with the Lough road.

Arn, Joseph and Speck talked about their journey and mostly about what was ahead of them. Joseph had decided that once he had delivered his message to Pluris he would go home to the Luff. He had been gone for so long now and his mother would be more than worried, he longed for the simplicity of the village, the comfort of the inn and market. Speck was less certain but determined, he had seen the Tower in his visions, in the book, in the words of the shaman and the poem. He had no doubt it held something of great importance for him and he felt no fear of it.

"Be careful of all those ghosts and ghouls in the forest my friend," the hunter joked, "they may creep up behind you," he waved his arms in the air.

"I am more concerned about militia and bandits on the road, than anything from fairy stories and children's rhymes." Speck retorted.

At dawn the company broke, they embraced and smiled, only Dance could see the tears in Arn's eyes as they walked west. "Is this truly what you want my love?"

"I could never leave you now. They are not the men I left the Luff with, they can protect themselves now. I will stand by your people and I will stand with you. Perhaps one day if willing, we will meet again."

"If the spirits wish it my love." They disappeared from view, headed for the borders of Kanegon.

"Are we doing the right thing Speck. Something feels wrong about splitting up. I know Arn will look after Febra as best he can."

"My friend I would be more worried about us than them. They have all the muscle, we are left with our wits to protect us. However the news is good, for I have mine about me and it will carry us to the Pluris road at least, I hope."

Arn had estimated they had a weeks walk ahead of them to where the Asten and Pluris road intersected with the Lough southern road. It was the busiest crossing in all of Vedian, any part of the country could be reached from that point, so they expected a lot of activity on the trail leading up to it. Strangely nothing could have been further from the truth, for the first two days they had not seen a sole and for the next three only an odd traveller who would move on by without as much as a greeting.

"Seems odd," Joseph said on their sixth day. "We are getting close now, we should surely be seeing more merchants on the road than this?"

"I agree, something does seem out of place, tomorrow lets be cautious in our approach to the crossroads, maybe just walk a little deeper into the trail, away from the road."

They talked about just about everything over a week, Vedian, the book, Arn and Febra but Joseph was intrigued the most by Speck's development.

"So what does it feel like?"

"It's incredible, for the first time in my life, I feel strong. Energised, like I can do anything. Afterwards I am spent but it is worth it." Speck smiled as he spoke.

"What do you hope to find in this tower?"

"I do not know, guidance perhaps? I just feel all the portents are pushing me towards it. I know its selfish leaving the Huskian's, leaving you Joseph but all my life I have sat in the shadows. The village never truly felt like home, they all put up with me but I always felt a little different. When I first read the book, when I read the incantations it was like I had come home. It just feels right. I hope you can understand that, I do not part company on a whim Joseph. In truth I would rather we stayed together."

Joseph put his arm around Speck's shoulder, "I know my friend and me too but we both have something we have to do. Once I have delivered my message perhaps we will meet back on the road or on our return home to the Luff."

Speck nodded but inside he knew his home would never be the Luff again.

They camped as usual, a small fire and heated some of the stew the Huskian's had prepared for their journey, it was a succulent meat, lightly salted to taste. They slept well under a cool night sky, their sleep undisturbed from the world around. They had become used to sleeping outdoors and awoke the next day refreshed, departing the road as agreed and approaching from an inward track, only fifty metres away but enough to give them some anonymity.

Mid morning they heard voices, multiple figures were up ahead on the road, some sitting, some standing and a vocal debate was being staged between two men. They crouched down trying to hear what was being said.

Both men were in armour, the closest was part of the militia from what they could see but the other one was different. For a start he wore full chain armour, not the lighter garb of the other man and his voice was well spoken, not the common tongue of a man raised on the streets of Pluris.

"These men are to join the Sixth ranks and march straight for Pluris borders, report there to Commander Grey. That is a direct order of the Scholatic council, I do not suggest you ignore it."

"What you mean. We have done what we were told, we took Kanegon in a couple of days, the boys just looking for a few extra gifts on the road. Ay boys!" he shouted out to the other men, who murmured agreement at his comments.

"I am not a fool Dulcet, so do not take me for one. I know exactly why you brought your men here, to prey on the merchants that convene at the crossing. It stops now, we have work to do."

"Something wrong with you lot. Hanging around with the scholars has made you soft." He spat on the ground, running his hand through his rough beard.

"Perhaps. It does not change the fact, that we have now occupied all major towns with the one key exception. We need to build before we look to take Pluris, it is by far the most well guarded by the royal protectors. As such we need all militia not holding in the other cities to the front in preparation. Your usual coin will be forthcoming"

"And if we wanted a little more, to do their bidding."

"Then you should consider again your demands as foolhardy and not befitting a man of your standing in the community." The well armoured man took a slight step forward, it was enough to make Dulcet back down quickly.

"Alright, alright. Men pack up, were moving to Pluris. Hold your moaning and grab your packs. That good enough for you Captain?"

"For now. I have business in Coralis, mind you arrive promptly and no more detours. Tell the commander I will be back to Pluris two weeks from today and if all goes as planned, we will have sufficient army to march."

The men quickly packed up their belongings, mercenaries they may be but they had all served at one point or other and knew how to follow orders and the benefits of doing so. The crossing had soon cleared allowing Joseph to speak for the first time.

"My god Speck, what has happened? First Asten, then Kanegon and from what he said Coralis as well, only the capital still stands free. Why would the Scholatic wage war on its own country? We must get word to the Crown Prince on two counts now, I have to move quickly, I am sorry Speck I had hoped we would camp here one more night before we parted but the urgency is too great."

"I want to go with you Joseph, the road feels very dangerous now but I just know Vedian may need other types of assistance in days to come and my path is not the same as yours." Tears came to the young mans eyes as he embraced his friend tightly.

"You take care of yourself Speck, I mean it, do whatever you need to keep yourself safe. Use what you have learned and be careful who you trust."

"Whatever I learn, I seem to unlearn! But you too, stay out of sight, those militia do not look the friendly type."

Speck stood and waved until he could no longer make out Joseph's figure in the distance, he paused for a moment and walked north off the main road. The junction ran west to Kanegon and Asten, east to Pluris there was no path to the north laid out. That way was just the forest and no one chose to go there.

For a land so limited in its wood and tree, it was a true irony they had a whole forest of trees stood untouched. Speck remembered his childhood the tales and rhymes of the haunted wood but in truth he had learned from the book why the forest stood untouched. The invaders had brought a herb lore that poisoned all the trees, leaving them brittle and grey, nothing in this land ever grew again but the old Redwoods continued to stand like huge towering ghosts reflecting a different time. It had been this that forced the Kanegon sailors abroad for logging and was the key reason wood had become so scarce in the land.

They called it the Forest of Malevolence not due to the ghosts or spirits that roamed within but the punishment that had been placed on the land, that was the true malice that forever was placed on Vedian. Speck had begun to wonder if it was a fitting punishment, he had looked at the book a number of times since they left, each night when they camped he would open it and get a glimpse of history as if he was there. It had become clear the enemy of Vedian had been brought to the shores not from hatred or greed but through need. They simply wanted to recover what had been falsely taken from them and the King seeing only an invasion went to war. A war that was as Great as any seen and as long as any held and for what, Speck mulled it over in his mind as he trudged through the tall trees, kicking at the brittle remnants that littered the ground.

He felt the first few droplets on his shoulders and then in the space of a moment the heavens opened with force, grabbing at his pack he pulled out the long hood and cape he had brought with him. By the time it was on, the rain was sheeting down, there were no leaves to shelter under, the trees stripped bare of foliage. He pushed on looking to keep a north trail, while there was no shelter from the weather, it at least ensured he would not be lost, as the sky darkened the stars became easily visible to navigate from.

Speck hoped he would be through the forest by tomorrow night at latest if he kept on a straight line. He sat down got out his leather sheet and tried to get as comfortable as possible in the damp and wet that surrounded him. He carefully pulled the book out, keeping it as near to his body as he could and pulling over his hood to protect it. He begun to read and the familiar feeling washed through his body.

He awoke with a start, looking around the forest was gone, he stood looking back at it, on a hill. What had happened? He remembered opening the book but could not recall what he saw and how had he got here, this had not happened before, he was still wet but the rains had ceased. Speck was confused and he turned to see what was ahead, in front of him at the base of the hill was a structure like none he had ever seen. A cylinder shaped tower, rising perhaps one hundred feet in the air, taller than any building he had seen on his travels but perhaps only twenty foot in diameter. Its building blocks were like a white chalk, deeply chiselled with indents, it lacked only one thing, a single detail to make it complete in his mind. The tower had no door.

Shel-Toro arrived in Pluris university as Joseph and Speck had parted ways, his journey from Coralis had been long and he ached. He longed for a warm bath and a sleep but matters had to be attended too. He had been pleased by SanPollan's news from Imanis, DeFache was under house arrest and could do no further ills, this became more crucial when he had become aware of what had befallen Asten and the death of Gru-Staedak.

That was not part of his plan but he had known there would be consequences. In truth the old man was becoming a problem, too outspoken for his own good, Shel-Toro knew it was for the greater good but he mourned a learned and respected brother falling in such a physical fashion. Had DeFache found out about these events it would have spurred him to an action, that up to now, Shel-Toro had worked hard to keep concealed. So SanPollan had proved very useful, coupling this with the removal of Madistrin he would soon be rewarded with a seat in the highs.

News of the artifact had gone silent after the affray at the university, his Captain had tracked it as far as Asten but with everything going that happened he did not want to be distracted from his main goal. There would be time to find these four from the Luff once Pluris was subdued. It was a disappointment, he longed to look in the pages crafted by a Scholatic great as

304

MonPellia truly was. What a shame they had no idea what they held, more than just a written tome. He allowed himself a smile, the benefit of the common man was his guaranteed ignorance in the way of books.

He was focused now on Pluris, once the Captain had concluded his business in Coralis and returned they would ready for the final step, then they would hold force in all cities and the Scholatic could control and protect. Shel-Toro breathed a sigh, it had been a long road, from the thinking, to the writing of lore, to the planning, the motivation of the council, years of work.

He knew a great scholar had to able to show patience amongst everything and he had been nothing but patient over the years. He had seen Vedian's squabble and fight amongst themselves for land, for goods. He had seen Kanegon become nothing but a home for lawlessness and bandits. Women and children scared to walk streets for fear of thieves and curs, he had been more patient than any could be. His cause was thought through, it had Scholatic infallibility through publication and debate with his peers. Yes he had seen it necessary to at times debate the more sensitive plans to a select part of the council but he could not be accountable for the poor behaviour of DeFache and Gru-Staedak.

A loud knock came at his study door. "Prominence, I am so sorry, he insists it is urgent, I have explained your long travels my lord."

"Who is it Burberry?" Shel-Toro enquired in a tired voice.

"Captain Parran from the Crown Prince royal guard my lord."

"Show him in." Shel-Toro seated himself, this was interesting, Parran must by now be aware something was wrong.

"My Captain please be seated, I am sorry my man has been tardy, my journeys do tax me these days." He gestured Parran to another chair.

"Thank you Prominence I will stand, I wish only to convey urgency. My liege is missing, he went to visit Imanis a few days past and has not been seen."

"That news is grave and unknown to me. For what was his visit in aid of my I ask?" Shel-Toro looked directly at Parran, eagerly looking to the read the soldiers reply.

"He was researching family history and Prominence DeFache had offered Imanis at his disposal."

A good answer Shel-Toro thought, that had been versed in advance, Imanis did have superb records of royal history, DeFache was quite the expert.

"I see. Well I have had no word from my learned colleagues. The ships captain?"

"Nothing my Lord, no sign of the ship or its captain."

"This is terrible news, I will immediately send envoys to Imanis."

Parran interjected, "No need, I have sent men to the island to search the coast for the ship, if there is any wrong doing, they will find it."

Shel-Toro noted the veiled threat. Parran was not to be trifled with, he had been Crown Prince Protector for a long time, he was not like most men, he was more of a thinker, if Shel-Toro did not know better he would say the man had a little Scholatic in him.

"Well Captain, my office and I are at your disposal. Let us ensure we keep this quiet, we would not wish to worry the people."

Parran bowed and begun to leave, "I will find whomever is responsible my lord, there will be justice."

"Indeed there will Captain, I will demand justice for Vedian."

Parran walked quickly to his quarters, he had asked his three closest lieutenants to meet him. He acknowledged them all briefly and with a heavy heart relayed what he had discovered, "He knows, I think part of him wants to tell me. He will ensure the people know soon as well, that will create unrest. Reports?"

The three men provided updates from the west, north-east and south-west, all the same, militia had occupied the towns under the Scholatic banner, curfews were in place. Finally men were massing on the Pluris eastern border in the foothills, over three hundred already and more arrived each day.

"What is your best estimate Rayan, when will they push?" Parran asked of the tallest and youngest of the lieutenants.

Rayan had served only a few years and had quickly escalated up the ranks, he was resilient and calm, a quality Parran held above all others. He ran the swords attachment of the Royal guards from Coralis. "My eyes tell me more are still joining from the main road and some up from the Lough, they are not just militia anymore, they appear to be recruiting mercenaries out of Kanegon."

"This fight will have little in the way of honour if that is the case but it will not be won in the field but in the pulpit. Without Madistrin or DeFache we lose the will of the people to the silver tongue of Shel-Toro. Until they are found, we must hold Pluris."

Rayan asked the question the others were thinking, "And what if they have been assassinated as we fear?"

"Then we will hold Pluris until the last men-at-arms remains, whilst the royal banner flies over Pluris we have hope. And when hope is gone, we will do without it and fight on, I am the last descendant of the Sabre Regiment and I will honour their name. Will you stand with me in a blood oath?"

Each man in turn drew a small blade and cut across their hands, a few drops of blood dropping into a cup placed on the table. In turn they touched the cup to their lips and far away beyond the forest line, Speck could see in his mind a door opening.

Chapter 16 - Tower of Ethindral

"To see them take the field was to see angels walk amongst men. Glorious in their tightly strapped leather, animated in their whispering robes. With staff and sword moving in tandem, turning and striking, slashing and slicing, they truly were titans of the battlefield.

And yet once stripped of the environment and trappings of battle and war these enchanters often seemed shy and quiet in their reverence.

As these oxymoron's walked the battlefields beside us, the fear in ourselves was only outstripped by that felt by our enemies."

'The Candlemen' - Battle Scribe Tiber – Vedian 575

"Everything is within my grasp and I choose to see that as an affirmation of my fundamental beliefs. I began imperfect and remain that way it seems. Not such a hard thing to accept."

The dawn light was creeping into the sky and from the tower balcony it back lit the majestic mountains to the north-east. Was it pure chance that such a conversation took place before this display of beauty and harmony? Or had it been predetermined so that the point would be punctuated with emphasis?

"Everyone takes part in the same struggle and decisions as us Lucent.", he spoke softly but still surprised Speck. "The enchantments merely underlines that need to us."

Remys continued as Speck stared out across the horizon, "The control we have over forces is directly linked to our belief system. If we study the great practitioners we find that those of a neutral aspect; such as the followers of the balance that seem so rife in our times, have much more subtle abilities. A typical example might be clairvoyance or premonition. But studying the exceptionally powerful cases we find that they lie at either end of the spectrum. The infamous Saban Monks wielded tremendous destructive power and it can be traced directly to their belief in a cruel and selfish world. What little we know of the Vedian mages of old points to tremendous morality and inner enlightenment, so we should not be surprised to find out that they hold skills of a creative and defensive nature."

Speck nodded slowly as he digested this information, it seemed that the magic he had thought of as a simple gift was in fact the fruits of the soul, more of a symptom of the wielders condition. What did his power say about him? Remys looked sympathetically at him, as if reading the troubling thoughts in his head.

"You may choose to believe that the power and yourself are one and the same, that nature has made you the way you are.", he peered at the boy to see if this thought had alleviated any of his angst. Remys secretly hoped that it would not.

"Down that path would lie too many troubling things.", Speck answered slowly, "I would be saying that I have no responsibility over my actions, I would be avoiding my powers of self-determination; if possible I would rather believe that my energy springs from what I choose my soul to be. If I chose otherwise I would create a self-fulfilling prophecy."

"I am deeply gratified to hear you say that, for it is my own heart-felt opinion that gifted ones are either formed by their powers or forge it on the anvil of their own will. I too was troubled by the darker side of my abilities until I earnestly set myself to controlling it."

"Have you succeeded?"

"It seems that I will never lose my ability to destroy, but my effort has not been without reward. Creative abilities I had never dreamed of are now available to me when the time is right."

With that he stood up and left the room, motioning Speck to follow him. It seemed that Remys must have been incredibly busy that morning for his room within the tower had all been recently cleaned and prepared with his bed made fresh wash bowl laid out and firewood for the newly cleaned hearth.

"Dash!", Remys slapped his own forehead, "What am I thinking not providing any food. It's a wonder we get so few guests here."

He entered a door that led from from the bedroom into the main tower and indicated he would be back in a moment, Speck sat and washed his hands, the clean water felt good on his skin. True to his word Remys returned with what appeared to be the

309

left-overs from a magnificent feast on a large steel platter, Speck wondered who the lonely candle man might have been entertaining.

Remys apologised profusely about not having anything ready for him and hoped the scraps would do for the moment, promising to provide something a bit better later on. The platter of cold meat and prepared fruit disappeared into the belly of the young man in short order, as left-overs went these were the best they had ever tasted. Remys sat and watched in a gratified manner as he rubbed his stomach and wiped the grease from his face.

"So Lucent tell me your tale. You have come a long way to be with us, what drove you to our door?" Remys sat down on the chair next to Speck and crossed his legs, as if to settle in for a long story.

"All my life I have felt so useless, so weak around others the opposite to my friend Arn, he is so strong and confident. When I tapped into this energy, I felt renewed, full of potential, it was incredible. Like nothing I have ever experienced and I just knew there was more in this world for me. I find it hard to explain Remys."

"Yes Lucent as do I. It is hard to explain love to one who has never felt its true embrace. Here at this tower you never have to explain yourself for every person who resides here feels it to. We are kin in our knowledge and this is our shelter."

Speck thought for a moment, "Why do others not come, I could not understand how no one was aware of it. Its visible from a good distance, even with the forest?"

"Our beliefs have their fringe benefits, there are two shields that hold us safe, one to cover the tower entirely. That only works from distance, once you are close it is viewable, the second is the enchantment that covers the doorway. That is a strong incantation and yet you saw straight through it. You are one of us, so that makes some sense I suppose." he appeared to be gazing at Speck's face, looking at it like a puzzle to be solved. "It is enough to keep out prying eyes and ears, our position near the forest keeps most away, the power of the mind is powerful when it comes to tales of childhood it seems. Now you talked of tapping into the energy, how did you perform this. It is different for everyone you see, how they discover their gift."

310

Speck took a deep breath, he wanted, almost needed to tell Remys everything a sense of needing to unburden himself. So he slowly recounted the sum of their adventures that had lead him to the tower. Remys had an attentive ear and asked a great deal of penetrating questions, quite often he would stop Speck to ask about Arn or Febra, some detail he felt had been left out. Before he knew it the morning was over and Remys clapped his hands together.

"Well you are quite the storyteller Master Lucent. Let us take some hot tea and perhaps you are ready for your lessons to commence?"

"What lessons are these Remys?"

"What you came for, knowledge, power perhaps," he looked back at Speck, "time will tell what you seek. Time to guide you through the maze that must be carefully trodden."

"I can not stay too long Remys. I want to learn, I truly do more than anything but I am concerned.." he did not get to finish.

"You fear for your friend Joseph, do you not? I could hear it in your voice, the indecision in the parting of ways in your tale. He must be a very special individual to drive you in such a way."

"He is my friend."

"Let us commence and we will see, you will find you have more time than you perhaps think, in these walls at least. Think not on it now, immerse yourself in the gifts we can share with you. Then we can seek which is the truth."

Joseph's path to the capital city had been a slow one, he had been forced to stay off the road due to the militia and the side trials were becoming more rocky and difficult terrain as the road veered east and north closer towards the Coralis mountains. By the time he reached two miles shy of Pluris he was forced to stop altogether. Across the road and for some distance in both directions a small army was camped, effectively the city had been embargoed. No caravans were being allowed to enter or exit and although he was careful to not wander too close, he could see all over the camp the crest of the Scholatic flying.

He crouched silently behind a boulder that sat upon the hillside to the north of the road, thinking about how he was going to get around the camp without being noticed.

A voice softly spoken whispered in his ear making him turn quickly, "No way through there lad."

A man dressed head to toe in a forest green leather stood in front of him. "Don't worry they can't see you from this elevation and they lack any form of attentiveness if they could. I am sorry to startle you."

The man smiled, Joseph was struggling to make out all his face shrouded in the hood he wore. "I assume you are trying to get back into Pluris?"

"My business is none of yours sir." Joseph moved to walk away.

"No you are right. I wish I had time to help you but I have my own matters to hand." The man started to move over the rocks, heading parallel with the road.

Joseph thought better of it initially but then decided to chance a question, "Do you know another way into the city?"

"They are not all here yet. Just move round to the north, the guard posts further round are much less dense. You can slip in under cover of night still. My farewell, safe passage."

Joseph reflected for just a second and ran towards the man, "What do you mean 'yet'?"

"I mean in a few more days, maybe a week or two that army will march on the capital and when they arrive you better hope your not still in it." He spoke with a forlorn voice, Joseph felt for the man.

"I know of this in some small way, I am sorry, I am just delivering a message into the city. I wish I could do more."

"No matter lad, you go about your task. I fear my chores will never end."

Joseph spoke before he really thought it through, "Is there anything I can do to help you?"

The man smiled and then quietly laughed, "We stand at dusk, in a city under siege, mercenaries and bandits litter the land and you ask a man that you have never met, never laid eyes on, if you can help them. Well my boy, you are either a gift or a fool."

"I...I...just....." Joseph stammered feeling embarrassed.

"I am sorry lad. I truly am but unless you can find the Crown Prince Madistrin then I am afraid your goodwill and honesty is for naught." He smiled again and pulled down his hood, his features were classic, a smooth shaped angular jaw with glass blue eyes and long blonde locks of hair flowed down to shoulder level. "I am Redrick my friend."

Joseph was confused, what did he know of the Crown Prince, was he missing? He had never been sure how to deliver the message but Elder Orn had been clear it was not to pass through another, an audience had to be requested for its delivery.

"This is grave news. Is Madistrin missing?" Joseph enquired.

The green clad man looked at him enquiringly. "Do you know the Crown Prince? Well, yes or no?"

Joseph was unsure how much to say or not to say to the stranger. "Can it be yes and no perhaps? I am on an errand," Joseph said cautiously, "I have to deliver something to the Crown Prince."

Redrick smiled ruefully "Then I fear you have journeyed for nothing. The Crown Prince has been missing for days, no one has seen him. Rumours are rife in Pluris he has fallen but the city is full of fish wives tales, so take this as you will."

"But my message has to go to him alone, I have to seek an audience you see." Joseph was uncertain of what to do.

Redrick turned his head slightly, "A message of that sort must be important, usually a request or dispute is handed via his court. A personal audience could only be requested from a very few. Who do you bear message from lad"

Joseph suddenly realised he knew nothing about this man, "I am not at liberty to say. I think I should be going." He started to move.

"Hold a moment, "I am not going to harm you. Just answer this. Is your message from a friend?" Redrick almost held his breath, could it be DeFache trying to make contact.

"I am not sure. It is not a foe of that I can be confident. It is a call for help."

"You are not going to give it up easily and I am not going to harm you, it is not my way. What will you do now, knowing Madistrin is not here?"

"I do not know. Who would be in charge in his absence?"

"The charge falls to the Scholatic but while his banner flies over the city it is not permanent. That is in the hands of his Lord Protector Parran and he will never remove it without proof of death.

"Then perhaps Lord Parran should be the one I seek out." Joseph mused on the idea.

"Perhaps. He is a trustworthy man, though he may have little time for you at present. Come, I will at least help you find a path in before we part ways."

"That's is kind of you, what is your business, I did not ask."

"Ah, that is one of understanding. I wanted to see what was amassing outside the city and how many. Information we need in preparation for any attack."

Joseph checked the words, "We?"

"I am Redrick of Coralis and I am part of a group of people who believe defending this city in the name of the Crown Prince is just and right. My town of Coralis has already fallen under militia control a week back, I have escaped to find Madistrin and seek his help. What I found was the same story across all of Vedian. Curfews and martial law in every town, with only the capital still standing free. Looking around us, you wonder for how long."

Joseph walked along the undulating ground, "Why would they do this? Who is behind it?"

"A fair question and in that part I can truly answer only the second part. The leader of the Scholatic high council is Prominence Shel-Toro, we are certain the plot is his. For some time there has been issues within the council, with members sidelined or removed from office while others grew politically beyond their measure."

"Can anyone not be promoted in the Scholatic?" Joseph enquired.

"To a degree yes but historically the council seats have always been given to the most learned and well written. The retirement of Gru-Staedak was against the principle of the council."

At the sound of his name Joseph looked sharply at Redrick, "Gru-Staedak, I knew him. He was dear to me for a short time."

Redrick looked at Joseph with a new found respect, "Then lad there's more about you than meets the eye. Gru-Staedak suffered few others in his latter days as I understood it. He must have seen something in you worth noticing. Fate is a funny thing is it not?"

Joseph smiled at Redrick, he had already warmed to the man, he reminded him of Arn, polished and rugged at the same time. Like a lost prince far from his throne. " I have been left to fate far too often in recent days and to be fair I think it has served me well. So I am going to chance her once again. I am Joseph from the Luff, I have travelled for many days with friends, we have been separated for reasons that would take too long to explain now. I have been asked to bring a message from the Elders of the Huskian's people to Madistrin for assistance with a man called Bast'wa." Joseph halted looking for an expression or reply.

"Well Joseph you are indeed quite the package of surprise. In all my days I have heard of few venturing down into the Inpur desserts and fewer still that made enough allegiance that they would be trusted with a message like this. It is easy to see now what Gru-Staedak saw. I know of Bast'wa, what ill has he brought on the Huskian's that they would reach out after all this time?"

The night had come down around them as they talked, Joseph explained their venture to Kanegon and their capture by Bast'wa, his gem trade and the deal with the Huskian's struck from a lie. Redrick was fascinated and frustrated at each piece of information.

"I knew he was amassing wealth, my own people have had dealings on a minor scale but he has friends in high places in Vedian. Not least on the council. He should have been put in his place long ago, Vedian has tolerated this type of behaviour for too long. I fear however that Madistrin can not help if he wanted too, the fight is at our door. However we will deliver your

315

message to Parran." He motioned to Joseph to follow, "Stay low, we can sneak in over the wall there, keep out of the lights."

They scrambled over the outer wall, at its lowest point, only about twelve feet high, there were militia outside the gates but no one troubled them in the shadows.

Joseph realised he had never been to Pluris, never seen its sprawling buildings or flint corridors, opulent market or pulpit square. At any other time it would have been quite the experience. They shuffled between the buildings quietly.

"I thought you said the city was still under royal control?" Joseph asked as they passed a statue that stood at least twice his own height.

"In the main it is but the Scholatic have spies everywhere and I would rather not be seen entering and I get the sense you should not either."

At last they came to a small house on a cobbled path, all the shutters were down and Redrick tapped out a rhythm on the door. It was pulled open by an old woman in a long robe and leaning on a stick. "What have you to say at this hour?" She peered out to look at their faces.

Redrick leaned in cautiously, "Sabre."

She beckoned them inside and pointed to a set of stairs that went down to a basement of some kind. At the bottom Redrick gestured to move three barrels that were on the centre of the floor to the edge of the room. Uncovered was a small trap door, he flipped the catch and raised the lid, below Joseph could see a ladder reaching down into the depths.

Redrick signalled him to follow, "Careful its slippery down here."

Joseph could see a light in the distance but his eyes were struggling to get a fix on it, he climbed down the ladder, everything felt damp, the air, the floor, he shuddered with the cold.

Redrick moved towards the light and took the hanging torch from its wall bracket. "Its not far now." They continued down a pathway of some sort of cave complex, the walls were thick with a green moss and the floor was like walking on eels.

The cave began to widen out into a larger area and he could hear voices murmuring ahead. Redrick nodded at the four men who stood around a large table, he shook the hand of the man who stood over a large map of Vedian. "Joseph this is his Lord Protector Parran, this is the man that can save this city."

They had scouted the borders of Kanegon for two days now. Arn was bored of waiting but Dance had insisted on patience that this was only a scouting mission. They had seen men come and go into the town, it was quiet at night, militia patrolled the streets and dealt brutally with anyone found out after curfew. Bast'wa's castle was heavily guarded, certainly a greater contingent than when Arn had last been there. He would know by now the Huskian's betrayal in the mines and had probably suspected of some further trouble. Or more worryingly Arn mused, he was amassing for an assault on the tribes.

Either way the hunter would rather they skirmished with a few soldiers while they could, under cover of night a sneak attack would be easy. They could be in and out without them ever knowing what hit them but his council went unheard.

"We need to draw the enemy to us, in the desert his force will be weakened and our skills enhanced. We need to get him out from his walls."

Arn pondered for a moment, "Then take the thing he holds most dear."

"Does he have wife or children behind those walls. A loved one perhaps we could take hostage?" Dance asked.

Arn nodded, "Yes we need to take that that he treasures most, his greatest love. My few short minutes in his presence tells me that will be no person but a prize. I'm going to steal his biggest and greatest gemstone."

Dance had agreed and was less than surprised when Arn insisted it would be him to slip into the complex. It made some sense, he was the only one who had been in it previously and a Huskian would stand out immediately in the walls of men.

Arn was excited at the thought of getting one over on the fat man he felt buoyed with energy. He equipped his two hunting knives at each side and a pouch empty at his belt. They had scouted an

317

entrance at a second floor window to the rear of the castle that could be accessed by climbing on an outer building and then up the large stoned wall. The face was full of foot and hand holds where the stone had eroded. Assuming they didn't break off in his hand, it should be an easy climb Arn thought.

He waited until the night had completely fallen over the city, the patrol patterns had been easy to identify and the gap was well over two minutes, more than enough time. He slipped through the foliage of the gardens, his leather boots careful to miss brittle leaves on the ground. He hoisted himself in one move up and on to the outer shed, resting for a moment to catch a breath and survey the movement around him. He could see in the distance the place where he knew Dance and the others were waiting, it was getting colder as winter emerged in Vedian, he grabbed a lock hold on the wall, looking up to plan his route to the second floor. He was a decent climber and he found it relatively easy to circumnavigate the ascent. As he moved to the penultimate hand hold, the rock crumbled a little but he was more worried about the noise than actually losing grip, he held himself tight and flattened against the wall but there was no sound below. He reached up again pulling his weight from his forearms and cautiously peered over the window that had now come into view. Inside was dark and quiet, he slipped in and rested in what looked like a reception room of some sort, it was heavy on furniture but Arn suspected every room in Bast'wa's house would look like that. Ugly and garish, befitting the man himself. Moving quickly on his toes he crossed the room, breaking the door a crack open to see out into the passageway, he had no idea where the valuables would be held but he was hoping his hosts need to show off would leave them close to hand, rather than in some vault in the bowels of the castle.

He moved through the passageway, carefully peering into rooms, looking for some sign of what he was seeking. At one point he opened a door to see three men undertaking some sort of lurid act, he quickly backed away, that was not what he sought. He was now in an adjoining corridor that led into larger rooms, one was clearly a sitting room, with various chairs and chaise longue laid out amongst huge rugs but nothing but rich tapestries and fabrics.

He could hear voices from the next room, very carefully he pried the door open, two men sat deep in discussion, one of the voices he instantly recognised. Bast'wa! His instinct was to rush in but he was not sure why, he could see a number of display cases at the right side of the room, this could be it. He looked around, searching out his target, on a lectern coated in a gold paint with two curled brackets and in each a ruby, each as big as a fist.

There was no way in the room without disturbing the men and if he did there was every chance he would not make it back out. Certainly no time to go back the way he came. He could see above the room there were wood joists that led into the room to the side, the walls not meeting at the roof, rather reaching up into a lofted area above. They were sitting with their backs to the displays, perhaps he could drop something down and fetch one of the rubies up? No, ridiculous idea, he would never be able to but it would be a good place to hold and wait for them to finish. He crept back next door, then slowly and carefully pulled himself up from the dresser onto the joists above, he could hear their voices clearly now as he, on all fours, moved along to where the two rooms joined. Then he sat and he waited. It felt like hours passed before they finally finished. Arn had hoped to catch some useful information about the Huskian's or Kanegon but almost all the talk had been of fashions and cloth, this seasons colours, how did people fill their lives with such irreverence. Once the door had closed and a few more minutes had passed, he dropped down onto a padded chair to make as little noise as possible. He moved to the lectum and went to reach out for one of the rubies, then his eye caught a stone the like of which he could only have believed existed in dream. It was a diamond in a steel case with a glass top and it was enormous. On the case on a copper plate was inscribed 'To his all knowing and all giving - Prominence Shel-Toro' then the word 'Adamas'.

Instantly Arn knew this was his prize, this would draw the fat man from his palace of affluence. He took the hilt of his knife and smashed the glass, grabbing the huge diamond, which barely fitted into his pouch. He darted across the room to peer outside the door and check for movement, out of the corner of his eye he noticed on the table a glass of water, left over from the conversation, just one glass.

As he put out his hand, the door swung open and he stood face to face with Prominence Bast'wa dressed in a ruby robe of silk, his portly stomach pressed against the svelte fabric.

Neither men could speak for a moment and then the shrillest noise Arn had ever heard as Bast'wa shouted, "Help! Intruder!" he waved his hands above his head, revealing far more of Bast'wa then Arn had ever hoped to see.

He pushed passed the shrieking man, running back towards his entrance point but already he could hear footsteps from that direction. He needed to take a gamble, he ran back and grabbed at Bast'wa, spinning him round, "Where is the nearest window out, tell me now or I will slit you like a pig" Arn pulled out his hunting knife and pushed it up to Bast'wa's formidable chins.

"I can not be harmed. I can not. There, there." He pointed at the door, one further down and opposite.

As Arn ran for the door, Bast'wa yelled, "I will see you hanging from the ramparts! You will be punished for this incursion of my person! I forbid it. Guards!"

He could hear shouting now, they were in the corridor, only a few seconds behind. He pulled open the door, a window stood like a beacon at the other side, he ran across and looked down. Nothing to jump on, he pulled himself up and outside, beginning quickly to climb down any hold he could find. Torch lights were springing up around the castle and he could see figures below, there was no time left! If he kept climbing, by the time he got down they would be on him from the grounds. Nothing for it, thirty feet or not, he had to jump and hope.

He spun his body and hurtled towards the ground.

The days Speck had spent in the Tower had seemed to pass without him noticing. Time had no real meaning when there was nothing to press against it.

No one chased him to be anywhere at any point, he came and went as he pleased, when his teachings commenced, it seemed to be when he was ready. There were no demands or requests placed upon him. Remys said to attain the best from oneself it had to be in a state of personal karma. Much of the time he meditated, looking to gain an understanding of his own thinking, of the way he saw himself. Later the incantations begun, small things to start with but Speck learned quickly and at times surprised even his tutor with the speed he took on board his new found skills.

There was little doubt Speck was at home in the tower, in the evening he would sit and read in the study. They held a sizeable library on history and the land, Speck felt less reliant on his book since his arrival. Yet he still kept it close, the book was his attachment to the others, he kept it wrapped until his pillow, occasionally he would remove it and touch the raised leather cover. He had chosen to not mention it to Remys but he could not put his finger on why. The tower was an amazing place, with very gifted people but beyond anything it seemed a lonely place. A feeling of solace and isolation was part of being one of them Remys had said.

He was not sure how many of them there were, he thought about a dozen different faces but they all wore the grey robes with cord and tassel to bind it, so at times it was difficult to be sure. As he slept that night, his dreams were filled with lights and sounds, the incantations came to him now in his thoughts and hopes. When he woke he could sometimes recall them and others were still an effort to bring into focus. However he was stirred from his machinations by a hand pushing softly on his arm, "Lucent, awake. It is Remys, I need you to come with me."

This was the first time he had been asked to be somewhere specifically since he entered the tower and in the middle of the night, it was odd. Speck threw on his robes and followed his teacher, shuffling down stairs and into the large study on the first floor. Inside everyone it seemed, was sitting around the hearth in a semi-circle. Remys gestured for Speck to sit down and he gave him a reassuring tap on the shoulder. There were indeed twelve including Remys, the only thing they had in common facially was age, there was no young features all looked like venerable men to Speck.

Remys addressed the room, "It is with no apologies I gather us together, I have received word that Vedian is under duress and I fear there will be many dangers to unfold in the coming days. The Scholatic have placed all cities under curfew, martial law has been declared. The Crown Prince is missing and only Pluris still stands under royal banner, men gather at its borders already."

There was a murmuring of voices at the shared news. Speck's thoughts immediately fell to Joseph at the mention of the capital.

Remys continued, turning to face the glowing fire, "We must as always choose. Do we involve ourselves with the dealings of Vedian or stay silent and wait for the time when we are needed. Let us hear from the voices of the tower now."

Next to Speck a long bearded man began to speak,, he looked as old as any man in the room, "We have waited a long time, we have seen neighbour against neighbour, Kanegon fall to ruin and shame, yet we have stayed our hand. For these matters are not ours to solve, we are not judge of the land and in this matter who are we to judge the Scholatic motivations? Do we know why they move now or for what purpose? They more than any would think before they act, perhaps there is greater good at work? We should not offer ourselves, little is their left for us in the world. Let us take comfort in the tower and know Vedian will find its own way."

Remys stood again, "Our thanks to our brother Harabat, his words are always valued here. Any more voices to be heard?"

For over an hour, each in turn they spoke, most reflected the first speakers views, they talked of tolerance, of non-interference, of not understanding fully the situation. Only one voice had shown any hint of supporting a move, the old man Cyrus, his grey wispy hair thinning with age swishing around his face as he spoke but even he seemed unsure of himself in providing a persuasive argument. Speck could instinctively see they would not get involved. He thought to stand and give a speech, to try and sway them to action but he knew it was no good. His words would land like the petulance of youth on shoulders that had stood for decades. He slumped down without uttering a word.

"Then we are decided." Remys called the discussion to conclusion and slowly each man wandered out from the room until only Speck. The young enchanter searched the fire for answers but none were presented. What did he really know of politics or Vedian?

"Surprised you did not offer a view master Lucent," Remys voice made him jump as he silently returned to the room, snapping Speck out of the fires hypnotic movement.

"I did not seem worthy amongst so many great men." Speck offered.

Remys laughed, "Yes, yes great indeed! They are but men who have spent many years in the solitude of the tower. Not an easy place to leave. Many of them have seen little but the tower their whole lives and some that have, would rather not see it again."

"But you have?" Speck queried, "Have you?"

Remys interjected "No, not for my part only Cyrus holds those links now and he is older than any, although he does not look it. You see Cyrus fought in the Great War. He stood by the sides of the once magnificent army and threw back the enemy from the shores of Vedian. Or so it is said." Remys winked conspiratorially.

"It does not seem right to me, for the Scholatic to turn the militia on to the towns and cities. They have always preached non-interference as I understood. How does this serve those principles?"

"A good question. However my brothers need greater motivation, we perhaps have sat too long, our memories are dimmed of the old days. We see men in robes no longer men in armour. I think Lucent our mind is made up I thank you for your words."

Specks mind turned to the book. The book could help him. Perhaps a way to persuade the others to act. He thought of Joseph walking into a city under siege, he was not big enough to understand the fate of Vedian but he would do something to aid the fate of his friend, if he could.

He ran to his room, pulled the book from its resting place, opened the cover and read.

"For gods sake get that water down here now!" Pinky shouted at the men carrying the pails, water slopping over them as they ran. Fire was everywhere, the whole rampart was ablaze, oil carried on their backs to pour over the walls was spilled across the stone, spreading the blaze. Suicide runs, they did not care now if they lived or died, the enemy was determined to achieve its goal and frustration was playing its part. Four days they held the last wall, four days and four nights, Pinky had never been so tired. Only a few remained now from the regiment, Paddy had fallen the day before but he fought like a bloody madman, throwing himself headlong into a wave. Captain Tress had taken a bad one in the leg, gash as wide as Pinky's arm but still he climbed up each day and fought on.

They had no more than a few hours left in them, no more. They had fallen back now, regrouping before the nights attack, just a few hours to put out the fires, grab some food perhaps, nothing else.

Once the worst of the fires were put out, Pinky walked like a corpse back to the keep, the make shift mess serving up to the few soldiers that remained. Tress sat on the floor with Fystal the battle mage, he greeted Pinky as soon as he entered.

"He goes it sergeant?"

"Still fighting Captain, got a few more in me yet, need to keep this rabble in line." He pointed to the other soldiers in the mess.

Tress beckoned him over and Pinky sat down, speaking quietly, "Last night Pinky. We wont go another."

"No sir." Pinky's voice was solid and true now, lacking his normal jovial chatter. "The men have nothing left to give and they have given everything."

"Indeed. Vedian could ask no more. I must ask you to lead the men in tonight I have another task to attend to Sergeant." Tress spoke oddly enough for Pinky to question.

"I don't understand sir. There will not be another night. What else is there to do?"

"Just promise me this Pinky. When you think of me, remember I was loyal to this regiment, always, you are my only family, my friends." Tress pulled himself wearily up and saluted before walking from the room.

Pinkerton looked to Fystal, "What was that about. What's he up to?"

"Let him do what he has to. Focus on what you now must do. One more time." The warrior mage smiled at Pinkerton, he had grown to like the sergeant over the days on the wall. There was something wholesome and honest about him. "If you could have one wish Pinky, on this night, what would it be?"

"Ah that's easy. For the Sabre Regiment to go out with honour and for them to never die," He laughed, "can you give me that mage, a little piece of immortality?"

324

Pinkerton slapped him on the back and wiped his wounded brow before grabbing his hand tight, "Good luck and good death enchanter." Pinky walked out onto the battlements for the final time.

Fystal thought to himself, I can not save you my friend but perhaps that which binds you. He opened the hand that had just shaken with Pinky and impressed on it was blood.

Madistrin stood crouched under the bushes facing the university doors, the dagger was held so tightly in his hand it was shaking. Next to him was the pale figure of his protector Lint. He had begged him not to come, Vale had threatened to tie him down but once he had regained consciousness there was no alternative. Lint would not let his Prince go into the university alone, so sweating freely and looking ready to drop, he had escorted Madistrin back under the cover of night.

They had calculated seven men for sure, two on the front doors and two on the back, the man on the internal door and two in the room. Quick and bloody, Lint's words and the only way to get to DeFache with haste.

Lint explained how crucial the first two kills where, "If the alarm is raised at the main doors, everyone is on alert, we then have five to fight, rather than the potential to engage one or two at a time. These kills have to be silent, we strike together straight to the neck of the opponent. Do not think my lord Madistrin, just act."

Samuel had scouted the gardens and watched the guards movements for them, they knew it was best to advance just after they received their food. They would be sitting, distracted and off guard.

Lint motioned and begun to move with stealth out from direct cover, Madistrin followed, his eyes perpetually on his target, twenty foot, he could hear the spoon clicking on the bowl. Ten foot, the sounds of them chomping down on the chicken, at five foot he could smell them. His knife rose, trembling with anticipation, the guard looked up and his mouth opened, food dropping out as his blade plunged down into the throat area.

Madistrin was showered in blood but he kept his other hand gripped tightly over the man's mouth as the life drained from him. As he breathed and looked to the side, Lint crouched over the corpse of the other man, he had never seen him attack, too focussed on his own charge.

"Well done my liege. Now quickly the boy will be inside, follow me." Lint led them on. As promised Samuel was in the corridor, he exchanged a quick few words with the soldier and then as agreed went back into the kitchens.

"Good news the door guard is not there. He must have gone to sleep, so its just the two in the room, remember we have the advantage of surprise but it is lost quickly. Do not hesitate." Lint walked quickly up the stairs, for a man with such terrible injuries it was not obvious from his movements.

The corridor leading up to DeFache's study was empty and quiet, they moved up on each side of the door and Lint counted silently before turning the handle slowly and opening it just a crack to see inside. He nodded to Madistrin, they could see a guard, the one DeFache had called Wilam, by the window looking out but not the other. Lint motioned for Madistrin to take the visible target, as they agreed he would attempt to engage any enemy in view, Lint would hunt down the other.

Madistrin moved in but made only a few feet before Wilam turned to face him, the Crown prince broke into a run the pain in his leg shooting up through his side, now in the centre of the study he could see not one but two of the other guards sitting together behind the book racks. The Crown Prince pressed forward as fast as he could and threw himself on the guard, attempting to push down with the knife but the man was quick and countered, pushing aside his blade.

On the other side of the room Lint was circling not one as they hoped but two men that had now got to their feet, he was looking for the place to attack, to find a killing blow that would not expose him to the other. He decided on another action, throwing the hunting knife straight at the leg of one guard, he roared with pain and dropped to a knee, enough for Lint to engage the other without reprisal.

Madistrin had been forced over, the weight of the stronger guard was upon him and his own blade was being pushed down against his mid rift. He knew it was just a matter of time but he tried to get his leg up to jar his knee into his opponent. It was enough to push him free momentarily but only for a few moments.

At the other end of the room Lint had thrown punches to the face twice, both connecting as the man tried desperately to land swings with the short sword but he was too close now and his blade strokes were clumsy. A third strike broke his nose with a crack, Lint moved for a further attack to completely disable him but it was ill advised. He had presented too much recovery time to the first opponent, the guard had pulled up and brought the blade down into Lints lower back, striking a mortal wound. As Lint fell he grabbed at the short sword and pushed it firmly into the beaten guards chest. It was his final action, as he fell from the world.

Madistrin would find it hard to recall the next few actions and seconds, it was hazy as memories can become but he recalled the weight being lifted from him, his opponent falling to his side, him crawling up to his knees to see a tall figure towering over a wounded man and ending his life with a scythe like stroke of a blade.

He blinked to focus and in front of him stood Umberto DeFache.

Chapter 17 - The Pathfinder

'Much has been written of the people of Coralis and their role or perhaps lack of it in the Great War. I have tried to take an unbiased view from the outside looking in and taken in consideration that these peoples heritage goes back hundreds of years. No one man decided their way, no single entity banished them to their fate. Yes it was the Prominence of the town that made the final decision to remain stricken from the battle field, to hold themselves separate from the matters that befell Vedian. I can not find the blame to be entirely placed at his feet with his ancestors demanding the way of pacifism from generation to generation. Could he have been strong enough to break the mould? Perhaps but it is understandable why he did not.

It should also be noted that while no documented evidence is shown for any individual fighting in the Great War from Coralis there were many of the town's people who took to the field as healers and stretcher bearers. They tended to the wounded on the battlefield and off and this I believe should temper our historical view, there was participation, it was simply a weak touch.

I think what angers people to this day is perhaps not what has gone before but the stubbornness to not learn from those mistakes. To not stand up and say yes our ancestors made the wrong choices but we are saying 'no more'. We will stand up for Vedian. I will continue to learn and document the citizens from my close proximity of the University of Coralis, giving me the greatest opportunity for insight and a dispassionate view. I hope one day i will be able to record their greatest triumph as they take up arms in the name of Vedian.

"The Way of the Pacifists of Coralis" - SanPollan - Vedian 961

Joseph patiently sat in the corner of the basement cave for well over an hour, he had passed on his message to Parran from the Huskian's but the soldier had given him little in the way of response. Food and drink had been brought and left while the five men went about their discussions and plans.

He struggled to take on board everything but he listened intently, there were over three hundred men now outside Pluris and they estimated a further two hundred were moving to join. Parran commanded just over one hundred men in and around the Crown Princes halls, there were a further fifty militia which they believed would be loyal in the city, however they feared how long they would hold under any form of attack.

Rayan the lieutenant from Coralis was the voice he heard most, "I do not see how we can hold the city with so few. If they attack from each side, north, south and west we would cave in immediately."

Parran asked, "How far are your men?"

"Three days out, they will join in time but the Asten swords are barely fifty, we serve to protect Coralis only and that has always been a peaceful city. As it has been for many years, never has the city been laid to militia control and placed under curfew, why would you? They are pacifists, the people will not fight." Rayan's voice was angry and frustrated.

"We could go out into the field, take them on with a surprise attack?" Redrick offered somewhat desperately.

"Now is the time for thoughtful tactics, not irrational thoughts. We would last no time with three to one odds. We need to thin them out, hold a line somewhere." Parran begun to pace up and down the cave, his footsteps echoing resolutely off the cavern walls.

Joseph joined the conversation before he could think better of it, "Could you not ask the people to defend their city?"

Parran stopped and looked around, "You sound like Madistrin himself, always putting his faith in the people of Vedian. I fear young man the news of his demise, which has been kindly shared by the council, has left the city in a state of uncertainty. Many think that any defence, or attempt at it, is foolhardy. They whisper that the council is now right to take charge in the absence of the Crown Prince. The people begin to think we are no longer a resistance under the flag but the aggressor. I fear the some are swayed by words not actions. These Scholatic are nothing but learned in the ways of manipulation.

"Yet you have not given them the opportunity to hear your side?" Joseph walked towards Parran, "Why would you condemn

329

democracy to failure so easily, that which you fight with your life to defend? Where is the sense in that?"

The air ran out of the room, Parran stared long at the young mariner standing in front of him, "I apologise, you are right. You speak with a passion that I would wish to hold for the people, perhaps you would forgive me, a long life of disappointment has perhaps scarred my views. e should try and get word out asking for support. If only DeFache were here, he could command the Pulpit for us."

Joseph took a deep breath, he was not sure where that had come from and felt lucky Parran had not taken offence, "What is the Pulpit?"

Redrick smiled, "Passionate you are, knowledgeable you are not. The Pulpit is the speaking point of Pluris, it is placed directly in the centre of the town and can be used by any who wish to address the people. However and this is its great irony, it is forbidden to be used by the people, only one of Scholatic descent can preach from the Pulpit. Therefore our only true hope would have been in DeFache's hands, he was ever held loyalty to Madistrin but we understand he has been held for crimes by the Scholatic, he can not aid us."

Redrick walked over to Joseph, "Wise words my friend but don't try your luck, sit down before Parran puts you down."

The other two lieutenants departed, Corn from the Lancers and Brown from the Pikemen were both sent to check on the town's defences on the south and west walls, while Redrick, Parran and Rayan continued to discuss their options.

"Even if we split and try to defend the three gates, the walls surrounding the city can still be scaled. It would be scant problem to send a group over the wall and to hit us from all sides. Only the seas to the west give us any quarter from attack."

Parran nodded at Redrick, "Agreed. However let us not give them up without cost. We should make each group small and mobile. Sharp quick attacks and retreat to set positions, collapse into the centre and convene on the marketplace."

Rayan cut in, "We could set up fire traps to ignite as we drop back each layer, it will push them back and give us time to retreat."

"Yes but there will be collateral damage to the city." Redrick pointed out.

Parran continued, "We hold the market for as long as possible and then the final defence is in the castle halls, a fitting place to make a stand in the Crown Prince residence. The walls there are thick and tall and it is all stone clad, no fire will burn it. We can fight there for many days I would warrant. They will regret their move on Madistrin, I will never forgive myself for not being at his side when they came for him. I will gave these Scholatic cowards a wound to remember me by. Now let us make preparations, Rayan speak with the smithy's, we will need as much armour and weapon as possible. I will get the fires prepared, Redrick we appreciate your help with the continued scouting."

Finally he turned to Joseph, "All I can give the Huskian's is a promise. If we live through this, if Pluris is held and we once again restore order, I will ride in the name of Madistrin and deal with Bast'wa myself but in honesty lad those may be empty words, our situation is grave. I would urge you to depart the city while you can and go back to your home."

"And will I find a different story in the Luff?" Joseph asked.

"All towns are the same, as we understand it, all under Scholatic law, with exception of one."

"Then if I can be of use to you sir, I would ask that I stay in your service till the deed is done and I can deliver your message back to the Huskian's as a positive one. I promised I would help them and I would like to deliver on that." In truth there did not seem any better place to be, he was alone now, his friends departed. Pluris needed every man, not just the ones named as soldiers. Freedom was not a right, he thought.

"What is a blood ritual?" Speck asked the question in a way that made it sound irreverent.

Remys looked less than impressed, "It is not the kind of thing you should be thinking about, of that I am sure. Your book is a little more than dangerous."

Speck was visibly shocked, "How do you know! Have you been spying on me?"

Remys laughed out loud, "No Master Lucent I have not. It is not a small trinket to conceal and we knew you must have triggered your skills from somewhere without the aid of teachings. It must be a very special tome to have shared such secrets. May I enquire to its author?"

"I believe a man called MonPellia." Speck answered calming down.

Now it was Remys turned to be surprised, "Well. That is an interesting piece of news. MonPellia was the father of the Scholatic from many years ago, he was responsible for the Moot of the Factions, do you know what that is?"

Speck shook his head. "Vedian was at odds with itself after the Great War had ended, Barons fought with Lords from the Taran's. The land bled and its peopled suffered, so MonPellia did what the Scholatic are forbidden to do, he directly got involved, he gathered all the leaders on the Isle of Imanis and assassinated them, forming in its place the Scholatic council, to aid the king in serving the lands of Vedian."

"He preached freedom with guidance, an interesting combination. It was MonPellia that is considered the founder of the Scholatic council, although you will never see much of his writings. He was perhaps a little too extreme for today's politic. Many say that the moot never happened, that the fighting just stopped through negotiation. I suppose in a way it did, he was just a very strong negotiator."

"Everything I have seen in the book surrounds the Great War. All it has taught me has come from that."

"Then you are privileged indeed, MonPellia was a great man by accounts and in service of the old Kings. Does he speak to you from the book?"

Speck thought the question odd and was too focused on his own thoughts and frustration to follow it up "Have you ever served a King as such?" Speck enquired.

Remys sat down and smiled, in that disconcerting way he did, "No. Those ways are passed. We teach the philosophy to a very few now. Our days of taking to the field are long in the memory, I myself am considered in these walls, well learned, You may be surprised to hear. Yet I have never set foot outside since I was a child, it is not our way now. Only Cyrus is left from the old order."

Speck was confused, "So we learn for what? Why do we study the teachings?"

"For knowledge of course. To grow in oneself and to develop, there is no better life." Remys seemed surprised at Speck's reaction.

"For what? To what end? How do we make things better?" Speck was struggling with the responses Remys offered.

"We make ourselves better Master Lucent. We become better in ourselves, we heal to become whole."

Speck was like granite in his response, "It is a selfish practice if it serves no other but ourselves. I have seen the Battle Mages, they were strong and proud and they did what they could to help Vedian, standing side by side with men in its defence. My path has just become as clear as the morning sky. I will not stay here to learn for no end. I am sorry Remys this is not what I was looking for."

Remys did not look to dissuade him in his words, "So what did you come looking for? You must follow your own course, there is a greater will at work."

"I wanted strength and the ability to help others but I realise now that I already had it. I see that now, it is not power to act, it is simply the courage to do so. I am sorry Remys but you are wrong in this, it is not enough to just do as you wish. I must leave tonight, I will go to Pluris and find my friend if I can and do what I must to aid the cause that you have been requested to join. I may not know all you do but one battle mage will stand when Vedian calls."

A voice came from the doorway, "I will go with you Master Lucent. Though it has been a lifetime since I last walked from without these walls."

He appeared in the doorway like a picture from Speck's dreams. Dressed in leather armour from head to toe and his ruddy red robe, there stood Cyrus. His grey beard covering him down to the belt and his long hair draped over his hood but in his eyes was a spark that lifted the young enchanter.

"I stood once on the walls of Bannermane with my brethren, I fought by the sides of Junas the Sword and Dior the Champion. One last time I will walk by their sides with you my young warrior.

May the hushed voices of our forefathers whisper in the ears of our enemy, that the battle mages of Vedian fight again.

Arn hit the floor hard, he tried to roll out of the impact but he felt the wound on his thigh open up as he landed. In front of him he could see the cover of the gardens, he focussed on moving forwards, there was little point in worrying who was coming, he could not fight them off in this condition. He half hurdled a low set of shrubs, the pain from his leg rising up to register with his brain. He could hear voices around him, they were close, he kept focus on the edge of the grounds and beyond the hills, somewhere the others waited. Each step pulled him towards them, towards her.

Dance had not seen him exit from the window, he had come out of the south side of the castle but she heard the commotion as the guards were alerted. She instructed them to move forwards, keeping as low as possible so they could to get a better view. A chase was on and she knew at the other end of it was Arn. Jumping to her feet she pulled the small crossbow from around her waistband, notched a bolt and fired it deep into the pack of guards that had exited the building with haste. It did no damage but drew their attention, enough to redirect them away from their target and towards the Huskian's.

She motioned for them to split up, in an effort to draw the attackers away she fired once more to ensure she had their attention, the second bolt landed firmly in the lead soldiers shoulder, he dropped to the floor. They were covering ground fast, she turned to run, pouncing across the grassy hills like a panther, graceful and quick. She was able to put enough distance between her assailants each time before turning and firing off another shot to keep their attention.

After a mile or so, the last of them gave up the chase, choosing to return to the castle and seek new orders. Dance converged on the meeting place they had agreed to earlier just off the road to Kanegon. She took a deep breath as she rounded the corner, the faces that met her were all her kin, Arn was nowhere to be seen. Panic hit her, "We must go back out, look for him."

"No. They will come back out in greater numbers, let us hope the hunter has done what he intended and given them reason to follow us into the desert." Gan-Ro spoke with authority, he was the Elder's son and an important warrior in the tribe.

"We can not leave him out there, we must go back!" Dance's voice was desperate and Gan-Ro could hear it.

"Your hunter did what was necessary if we do not return now and give word, then we undermine him and negate his actions."

"Your right Gan, you go back to the tribe, tell them we have disturbed the nest and to be ready. I will stay and search for Arn." There was little point arguing with her and the Huskian knew it, however he also knew that if he left her alone and any harm came to her, it would be on him. Besides the hunter would never approve and he liked him."

The strike was quick when it came, Dance barely felt it before she lost consciousness.

Gan-Ro pulled her up and over his shoulder, like lifting a lamb, "We march now, the hunter will have to find his own way."

The scouting party found their way back to the village the same night Joseph had met with Redrick. Tired from the journey at a full pace, Gan-Ro had to tie up Dance eventually to stop her from leaving. He dropped her in front of his father's tent, casting a look at Febra "Perhaps you can talk some sense into her." The Luff girl just stared back at him.

"Or perhaps not."

Gan-Ro explained to the Elder what had taken place, that there was a strong chance they may pursue them back through the Inpur desert.

"Good, this is good. The hunter was clever to pull them close. We have warriors from the other tribes on route, we will be readied for an attack by tomorrow night."

Dance, who Febra had seen the need to untie, now stormed into the Elders tent, "You had no right Gan! No right. It was my decision."

Elder Orn's voice rang out like a horn, "Your decision. It is not your decision. The spirits guide you and they would seek the safety of the tribe before anything else. Your selfish words do the Huskian people no good."

Dance was cut down like a disrespectful child. She murmured an apology and walked swiftly from the tent.

Febra watched as she came out, "He may be back yet. He's a survivor."

Dance turned to face the girl, "I love him Febra, I would give anything and it shames me."

Febra scratched in the dirt with her knife, her knees pulled up to her chest "Would it not be good to live in a world where that would be enough save him?"

Redrick flirted openly with just about anyone Joseph had discovered, he didn't seem too choosy about age or gender, he just seemed to enjoy the chase. As they sat in the Copper Tavern, a haven for the Pluris common man, drinking mead and talking with locals. It was night on the second day of his stay in the capital, he had spent the afternoon running errands, fetching foodstuffs, filling water skins with the stable hands. It felt good to be doing something, Joseph was fully aware his competence was not with a sword and shield.

Redrick had stayed close, popping up every now and again to check on him. He was full of chatter and funny stories, he seemed to know everyone.

"So I told her, maybe the second time but not in his shoes!" The crowd that had gathered at the bar, fell about at the punchline of his story. Joseph wasn't sure he got it but laughed along all the same. It felt like being with normal people for the first time in a long time, this could as well be a night in the Luff, all be it on a grander scale. There must have been almost a hundred people in the wide tavern, one big floor, like a barn with tables. A lot of patronage were local soldiers and some from the royal house he noted. The Innkeeper was a man named Norris Batchley. Rather thin and petulant, if his role was to perform as the fat jolly host it was an anathema to him.

Norris filled Redrick's mug with ale, he was a good customer, he made others laugh and the more they laughed the more they drunk. "You in town long?" Norris enquired hopefully.

Redrick mused, "Well that depends on a number of factors my good Norris. Do you have anything to compel me." He grinned in a comely fashion with those raised eyebrows.

Norris tutted and went off to another part of the bar. "You shouldn't tease him. Anyway why would you?"

Redrick leaned in to Joseph, "I could be dead tomorrow, one should never close down any avenues. Now what time is it?"

"Almost midnight" Joseph replied.

"Then we should be off. That is assuming you are coming?"

Joseph looked at Redrick, "Where are we going at this hour?"

"A little scouting mission from Parran. Think its time we put your skills to use Joseph."

"I am not so sure I have any skills."

"Well, still waters run deep and all that." Redrick smiled. "We need to check on their numbers and its safest after dark."

They departed The Copper Inn and moved down Broad Road until it intersected with Iron Lane. Redrick led them to the outer wall which stood twelve foot high. "Hardly Bannermane is it?"

They climbed on a cart that was sitting by the wall and Redrick stacked up some boxes, he climbed up and motioned for Joseph to get on top of his shoulders. It was a fairly simple task for two men to get over the wall, what damage could five hundred do, Joseph thought.

They dropped down with little noise, they could easily see the lights from the camp just a mile or so down the main road. A few squads were placed near the entrance points to discourage those looking to leave or enter but their attention was focussed on the gates. They slipped through the front lines, keeping off the road and near to the rocky hills where they had first met. Redrick used elaborate hand signals to direct Joseph, some of which were clear and others made little sense.

As they came within a few hundred yards of the camp, Redrick pointed up, they scrambled over some boulders and gained higher ground, so they could get an elevated view on the proceedings. Joseph recalled the conversation of the previous night, Parran had talked of three hundred men and and a further two hundred to arrive.

It can't be right, Joseph looked alarmed at Redrick but the tracker was doing his own sums as he scoured the camp.

Finally Redrick spoke, "There's got to be seven hundred men already. Tell me I'm imagining it lad."

"No. At least and on the road I can still see more coming in from the west." Joseph's voice had a hint of tremor in it.

"No way can we hold against a force that large. They will over run us in a day. Where the hell have they got them all from and how long have they been plotting to mobilise such an army? They must have combined forces with militia, Scholatic guard and recruited every mercenary in the land! Nothing more than thieves and bandits for the hire, probably recruiting them out of Kanegon. We can't fight this."

"Let's get back to Parran, we have to tell him. We need more help."

"There is nothing more Joseph. We have all the royal guard and the swords arrive tomorrow but there is no one else loyal to the Prince."

"Perhaps there is." Joseph spoke softly to himself.

They made a quick return to Pluris, making straight for the caves below to find Parran and the others. Joseph was becoming familiar with the cold dampness of the lair, it was almost refreshing.

Parran acknowledged their presence immediately, looking to Redrick for an update, "What does your scouting tell us?"

"Grave news my friends. The numbers have swelled to higher than we could have imagined. It is a desperate scene, over seven hundred strong in ranks."

The other men, seasoned in battle, took a literal step back in amazement, Rayan shook his head, "This plot has been long in the making, if the numbers have grown so. We can not hope to hold against so many."

There was a pallid silence over the group, as Joseph raised his voice, "Please if I may, I have an idea. We could get word to the Huskian's, ask them for aid. They are an honourable people, they recognise the old bonds with the Prince."

338

Parran snapped back, "The Huskian's can not defend themselves, they come to us for help. What use is this?"

Joseph continued unperturbed, "I believe they will come if you ask and they understand the need. They know much of betrayal. Please will you send a rider and plead a case."

Parran calmed, "Aye I will. Any ally would be a willing guest in our present situation, though I hold out little help. You say they have but a hundred warriors, that would not be enough."

"Perhaps sir but you may not have seen the Huskian's, they are a formidable people, one hundred of their best could equal many more of the enemy."

Redrick nodded, "I agree, let us send message with haste in the name of the Crown Prince. With promise to aid them in return. I fear though it will not be enough and even if they agree, I doubt they will arrive in time."

Joseph continued calmly to speak, "I agree, we need more than just the Huskian's and if we are to ask another peoples to aid us in this hour, then should we be afraid to ask our own? Tomorrow, Scholatic or not, I will go to The Pulpit and tell the people the truth and we shall see who they will follow."

Shel-Toro looked out over the city from his tower in the southern end of the university. It bustled with activity, people going to and fro, chores undertaken, tasks being done. He enjoyed watching the people go about their daily lives, it was a reminder to him of the responsibility he had, they were so simple in their view of the world, how could he have once thought that they could honestly protect themselves. Folly of youth perhaps? With maturity he had perhaps seen clearer the dangers ahead, others like DeFache had slowed his hand. His principles of non-interference had been stubborn and no doubt well intentioned but that was not enough for a Scholatic of his standing. It was important to think bigger. There was no doubt in Shel-Toro's mind that the people of Vedian were standing on a precipice. A judgement of their own making had been called, they had grown more ruthless, more unruly by the year. The town of Kanegon had become a pool of crime and unrest, a place for men to gather and spread their venom. The rise of Bast'wa as a respected merchant and leader was symptomatic of how far the place had fallen. A despicable man, the thought of his presence turned Shel-Toro's stomach, however he had been necessary to raise the funds for the mercenaries. After this, he thought, I will take great pleasure in throwing him to the people that he has dominated for so long.

There was only one outcome to this impurity, war and death. That's is all he could see, there was no other alternative. He could see as clearly the road laid out as he could the read the words in a book, there was no redemption for them and he must now step away from the preferred path of guidance for just a time. Time enough to change course, it would be hard on the new road, he had steeled himself for the delivery of a heavier hand. Control would be met with defiance, then after a time there would be acceptance. Some then would call the job done but he knew that was not enough, he had to ensure they did not return to the old ways, the Scholatic would rule Vedian with Shel-Toro at the head of the table and he would punish the people for a period of five years, harsh punishments for any crime, any step out of line would be met mercilessly. If a man stole, he would suffer the consequence, if he brawled drunk, then he would be beaten. These would be good strong teachings and serenity would be achieved through the lessons he would hand out. The people one day would whisper his name, quiet at first, he knew that but eventually their reverence would come to the fore.

It just took commitment, Shel-Toro knew that, it was so easy to be swayed or for a single example to prove another way was an option but he was now adamant in his resolve. He stretched, his long robes rising off the floor and resting on his soft sandal. In the distance over the wall he could just make out their growing numbers. A thousand men Bast'wa had promised him, every man that would take payment would be sent to Pluris. It was not that he needed that many but the show of force would be a crushing blow to the people, they would see if was only the Scholatic that could protect them. Picking up some scrolls of papyrus from his desk, he flipped through to ensure he had his script for the speech. He did so hate to be unprepared when speaking to the common man, it was so easy to use words they did not understand and he so wanted to be understood, it was important to him they appreciated the efforts he took.

His assistant rushed to his side as he moved to exit the room, his robe was straightened and collar pulled taut. He waved the help away, striding down the winding stairs of the tower, an announcement to be made, the last in Pluris for a while, until the city was safe under his control. He felt oddly at ease as he moved through the common folk, a small parade of Scholatic assistants following behind as he strode forcibly forward, through the market square and towards the huge podium that stood at its centre. The pulpit as it had been christened over five hundred years hence. A solid marble lectern, mined from the purest white stone, it stood as a symbol of the Scholatic, a principal of words above action. A sign of breeding and purity that comforted him. He would move from the city soon, before the push began, his Captain had assured him this would be the right time, before anyone took the chance to take him a hostage or worse still carry out an assassination.

Shel-Toro mounted the three steps that led up to the raised platform and unravelled the scroll containing his speech, carefully placing it under the arm that reached across the lectern. He looked out, a few people had begun to gather and word travelled quickly in the city, there would soon be more arriving.

It was not the traditional way to pre-announce a pulpit speech, it was just a case of taking the stand and giving time for a strong crowd to gather and interest to grow. Although often speakers would send out banners or messengers to make people aware of their arrival. On this occasion Shel-Toro had decided to allow the the crowd to naturally become aware of his presence at the pulpit.

He begun as all Scholatic speeches did with the odes to previous incumbent speakers, normally a full fifteen minutes of Scholatic self congratulations to those that had gone before.

"And to His Prominence Rel-Tulo of the University of Asten in the year of Vedian 876 who at this stage made such a speech that the people cheered and waved their Vedian flags."

Joseph stood and watched with some confusion, the crowd was deep now and he was a few rows back from the front, he couldn't make out what any of these thank you's were about. Redrick had told him to come and watch a pulpit speech being made but all he had heard was a man waxing lyrical about other men he had never heard of. Redrick could see he was unimpressed, "That is Shel-Toro the leader of the Scholatic council, the man who is about to lead that army outside the walls into this city."

"Well then what are we waiting for? We could attack him now and hold him hostage." Joseph looked eagerly at the tracker.

"Yes we could but take a look around you and above." Redrick pointed at the university tower.

Joseph looked up and back to see archers bows notched, he began to pick out figures around the crowd wearing the crest Shel-Toro wore on his robe.

"The personal guard of the Scholatic and that man standing behind him in the plate armour is the Captain of his Protectorate. However and more importantly, any move made on him here would be looked on as an attack by the people. They look to him in Madistrin's absence for rule and law. If we moved on him now, it would surely backfire on us and we would reinforce our position as the aggressor.

"So we are neutralised before we have begun." Joseph stared at the Captain towering behind the pulpit stage, he could not get away from the feeling he had seen him before. He snapped his attention back to Redrick.

"For now, let us listen, for he is not out here today by chance, he will look to weave a web for the people to be caught up in."

Finally finishing the introductions, Shel-Toro begun proper, his voice was crystal with its clarity and deep, the type of voice that could enrapture a man.

"It is with the greatest sadness I am called to you on this so fine winters day. With every morning I wake in the arms of Vedian, I give thanks that I am blessed to be counted amongst so many honourable peoples of Pluris. Yet my heart is heavy as the smithies anvil, for my great friend, my oldest ally has left us. You have no doubt heard the rumour now, as have I, that his Crown Prince Madistrin has fallen and like I, you have said, No! We do not believe these ill words! But my brothers I can no longer be a fool to myself, though I wish it is otherwise, we are alone in this world, the royal line has ended."

A silence was over the whole market area, every man and child was held by the voice that resonated over the throng.

"And Vedian has suffered. Have you sir?" he pointed at a man in the crowd, "Have you not been the victim of crime in our fair city? Thievery as blatant as day, do you sir not fear for your wife and

342

your home? We have entered an age where the decent, law abiding folk are second class citizen to the blaggard and cur. Enough I say! My heart has only enough blood for so many, yet it bleeds on and on for you, for each of you. I would have it differently but no, my hand is held, I am Scholatic, I can not interfere, I can only guide. So I sit up there in my tower and I watch and I hope for you all, for safety and stewardship. I wish there was more I could offer..."

Shel-Toro tailed off and moved as if to finish, he pulled up his paper and gave a last forlorn look towards the crowd. Then a voice shouted from behind Joseph, "Help us."

Followed by another, "Save us from these criminals! We need the Scholatic!"

Shel-Toro, turned and moved his hands in a placating manner, "You would not have it so my friends. It is not our way. If we were to help it would come at too great a cost, I will not pay that, I will never pay that. It fills me with hope that I wish for it but I know those wishes are not truly in your hearts."

Joseph looked up at Redrick, "What's he doing?"

"Hes making them believe."

More and more shouts came from the crowd, "Please, we need you."

Shel-Toro again moved to depart, then as the demonstrations increased he turned and held up a hand, "I can not thank you enough for your words. It means so much to be honoured by you but I must say what would you have me do if I could find the power?"

"Defend us. Save us. Keep us safe." The crows was boisterous now, it seemed to Joseph everyone was shouting.

"In other towns in Vedian there have been such cries for safety, we have done our best against our judgement to help. To gain control for the people, we have used the militia, we have even introduced curfew to stop the thieving and do you know what we got in return?"

The crowd shouted as one, "What?"

"We received only words of disappointment, words of loathing. Too much control, too much love. I could not hear those words

343

from my blessed Pluris. I ask myself can there ever be too much love? I can not help, as much as it pains me. For though my heart is strong as the Coralis mountain and deep as the roots of Malevolence, it would surely break if you could no longer believe in it."

"Please, Please. Shel-Toro. Shel-Toro. Shel-Toro." The chant came like the sound of a drum, again and again the crowd pleaded.

For the last time, Shel-Toro raised both arms above his head, "I wish I was a stronger man, I wish I had the strength to hold back the tide of your words. Yet it washes over me and so I, a weak man, choose only to bathe in it.

I choose the people of Pluris!

I choose to follow your words over all others! I am the Pathfinder and I will make you safe, I will bring militia to the town and break any that endanger our serenity, you have my promise. No matter who opposes us and what lies they weave, we will endure. Praise be Pluris and its glorious citizens!

It was long after Shel-Toro had departed the pulpit that the cries and shouting finally ceased and for the first time in his life Joseph understood the power of words.

Chapter 18 - The Pulpit

"It takes a lot of luck to win a battle, a lot of guile to win a war and a bit of both to survive either.

I have fought in every major campaign, commanded men to retreat from the shores of Kanegon and to stand at the fortress of Bannermane.

Now, on the final day of the final hour at the keep, I see enemies every side of me and I will not wake to see another dawn.

Of this, I fear, nothing.

These words I scribe as warning to those that come after me, look ever out at your foe, from walls, seas and shores but never fail to hold an eye inwards.

For there, lurking in the dark, closer than any should reach, lies the real evil. That who was once a friend.

For treachery is the greatest betrayal and from that fate, there is no return, no respite, no victory."

'The Great War: Bannermane' - Last words of Commander Dior – Vedian 501

Speck looked up as he pushed the book firmly into his pack, above him stood Remys, staring silently.

"I am sorry Remys I know you would have me stay but my mind is made up, I must go." Speck rose and touched the hand of his mentor, grasping it firmly and warmly. It would be wrong to say they had grown close but they shared a mutual understanding and Speck appreciated what Remys had shared with him. It had felt to Speck like he had spent weeks in the tower rather than days, time just seemed to draw out inside its majestic walls, allowing you to accomplish more with less.

Word had passed round quickly and most of those that had gathered the previous night were at the stable front ready to see them depart. The air had a slight frost in it and Speck pulled his cloak close as the door opened, winter was here now and outside the walls there was little protection from its elements.

Remys finished tending to the horses he had offered them, two black stallions, strong and capable.

"Take care of them now, they will come home if you have no further need of them." Remys placed his hand near the horses mouth for it to sniff, drew it away and then firmly stroked the beasts neck.

Speck made a final effort, "I wish you would come with us Remys, with you at our side we would be formidable"

Remys grinned, "I doubt that my lad, I have not stepped out from this haven in an age. I know nothing but its comforts, what would I do out there?"

"But everything you know, everything you taught me!" Speck protested.

"All I learned from others. Not tested in the outside world Lucent, to be studied and meditated on in our home." Remys genuinely seemed uncertain of the point Speck was making.

"I can not be as you are. I can not exist in a place that learns and prepares but never acts. I wish you well Remys and to all of you." He waved and looked across at Cyrus, the old man was saddled and mounted on his steed, at his side he held a ornate staff with a seven pointed star at the head, it was thick but Speck could not make out the material it had been crafted from.

They began to walk the horses forward slowly, Cyrus turned to Speck, "They know nothing else lad, this is their world if you take them from it they would be lost."

"Yet you willingly choose to come with me, to help me. Why?"

"Unlike them, I once lived outside the walls, it was a long, long time ago but I recall the feelings. I remember what it was to wield power not just control it. That's the fun part lad." Cyrus smiled and winked at Speck.

They cantered through the northern grasslands, the horses comforted by the flat grounds and fresh breeze. "Which way should we head? I came up through the forest to the south."

"Horses will not go that way, we will stay due east, link up with Coralis before taking the road south to Pluris. It will take us through the mountains but I know of a safe pass.

"Is it true what you said last night Cyrus? That you fought at Bannermane. How can that be true, you look, well old but not that old?" Speck was more than curious to hear any more of events that he had witnessed in the book.

The aged enchanter pushed away his grey beard from his face, tucking it under his tunic, the wind whipping it up into a tangle. "Time is an odd thing in the tower. I am older than any living thing has a right to be and I was there but not with as one of the great names you will be familiar with perhaps. I was a novice, only just initiated into the order back then. A baptism by fire, that it was. But yes, I stood at the keep on that final day, with the leader of my kind, Fystal and next to him Commander Dior.

"Fystal and Dior. I have seen them!" Speck said excitedly. "I would hear more of all of them and especially Tress."

"Captain Tress did not stand on the final day, I never did know why. I remember seeing him the night before and then no more, It was odd, he was not the sort to be apart from his men in battle but it was madness, who can tell what fate befell him at that time. It was a miracle any of us survived it."

"How did you? There were so few left to face the enemy." Speck almost forgot the pain in his backside as Cyrus spoke about the history that he felt now so attached to.

"Well that was the strange thing lad, that morning we prepared for the onslaught at dawn. Maybe a hundred left all told, only the very best mind or the truly lucky had survived so many days of fighting. Hardened veterans from the swords and a few lancers as well as a handful of the Sabre Regiment. Magnificent they were, I can see them even now, never has a group of individuals fought as one on the field, they could splinter an attack like a chisel into wood. With them was Janus the sword, probably the finest man at arms I have ever laid eyes on, so quick! Like a fish darting through the current, that silver armour flashing all around, word had it a smithy whose daughter he once saved from bandits forged that for him. Probably not true but these tales are what keeps men like Junas alive in the memory."

"You were saying, the final day." Speck tried to get the old man back on track.

"Oh yes, yes, well one thing does overtake you know. So we mounted the keeps narrow ramparts, looking down the throng

347

had amassed below, they had overrun everything. A horn bellowed from beyond somewhere, it always started with that blasted horn they would sound. I remember Fystal speaking with us, preparing us for the final hour, just him and I, my old mentor Corneal and a handful of others. All that was left of the battle mages but still we stood, he never offered for me to leave and to be honest by then if he had, I would have said no."

"What instilled you to be so brave?"

Cyrus roared with laughter, "It's not bravery son, nothing as grand as that, its camaraderie. I had been with those men for days and weeks, fought, sweated and bled and while we did stand apart from them its true, I could never have turned my back on them. Battles are not full of valour and great deeds, just men sharing a common instinct to protect one another. A bond if you will."

"A bond in blood?" Speck threw it in and immediately realised he was on to something.

Cyrus shifted on his mount, the grassland was turning to hills and in the distance the Rinslake Range, mountains that ran from the very northern shores down south, cutting off Coralis and the town of Medwere from most of Vedian.

"We should stop soon before we enter the range proper, get some shelter in the hills and a bite to eat, I for one am famished." Cyrus's attempt to change the conversation just goaded Speck into reigniting it.

They set up a makeshift camp, Speck lit a fire with the materials packed on the horses and prepared a broth of rabbit soup. Remys had ensured they were well stocked for their journey and they washed the food down with a Vedian red.

"Oh yes, very good. That is from the Lough lad, a strong dry wine deep in the south as befits its origin near the borders of the Inpur desert. We have a good cellar in the basement, I have often pressed my own grape from the northern plains area just beyond the tower. Its a fruity wine as you tend find in the north but good with a chicken."

"I never had much wine in the Luff, we are more a mead drinking village." Speck was enjoying his first tastes of the southern vineyards and gulped back the small mug.

"Its never too late to learn, before this trip is out, I will learn you in the world of Vedian wine."

"You have learned all the enchantment and energies in the world and you would spend our time teaching me about grapes?" Speck smiled.

"I leave the teachings to Remys, I promise you will get a lot more pleasure from this than you will ever get from the other."

They cleared up and nestled down in their blankets to sleep but Speck was just waiting for the right time and Cyrus knew it.

"All right, all right! That retched book has cursed your mind it seems. Remys mentioned that to me. Alright I will speak of it although I was bound not to lad. So hold your tongue if you will. The night before we stood at the keep on the final day Fystal came to us and requested we join him in performing a ritual. It was an odd thing to make a request. Normally I just got told what to do and I did it. I liked that, made things simple. We sat huddled by the fire and he said if I chose to, I would be part of performing the enchantment. Well what do you do with that? I asked him what would you have me do and he replied ' As your heart takes you and your head wills you." To be honest, I just did what I thought they wanted me to do, I was a bit beyond soul searching back then. So Fystal, Corneal and the others joined for an enchantment that I had never performed before and never would again."

Speck was desperate to know, "What was it Cyrus?"

"A blood oath. We bound blood that Fystal provided, from who knows where, to the souls of the Sabre Regiment. A complex binding and completely draining, had we been required to fight the following morning it would have been for naught. I could barely stand at the end of it let alone hold sword and staff. What it did, well what he intended was to bind members of the regiment together so they could be called on again." Seeing Specks face, Cyrus shook his hands, "No, no, its not bringing anyone back from the dead, we do not have that kind of power. Its more the spirits of them. For a time to call on their essence, I don't really know what it does to be honest, it was never mentioned again. It seemed a huge waste to me at the time, sapping our strength in the final hour and for what?"

"Could you do it, if the time was right?"

349

"Do what?" Cyrus nuzzled down further into his blankets.

"Could you perform the Blood Oath?"

"I would not tamper with souls of the dead. Not unless the horde was at the door and Vedian was in its final hour. Now go to sleep, we have a long ride tomorrow"

So you could, Speck thought as he laid down.

Arn was cold, the night spent curled up in the gardens of Bast'wa Castle had not been a comfortable one. He was pretty sure his wound had opened, blood once again had stained through onto his trousers, his ankle hurt where he had fell and the frost formed on his hands.

The guards had patrolled all night, his only option was to lay low and wait, eventually he had fallen asleep at the base of a burberry bush, its winter flowers tickling against his chin playfully. He carefully looked around, no one was in sight, no obvious patrols, in fact the whole castle was quiet. He looked up over the bush, his head turning in panoramic rotation across the outbuildings, he could make out a few servants moving about and the gate guards but apart from that it was unnervingly silent.

His first instinct was to run, to find Dance and the others. He patted the pouch hanging from his belt, instantly he felt the comforting shape of the precious gem. It just did not feel right to him, the place should have been crawling with Bast'wa's men, this was no trinket he had stolen. He decided to get a little closer, he crept up to the outside wash house which housed one of the wells that fed the building. He could see a young stocky woman filling two buckets with fresh water, she was dressed in linen and hemp, the hem gathered and tucked into her work boots.

Arn considered grabbing her and getting information but she might cry out before he could stop her and then a simpler alternative solution presented itself. He moved round and entered from the open doorway, "Good day to you lady, works never done hey?"

She briefly looked at the hunter, taking a glance up and down quickly before turning back to her duties, "Indeed not in this house."

She was a large woman, chubby in the face and full in the figure, "You new around? Not seen you before, reckon I would have remembered."

Her slightly flirtatious opening was all Arn needed, he was in like a dart, "Yeah my first day, I'm lucky to have fallen on such fair company for my chores."

She giggled which seemed to suit her, Arn took a deep breath in and went again, "Bet you are popular round here. You must fight those guards off."

She pushed a hand towards him brushing his tunic, "Be off with you! Your a right one you. No one to fight off anymore, now they've all gone."

Arn's interest was piqued, "Bet you scared em off. You don't scare me like that mind, I won't go where they gone, wherever that is."

"Pluris they say, the capital, all of em up and left early this morning and his Prominence, castles as good as empty." She looked around, "In fact, no one to really check up on us, you know." She stood up and moved towards Arn.

Arn could not quite work out this turn of events. Why would they all just leave, surely Bast'wa would seek out his lost prize and what of the Huskian's, it made no sense. He came back to reality as the woman was picking open the buttons on his tunic.

"Well yes that would be lovely but err, I have to, sorry, its quite the loss you understand." He started to move away.

She snorted, "Oh you're one of those are you, One of Bast'wa's boys."

Arn took her comment as a positive, "Yes that's right, sorry."

She turned back to her chores and mumbled to herself, "Should have known, too pretty to be a woman's man."

Arn was unsure what to do but decided he needed to get word back to Dance and the Elders. He kept low as he made for the back of the gardens and then sped up, fast as his leg would allow as he hit the grasslands. The hunters thoughts turned to Joseph and Speck on the journey, he was not one for feelings of guilt, rather living in the moment and enjoying life for what it was. He could not shake the feeling something bad was happening, why had Bast'wa gone to Pluris with his personal army? The next days march went on forever and Arn had to stop more times than he wanted too, resting his leg and gathering energy.

Finally at the borders of the Inpur desert the hunter was greeted by a Huskian scout, he offered food and water enough to finish the journey, ensuring Arn was clear on the route to take through the sands. Even ensuring his wound was properly bandaged before letting him go on. He did not wait for nightfall rather pushing on in the sunlight, his head wrapped with his cloak made for an odd look, but Dance had drummed it into him how important it was to keep protected from the deserts elements.

By the time he arrived outside the camp, four days and nights had passed, he was exhausted. He stumbled into the shade of Elder Orn's canopy, Febra stood over him.

"You look terrible but I told her you would be back." She took some water with the ladle and passed it to Arn.

"Thanks. Where is Dance and Orn, I need to speak with them."

Arn did not get to finish, Dance had heard his voice and came running from the main enclosure, "Oh my god Arn." She ran into his arms, hugging him tight.

"I am alright, no real damage done. Bast'wa has emptied his castle and they have all gone north. They march for Pluris, I don't know why. It doesn't seem right, after what we did I was sure he would come looking. Whatever is calling him there must be of great importance."

As he spoke a man dressed in light leather armour and a helm bearing an ornate crest walked from the mouth of the tent with Elder Orn at his side.

"Indeed it is. They are being called to Pluris, as are many others by the voice of the council. In a few days, when their numbers are at a throng, they will take the city."

Arn was confused, "Who, who are you?"

"I am Tarnell of the Crown Princes royal guard, I have been sent here by Commander Parran with a message for the Elders. Vedian needs the Huskian's aid or in a week we fear Pluris will fall."

Joseph held the sword tight in his hand, it was heavy, like trying to hold a brick with your arms stretched out. His wrist strained at the effort.

"Christ lad, the enemy is not going to cower with you holding that limp stick. Imagine your greeting a woman" Redrick looked at Joseph, "Oh lord, don't tell me you have never! This is desperate indeed. You can't go into battle with that cherry unblemished, leave it with me, I can see to this. Now arm up, lets see how you handle a blunt weapon." Redrick picked up a one handed mace, swinging it around his head before attacking from over his shoulder. Joseph did not like the sound of whatever Redrick had planned for him but right now he needed to concentrate. This had been the fifth day he had been the recipient of his enforced tutoring from the Coralis tracker.

"A man should never die from ignorance," he had said, "we need to lick you into shape, you look like a long sword kind of man. I think a shield too, small buckler, keep you alive a bit longer, well at least the first skirmish." Redrick grinned in that annoying way he did, it was hard to get angry with him, he always seemed to lighten a mood even as dire as the one they found themselves in. Parran had suggested they had one or two more days at the most before they were attacked. Scouts reported a large contingent moving up from the south, part of Bast'wa's personal guard. Joseph did not look kindly on that name and he explained to Redrick the run in they had with the diamond baron.

"Long has that fat man preyed on the people of this land protected by the Scholatic themselves no doubt. I wondered how he was allowed to trade so freely, now we know. Surprised he is making the trip himself, I had heard he has not been out of his castle for years. He must be desperate to make a good impression."

They practised for hours, Redrick showing him how to counter a variety of blunt weaponry with his small shield, it was surprisingly versatile. At the head it was notched to allow his sword to rest, enabling a stabbing motion while staying protected. It was just so heavy, Joseph asked for a lighter weapon but Redrick insisted this was the sword for him.

"When the day comes and you take to the field and can not feel the weight, you will have become a soldier. Anyway you'll be surprised how the fear of death removes other such sundry concerns."

As Redrick called a break, they sat down outside the bulwark, the entrance to the Crown Princes halls, the solitary flag still flying overhead.

"Will you fight on the front lines when they come?" Joseph enquired.

"Oh god no. That's for the new recruits like yourself. I am best working from the rear" he did one of his infamous winks.

"Is nothing sacred with you Redrick, nothing serious? I may die soon."

Redrick took note of the tension in Joseph's voice, "We all die Joseph, its a great inevitable part of living. With all the chance, fate and circumstance that occurs in our life, death is the only certainty we can be reliant on. Its comforting when you think about it. The one thing that will happen. So once you accept that, everything else is easy really. Anyway you won't be dying on the first day, I promise you that, for you will have the protection of the greatest archer in Vedian!" He stood up beating his chest.

"I have a friend, who might have something to say about that." Joseph smiled thinking of Arn, he would like the tracker, they were from similar stock.

"Then bring him on and we shall duel and dine! For you can surely not do one without the other."

Then suddenly, Redrick's demeanour changed, his face solid and taut, he leaned in towards Joseph, "I promise you, no blade will touch you on the first day." It was a brief change and soon Redrick was off again, with his stories and songs.

They had moved inside the halls now, Redrick had said it would be safer to stay inside its walls rather than the inn. The place was impressive, it was not quite as formidable as a castle but it was not dissimilar in style to one. Joseph immediately noted that it had an outer wall and an inner keep, the grounds in between holding the stables and servant housing. The outer wall was built with a wide allure to allow patrolling all around and the raised platform was suspended above the ground below leading into the keep. Also on the external side an overhang with sockets were cut in the floor to allow defences to be deployed, there was no moat but there was a massive gate made from the deepest stone with ornate steps leading to the barbican area that led into the castle proper.

"Why does the halls have these type of defences? I thought buildings where only built with barbican's to repel attack. Surely no one would want to attack a place like this? You know, under normal circumstances."

Redrick bit down on a over ripe apple, "That's because you see a city with a building in it. Pluris was founded from the halls. The city was built around them, originally it would have stood alone, so it has been forged with its own protection. That now looks out of place, as it is a building alongside many others.

Joseph acknowledged the point, "So if we fall back here, how will they attack?"

Redrick threw the bitter apple aside, looking around as if to see an entry point. Well two options and its not if, its when. Either they try to take the bulwark through the gate but the stone corridors in their are tight and they have a huge disadvantage as they can not use their numbers to hurt us. You can barely get three abreast through there and anyway, I doubt fifty thousand men could get through the main gates. Its stone is thicker than any other built. The other option is you take to the outer walls, That's the way I would go, throw numbers at the walls with ladders and support them with archers. Can you imagine Joseph a thousand men attacking at once, it will be like nothing that has been seen since the Great War. We may make a song of us yet, well maybe a limerick for you."

"If they take the inner walls, I suppose we fall back inside the keep?"

"Yes but once they take the walls our time is limited. Sooner or later they make the gatehouse from the inside and open come the gates. Then its over."

"There really is no hope Redrick, even if the Huskian's come in time. Is it worth it to the people? Will a ruling of the council really be so bad I wonder?"

Redrick nodded in agreement, "In all honesty probably not. They may even make things better in a way but I was born in the city of Medwere in the taran of Coralis. Do you know much of it Joseph?"

355

"No I have never been and have heard little to be truthful."

"Well long ago my people laid down their arms. They choose to live a different life, one of pacifism. They will not raise arms against anyone, even an aggressor, they will not fight in this battle nor did they in the Great War. They believe in peace and a principle of non-interference. It has served them well and after all these years, until a few days ago the town stood unoccupied."

"So they stand by, while their fellow man dies around them? They does not seem very honourable."

"Perhaps. Sometimes it can be the most honourable thing to stay one's hand. To say I will not strike." Redrick seemed lost in his thoughts.

"And yet you stand here, ready to defend a city that is not yours?"

"Oh I am an outcast. The people long ago cast me out for raising my hand against men that came and attacked our town. I live on the outskirts, always with an eye on Medwere and its citizens. My people believe in the good in men, perhaps I have spent too much time seeing only the evil that they do. I am here in the most for Madistrin and Parran, his men have looked over Medwere for many years, ensuring they are protected from distance. I would see some of that debt repaid. So that is why I will stand young Joseph but the question is why will you?"

Joseph shuffled on the floor, looking up into the marvellous hall, his gaze stopped at a tapestry that depicted a scene from Bannermane. "I was asking myself that until I heard Shel-Toro speak. You may be right, things may be better under the council and the Scholatic hand may hold a stronger law and order in Vedian. We may be safer and eventually even happier but there will be a cost, it was in his eyes and his words, free will. That will be the price the common man pays, I am not prepared to pay it Redrick. So that is why I will stand."

"Well said lad. Well said."

"Your prominence we are ready, Bast'wa has arrived with his contingent. We are at as a full a number as we can muster, shall you give the order?"

Shel-Toro rubbed his brow, he was uncomfortable away from the walls of his beloved university but his Captain had ensured him it was safer to leave Pluris and join the army outside for a few days, until the deed was done. He dabbed some water from a bowl that rested on a side table, "I think we have enough to make this strike as painless as possible. Of course you know best in these matters Captain, you and your protectorate should make the final decision of timing."

"I think dawn, they will see our numbers in the light, it will force some desertion, I see no issue entering the city, they will fall back to the halls and then we will go from there. We have had the other towns building siege ladders and they are beginning to arrive to camp. All is in hand, I would like to have had a few more archers but most of these men only know the sword. There may be casualties from the city my lord, not all these men are from my choosing."

"No, no, I understand. It is not ideal but we have had to cast our net wide." Shel-Toro hardly seemed to register the concept of collateral damage. "I assume Bast'wa awaits an audience."

"Indeed sir, he has been asking for some time."

"Well lets get it done so I can be rid of him, show him through and gather San Pollen and the others, I would have a meeting of minds once we are done."

"Of course, I will ensure it." The Captain saluted and moved out of the ornate tent, motioning for Bast'wa to be presented. He moved around the camp from fire to fire, some men he recognised most he did not. He was uncomfortable fighting with so many mercenary types but his hope was superior numbers would crush their opponent before the battle could begin. He noted Dulcet and his men gathered up around a cooking pig, they laughed and howled, not his choice that was for sure. Blaggards and curs not soldiers and little discipline, he walked to the officers tent to seek out Commander Grey.

While Grey was technically superior in rank to him, everyone knew he was in charge. Grey had served alongside him for years now as part of the Scholatic protectorate, he was ten years his senior and his best battle days were behind him but he was an incredible tactician and the Captain respected his view. The men acknowledged each other with a barely perceivable nod, "We have confirmed ready. Just to decide when."

The older man, shifted in his chair, his plate armour clanking against itself, "Be a shame not to give them a sighter. The clever move is night of course but why hide when we have such numerical supremacy. My vote would go for a dawn start and lets make a build up, so they get thinking time."

"My mind as well. Let fear be our own ally and we can finish this quickly."

"Don't be too eager my Captain, Parran is no boy, he will not fold to our charms easily."

"No but a few of his less loyal men may. We take the field tomorrow at dawn of winters night."

Grey stood up and brushed his remaining hair at the side, "Be good for one more, I have missed it Captain. I will brief the lieutenants."

The Captain stood with the cool Vedian wind whipping across his face, his cloak swept up, reaching out to the east. One more for Vedian, he thought.

Madistrin stood as upright as he could, leaning on the dark wood cane DeFache had kindly provided. He had offered some words, although they seemed quite inadequate. They buried Lint in the gardens, under a sycamore tree, Madistrin placed a white rose on his resting place. DeFache stood by his side, he did not know if Lint had family, often they did not but he would attend matters on his return. It was a strange concept to owe someone a debt that you could never repay.

DeFache offered a verse from the eternal book and then bowed and turned away, motioning for Madistrin to join him. They had run off the last guards with the servants help and first exchanged information of Madistrin's betrayal on the ship as well as the rise of the council in Vedian. The Scholatic had then called for word to be sent to the mainland by the only vessel they had left, a rowing boat. They needed to request a barge to cross and collect them, DeFache considered the two of them going in the row boat but the voyage could be rough in winter and it was a further risk that they could not afford.

"It is a days journey there and a night voyage back in a suitable vessel, we can have transport here by dawn all being equal. We will be in Pluris by tomorrow dusk, the day after winters night." DeFache sent two of his trusted servants, promising they spoke with no one and just secured passage with haste , he gave them coin enough to ensure it was done four times over.

"Yes that makes sense. One more day will surely make little difference, you perhaps take the time to fill me in on the background to the council's doings over the past months. I would best understand the motives for these actions. Also the charges they have made against you Umberto, why would you risk your place at the table for the boy?"

"You have spent a little time with him?" They walked back to Imanis, entering his main doors and traversing the long staircase to the study.

"Of course, under trying circumstances. I can see he is a special lad, there is a great sense of honesty about him. It leaves you somewhat bare." Madistrin leant his cane against the study chair and sat down, relieved to take some pressure off his leg.

"Indeed. I thought long and hard on asking him to move into the university walls but I felt it was right for him. I wanted to ensure he was safe and that seemed best served keeping him near. He has worked long and hard in the gardens, he is a skilled botanist, I realised that some rules are outdated, they needed challenging. I think as I get older I begin to question the things my youth took for granted."

"Well you are, as always have been, your own man DeFache and right now I am glad of it. Shel-Toro seems to stretch out across all of Vedian, I hope you will be able to advise me when we return on the best course of action to take."

DeFache strode around the study with purpose, sometimes scratching at his temple in thought, other times stretching out his long legs, he rarely stood still.

"The course of action may not be one you want to take. I think Shel-Toro looks to take other the governing of Vedian, to wrest it away from the crown and place the council at the heart of rule.

He sees himself as a saviour I think, his intentions are not as misguided as you may think."

"I doubt that. He is mad if he thinks that will wash with the people or the royal guard. I can surely appeal once in person to halt this madness."

"I wonder my friend what your brother would do in such a circumstance." DeFache peered out of the corner of his eye at the prince slumped in the chair.

"My brother would have fought himself had he seen a reflection, you know that Umberto. Are you trying to shame me to a war?"

DeFache stopped pacing for a moment and stared at Madistrin, "Perhaps just looking to goad you into a fight. I suspect things are much worse than we know, I am unsure what we will find when we are back on the mainland. I would simply have you open to all options."

"Fair enough. However I do not think Vedian needs sight of a cripple fighting at its walls."

DeFache smiled and thought to himself, that may be exactly what we need my friend.

It had been a long two days ride through the Rinslake Range, even using the pass, conditions where hard on the horses. Speck leant over his beast, nuzzling into his mane, he had rarely felt such a biting cold thrown at him. As they moved through the rock formations they could begin to see the outline of a city emerge, Medwere.

It appeared to gleam with the reflection off the huge frozen lake that surrounded it, Speck had never seen anything like it.

Cyrus rode close, "Its still a couple of hours, lets set down here in that cave entrance for shelter, I'm losing the feeling in everything!"

They pulled into a six foot recess, enough to use the kindling to get a small fire going and shelter the horses from the wind. They ate cheese and bread, it was too hard to cook and they knew a hot meal was close at hand now.

"Lets push on and just get it over with, I can feel a warm bed in arms reach, I don't want to spend anymore time out in this than we have to." Speck rubbed at his arms.

"You're probably right Lucent. Its been a long time since I travelled like this, I forgot how uncomfortable everything is. Lets water the mounts and then do the final leg."

As Speck went to the packs to pull some water for their horses, two figures came upon them, the elements having almost completely shielded them from view up to now.

"Hail." A voice came from the first man as he stopped at the cave entrance. "We are merchants out of Medwere, might we share this space for nightfall is closing in."

Cyrus waved his arm in front of him, "It is yours gentleman, we are now moving on, feel free to enjoy the small fire with our compliments."

The first man was squat and overweight, the second similar in height but thinner, both wore travelling cloaks and had large packs. They moved to take the weight off their backs before the thinner man turned to Cyrus, "Are you heading to Medwere?"

"Indeed yes, we have family there." Cyrus responded, mounting his horse.

"You would be careful then, towns overrun with militia. Curfews on dusk until dawn, don't be seen in the city between then, or you'll be for it. We had hoped to travel on to Pluris and sell our wares but word has it the road is now blocked."

The fatter man added, "I heard Pluris will be next for militia, some say there is an army on its door. I don't know though, I ain't seen an army."

"That's because you haven't been there. Mo Loins he's a smithy in Medwere, he knows. He says five hundred men have gathered. Well that's not right is it but I didn't want to say, cause Mo is a good man not usually the gossip type but these are strange days. Anyhow thanks for the fire and careful now."

Cyrus paused seeming to think for a moment, he then turned to the merchants, "Do you have foodstuffs to sell?"

The fat man smiled, "Aye we have indeed, let me show you our wares. Well this is a bit of luck. First in a while." He pulled off the heavy pack, unclipped the straps and pulled out a bundle of goods wrapped in a large pelt. Rolling it out on the cave floor to reveal its treasures."

"Got hard cheeses, boiled rarebit, salmon from the lake, very good bit of fish that." The man seemed beside himself with the prospect of some adhoc business.

"We'll take all the cheese and those two wolf pelts plus any kindling you can spare." Cyrus pulled a pouch up from his belt.

"Those pelts are northern wolf skin, very good price in the towns they fetch, especially down south. I would need three copper to see us right."

Speck spluttered, "Three copper! Were being robbed!"

Cyrus pulled out the coin, "It does not matter, here." He passed over three copper coins and they packed up the purchased goods and waved farewell to the two merchants.

Speck turned to Cyrus, "Am I to assume our warm beds have been put on hold."

"Pluris is in greater and more urgent danger than perhaps we knew, if their stories are even part true. We can save a day going south from here and joining up on the road, once we get closer we can reassess. Now we must ride and I think ride hard, prepare yourself Lucent, this is going to hurt in the morning."

"It will still be two days until we reach the city?" Speck asked.

Speck could hardly hear his reply in the wind as he rode ahead, "We should arrive on eve of winters night, if you do not insist on talking all of the way."

Joseph had been restless all that day, he had practised with Redrick in the morning but his mind just was not on swordplay. He had performed some chores in the halls, moving arrows up to the ramparts and oil from the stores. His mind kept returning to the words of Shel-Toro, how he had mesmerised the people so easily, like cattle being led to slaughter. He found himself wandering the streets as the sun went down over Pluris, the markets were open late, traditional on the eve of winters night.

He could smell the roasted pork and game but he had no taste for it, lamps and torches lit up the square and his eyes fell on the pulpit. What would stop him going up there? Nothing. There was no guard. The Scholatic had left the city according to Parran. He moved but then a fear got hold of him, what would he say? Who was he to address the people such? He was not a scholar, or even a noble, the best he could hope was that a few words would escape him and he would not make an ass of himself, so the locals didn't beat him for his folly.

Around him the city lived on, the smell of roasting permeated his nostrils, it was a warm homely smell, it reminded him of the Luff. And that was when it struck him, this was not just about Pluris, or these people, it was about every man, in every town and village.

No one had the right.

Like a migrating bird at the onset of winter he was guided by nature. Three steps and he was at the base, two more and he had reached the bottom of the lectern and then he rose and as loud as his voice would carry in the air, he shouted, "My people, please!"

Some stopped to look, others briefly distracted before turning back to their business.

He tried again, "I would speak to the people of Vedian. Please hear me."

There was some commotion now, a few of the traders had stopped and begun to wave their arms, "Get down lad before they throw you down!"

A small group of townsmen had moved from the market stalls in front of the platform, "You're not allowed up there you fool, get down its for the words men only. Come down now!"

Joseph pushed on regardless of their protestations, "Outside these walls is an army, it has been raised for one reason and one reason only."

Some of the shooting had stopped and more folk moved from the market to gather under the pulpit.

Joseph shouted to try and garner more interest, "Hear me now. Hear me people of Pluris" More stopped and shuffled towards the pulpit area.

"A few days ago the leader of the council stood here whispered promises of peace in your ears. He offered you law and order and you took it like a suckling lamb! Did you not once go back to your homes and question the price? He has militia in every other town in the country, curfews in every city, men are beaten for mere misdemeanour's, he will bring you justice. Oh yes! But it will have no heart, no compassion, it will not be for you, only for his greater good. What are we without our freedom, without our will to choose between right and wrong? Have we strayed? Perhaps. Vedian is not what it once was but it is still ours. We that live on its land, farm its fields and harvest its oceans. Not they who languish in their towers, what right do they have? Tomorrow a thousand men will storm this city and take it by force and they will promise you comfort. If you take it, if you lay down and curl up under the shadow of their promises, you betray all that Vedian stands for. Once we stood and held our lands against the invaders from far shores, it was easy to spot the enemy, with their ships and arms. Now we enter an age, where our greatest threat is in the poison that men weave in their words. Where education and learning are weapons that are used to subdue us before we are even men. It is one thing to stand in front of your enemy, to choose to fight and perhaps to die for that cause but we are denied even that! They tell you tales of the Crown Prince, of his loss, yet they do not reveal it is them that took him from you!"

A gasp went up in the crowd, the whole market area had stopped, every man, woman and child was turned to face Joseph.

"You are beset on every side but I do not fear the army and their thousand swords, for that I can touch and I can feel but those words that cut through our very heritage, the demand that, which if our wits where about us, we would never give in to. This I can not fight alone. I am but a man of Kearn Luff, a simple fishing village of Vedian, I have worked the land and seas and would be happiest doing both again. Yet I am here instead, I stand here, where I am forbidden to stand and why? Because of their repression! Because of their thraldom! It is enough. I say enough! Lies have eaten away at this land since the death of our first prince and I tell you now his death too was a lie! Spun by the men that would feed you this peace, this false sanctuary."

364

The crowd were fixated on him, frozen in a moment, mouths open, eyes wide, each word soaked up.

"Now on this winters night, I ask you, men and women of Pluris, stand with us, with the royal guard of Madistrin the rightful heir who represents the people. Fight to protect the one thing you can not allow them to take, your free will. And if within these walls you forfeit your life, I can tell you now and with certainty, you will feel no remorse even after the last breath escapes you!"

Chapter 19 - Winters Night

If we be brave enough and if our souls

be wise enough in Vedian's embrace,

We may find a place, a glorious place

to share our brothers face.

Yet only can you find this goal

this endless nirvana of hope,

If prepared we are to share our blood

in defence of nations scope.

Oh blessed transgressors! Oh divine sinners!

We have room for you all on the tapestry of conflict.

No man will be turned away, no man can be lost,

If he fights for King, for Vedian, ne're will there be cost.

Into her arms, she will call you,

Into her bosom she holds you,

No love have you ever held in rapture,

Greater than this land our enemy would capture.

So stand now man of Vedian,

March now soldier and sons,

Destiny awaits you in this glorious theatre

An eternity for Vedian's blessed ones.

'O Blessed Vedian' - Richmond the Laureate - Vedian 551

Joseph had eaten a light breakfast as Redrick had advised, a cut of bread and some pork rinds left from the night before. The atmosphere in the main hall was a nervous one, soldiers talked quietly, others silent, burdened with their own thoughts. The Asten Lancers had left first, positioned in two groups of fifty men, Captain Corn had departed with them and as agreed with Parran he would stand at the north and south gates.

"I can not see much reason they will not knock on the front door but we should be prepared for them to split their forces and move north and south as well. I will divide my force to communicate quickly if the need requires." Corn had raised his hand to salute the Commander in the traditional way and left well before the sun rose.

Parran spoke with Redrick and Rayan, he was cold and efficacious now, even more so than usual, "Rayan will hold a troop of the Coralis swords here to manage the retreat and defend the bulwark. Corn I think is right, they are likely to push their weight to the main gate west, Brown will take his seventy pikemen to the front plus the rest of the swords." He ran his hand down the thick scabbard, feeling the familiarity of its dents and scratches to the touch, then paused and whispered so only Rayan and Redrick could hear. "What of the concealed entrance that leads up to the halls from the docks to the east? Would the Scholatic know of it?"

"To my knowledge that is a well guarded secret. Madistrin was careful to keep silent on the matter, it is only known to a trusted few and in any case it is barely a man wide at the tunnel, easily defended. We should post a couple of guards at the base of the interior steps, just in case." Parran nodded at Rayan's words to confirm his agreement.

"We are lucky so many recruits came forward last night, another hundred men trained or not will help the first push." Redrick looked across to Joseph who seemed unmoved to the activity around him.

"I doubt any of them will last the day and most will run at the sight of the enemy." Parran stopped seeming to think better of his words. "Yet it is good to have the people with us. Madistrin would be proud. The boy has some guts, I will give him that, I would rather face the whole army myself than stand up and talk in the way he did. My god I think I would have followed him!"

Redrick chuckled, "So the old warhorse still can still be touched can he?"

Parran gave him a look, which was enough to stop his laughter. "We will still have only two hundred men at the main west gate, Rayan stands with the Coralis swords, what of you Redrick? I have no order to give, where would you choose to stand?"

Redrick paused and called over to Joseph, "Lad, come hither, I would have words with you."

Joseph pushed aside his plate and stretched his arms up as he pushed back the bench he was sitting it, "Yes Redrick?"

"We need to take our positions, where do you stand?" Redrick looked directly at Joseph's eyes, looking for some sort of sign or expression.

"With the people Redrick, where else could I be. At the west gate." Joseph did not think or stutter, he just replied with earnest.

"You see Parran it is a foolish question, or perhaps a question for a fool, either way the answer remains the same. Across thirty feet from the main gate is the millers house, it has a stone chimney. That's is where you will find me, keeping a promise."

Parran reached out and clutched the arm of the tracker, "I am glad you are with us, fight well and luck be with you." He turned to Joseph, "And to you, keep your back to another where you can and your eyes open."

The commander marched out with the Royal Guard, forty strong they left the halls on the morning of winters night.

Redrick checked through Joseph's equipment, ensuring his chain tunic was pulled tight and his buckler straps taut enough that the shield would hold even without a hand grip. "Have you managed the weight of that blade yet?"

"It still feels heavy, are you sure I would not do better with a lighter blade like we equipped the other townsfolk with?"

"I am sure, we will check again tomorrow, see how you fare." Redrick finished checking his own armour, all leather from head to foot, with a matching neck brace and wrapped helmet that left nothing exposed but his eyes.

"Is one day really going to make a difference?" Joseph asked belligerently.

"Normally not but this day will likely be the longest in your life, at times the seconds will pass like hours, it will feel like it goes on forever and there is no end. If at any point night or day you get a chance to rest I would encourage you to take it. Fatigue is your greatest enemy, that is if we discount the thousand or so men out there all waiting to kill you." Redrick roared with laughter, it seemed to Joseph he found nothing more funny than himself.

"Captain Corn sir, the men are set at both gates sir!"

"Thank you Lieutenant, hold the south watch and report to me with a runner if you have sight of anything. I will hold here with the north gate in the meantime."

"Question Captain." The soldier stood patiently waiting permission to ask.

"Given as always Lieutenant." Corn liked the military lifestyle, respectful and ordered. Lieutenant Milton Elk had been with him for ten years and he trusted no man under his command more. A stalwart shining example of military upbringing like his father before him, tall and muscular built for the role.

"If the force pushes west only, will we join the defence sir or hold the north and south gates?"

"Fair question. I think we need to keep our mind open, for now we hold, the last thing Parran needs is a sting in the tail and it would not take many to come through from behind him to do that. I know its hard for the men to stand watch while the others engage but we all have a job to do." He saluted to Elk and the lieutenant departed for the south gate.

Lets hope they do not choose to come north or south first or their minds may quickly wish they were watching the others. Fifty men won't last long, just enough time to send a runner and report numbers. Either way he would do his duty, that was what being a Captain was to him and he would be damned if anything was going to change that.

So he stood and watched over his men waiting for the dawn of winters night to arrive.

Captain Brown stood facing the tall west gates, the main door to Vedian closed for the first time in many years. It stood fifteen foot tall, two huge panels over three foot thick and reinforced with joists across. It had taken four men to push them closed and more to drop the huge wedge that locked them into place. However as intimidating as it looked it was made of wood and that could be burnt. It would take time but sooner or later they would come through, hordes of attackers and he would hold the line first, his pikemen were best placed to greet the inaugural attack with their sixteen foot polearms. He organised them in ranks of six, each group locked together shoulder to shoulder, ready to face infantry advances first from distance and then once the initial attack they would draw on the short swords at their belts, moving hand to hand.

Twelve teams set before him, he would hope for each pike to take a victim or two before being discarded, behind them the hundred or so men recruited from the city, each dressed in bits and pieces of armour they scavenged from the halls stocks, some carrying flails others swords, they looked like a noisy cockerel could scare them off. He had often believed he would die in battle as had his ancestors before him, his father a famed member of the glorious Sabre Regiment, if only he could be here to see him once more, to see the man he had become on the battlefield. He walked through the ranks, inspecting the men, talking with some, encouraging others.

"You Lancepesade Hamman, that spears been notched man!" He addressed one of the ranks.

"Yes sir, indeed sir. I struck it on Lancepesade Brines helmet after he took my woman sir!" Hamman stood up straight, his eyes looking left to his colleague.

"Is this true Brines, did you take Hamman's woman?" The Captain addressed a stocky soldier of short build.

"Yes sir, that is a truth sir but in my defence she looked like a man."

The whole troop begun laughing and Brown joined in with them. These were his family, the brave men that stood now around him, he was at truly home here.

And on the morning of winters night, he stood watching over them.

The halls were quiet now, a few of Madistrin's loyal servants went about clearing out the eating area preparing drink for any that would need it throughout the day. Rayan had placed the troop out on the bulwark ramparts that were accessed from a large staircase and then extended out from the halls and linked to the defensive walls, it faced directly towards the main west gate. The north gate was obscured by the university but the west retreat would be covered perfectly from this vantage point.

Most of the Asten swords were decent bowman as well, so thirty were placed on the walkway with arrow stocks and the other twenty in the base of the bulwark ready to pull the gate in case of retreat. Unlike the west gate to the town the bulwark gate was crafted from the thickest stone and Rayan's concern was not the enemy penetrating it rather than how they would close it quick enough once the men were inside. The retreat was though the marketplace and past town buildings, they would be pursued and he was reliant on his archers to give them enough cover. It would be tight.

His thoughts turned to the battle, if they could hold outside for the first day and night, perhaps enough time for the Huskian's to arrive before they were pushed back to the halls. He caught himself, why would they come? Vedian has had no contact with them for years, it was idle wishing to think they will ride to our aid.

He walked back from the ramparts along the walkway that crossed into the main building and through the double doors that led to the stone staircase and down into the hall, picking up his kite shield, the reverse teardrop shape adorned with the crest of Vedian. He slung it across his back, using a guige strap to hold it in place and looked down at his weapon. Most of the swords preferred the arming sword or falchion, they were trained in most blades but oddly he had always found the flanged mace a more versatile weapon, perhaps it was the weight, it was only two foot but sturdy in his grip. He handled it like a treasure, caressing it between his hands, its penetrating edges catching the last rays of moonlight that wisped through from the windows above. The Captain of the Coralis Swords, wielder of the mace! Oh how they had loved that in Asten at first! Yet time and again he had silenced them at tournaments until he stood as Vedian's Coralis champion for four years running now, even Junas the Sword had not managed that achievement.

He moved down the stone stairs and out into the courtyard, the cold morning air striking against his face and crisp grass cracking under the weight of his passing. He passed into the lower bulwark and exchanged words with his men, for five years he had stood guard over a city that did not want him or his men. Yet he had defended Coralis as Madistrin instructed, with never a word of thanks from its people.

He wondered who was watching over them now on the morning of winters night.

Parran surveyed the west gate, Browns pikemen were in place, he could hear them from the marketplace, that was no bad thing, if he could hear them so could their enemy.

The townsfolk would be found out quickly, only a handful would survive the first hour, it was the natural order of things. Those that made it would be stronger for the next encounter.

Behind them he had positioned the Asten swords, around fifty men, under Lieutenant Ank, a rather unpleasant individual that he was not convinced by. His appointment had come via a Scholatic request after he had performed some duty for the Protectorate. Madistrin had told him it would be politic to allow the appointment, he had conceded.

An officer needed to have the confidence of himself and his men, Ank had neither and that worried him. Still he had done nothing directly to suggest he was anything but loyal and right now Parran needed everyone. He held the royal guard with him at the rear, just at the front of the market place, half way between the west gate and the hall walls. From here he could survey the battlefront and be in a position to call a retreat. The men around him were the best, hand picked by him from swords, lancers and pikemen throughout Vedian. It was considered a great honour to serve amongst the royal guard and a position of respect in the city. Most were venerable, some as old as fifty, lifetime military men, no longer designed for battle but more for the show. Even their armour was more pomp than it was practical and yet Parran could not see his way to dishonour the Crown Prince by wearing any other.

A fine thin plate armour, crafted from metal but enough only to see off a swung blade, any firm blunt weapon could gouge through its defences. The shields were smaller versions of the kite the swords used, called heater shields, made from tough wood and covered in a hard leather and thick papyrus, they were painted in gold with the royal crest. As well as a traditional long sword they held a glaive, a polearm of six foot with a single edged tapered blade. The overall effect was intimidating and impressive if far from battle efficient.

To Parran though it was more than that, his armour and that of his men's represented the man he believed in. A gentleman and Crown Prince that he had served most of his life and that he respected above all others. If he had asked him to take the battlefield with nothing but the clothes he had brought into the world, then he would have done.

On the morning of winters night he stood for his men, for Vedian and above all for Madistrin.

Redrick pulled himself up onto the window ledge and grabbed at the joist that secured the roof to the millers home. The thatched roof snapped as he grabbed at a hand hold. Not the best place to be if they decide to start shooting fire arrows he thought to himself.

He nestled into the chimney stack, the brick and clay support perfect to defend from. He pulled a longbow off his back, a single crafted wood weapon, he had picked it up in Kanegon a few years back. Supposedly, if the merchant was to be believed, carved from the grand oaks from across the western shores. Most archers could shoot five maybe six arrows a minute, the tension on the shoulder and fingers too much to enable much more over a prolonged period. Redrick had spent many days in the rough mountains of the Rinslake Range, hunting in and around Medwere, he could fire a bow when his fingers had lost feeling and the muscles in his left side were over developed as a result.

Nestled in twelve groups around him and gathered with reeds from the Medwere marsh were twelve arrows. One hundred and forty four, enough to take more than one tenth of their force down if they left him be. He smiled to himself, he needed to get the lion's share off before they breached the gate, once through they would burn the closest buildings and he would have to find new lodgings.

On his back was two quivers crossed over, he placed two stacks in each and looked down at the courtyard below.

He could see Joseph standing with the other recruits, he looked completely lost, out of his element and depth. If Redrick did nothing else this day it would to ensure the lad survived, he was special in his normality, he had quickly become dear to the tracker.

He stood on the thatched roof of the millers home with one solitary aim on the morning of winters night.

The sound of voices was all around him, he stood three rows back with the townsfolk, they had been organised into groups of twenty and told to stay together as much as possible when the fighting started. Some of the men looked petrified at the prospect, others accepting of their fate. A few were retired military and had a look of despair more than fear, a lifetime working to get out of the militia, now at the final hour pulled back in through obligation, shame or a mix of the two.

The thought arrived with Joseph that these men were here because of him, they stood alongside the military due to his words. He had to check himself, to accept the reality of that. These men stood due to what he, Joseph the sailor from the Luff, had said and he now strolled around them like a lost lamb. No. Unacceptable to bring a man this far and abandon him to his own fears.

He picked himself up, physically drawing on his frame to deliver presence and give himself confidence. Beginning to walk through the ranks, smiling and acknowledging each man as he walked purposefully, he had seen Redrick do it often enough now. A little banter with some, a laugh with another and where he went the mood lifted.

"Good morning Joseph, it is good to have you with us." A young man, barely older than himself held out a gloved hand.

"And to you sir, could I have your name on this day?" Joseph smiled and shook the outstretched offering.

"I am Will, the Millers son. What you said sir, my father said it moved him like no other since the days of the princes brother. He said there was no point having a home and business if it was at another man's behest, mother was unhappy but were here. For you." His voice was earnest and it jarred Joseph.

These men could die here, on this morning they could well stand and die, Parran had as much said it, most of the ones that chose not to run would be dead in the first hour. What he had asked of these men was to sacrifice themselves and for what? Joseph begun to wonder at his own words, were they born out of a selfish need, did their free will really mean so much, was it worth a families life? Joseph looked at the millers sons face and knew that this was not the time to share any doubts of his own.

"It is good to have you with us Will." Joseph noticed at his side he held a crudely constructed morning star. "A strong weapon, do you know much of its use?"

"My father was in the militia for a time, he has shown me how to use it. He says the morning star is a favoured weapon of a common man."

Joseph put a hand on his shoulder, "It will serve you well and there will never be anything common about you Will. You stand today with some of Vedian's finest, shoulder to shoulder, we are kings among men my friend!" And then seeing the reaction on the young mans face Joseph shouted it for all to hear. "Kings among men!"

The townsfolk as well as the pikemen and swords joined in, "Kings among men!"

As the roar went up it was deafened by an almighty cry from beyond the gate and the stampeding of boots on hard frost covered ground. The dawn broke and light chiselled through from the west to fall on the courtyard.

As the horde advanced on the western gate, Joseph stood steadfast at Pluris on the morning of winters night, a sole man from the Luff, a king among men.

"Should I scout ahead, I could cover the ground quicker perhaps?" Arn for the fourth time that day questioned Dance.

"We need to hold a forced march and no more love. There's no point reaching Pluris with nothing left, we should make it by tomorrow night."

Tarnell had explained that the army was at the door, he had made the promise to the Elders of future aid and asked for help. It had taken time for Elder Orn to once again reach out to the other tribes but eventually they had agreed to provide assistance. Longer term a debt owed by the Crown Prince seemed a way out of their issues with Bast'wa. They assembled a force one hundred strong, enough were held back to guard the camps. It had been a long time since Huskian's fought abroad from their home, most had never been past the borders of the Lough taran and some had never left the Inpur desert. The thought of a chance to engage Bast'wa and his men was enough incentive for most of the tribes.

Dance had envisioned herself taking charge of the force but in an unusual move for their people, Elder Orn had chosen to lead his tribe. With no horses to their name and most unfamiliar with riding they had no option but to march, Huskian men were made for combat and not speed, the females of the tribe fared a little better, their force made up with over a third females. Arn never thought to question the difference in Vedian culture, where women were not deemed acceptable to hold positions in battle. His relationship with Dance had already taught him so much of what she was capable of, he had no doubt her kin were of the same ilk.

They had made the journey through the Inpur and up over the Lough in good time and by the evening of winters night they had almost crossed half way the journey to the Pluris crossroads where a few weeks hence, Joseph and Speck had parted ways.

"Tarnell confirmed there are a thousand men attacking, one more day could be one too many. He says only two hundred men defend the city." Arn struggled to hide the frustration in his voice, he had asked after Joseph and Speck just on the off chance. Tarnell had recognised his friends name immediately, explaining that he had seen the young mariner with Commander Parran. His friend was alone with an army at his door, he should never have left him. It was selfish and he knew it, his guilt was threatening to engulf him, this was not the first time he had parted company by choice, they had done so in Asten and Arn had promised it would not happen again. But then he had not expected for love to sneak past him while he was not looking. He looked at Febra, walking as ever next to Elder Orn, she knew it too, what ever fate fell on Joseph was on both of them.

Dance called a halt to the march and spoke briefly with Elder Orn before turning to Arn, "We will camp here off the road, then we start again tomorrow morning, we will push straight on and should make the city after nightfall, Tarnell has told us we should approach from the south gate and he can get us passage. Although by then, we may have to react to circumstances as we find them."

"Let me scout ahead, please Dance. I can find out what is going on, prepare you better." Arn pleaded and Dance knew her love for him would no longer stay his hand.

She nodded but asked him to wait until she had spoken to Orn. A few moments later she returned and motioned for Febra to join them.

"I have news, the Elder has decided Huskian's should enter with purity to the human city. The spirits have spoken and he will allow you to move ahead Arn but only if Febra accompanies you." She cautiously eyed Febra to see her reaction, it had been her that pleaded with Orn to release Febra, she knew he would go on ahead and with the girl at his side, she believed his chances of survival were improved.

"Strange turn of events. I assume hunter you would look to move forwards tonight?" Febra turned to Arn.

"Our friend is in that city and I can not sleep wondering what has become of him, we are both fast over ground, we can be there by the morning if we travel hard. Will you journey with me again, whatever ill has befallen you, it changes nothing. I believe Rundell would wish it for us."

Febra tilted her head to one side, "I believe he probably would. Lets just hope you can keep up hunter."

Arn looked back at Dance, embracing and kissing her passionately, "I am sorry, please understand, I do love you and I will find again you before you enter the south gate and bring you word. My heart is torn but it will be damned I am sure if I do not help my friend."

"Go. Be safe my love." Dance reached out to touch his hand again but the hunter was gone. She watched them run under the moonlight until they were just shadows amongst the winters darkness.

It seemed to Speck the wrong time, a day and a night out perhaps from Pluris, Cyrus estimated. He was shattered from riding and the horses needed a rest as much as him. What he should do right now is get some sleep but he felt that familiar urge and he carefully pulled the book from his pouch.

He turned open the cover and the feeling washed over him, warm and comforting now, it was a truly holistic experience and he bathed deep within it.

Captain Tress stood in the lower keep, his breathing hard, his armour gone, in his hand a dagger. At his feet, the body of one of their own, a man from Asten, he did not recognise his face. Had madness finally gripped him? Was the stress of battle taking its final toll?

He looked carefully around the corner, two more guarded the door to his cell, no point trying to reason. These were Dior's personal guard and they would be under orders to let no one pass not even the Captain of the Sabre regiment.

His hand was shaking slightly, he tapped on the wall with the hilt of the dagger, the sound echoed around the old walls. He could hear footsteps coming closer, as the man rounded the corner he was on him, no point in even trying to disarm him, these were good men, veterans, it was a killing blow or nothing. He brought the blade up into the ribs, twisting and pushing again, before retracting it. He had come into view and the second guard who was shocked at the realisation of who he faced, turned and advanced, cautiously.

Tress thought to apologise, to say something to explain his actions but he would have struggled to do that to himself. The guard led with his shield, pushing out with the heater to push Tress off balance. In turn the Captain took a step back and reversed the blade in the back of his hand, bringing it up, looking to catch the face. The attack glanced off the top of the shield.

"Traitor scum! What are they paying you!" The guards hatred was struggling to keep under control at the sight of Tress's betrayal.

He did not bother to respond, he needed to focus, he thought to throw the blade but checked and rolled off the wall as the shield slammed into it, followed swiftly by a cutting falchion swipe. He was almost close enough, he grabbed into melee range and at a right angle drew the blade into the neck, working past the protective armour and burying it deep in the flesh.

Breathing hard he tried to steady himself, reaching for the keys on the waistband. He unlocked the heavy door and pushed it open, inside sat the shaman. He looked at the Captain, covered in blood and visibly shaking now.

"I have been waiting for you. Now we can end this, if you have it?"

Tress pulled from his pack a small ornate crescent moon, carved from wood and embossed with colourful paints and handed it to the shaman.

"We have to leave now. We have a few minutes before they realise something is wrong. I have secured passage out for you once over the wall."

They moved quickly through the keep, up the steps. Once they reached the upper levels everyone was too busy to notice one more man with their Captain. Larger than most but just another man defending against the onslaught.

They reached the back of the keep and Tress lowered a rope down the outside of the building, a tug from below confirmed it was time.

"You could come with me, we would protect you." The shaman offered.

"Nothing can protect me from what I have done. My treachery is complete, leave."

"What you have done will save two nations."

"Perhaps but my name is damned." Tress turned and walked back to the walls as the shaman lowered himself down on the rope and slowly disappeared from view. As he approached the walkway he saw Pinkerton wiping down his sword with a thick cloth. He looked up at the Captain from his sitting position and smiled. Tress walked past his lieutenant and bent down to pick up an old longsword discarded from the previous days fighting. He stood alone on the battlements, Captain Tress of the Sabre regiment, for the final time.

In the distance horns blew and the enemy advanced once more.

Speck looked up and the realisation of a secret locked away dawned on him in its entirety. Vedian was not the oppressed, they had been the aggressor, they had stolen and held in chains a captive from their enemy. The only reason the shores had been crossed was to seek out what had been taken from them. The King could have given it at any time, he could have released the shaman and returned their artefact. Why? It made no sense to bring a war on Vedian for what benefit?

He looked across at Cyrus who was covered in the pelts bought from the merchants, "Why old man? Why did we go to war?"

He was met only with the deep snores from the enchanter and he stirred turned over and fell back to a deep sleep. Speck was too wide awake to even think about sleep, Tress had turned on his own people to right the wrong the king could have resolved long ago, so many dead.

Slowly Speck drifted away, minutes or hours passed and the pace of the day caught him, he slept but the images confronted him, there was no peace in sleep.

When he awoke it was to a cold and frosty morning, Cyrus had a fire burning and they shared a small breakfast before loading the horses and riding again. As they slowly twisted though the mountain paths it was the noise Speck heard before they could see any sight, a throng of crashing and shouting, cries and curdling screams. The mountain cover still obscured Pluris from view but they were close now, enough to know a battle was being fought. As they neared the end of the range Cyrus had them dismount their horses and walk.

What faced Speck would live long in his memory, the site of hundreds of men pressed against the walls of the city, of fire raging at the gate and from the city. Behind hundreds more men stood in troops awaiting their orders.

"My god Cyrus, we are too late!"

"They are not yet in the city, so the battle still is not lost I think. However a way in seems to be the issue. We should scout round to the north gate, to see if it is under siege as well."

They moved cautiously through the hills, careful to draw no unwanted attention to their passing, Speck was fixated by the battle as it raged around the city.

As they came into view of the north gate, they could see a smaller battle, perhaps a hundred men pressing with a singular battering ram being used to assault the entrance. Speck had never seen such a contraption, it was like a small out house on wheels, within men were pushing it forward and in front a long arm that was reinforced with metal at the head. Time and again they drove it against the heavy gates.

"We need to help Cyrus. The gate will not hold against that for ever." Speck was eager to engage.

"Hold steady Master Lucent, if we reveal ourselves outside the city, it will be us in the real danger. No we should enter with stealth, to show our hand too early I think will be a mistake."

As Cyrus pondered the best way forward Speck was lost in the image of the scene from the main gate, how could they endure such a force? His mind turned to Joseph, his friend was in there somewhere, he was certain of it but he needed to be sure. He concentrated, closing his eyes and as Remys had taught him he focussed until everything else in his mind was blocked out, until just one image remained. Then a spark of light and for a moment, for a fleeting moment, he saw his friend, Joseph illuminated in his mind as if he were standing next to him. His friend was alive! And he was in trouble. Speck knew there was no more time.

The first few minutes all Joseph could hear was the alternate thud of the rams striking against the gates. One then the other, a dull and ominous reverberation that echoed in the ears of the men. Then the skies filled with a hundred arrows and orders were shouted for cover, Joseph pulled his buckler tight to cover his head and squatted as low as he could.

Parran ordered the few archers they had to return fire but for the first hour they simply stood and waited. A greater test Joseph had never endured, with the thud of the rams and the whistling of the arrows punctuating the silence.

Surely they should be doing something he thought to himself, the gate would not hold for ever. Occasionally he would turn and look back to see Parran standing silent, expecting him to burst into action.

Then it came, a resounding crack, the gate latch begun to splinter, a huge cry came up from outside, men whooping and shouting. A swarm of arrows turned from black to red. Fire was thrown down into the gate and further into the city, most landed harmlessly but a few took hold in straw or the few bits of wood in buildings. A second volley and a third came this time all hitting the gate, peppering it on both sides and the smell of burning hit Joseph's nostrils.

Again the rams struck and the gates held.

A few of the men standing in the group Joseph was in were trembling, some had taken wounds from the bowmen and retreated back to the halls. He could see their courage failing each time the rams struck at their target, if they did not do something soon, they would lose them.

Fire had now gripped the top of the gates, they were blazing and the next ram splintered again at the huge latch that held them tight. Surely one more push and they would be through. Joseph looked round once more desperately hoping to see Parran moving to action.

Still nothing, not a movement or sound come from the stoic commander. From each side of the gate emerged two men, each rolling out a linen that met in the middle at the base of the gate. The cloth was a metre in width and looked damp, then beyond that a second layer and a third, so the cloth ran over three metres deep almost to where the first line of Pikemen stood.

The next moments happened so quickly, it was hard for Joseph to register in what order they commenced. The siege weapon struck again, this time the latch broke and the gates pushed open, the rams rushing forwards with their own momentum. A single voice, Parran's, shouted from behind him and arrows cased in fire were launched to the edges of the rolled out mats.

In a second the whole scene was engulfed in flames, the rams and the men in them encased in fire. The screams and shrieks rang out in through the cold air and the gate once more became impassable.

Rather than waiting and allowing the fire to die down as it eventually would, more rams were pushed forward with cries from beyond. Forced into the gap that had been made, they instantly caught fire as well but enough momentum had been achieved to press a gap through the gates. The attackers pushed forward like hunting dogs, heads down they rushed for the space with fire at either side.

Browns pikemen were instantly mobilised, a single troop moving to the breach, advancing in time with the enemy. Slightly tipping their long weapons to greet the attack, they pierced the first men and moved to the side and back, allowing the next troop to engage. Brown called the organised rotation again and again, then as the bodies begun to pile up, the flames subsided and the gap was widened. The enemy ran hard this time in much larger numbers, the pikemen held strong but there was more than a single troop could hold against, the enemy hurled themselves over the top, some impaling on the huge spikes, others pushing back the lines with the sheer force of their weight.

Brown called them to group in a wider order, three troops pushed against the line but a few began to break through, throwing a mixture of hand axes and short swords randomly into the defenders.

Now they were too close and the long pikes lost efficiency, Browns men unsheathed the short swords they carried, engaging hand to hand.

Joseph looked around and sought out the face of Parran, the commander looked at him and nodded.

Joseph cried out and called the men around him to support the pikemen. His first experience of close quarter battle was more brutal than he could ever have imagined. There was no skill, no ability that could navigate this melee of blades, shields, kicking and brawling. He tried to pull his sword up to strike an attacker to his left but it got caught on the shield of another defender. The best he could do was raise his buckler and slam it into the enemy for a dull glancing blow.

Over a hundred and twenty pikemen and townsfolk engaged in the battle now but the enemy numbers pressed and pressed through the gap and slowly as the fires dimmed, the entry point widened.

For the first time Joseph and the men around him had been pushed back to the right side of the gates, he had some room to fight. He pulled up the sword and swung it, cutting deeply into the back of a long haired assailant, dropping him to the floor, Joseph moved in for a finishing blow, as he did an arrow whistled past him. He turned to see another man who had come from his blind side dropping down. His first real lesson, Parran's words ringing in his ears, from that moment on he sought out another man to fight behind, always looking to have another at his back, he found Will the millers son. They engaged back to back instinctively and pushed themselves forward, Joseph catching a single word of instruction to the young man, "Together."

For the rest of the morning they fought, sometimes with the townsfolk and other times with Brown and his pikemen. He lost count of how many arrows had passed him, striking an as of yet unseen opponent. The long shadow of Redrick was watching over him.

After an hour of battle, he could feel the line buckling, it was an odd sensation, the fighting became concentrated at the centre and then a man fighting next to him would fall and a wedge was driven in. It was confusing at first and then a feeling of panic begun to rise, the notion that he should run filled Joseph, he could see it in other faces. All of a sudden he and Will were cut off from the group they had been fighting with, it happened so fast they could not react. They ran against the men pushing them hard, trying desperately to break through but they were thrown back by the weight of the attackers. In his head Joseph could hear the retreat being sounded but he could not react, a dozen men had now surrounded them and they were backed up almost to the outer buildings, there was no way out. Joseph looked across at Will who was holding the morning star his father had given him tightly in two hands.

The inevitable charge begun as the men looked to finish the small prey and then between them a wall of fire sprung up from nowhere, dividing them from their attackers. Flames twelve foot high stopped their assailants in their tracks. Behind him a voice,

Joseph looked round and up to see a long arm dangling down, he grabbed it and was hoisted up onto the rooftop, now burning around him. He grabbed down and pulled up Will.

"Well I don't know where that fire came from lad but you are blessed indeed!" Redrick smiled and motioned them to follow him over the building top which now burned slowly. "We have to get back to the halls, Parran has sounded the withdrawal and once the gates close we are in trouble."

They ran over the rooftop, dropping down on the other side and slipping between the buildings, making for the safety of the bulwark. The fighting still raged around them, Browns pikemen desperately trying to hold the retreat, to enable the remaining soldiers to make a safe return to the halls as Rayan's men gave covering fire from the top of the wall.

"What did we achieve?" Joseph shouted at Redrick as they ran.

"You're alive lad, that's all you can ever hope to achieve in battle!"

Chapter 20 - Blood Oath

"It is oft the case in historical terms, that we look back on a moment in time and seek to paint its picture in glory. A recollection bound in reverence and hope for the future, more than an actual record of facts and truth. When it comes to the Great War and the legendary Sabre Regiment, nothing could be more the case. Stories, tales and fables both spoken and written shroud the men of the regiment in majesty and immortality. So I set out in good faith to collate and record just the facts, to piece together what is actually known of the regiment. I have probed, read and questioned in an effort to cast light on their experience, skills and achievements. To be honest it has been like sieving a flour that forever pours. Everyone seems to know something about the Sabre's history or knows someone who does, every man has an affinity to them, everyone a story to tell.

As I pursued the elusive truths, I began to wonder of the point to it. For the first time in my lifetime as historian and archaeologist I questioned the purpose of fact.

What could a truth add to the myth so fully formed. A legend that could inspire a child at the mere utterance of its name, what part could fact play than to pour scorn on innocence?

So I laid to rest the History of the Sabre Regiment and instead choose to publish a work of their triumphs from the mouths of men. For once in a while, just sometimes, we need the dream more than we need the reality."

'The Sabre Regiment: Tales of Triumph' - Karl of Bannermane Archaeologist & Literary Commentator - Vedian 981

The leather partition was wet from a fading morning frost, water dripped slowly down onto the Captains helm as he waited.

"Sorry to keep you, how did the morning fare Captain? SanPollan and I were just discussing the use of the siege weapons, very interesting how warfare has evolved over recent times. The roof built to shield the men from arrows as they operate the contraption is very clever."

SanPollan stretched out his long arms, "Yes, I was most excited to watch the gate and then you sent in the next rams almost immediately knowing they would catch fire and the men inside perish. Could you explain more of that decision Captain?"

"Men die in war your Prominence, the decisions I take are to decide how and when. Taking the gate main gate was our primary objective on the first morning, we have achieved this." Nothing in the Captains voice showed any sign of frustration as he answered the Scholatic's questions patiently.

"What will be our next move? Will you assault the keep today?" The Scholatic from Coralis mused.

"I think it for the best my lord, the sooner we can press them, the sooner their numbers will dwindle."

SanPollan laughed, "Oh yes Captain. We will have this rabble out by sundown no doubt."

"The halls is not that easy to take my liege. The Bulwark is well defended, it will come at a cost of many men but we will take it, not today, or tomorrow, the next I think." The Captain bowed and after waiting for confirmation from Shel-Toro, he departed.

"Hes a fierce individual your Captain. Lacks a certain character at times." SanPollan plucked at the succulent grapes that rolled on his plate.

"He is a man from a different time. He has served the Scholatic all his life and we are lucky to have him. The Captain will deliver for us the final piece that is Pluris, then the council will control Vedian and we can begin to guide these men as they need to be."

"A firm hand." SanPollan offered.

"I look at these men in our own camp, I see thieves and charlatans. I think to begin with we may have to take a more severe touch. It will be for the best in the long term." Shel-Toro nodded to himself.

"Do you not fear the peoples unhappiness at those actions?" SanPollan looked up from his plate briefly catching Shel-Toro's eyes.

"I will never fear the repercussions of my actions when they enable a greater good for Vedian. We can not let man's perchance for expressive emotions, weaken our resolve for balance my friend."

Joseph walked from man to man, checking wounds, speaking constantly in an effort to keep up their spirits. Of the one hundred men that had joined him in battle only twenty three remained, some dead a number fled in the retreat he suspected. And why wouldn't they. There were just so many of them, the heat, the confusion, he had never experienced anything like it.

Joseph acknowledged Will who sat tending to his fathers wound, a gash on the arm that he was bandaging. The lad had fought well, clinging on to that old morning star like a hard won prize.

"How goes it miller?" Joseph shouted across.

"Pah! Nothing a scratch. I have had worse from the quern-stone. Did you see my boy out there? Did you? Like something from the old days." The miller clasped the young mans shoulders, the pride smouldering on his weathered face.

"Indeed I did." Parran had wandered over. "You are a natural and that is a gift few receive. When we make it through this miller, you bring your boy to me, I will find a place for him worthy of those skills."

"My lord, it would be a great honour. I can not...."

Parran raised his hand, "You have nothing to thank me for. I would thank you and all of you who stand with us here. Joseph I would speak with you." He pulled the young mariner off to one side.

"These men remaining are more loyal to you than to anyone here, you take formal command of them now. I will place you on the ramparts to the north of the keep. Do you take the charge?"

Joseph was surprised but he did not question it, "Yes. I will."

"Then eat quickly, they will come soon."

"Our numbers Commander, how many do we have?"

"The north and south gates were only pushed enough to hold the men in place, so Corn took little in the way of losses, his hundred lancers broadly stand. Browns pikemen as you saw took the brunt of the attack, their seventy are now thirty and we lost ten

388

from the forty swords. Plus the twenty swords we held in the bulwark and you're twenty or so left of the townsfolk. A few over two hundred remain."

"Is it enough?" Joseph asked.

"Its never enough but we can hold the keep for a while with those numbers. Now eat."

Joseph grabbed some bread and wandered further down the room to find Redrick sitting at the long bench, he was chomping down on some rabbit leg while regaling the soldiers of his many deeds completed that morning. To hear him you would not know there was anyone else fighting in the battle. He spied Joseph moving in his direction, "Aha! I spy our new lieutenant. Come sit my liege, I am but a servant to you."

"Quiet Redrick. I am not your commander."

"Oh but you are my good sir. For I have been assigned to your little outfit. I should fit in perfectly no doubt, these all seem like excellent warriors. I think one of them over there was actually fighting with a farming pick! What bravery! They shall sing of Joseph and his mighty tinkers, the exploits of his masterful smithy and bread maker!" Redrick was beside himself and the men loved him for it.

Joseph gnawed on the bread, washing it down with a strong ale, he was ravenous, as if he had not eaten only a few hours earlier. He barely felt the small hand resting on his shoulder, "Hello my friend."

That voice, instantly Joseph recognised it, how could he not. He spun round and in front of him stood Speck. "Well in all the world! How did? Where did you? It was you wasn't it? The fire that saved Will and I, I knew it!"

"Yes and it bloody nearly killed me projecting that far. What the hell have you got yourself into?" The young men embraced, Joseph had never been happier to see his friend, a familiar face, someone to share these experiences with.

"Where have you been Speck?" Joseph only now noticed the old man standing behind him, "And who is this?"

"I am sorry," Speck shook his head, "Apologies this is Cyrus." They greeted and Speck explained about the tower and meeting the other enchanters, his training and finally Cyrus.

"Well you have been busy Speck, I knew you would do something like this, something amazing. You are special my friend, I think you have always been."

Cyrus interrupted the reunion, "I would speak with whomever is in charge lad, with haste if you would."

"It is Commander Parran but he is very busy." Joseph was trying to be polite to the old man.

"I think he will see me, tell him Cyrus of the battle mages has returned."

Joseph did as he was asked, expecting a short shift from Parran but as soon as he spoke the name the Commander's face changed. Looking almost excited, not an expression he had seen from the experienced campaigner. His pace quickening as he covered the distance through to the hall, leaving Joseph in his wake.

"Cyrus! It is you, I would know that armour anywhere. Where are the others?"

Cyrus shook his head, as he shook the other man's hand, "No my friend, we will never again come abroad in any number I fear, my brethren are not as we once were. It is just I and the lad here. But I once stood with your lineage Parran at the walls of Bannermane, so perhaps I can still be of some assistance.

"There is no honour greater that I could imagine than to have you here. My grandfather spoke of you, I thought you to be dead."

"Just old. Very old but enough of that, brief me on what has gone and what will be." The two men walked off to speak, leaving Speck and Joseph once more.

"You look different some how Speck, older maybe." Joseph cocked his head trying to discern the change he saw in his friend.

"As do you. I would never have had you as a soldier and a lieutenant I hear from the men at your table." Joseph looked embarrassed.

"I just want to do what's right Speck. This council, these Scholatic, they speak with honey but the taste is bitter."

At that moment, shouting came from the outside of the halls and from further out Joseph heard the sound of horns being blown.

Redrick scrambled over the bench and motioned towards Joseph, "It is time, we should take up position."

They climbed the internal steps leading to the walkway and crossed out to the rampart wall that faced north, they could see far out past the university the Rinslake mountain range standing ominously on the horizon. Below Joseph could see the various towns dwellings, some smouldering from earlier fires. There was no one on the streets, the market place empty and desolate, the city was a shadow of its normal hustle and bustle.

"Surely they will attack from the west wall not here? The walls are high and there's so many buildings, very little room. Has Parran put us here to keep us away from the fighting?" Joseph said with more than a hint of frustration.

"Perhaps but I think the enemy may try on all counts. Don't let your guard down, I will check on the bulwark and return in a few minutes. And don't worry lad, we'll get our chance, that I can promise." Redrick disappeared along the wall as it turned to the west.

"How did you get in the city Speck?" The thought had just occurred to Joseph, he had no idea.

"There were only fifty or so men pushing on the north gate, Cyrus said it was a punitive number just to keep the defenders in position and away from the main push from the west. I was almost stone cold out after my efforts to aid you, I think he distracted them somehow but I'm not sure. Next thing I knew we were being helped through by Captain Corn's men. He seems like a good man."

"Yes. I don't know him well but Parran seems to think highly of him. A military man through and through I believe."

"They brought us straight into the halls with the retreat, took me a while to find out where you were."

Joseph looked long and hard at his oldest friend and spoke quietly, "We're not going to make it Speck, their numbers far outstrip ours. Parran has requested aid from the Huskian's and maybe Arn's presence there will help us but even then, they are so few. I can not see any fate for us but a dark and bloody one. Its good to have you with me, everything just feels lighter now."

"Don t give up hope just yet my friend. I have learn a lot in a short space of time and one thing is certain, that old Cyrus has a few tricks left to play. The biggest of which, I am going to try and pry out of him. When Redrick returns I will seek him out."

Speck told Joseph about his visions the book had shown him and about the blood oath the mages had completed at Bannermane.

"Cyrus says it can release the souls into others." Speck concluded.

"What good will that do us?"

"Honestly I do not know but I don't think these battle mages performed such a ritual for nothing and in such dire circumstances. Cyrus knows more than he's telling." Speck picked at the skin on his thumbs with his teeth. "Wouldn't that be something Joseph, the Sabre Regiment. I have seen them, they were amazing, shadow dancers on the battlefield, organised and polished yet brutal. If its a miracle we need, well perhaps...perhaps." He trailed off lost in his own thoughts.

The sounds of voices could be heard from the wall, orders being shouted and a constant thudding as the war on the bulwark gate began. Below they could make out some of the attackers congregating, only a small troop, they seemed to be working out what to do.

The miller looked at Joseph, collapsing back quickly into the hierarchy of the military rule, a lifetime in service reasserting itself. "They will bring ladders sir, should we fetch oil?"

"No. They will need the stocks for the west wall. We will repel them as they place, get a few picks from the store." Joseph eyed their oppressors, watching carefully as the long ladders were brought in and pulled into place, just as the miller predicted.

The numbers had swelled now, almost a hundred men were below the north wall and they began to fire volleys of arrows up to the ramparts.

"Down! Cover!" Joseph cried, as he and Speck tucked tightly into the raised wall to shield them, his small buckler raised up over his head. He heard the clank as the long ladder was hoisted up and swung forward to strike the wall. Men below scrambled up as quickly as they could, before they had raised their heads, four ladders where on the wall and each had five men ascending at speed, skittering like insects making quick work of the long climb.

The miller arrived carrying a handful of long pikes, "Everything I could lay my hands on sir."

Joseph took one of the long staves and hooked the curved end under the final step, pushing against it, the weight of five men surprised him. Will immediately ran to his side pushing together they used the rampart wall as leverage, pushing down on the pike. As it begun to move the ladder away the pike broke suddenly, the men below held tight and managed to ride the vibrations and continued to climb.

The first man on the wall could only claim one foot before being swatted off with the millers mace, as he screamed it seemed to accelerate the others advance. They began to swing up over the wall: one, two, three.

Joseph pulled Speck behind him and engaged an attacker climbing up from the third ladder, he swung his sword cutting deep into the the man's torso just as he got a foothold on the rampart. A second stabbing attack felled him to the floor but the successful ascent was buoying those below and more took to the ladders.

Will swung into place next to Joseph, his morning star flying through the air, bludgeoning against the enemies rising up from ladders one and two, he crushed the powerful weapon into a tall man's skull and backed up into Joseph. He heaved at one of the ladders trying to dig into the wall to give him more power "They're too heavy now, I can't move them."

From the other end ten men had mounted the battlements and were engaging what was left of the townsfolk with the miller at the lead. Joseph turned to Speck, "Have you got anything that might help?"

Speck tried hard to think but nothing was appearing with any clarity, "I am sorry, nothing. I have nothing."

"Then this time, you sit behind my shield." Joseph pushed forward and met the assailants, dropping forward and pushing his buckler up into the chin of one, opening his neck guard to a piercing follow up attack from his blade. He tore the sword across without thinking, it seemed to glide now, no weight on it at all.

With each one they took down, two more mounted the wall, soon a pitched battle was fought with over fifty of the attackers, their line was pressed and Joseph could feel it cracking, he was losing men, the millers group were beginning to get cut off as they swamped from the ladders further away. Joseph could feel desperation welling up, it began in his stomach and washed up with heat through his body, he thought for a moment he might pass out. He pushed hard trying to break through to the other party, hacking and stabbing, furious in his determination to break back into the line. "I can't get through! Redrick! Redrick!" He hollerred the name, kicking out to push the men back that separated the two groups.

Moments passed, then he heard it, the whistling of arrows, a tall man dropped in front of him as if his legs had been cut away. A second to his left fell crying from the wall, slowly they began to drive a wedge back to the miller, who stood now alone, his compatriots laying dead or mortally wounded. Joseph could see he was injured, his shoulder was dropped, blood covered his tunic and stained the leather, his shield long since discarded, he gripped the stout mace in one hand, the other limply hung to his side. They charged into the pack, Will beside him, pushing two men off guard so quickly they lost footing and stumbled from the precipice.

Joseph could see Redrick now, he had drawn his short sword and falchion and was striding towards them from the other end of the wall. They met the group from both sides, Joseph and Will cutting through to flank the miller and Redrick engaging from behind them, they soon stood breathing heavily in the afternoon sun. They had finally managed to kick the ladders back, as the attackers held, unwilling to make a second push at this time.

"Father, we must get him to the hall!" Will was carrying the full weight of the man on his shoulder, losing consciousness the miller grumbled some unintelligible words.

"Speck, help Will and find an apothecary in the hall." The young enchanter moved to the other side and together they pulled the miller from the battlements.

"No time to look pretty lad, we need to help, the fighting to the west is far worse. Leave a few here for watch and word, we need to move now."

Joseph signalled for three of the men to hold position and send a runner if the attacking begun again, ten others remained who left with Joseph and Redrick for the Bulwark wall.

Speck helped Will find his father aid and checked everything was in hand before departing, he found Cyrus in the main hall. "I expected you to be out there." the young enchanter questioned.

The old man wiggled his fingers, "Lighting fires and crackling bolts of lightning no doubt. Plenty of time for that lad, my turn will come, I know what you are going to ask, I know because I have thought of little since Rinslake. Now, having seen what we are up against with my own eyes, I am certain these are desperate times, was there any other situation that this was designed for? I do not know, I was a boy at Bannermane for god sake. I barely knew what I was doing, had only been in the order a month and off I was to fight the greatest battle in history. Funny thing about history Speck, you don't realise you're in it. Everything I have heard, every story and every song, tells me it was immense, incredible, I was lucky to have been there and perhaps I was. All I remember is losing most of the people I had come to admire and that no one left that field of combat the victor.

He looked round the huge hall, eyeing the tapestries that hung from the walls, some depicting scenes from Bannermane. Pulling on the bottom of his beard hairs he pouted and clearly rolling around ideas in his head, finally continued. "If we do this lad, I don't really know how much effect it will have. Or indeed if it will work at all. This oath was constructed with some of the greatest enchanters that have ever trodden on Vedian's earth. It was designed to be reclaimed with such power as it was created. To raise an army of souls of the Sabre Regiment, to bring them to life in others."

"What would that mean to those it inhabited?" Speck asked at the prospect.

"Difficult to say, they would be washed clean, if they survive over time they may gain hold again. I do not know Speck. But you miss the bigger question, we need men to take part in the ritual, we would need volunteers."

"Who would put themselves up for such a fate?"

"Normally I would suggest the desperate, we'll be in no short supply of those by tonight. I think we will only manage a few, the ritual was supposed to ignite a regiment but with only two of us to fire it, the best we can hope for is half a dozen perhaps. Yes five men."

"Five! Five! What the hell good are five men going to do. Five men can not hold the keep?"

Cyrus laughed, "You have seen Bannermane have you not, you have witnessed the battle, then you have seen nothing boy! I have stood side by side with those men, I have fought and bled with Tress, Pinkerton, Brown and Junas the sword. I would trade any one of those for a hundred of these men. You are right, five men can not win you a war but they might, just might, win you a battle."

The afternoons fighting at the west wall had not gone well, the bulwark gate still held but the siege bombardment had come first from a single trebuchet set up just inside the city walls and then from archers and finally direct engagement on the ladders. At one point over fifty ladders were primed against the west wall, the attackers swarmed the battlements, desperately pushing to get access to the gatehouse within and the release of the lower doors. Each time Rayan had pushed the swords in, mobilising as a swift counter unit, attacking where the pressure was, filling voids as they almost caved. Gallons of oil they had poured down below on the aggressors, fires still burnt below at the walls base, the smell of flesh burning in the air countered the fresh winters night aroma.

They had held at a cost and at dusk the enemy had retreated back, Parran gathered the Captains together, gaining updates on personnel, the wounded and making plans for night watches.

"My boys are thin sir," Brown reported, "we took heavy losses in the morning and a few more this afternoon, you have only twenty pikes remaining. But we took our share, I can say, fought like dogs they did, my boys." He pushed his gloved fist firmly into his other hand, it had been a tough day for his men and he felt it more than most.

"Corn how fare the Lancers?" Parran's face was like stone, no emotion leaving him.

"We took the brunt of the action on the west wall as agreed, my hundred is forty lighter for it thirty dead and ten more will not fight. We are ready again to do your bidding Commander, sixty lancers will stand." Corn stood awaiting further orders, it had been a difficult afternoon but they had acquitted themselves well, he stood proud.

Parran turned finally to Rayan, "Your swords were brilliant today Rayan, tactically they were adept and efficient. We will need more again tonight from your fifty, I think they will come again before the day is spent."

They all nodded in agreement, the enemy would come tonight thought Parran and now a little under one hundred and fifty remained to challenge them.

Cyrus announced himself with a cough, "Sorry gentlemen but I have a request."

Parran's demeanour changed ever so slightly, "Yes of course, speak."

"My young colleague and I have a possible way to help. I can not counsel you of its success as I am not sure myself. We have perhaps a way to bring some much needed experience to the battle."

Cyrus explained the Blood Oath, each word out of his mouth dropped the Captain's jaws further and further open, until he had finished and no one spoke.

"I will do it." Captain Brown said in such away that his intentions were clear. "I have but a few men remaining, Corn I ask you to take them into the lancers fold, I trust you as no other."

Corn acknowledged the gesture, "Honour is mine to do."

"Please be clear I do not know how this will go for you." Cyrus spoke directly to Captain Brown.

"One chance. One chance to fight with my forefather. I would risk everything."

"You have our agreement, offer it to the men. Not sure you will get many volunteers Cyrus, it has been a long time since enchanters walked alongside soldiers, they will fear what you offer." Parran warned.

Cyrus left and shared with Speck the agreement, they went around the men talking with them in groups, most backed away not embracing concepts unknown to them and fearful of the effect on their souls.

"At least at the end of their swords I know my fate old man. Sorry no way!" Was a response they heard again and again.

The dozen townsfolk that remained were no different until the miller spoke, "I am no use now, my arm is shot, I won't raise a shield again. If another man can do better with what is left of me, take it."

Will protested but his father's mind was made up. Lieutenant Elk from the lancers also came forward, he had heard that Captain Brown had put himself forward and wanted a member of the lancers to be represented. "Anything those pikemen can do, so can we lancers!"

Brown laughed, "Excellent lad, there's nothing like a bit of company rivalry in the face of absolute annihilation of a mans soul!"

Cyrus joined back with Speck to see how it had gone, "We were lucky with the lancers lad, that will pull out one from the swords too, no chance they will be the only company left out. With the miller that's four, so one more."

By the time the evening meal was served up and the men had eaten their fill of beef a fourth from the Asten swords had as Cyrus predicted, come forward. A young man named Trip had by all accounts been shamed into it by his unit, he did not seem that keen but nonetheless volunteered.

Cyrus led them out to the ramparts with Speck following close behind, the smell of burning had subsided and the evening air was permeated with a chilling breeze. The air coming down from the mountains and battering Pluris from the north.

The old enchanter instructed the four to stand in a semicircle around him and Speck, he appeared to take a final look past them, expecting their final member to dramatically arrive but no one came forward. A mug of sweet smelling broth was passed around them and Cyrus instructed them to sit down on the ground, soon one by one a drowsiness washed over them and they fell quietly to sleep.

"It will go easier on them if they are not conscious for the transfer, now let us begin."

They had run all day, never once had Febra complained, Arn's lungs were burning with the exertion. He knew they were close, the Rinslake could be seen ahead and light shone through on the darkened horizon, it looked as if hundreds of torches were burning in the distance.

"Is that a camp?" Febra squinted against the clashing mixture of fire and darkness.

"No, too big surely." Arn was starting to become concerned, he changed their trajectory so they approached from due south, well away from the east to west road. They negotiated rocks and rough thickets but soon the truth was revealed, a murmuring of light now had become hundreds of individual torches, spreading through the camp.

"My god, there are so many! We have to get word into the city." Arn searched the horizon.

"What good are a hundred Huskian's going to do against that. It will be a slaughter." Febra said dismissively.

"We need to ensure the timing is right, communicate with the Commander inside to co-ordinate an attack. There on the south wall." Arn pointed to a point left of the south gate where a handful of men had positioned themselves. A market cart was abandoned outside, giving just enough height to gain the wall.

Quietly they slipped over, the men less interested in anyone getting in than getting out it seemed to Arn, their gaze turned towards the city rather than away from it.

"Looking from the corpse line they have that large building under siege." Arn pointed to the bulwark and its halls.

"We will not get in without attracting attention." Febra noted the militia on the streets everywhere and outside the bulwark gate, many men had gathered, waiting.

"We could probably climb the wall. Of course we might get an arrow before they know who we are, from either side." Febra slightly grinned.

Arn saw the girl he had left the Luff with for the first time in a long while, it felt good, "I think we should try from north and south walls, one of us must make it to communicate with the defenders inside."

"I will take the south, I am smaller and quieter, more chance I will make it without being noticed? How do I know the Pluris men will listen to me?"

"Because we are all they have got that stands in the way of a thousand men on their doorstep, they will listen, now we must move with haste."

Arn smiled and put his arms around her, she did not resist, neither did she return the embrace. Nodding she turned her back, pulling up her cloak to shroud her lithe form and skittered into the night.

The hunter slowly ventured over the south outer wall and a few paces at a time, always scouring the night for movement, begun to work his way carefully and slowly around to the north face of the halls. The buildings were in plentiful supply and there was a lot of cover to hide in the shadows. He looked up for a set of potential handholds. As he begun to pull himself up a single horn sounded from beyond the gates. A rumbling of sound and voice cut through the quiet, quickly turning to cries and shouting, he looked up and grabbed another hold, pulling himself up, he climbed as fast as he could, they would be all around the wall soon, the night attack was beginning.

Redrick shouted at Cyrus, "You have to get off the ramparts man, none of you are safe here!"

"We can not interrupt the oath now, it has to run its course. They can not be moved."

"Well in a matter of minutes, you may well be surrounded if they take a hold on this wall. For Vedian sake man, can't we carry them inside?" Redrick pleaded.

"No the enchantment is locked, it must run its course or their fate could be worse. There is still time for one more."

"Not bloody likely! I am too pretty to be possessed and I doubt their fate will be a lot bloody worse than a pike in the gut or getting trampled but you know what's best. Joseph we need to create a wall around these four, get your men."

Twelve of the townsfolk now stood, only the hardiest that had began the day with Joseph remained, one or two veterans, a few

400

lucky ones and some jewels of war like Will, that had sat latent in plain sight all their lives.

"How are we gonna stop them pushing us back?" the millers son asked.

"Can you weave some enchantment to help old man?" Redrick turned to Cyrus.

"We are spent, the oath took everything we have. No further enchantment will pass this night I am afraid."

"Well That's great. I say get a load of them, these mages are about as useful as old washer women."

The men around Redrick laughed.

Cyrus moved forwards and stood next to Redrick, "I said we could enchant no further this night, I did not say we could not fight."

"Great me old grand pappy and his boy, were saved lads! Well beggars can't be choosers, come on old man lets show them you still got it. What ever it is."

The thudding of the ladders being hoisted into place resounded and within a few moments they were upon them, fierce faces bellowing cries of hate filled the air. Joseph looked round to Speck, "Stay behind me, please."

Corn's lancers pushed back at the first wave that took foothold on the ramparts but quickly had to drop down behind the walls, as volleys of arrows rose up and shattered down upon the cobblestone. The shafts covering a second assault, gave enough time for fifty men to gain an advantage and crest the wall. The remaining pikemen now under Corn's command pushed hard, throwing back some of the attackers but the numbers continued to swell, this was no evening sortie, the Captain was throwing everything forward. Joseph could see below the bulwark men queuing to get a hold on a ladder, hundreds swarming below like insects.

Parran's voice cut through the noise, "Rayan your swords to the north wall with urgency."

The men flew past them, running to deal with whatever danger fell on the north wall, in their wake the space was filled with the enemy. Like water gushing through a leaky barrel, they saw the dozen men standing in a circle around something and rushed forward to meet them.

Redrick had drawn his blade, shouldering his bow across his chest, he leaned forward to cut swiftly at the head of the attack, felling a running enemy with two shots across chest and face. He pulled back, determined to hold the shape and protective circle intact.

The sight of one of their own cut down, threw the others into a frenzy, they rushed forward towards Redrick, thrashing their blades towards him. Joseph and Will standing either side tightened up and pushed forward to greet the assault, a melee ensued, close quarter fighting, with long swords and larger weapons almost redundant. The force of the attack instantly threatened to wash away the small number of defenders but as Joseph was pushed and the forces around him seem to close in, they were thrown back.

Spinning violently, the staff come crashing down on one, followed in an instant by a driving sword, the old man moved with grace through the throng, creating space to move and fight where there was no right to have any. He swiftly turned and bellowed down at Joseph, who had dropped to one knee, "More time lad, we need more time!"

For endless minutes the ramparts pushed and pulled back and forwards between attacker and defender but for every one they killed or struck a wound, another one would climb up. They were slowly being pushed back from the wall and as they were Joseph's group were becoming more and more exposed, having nowhere to retreat to if their charges were to be protected.

Only a few remained now, with Joseph and Will on one side and Cyrus and Redrick the other, just two additional men stood. In the centre continuing the enchantment Cyrus had taught him was Speck, surrounded by the four silent bodies, waiting for any sign.

Redrick looked up, his breathing heavy, the wounds to his forearm and face dragged at his energy, "I will not fall here before you do old man! You understand that, it would be embarrassing."

As he spoke, in front of him a huge opponent came forward, carrying a two handed maul and dressed in wolf pelts and thick hide armour, he growled as he pulled himself up, towering over the tracker. He swung the massive weapon, bringing it crashing down in Redrick's direction, it missed marginally, striking into a fallen corpse. He was quick, Redrick thought, quicker than he had any right to be given his size, the tracker moved to the side, looking for any advantage he could carve. As he looked for an opening the maul was thrown towards him and the huge opponent lunged in, delivering a volley of blows to Redrick. The shock of the attack caught Redrick by surprise, his blade dropped as he rose his hands to defend himself, a second and third huge hand bashed down against his face.

"Fight me! Wastrel of the herd, you are no son of Vedian!" The words seemed to strike a chord and the attack of Redrick was halted, turning to look at his next victim, there in the centre of the broken circle stood Speck, standing with a sword in one hand and the other in front of him was glowing.

The huge opponent rushed forward, pushing Will out of the way and lumbering forward to meet its target. Speck took a single pace forward, to provide a stronger stance and pushed out his hand, Joseph could feel the force move invisibly through the air, so near to him. The huge brute was taken from his feet and thrust up and back, striking down three other men as he fell. Joseph saw the opening, launching himself forward and driving his own blade deep into the side of his armoured hide.

Around him they kept coming, the line had completely fallen and once again Parran's voice cut through the night air, "Royal guard to me!"

They moved as a single vessel, completely unified in their action, men bonded by training and time, working to a single goal. At their head the Commander who had led them for decades, his long weapon turning and piercing, efficiently cutting in and out of the enemy, carving like a chisel into the growing throng of attackers. They made route for Joseph, driving a wedge into the rampart, their dress armour like an invisible shield reflecting the moons rays. As they arrived, Joseph could see Rayan's swords once again joining the fray at the west, the enemy slowly but decidedly was pushed back from the wall and as the last men fell from its height, so ended the first night of the Defence of the Halls of Pluris.

Parran greeted Rayan, "Just in time my friend, how holds the north wall?"

"Not good, a hundred and fifty, we barely held them back, if it wasn't for the stranger I would probably not have made it." Rayan was walking stiffly and held one hand against his hip. "Commander Parran may I present to you the hunter..."

"Arn!" Joseph shouted and ran to the figure emerging from behind Rayan. "Where did you come from?"

"That's is a long story but no time now. I must speak with your commander."

"You have my ear but let it happen while we tend to the wounded." Parran reached down to look at Redrick, his body lay still on the floor but his breathing was still apparent.

"Oh no! Arn I must tend here first, do not disappear on me." Joseph rushed to Redrick and with Will's aid they carried him from the ramparts.

"The Huskian's will arrive tomorrow, they await three blasts of the horn and will attack from the south at my call."

Parran eyed him briefly, "You lead the Huskian's and yet you are not one, these are strange times. How many strong is your force?"

Arn stammered slightly, "One..one hundred my lord."

If there was disappointment in Parran's voice, Arn could not perceive it, "This is good news, it will help the men after tonight. We have taken heavy losses, although we inflicted twice as many, I fear it is not enough."

Parran invited Arn inside for food after the last of the wounded had been brought into the makeshift infirmary.

"I must speak with my Captains, you are welcome to join us as you represent the Huskian's."

Rayan arrived, his leg strapping around the hip could not stop the flow of blood which already soaked his bandages.

"You look ready for death Captain." Parran smiled at Rayan.

"Think my running days are over but in this fight we fortunately don't need to go far to find trouble."

Parran nodded and patted his Captain on the back, "Where is Corn?

Rayan bowed his head, "He fought bravely my lord but he was taken by an arrow and fell from the wall."

"Grim news this night." Parran turned to Joseph, who had joined them, "Redrick lad, will he live?"

"Yes they think so but he has yet to regain consciousness."

"Let us check numbers then, Rayan the swords?"

Rayan shook his head, "We were outnumbered three to one at the north wall, I lost half my force, twenty five swords remain. As for the lancers and Browns remaining Pikemen about a third will not fight, most to deep wounds. So that gives us sixty of them."

"Less than one hundred and if the Huskian's arrive tomorrow as Arn hopes, we double our force. The enemy must have lost twice our number at least but that still leaves them six hundred to seven hundred men. If they push in the morning, which no doubt they will, we may lose the Bulwark before the Huskian's lay a foot in Pluris." Parran pondered his next words carefully, "If the bulwark falls and we retreat to the halls proper, we will not hold for more than an hour or two, it is too wide and we are too few. Our hope lies in holding the walls until the Huskian's can mount a charge from the rear, pince their force, even that hope is small. I would make one more stand tomorrow in the name of our Crown Prince Madistrin, to make it worthy of his name."

Cyrus walked in from the walls, the old man was dusted in blood, his beard stained and his armour cut in multiple places, he looked even more intimidating to the soldiers that saw him, they seemed to shrink at his presence.

"We have lost the Trip, the lad from the sword I am afraid, however four of them survived the ritual and Speck is now with them."

"Three surely? " Joseph queried. "Only four begun the ritual?"

"Well that is the strangest thing. I knew once active we had capacity for the enchantment to hold for five. It seems we had a late volunteer, though by the Kings of Vedian I know not where she came from."

"She?" Parran was startled by the thought of a woman involved.

"Yes. They have awoken and it is like nothing I have seen. They remember nothing of who they were, those people have gone. At least for now, perhaps forever."

"And what has replaced them?" Parran asked his voice echoing the slightest tinge of fear.

"From what I can make out, they are four men of the Sabre's but let them make their own introductions when they are ready. For now, we must make plans for the morning. Come Parran I would speak with you alone."

Joseph returned to Redrick's side, the cut on his face was nasty if superficial, although he was sure it would be more than that if it damaged Redrick's good looks. He chuckled to himself thinking of how the tracker would respond to such an indignity. The wounds on his forearm and legs were deep, the apothecary had done all she could to soak and clean them, he was stitched and dressed but still he did not wake. "Come on my friend, we need you out there. The troops need your voice and I need you most of all." Joseph quietly spoke the words, he had grown very fond of Redrick over the past days, he had a talent to not judge people, just accepting each and every one for who they were, it was something quite special Joseph thought.

Arn walked up and thrust an arm around Joseph, "Whatever have you been up to since you left! I would not recognise the young man that left the Luff all those weeks ago. I am happy to see you Joseph, I am sorry I ever left in honesty. I would ask for your forgiveness but I do not deserve it." The hunter seemed ashamed and he bowed his head at the thought of his actions.

"If every man made decisions on love, I have no doubt we would all live in a better world Arn. How on earth did you get into the halls?"

Arn explained his journey with Febra, his scaling of the wall and how the fighting had broken out as he climbed.

"I was just another assailant to the wall, until that is I begun to deliver some blows to the enemy, you should have seen their faces! They did not expect the attack to come from within, at one point I thought I was going to be overwhelmed but Rayan is an amazing fighter, very gifted, he and his men fought through to me. You know Joseph, as I stood there surrounded by them, my thoughts were not of Dance, not of Vedian, not of the Luff but just to find my friends. I am sorry I let you leave, I will stand by your side here now, until whatever end we are given. I hear you are a Captain of the People!"

"Shhh Arn. I am Captain of nothing. Only Will and I remain from the commoners, hardly an army to lead."

"Well you have me now and Speck I don't doubt. I will follow you Joseph and if we can make it until midday perhaps time for the Huskian's to arrive, we can deliver a bloody nose to this council. One that will even wake Rundell from his slumber."

Joseph smiled. "Indeed. Oh what I would give to have him by our side now."

"He is with us Joseph, in our hearts. He gave everything for the King and we fight now in his brothers name, we will give no less. Now let us find that little wordsmith Master Lucent, see what on earth he has been up to, there are still a few hours until dawn and I feel little need for sleep."

They walked together through the hall and out onto the ramparts, there above the west gate at the head of the Bulwark stood Speck, at his left Captain Brown, on his right Elk from the lancers and the Miller. Speck turned as he heard them approach, as the fourth figure came to view the realisation hit Arn like a hammer.

"Oh no. He said she."

Joseph looked quizzically at the hunter and then he saw her, a tiny figure emerging from the background to stand with the other three.

Speck looked just as confused, "I don't know where she came from. One minute I was completing the enchantment and then that huge attacker set about Redrick. When it was over she was laid down next to them. She must have joined just before it completed."

"Does she know who she is?" Joseph asked.

"She is Febra no longer, no more than the rest but I will let them introduce themselves. Please get the others, it is time."

A few minutes passed as Joseph fetched the others. Rayan, Parran and Cyrus arrived on the ramparts. Speck spoke with an air of authority, "I will let these fellows introduce themselves."

Captain Brown stepped forward, "I am Pipe Major Brown of the Sabre Regiment."

Next was Lieutenant Elk, "I am Colour Sergeant Pinkerton of the Sabre Regiment."

The look on Rayan's face was incredulous, "What trickery is this Parran, I am less than comfortable with this enchantment." Parran raised a hand to silence him.

The miller moved forward, "I am Captain Tress."

Finally Febra stepped forward, tiny in stature compared to the others, her voice so familiar to the men from the Luff, announced softly, "I am Junas the Sword, of the Sabre Regiment."

"So we few stand with our fathers and heroes of old as they once did on the walls of Bannermane." Cyrus looked at Parran, "Will you and your men stand at their side Commander?"

Parran sighed, "I would have nothing more than to stand by one of my forefathers but these can not truly be they. It is a magic I do not understand and do not wholly trust. Yet we have so few left, would I be a bigger fool to turn away their aide if they are but a shadow on the men they portray. So I suggest it leaves me with one question. Will you, members of the Sabre Regiment, stand with me?"

They responded as one, "We fight for the King."

Parran would never forget the next moment, a recollection, a voice that shook him to his core, that raised every hair on his body. A moment of sheer exhilaration, to be filled with hope when none remained, as the sounds rose from behind him.

"Then you will stand with me! For I am the rightful heir and king to these lands. For I am Madistrin!"

Chapter 21 - The Price

"The weak made strong"

Inscription on 'The Quelling Blade' - Sword of Kings

A melee of confused conversation followed the arrival of the Crown Prince. Joseph, Speck and Arn sidelined as Parran, Cyrus, Madistrin and DeFache quickly caught up on the events that had unfolded over the past few days. With only a couple of hours left until dawn the three of them stood in the great hall.

"He doesn't exactly look like a king does he?" Speck offered.

Arn shuffled two copper coins between his fingers, grating the metal together, "I imagine they come in all shapes but I know what you mean. The Scholatic with him, DeFache, he looks important."

"I know of his name. Gru-Staedak talked at length about him, he was his student I think. He said he was a trustworthy individual with a good heart. I wonder if he knows about the old man?" Joseph poured himself a small mug of ale, as his mind wandered back to his days in the gardens of Asten.

He looked over his shoulder at the sound of footsteps approaching, "Now I just know you have poured that for me." The silver tongue of Redrick danced across the hall floors to greet him.

"Redrick! You should not be up, when did you wake? I asked them to get me."

"Yes. Yes, let a man get a drink. Only a few minutes ago, I wanted to surprise you. It seems things have been busy without me." He pointed across to Madistrin who sat at the huge hearth with the others locked in debate.

"I thought you were dead." Joseph handed him the drink.

"Lad I bedded three women of Kanegon at once! Do you think a few blades will take me down!" He beamed a smile at Joseph.

"Redrick this is Arn, my friend from the luff, he has brought word from the Huskian's, they will arrive later today."

"Then he is a guest warmly welcome. Hunter type I see, nice bow, ashen I think." Redrick shook Arn's hand warmly.

As Redrick sat down, DeFache and Madistrin moved over from the fireplace and while the Crown Prince exchanged warm greetings with Redrick, the Scholatic stood in front of Joseph, "I wonder if I might have a few moments alone with you."

"With me? Umm yes of course." Joseph was surprised and it clearly showed.

"Let us move outside, the air is clear at this time, cleanses the palette of thought I find." DeFache walked towards the staircase that led up and onto the walkways, Joseph trailing behind.

"I appreciate you do not know me but I am led to understand that we have someone in common. Is it true that Gru-Staedak fell at Asten?" DeFache looked out into the dark skies, his voice calm and crisp as the air.

"It is true. I am sorry, for I know you were dear to him, he spoke often of you in our short time together. I have not encountered one who held such wisdom and tempered it with such grace and the ability to communicate with ordinary men. He died defending us all." Joseph's voice cracked slightly at the recollection of his demise.

"Your words comfort me, Gru-Staedak must have seen something in you to talk so openly and from what I hear from Commander Parran, his judgement was as sound as ever. It is good someone was able to honour him, for I fear I did not. He talked and I did not listen, he asked me to see what was going on but I would not, too blinded by Shel-Toro's words. He saw this, he knew this would happen and he asked me to support him openly and I refused. I thought him to be old and too quick to see conspiracy in our ranks. How wrong I was and I can never tell him how sorry I am, not for my errors in judgement in the truth but not having the will to believe in him, the man. We Scholatic are supposed to be great thinkers and yet you saw in him what I could not." DeFache trailed off, lost in his own thoughts.

"I do not know of what went before but I can tell you this, when he spoke of you, he was the brighter for it, he loved you as a father would a son."

"And that Joseph makes my error all the more tragic." DeFache's voice was empty, Joseph wanted to tell him everything was going to be alright but he wasn't sure how, he was this revered Scholatic and Joseph just a sailor out of the Luff.

"Perhaps the wrong can be corrected here, the old man loved Vedian and the people in it. Here on these battlements amends can be made."

"Perhaps but I can not look past the practical, we do not have enough to hold the halls for another day. Madistrin's arrival will rally the troops but it does not change the fact we have but a hundred. I am not accustomed to hoping for miracles."

"Sometimes I think you just have to believe, like Gru-Staedak did in you."

DeFache's tall frame seemed to relax slightly, his short beard almost breaking a small smile. "Now I understand how you took the Pulpit."

In the final hour before dawn, Madistrin visited every one of the hundred men in the keep, as well as the apothecaries and the kitchen staff. Each he shook by the hand and had words of encouragement and thanks, finally he approached the three from the Luff. He was dressed now in his armour, plate mainly, some chain on the left arm and leg, the weight too heavy on his injured side to burden any more. On his back the shield of his house and in a long scabbard the sword born by his brother before him and every king for generations, simply known as 'The Quelling Blade' a longsword cast from silver and cut with runes along the metal. The hilt steel, wrapped in thick leathers, hardened and embroidered in red hues.

"A mighty sword my liege," Arn offered, "Forged by the House of Histevirrillm, I would wager."

"Then you would know the smithy craft well hunter. It is indeed from my friend Durgal's line and I would wield it in lieu of his sacrifice at Asten. The news I have been borne since returning has been nothing but ill. His demise was amongst the worst but I see your friend wields a weapon from the same house." Madistrin pointed to the sword sheathed in Joseph's scabbard.

Arn looked with surprise, immediately identifying the figure of eight mark at the base of the hilt that Durgal had showed him in Asten. "Well Joseph, you wield a formidable weapon, that you should share a smithy with the Crown Prince indeed!"

411

Joseph looked shocked and turned to Redrick for explanation. The tracker grinned wide and chuckled, "Did I not mention it. I thought I did? That sword has a line that goes back to the Great Wars, it is a sister blade to...well perhaps another time. Suffice to say it was cast by the best blacksmith house in Vedian. Let us toast to Durgal and the House of Histevirrillm."

They all raised their mugs and the tracker from Coralis proceeded to introduce the three from the Luff to the Crown Prince, who spoke with a friendly tone.

"What could I say about the men from the Luff that has not already been said. For I have been back in my house but a few hours and my Commander waxes lyrical about you all. Is there anything I could honour you with?"

Arn, looked to Speck and he to Joseph, they knew exactly, "There is one thing my lord, we would ask you when this is over and Vedian stands free, to right a wrong." Arn spoke and the others nodded in agreement. He recalled as briefly as he could the tale of Rundell, of the poisoning and his eventual banishment. Madistrin slowly took in the story.

"My brother was dear to me, like no other man that has lived, he was what could be great in a king. In many ways, all that I am not and he was taken by a mans error, that cost this kingdom dearly and in many ways has delivered us to where we are today. Yet should a man be punished for his lifetime and beyond for a mistake made in good faith? I will agree on one condition. Rundell will be pardoned formally if we hold these walls until the midday sun rises at its peak. Can you do that?"

The three nodded and Joseph spoke, "He saved our lives and was our friend, we owe him this stand. We will hold."

As the young mariner finished his words, out onto the ramparts walked the Sabre's, dressed now in chain and adorned with weaponry, they emanated an aura that none who looked upon them could articulate. When they spoke it was with the voice of the incumbent host but not with their tone or manner, it was most jarring with Pinkerton who seemed to ramble on constantly to his colleagues or at times himself.

Tress bowed as they approached Madistrin, "My liege, Sabre Regiment ready."

Madistrin nodded, "Do you know where you are?"

Pinkerton looked at the other three, "Yes sir, Pluris sir."

"Perhaps I should word if differently, do you know what year it is?"

Pinkerton gave a slight raise of the eyebrows and Tress caught him and moved to speak,"We know, we are out of time my lord, we were drawn here by an oath, a promise to each other. We will fulfill that in the name of the Sabre and the name of the King. Beyond that there is nothing, in truth there never was more than that."

Pinkerton seemed to hardly able to resist chipping in, "We're not mad you know, well I'm not can't be sure about Brown."

Tress turned, "Not the time Pinky."

"No sir, never is."

Parran had advised Rayan to man the south wall with the remaining swords until they were outnumbered and then to fall back to the west, there they would stand together. The royal guard would stand at the western wall with Madistrin as he demanded, Parran tried desperately to get him to agree to stay back from the fighting. "My brother would be here Parran, you know it. I am not him I know but I would honour him such and the people here who have fallen before me."

The pikemen and lancers that remained stood to the left side of the Crown Prince, the three from the Luff with Redrick and Cyrus and the Sabre Regiment held the right side. Less than one hundred men stood upon the wall as the dawn broke on the day after Winters Night.

Shel-Toro was angry and he could not hide it, "This is unacceptable! Am I to be lied to by everyone! You said he was dead. This will not go well for you SanPollan."

SanPollan was desperately looking for a way out for the predicament, he had come so close, "I have been sorely let down. My advisor's have costs to bear but let it not fall on me, in all good grace I am the innocent party in this."

"I sorely doubt that." He turned to the guard at the entrance of his canopy, "Get me The Captain now and that Bast'wa, he may yet be of use."

413

Shel-Toro paced up and down the rug that had been laid out, a thick wool caressing between his toes did nothing to calm him.

"Your Prominence."

"We have no more time Captain, this needs to end before word gets out of his return. Once the place is broken and he is departed in battle, I can speak to the people of his deceits. It ends now this morning. Can you make this happen for me?"

"We will push our full force to the west wall and a contingent to the south, if we gain the south wall we can surround them and make for the gatehouse. There will be no halt, no respite, we take the bulwark and I will deliver Madistrin out of bondage."

"As always Captain, a voice I can rely on. Bast'wa I see you have finally arrived, your men are needed."

Bast'wa was slightly out of breath from the call, he stood panting dressed in an open necked silk shirt and matching trousers, "I came with haste my lord, pleased to hear your call. How can a simple merchant be of service."

"We need your men on a full assault to the south wall, it must be taken, we will push hard pull their forces to the west, then once taken you can strike from behind."

"My Captain, It sounds truly ghastly, I may take many losses if we push so aggressively. What compensation would a poor man receive for his dutiful service?" Bast'wa smiled pathetically at the stoic warrior.

Shel-Toro weighed up his options carefully before replying, "I will give you Kanegon to run as you will, with the council in mind as always. All the shipments in and out will be yours to tax."

Bast'wa was elated, "You are too kind to me, too kind. My men are at your disposal Captain I will send my man Dulcet to lead them. He is a blunt instrument but you will find him effective."

Shel-Toro locked on to The Captains gaze, "No second chances now, it must be this morning."

"I will lead them myself."

As Joseph looked down and cast his eyes across the city, there was silence, nothing moved in the usually sprawling and busy

414

back streets. All the citizens had barred themselves inside, nothing walked in Pluris save the geese loose in the market and an occasional hound that wandered into view.

From beyond the broken west gate he could see them lined into ranks, waiting for the call to arms, hundreds of men still faced them. The horn sounded in the distance once and they began to file in troops of around fifty men, each bearing the huge ladders and a small attachment of archers, at the head he could make out a group of armour clad soldiers, all dressed in glistening plate, ornate and beautiful in the dawn light.

As the first group entered the city, they began to move from a march to a light run and as the distance closed on the bulwark and its thick walls, they pushed into a sprint.

Parran shouted and the few remaining archers leaned forward firing down onto the pack, searching out the ladder bearers as they hauled up their precious cargo to the walls. Each man that fell was replaced almost instantly by another and as soon as the ladder was up, the next troop had emerged. Parran saw quickly two more units break off to the south wall, "Send word to Rayan on the south he has his work cut out for him". A runner was dispatched to the other wall, as Joseph helped pour the remaining oil stocks over the rampart and down onto the climbing masses. Shrieks and cries as men burned, one ladder caught fire and took with it the seven men plus two more below as they fell but still more and more came, the city was full with soldiers from the outer wall to the bulwark gate, lining up to take the walls regardless of cost.

As they began to ascend Parran lined up the units with shields out, with each new assault, he called the men to push forward, pressing with their shields as one line. He at the centre with his tall kite shield thrusting forward at the enemy. Time after time they reached the top and were buffeted from the wall by the impenetrable line of shields. Slowly as the morning wore on their numbers dwindled and holes began to appear in the line. Each time Parran called and they tightened up, the line growing just a little shorter.

"Too many archers!" Redrick called firing another shot down to an ascending soldier, "They are picking us off."

As Parran contemplated the counter, shouting reared up from the south wall, "Fall back! Fall back!" Rayan came stumbling back with just a few swords, the enemy was tight behind them as they desperately tried to hold them at bay.

Before Parran could make a decision Tress turned with the other three Sabre's and launched past the retreating swords and plunged themselves deep into the enemy. Pinkerton and Brown at either side cutting into the opposing force directly, shields out to the sides to protect the flanks. Then she came and any man who stood on the ramparts that day would never forget it, even if they would struggle to find the words to describe her. In her hands two swords, lightweight scimitars, curved blades spinning and cutting as her svelte form moved from opponent to opponent. The grace of Junas the Sword that Vedian had not witnessed for five lifetimes, coupled with the feral ferocity of the girl from the Luff, if there was beauty in battle this was it Parran thought.

Yet for the men from the Luff, they just saw their friend, the girl from the market who was responsible for this long journey and to each other they smiled.

Joseph was shocked back into the moment with a cry from Cyrus, "Look to the front!"

The line was buckling, a few of the climbers had began to make the wall outside the edge of the shrinking line, gaining footholds and attacking from the flanks. Cyrus pulled out of his position in the line and ran across the ramparts, pushing out with his long staff, as he drew his sword in the other hand. The pikemen were in desperate trouble as they became overwhelmed, Cyrus hacking and bashing to try and gain back the ground lost but there were too many joining, the line had split now and a group were cut off from the others. At the left Cyrus and the pikes, in the centre Parran and the royal guard still pressed the nearest to the wall and on the right Joseph and his four. Behind them the Sabre and remaining swords continued to fight, if that was lost it was over, Joseph turned to Speck as he cut across an attacker with his buckler, cracking his jaw. "If you have anything to amaze with, this is the time!"

Speck pulled further back nestling himself behind Will and Redrick he concentrated and his mind pulled forth an image from the book and then screaming, everywhere. Every ladder on the wall had suddenly combusted, men were diving off, crushing others below, gaps opened in the climb and Parran saw an opportunity to push back, driving the Royal Guard forward, shields raised kicking out the ladders below.

Will shouted to Redrick, "Cyrus is surrounded, we have to help!"

"Don't lose the line boy! We can not afford to buckle on both sides!" Redrick had long since discarded his bow, fighting now with his sword, his face covered in blood spatter, his armour soaked with old wounds and new.

Speck looked across still drained from his enchantment moments earlier, he saw the old man swinging staff in one hand and sword in the other, over twenty men had now surrounded him completely severing the left side of the wall from any support. Realising his predicament he dropped the sword and reached out, one man dropping to the floor holding his throat, then another and another, as if the life had simply left them in an instant. Still using the staff to fend off blows but with each one that dropped another stepped forward and finally a short sword found its way from behind him, it brushed through the thick leather hide and nestled deep in his back. He dropped to one knee, looking back to find Speck as the killing blow came inevitably down. He held out his hands and drew deep down inside himself, as the blade struck through his neck his hands clapped together and a force shattering the air like a tornado, a whole host of attackers thrown instantly to their death from the ramparts, the nearest seeming to implode and shatter into nothing. He lay on the cold floor surrounded by no living man as the last life within him slipped away and with it the final survivor of Bannermane passed from the world.

Parran forced the Royal Guard across to the left, removing the few men left standing, startled and shocked by what had just gone. The south wall was open and The Captain had been quick to fill the breach, men streamed up the ladders, only the width of the rampart was holding back the surge of bodies.

"Ain't gonna be able to hold this forever Captain." Pinkerton offered as he swept his sword down upon another assailant.

"We just need to hold for long enough." Tress replied as he ducked down to dodge a flailing blade.

"What we waiting for then Captain?" Brown asked, his shield bashing forward.

"Waiting to be told that we don't need to stand here anymore. When that time comes we can rest. Now shut up and fight!"

They were under siege on all sides now, the final enchantment of Cyrus had given them a bloody respite that saw the end to a hundred of the opposition but that was all it was a respite, the ladders were back up and full again, the line barely holding and behind them the gap was narrowing as the sabres were beginning to lose ground.

Arn had waited for as long as he dared, he called across to Parran, "Now commander, the horns."

Parran waved and a bugle sounded quickly three times in succession, the hunter looked out expectantly but nothing changed. The landscape remained the same.

Redrick screamed at Parran, "For Vedian sake pull it back, we are going to lose it, there's too many!" He could feel the pressure all around, men struggling to hold their tiny piece of the ramparts and losing just an inch here and there as more bodies came forth. As the words formed on the Commanders lips the south line stopped pushing and bodies parted like a wave, from the walkway emerged a line of plated soldiers that Joseph had seen earlier from above. The Captain flanked by four of his trusted lieutenants moved toward the Sabre's, shouting.

"Is this what its come down too Parran, you bring a girl to fight us. Have you no honour?"

Pinky smiled, "I think you're gonna regret that."

A roar went up from the men on the south wall as The Captain moved into battle, he was a huge man but moved quickly and Tress was careful to wait, not to commit himself until he had the measure of the man. Pinky met the two left with Brown, the other two fell to Junas.

Parran called out loudly, "To the Halls, to the halls."

Using the royal guard shields as protection they began to quickly move down the steps that led from the ramparts, pushing back at the enemy, allowing the remaining few defenders to fall back.

"Now Sabre's! Fall back." Parran cried.

Tress looked around, instinctively he knew they would not make it, there was not enough time to get everyone behind the hall doors and close them before they were consumed.

"I'm sorry to tell you boys but that's one order we are gonna have to ignore."

Pinkerton could feel it as well, his battle hardened senses alive to the issue. "I'm not running from these pig lovers. Bollocks to orders sir."

"Yep just this once Pinky aye." Brown smiled.

"Just one question Captain, cause I have to ask see. Why did you do it?"

Tress stepped back and breathed in, "I did it for Vedian Pinky, I did it because in my heart I knew it was right and above all, I did it for the Sabre's."

Pinky looked at his Captain, "We always knew it sir, even when they cast out your name. We always knew in our hearts."

Tress nodded at each of them in turn and the Sabre Regiment formed into line and for one more time they charged together headlong into the enemy.

Joseph slammed his back against the heavy doors, his breathing was quick as he slumped down onto his backside. Around him the few remaining men collapsed into chairs, some on tables or most just upon the floor.

Arn wiped the mixture of blood and sweat off his brow, "She will be here, I know she will, we just need a bit more time."

Speck raised his eyebrows, "Look around us, there can't be more than a handful of men who can still fight. When those doors give in, its over."

"I am sorry about your father Will," Joseph turned to face the millers son, "he was a brave man and braver still to volunteer. Without their stand we would never have made the halls."

Parran walked across to where they sat, "Rayan is dead, it is amazing he fought as long as he did with that wound. The last of my Captains."

"Well I'll take that as a compliment shall I" Redrick looked up at the commander.

419

"I have never considered you in the same way, they were military through and through. You have too much chat for the life." Parran rested a hand on his shoulder. "Still, I am glad you are with us."

"You see Joseph, I am more lover than fighter, even our good commander recognises my true skills." Redrick laughed.

Speck felt angry, Cyrus was dead, they were soon to be, he could not understand this was a situation to make light of, "You should have more respect."

Redrick looked at the young man, he could see the pain he bore in his loss, "If my words caused offence I would revoke them. I joke because I see no reason to do anything else. I will show my respect to Cyrus and the Miller and all the others the minute those doors open. My respect will fall hard on each and everyone that walks through that door and it will carry on until there is no more of me to give. Respect comes through actions and I promise young enchanter, mine will be felt."

Parran nodded, a new energy seemed to fill him hearing Redrick's words, "The final stand will be out of respect for those that gave their lives to this point, ..." he was interrupted by Madistrin who walked with DeFache at his side.

"Will you offer me such respect Captain?"

"My Liege?" Parran looked confused.

"I stood on the battlements did I not. Yet at every move or turn you pushed me behind you, your shield always protecting me before yourself. I am not a child, I ask only what every other man asks that stands here. The chance to show my respect and if it means my death, then so be it."

Parran looked visibly distraught, "My lord, I am sorry. I just, I am your protector."

"Yes but the time has gone Parran. I would have you treat me like a man, let us break bread and drink wine and when the time comes stand shoulder to shoulder with me as your kin. That is what I wish, not as a Prince or a King but as a man, as your friend."

Parran kneeled in front of him, "You make me unworthy lord. You have my bond."

"Then let us not hear another word of it. Wine! Let us drink until the knock comes at the door!"

They sat and they drunk and laughed, alongside the seven royal guards, four men from the lancers, the three swords, the six of them and one sole pikemen who remained from Brown's regiment. All except for DeFache, he quietly wandered from the hall, more comfortable in his own company, slipping into the kitchens and down to the cellars. From there out to the passageway that had led Madistrin and he into the halls, an old escape hole that led down under the docks. There was nothing he could do to help right these wrongs in there, with sword or shield, he needed to use a more powerful weapon. He grabbed a horse from the stable and pushed out through the north gate, now empty of guard with all attention turned to the hall.

Minutes passed quickly, they expected the fighting to halt outside as the superior numbers consumed the Sabre's. Yet still they heard the sound of battle rage on and then it began, a shout and then a crash as the doors took the weight of a ram hitting them. Again one, two and then the shout, again the huge thud. The thick wooden joist shuddering at the pressure pushed against it.

They stood all twenty six men together, Madistrin had sent all servants, kitchen staff even apothecaries away, through the passage and told them to return to their homes. There would be no healing through this, no evening meal to be cooked and served.

Will pulled up his morning star, the chunky weapon chipped and dented but familiar and solid as he gripped it tightly with both hands, he no longer felt the need to make his father proud. He knew he was proud of his son long before this begun, Will stood now for his own reasons. If he could walk away, with no cost no, no impact, he wouldn't. He had seen the power of camaraderie even in death and the taste was no less sweet for knowing he would be next.

Madistrin looked to the man on his left, "What is your name sir?"

The stocky man hoisted up his long pike, "Brine's of the pikes your majesty lord sir."

"I am proud and honoured to stand alongside you Brine's. Perhaps there will be room in your regiment for me yet." Madistrin warmly smiled.

"Plenty of space my lord sir, just as well you're not married though." Brine's grinned.

"Why is that?"

"I got a terrible reputation with other pikey's women!"

A roar went up as they all laughed at Brine's words, quickly drowned out by the crack of wood, splintering as the doors flung asunder. They poured through the opening, clambering over the wood and met the twenty six with impact.

Parran's glaive sung through the air, skewering two men together before pulling the long polearm back to slice across another, the receiving blows absorbed in part by his battered armour.

Will looked at Joseph as they prepared for the onslaught and they shouted as one.

"Kings among men!"

Joseph and Arn were tight in a triangle with the millers son, the bloodying blows from the mace, coupled with the slicing of the two blades, cut down one after another as they continued to swell at the opening. Arn's light armour allowing swift movement, dodging blows and cuts as they reigned down upon him, Joseph's buckler flexible and used resourcefully as he parried and set up killing blows. He could hear Redrick's voice from the side as fought, "Can you feel it now lad! Is it still heavy?"

Inside Joseph smiled, he felt nothing, Durgal's crafted sword now just an extension of movement in his arm, the weight that had first pulled down like a stone, reduced to nothing. "Like a feather!" he shouted back.

"And you use it like one! Fight boy!"

They fought like men possessed, creating an impervious wall for a few short minutes, a barrier that nothing could pass. If a song would be written and tale crafted, then it would be of this moment, crystalised as they were, more myth than men.

Then a crack emerged.

One of the swords tripped across a corpse and like a house of cards the wall caved. The throng pushed into the right immersing the remaining swords and quickly finishing them in a flurry of stabs and cuts. Out from the halls a horn sounded but they did

422

not hear, the pressure now mounting from the front and the left flank, then Will fell, caught by a glancing blow to the temple, he dropped to the floor motionless. Joseph and Arn tried to close the gap to help but it was all they could do to hold their own opponents.

As the attackers pressed the advantage Madistrin cut deep into one assailant only to find he had over stretched and his legs swept out from under him. A sword swung down towards his chest and he saw his final moment had arrived. From his left side a long pike was thrust above him blocking the death blow and swinging up to strike down its wielder. Brine reached a hand out and pulled the Crown Prince to his feet and they stood side by side again, the would be King and man of the guard, equals at the table of battle.

Shouting from outside now could be heard inside the keep but still they did not register it, the royal guard desperately trying to hold the centre with Parran, one fell to a crossbow at point blank range another from a flail striking the neck and shattering the windpipe. As men fell they were pushed back and back, until just a tiny few stood underneath the hearth, Parran at the centre, his shining armour dulled with running blood, his glaive still held out in front of him, to his right Arn and Joseph both panting and sweating freely and on his left the pikeman Brine and Madistrin.

Joseph took in a deep breath as the attackers rushed to consume them. Their weapons struck a few inches in front of Joseph bouncing off thin air, an invisible wall. Again and again they struck with swords and shields to no avail. Their assailants faces were a picture of frustration and confusion as they continued reigning down their weapons to no avail.

Outside the noise grew louder and louder and for the first time the sound seemed to drench through to them. Some of the men who were in the hall had turned around and began to face out towards the bulwark. Joseph could hear the sound of fighting and shouting clearly now and he looked at Arn.

"Its Dance! They're here!" Arn shouted.

Far below the Huskian's had heard the horn blow three times, they had charged hard at those assaulting the south wall, out of sight of the defenders above. One hundred tribal warriors that had not been abroad in Vedian for hundreds of years bore down on the mercenaries with a reaping judgment. Most wielding the 'Kibaranyembe', a stone club with a thin axe blade slotted in the top, thrashing and slicing into the back line in a frenzied attack. Commander Grey who was leading the south wall attack from the rear line barely had time to unsheath his sword as the sight of the howling Elder Orn wading into battle with Dance at one side and his eldest son the other, bore down upon him.

It would be one of the greatest points of battle and military debate in future Vedian times, if the Huskian assault would have won the war that day. If one hundred of these mighty warriors could have driven the whole army from the field. Yet it would only ever be conjecture, for as the Huskian's drove into the south wall offensive, the west wall assailants come under attack from a most unlikely source.

Some of the men assaulting the keep started to grow angry and reigned blow after blow down on the seemingly unassailable wall that protected the six men. Joseph could make out directly in front of him the face of Dulcet the mercenary they had seen at the crossroads all these days ago. His viscous face twisted as he pummeled down at the unassailable wall Then shouting again from the wall could be heard of 'retreat!, retreat!' and the attackers in the keep stopped their assault turned and ran.

The six looked at each other in astonishment and Parran first to react moved forward, looking out to see what could have happened.

Joseph searched for his friend, he knew he was close and then realised there were not six but seven at the hearth. Tucked into the recess of the unlit hearthstone sat Speck, almost passed out from the exertion of his enchantment, "Did it work?" he said barely audible.

"Yes Speck, you saved us."

Joseph turned to hear Parran's voice, "Never have I seen anything like it!"

They all rushed out onto the ramparts, now clear of the enemy except the corpses that remained, they ran up the walkway and looked out on the city below.

Below them the sights was full of Huskian's, battling with a few remaining assailants who were trying desperately to run from the south wall and beyond that nothing but a sea of fire. From the west gate to the camp on the main Vedian road fire roared and men burned, every piece of earth was scorched and nothing stirred. In the distance they could just make out men running.

Joseph looked around trying to take in what he could see stretched out in front of him, then he realised where was Redrick? He spun jumping down the stairs and running back to the halls, his eyes casting over the dead and he saw him.

Slumped over another figure in armour he lay face down, Joseph threw himself to the floor and cradled the figure in his arms, carefully turning him over to lay his head on his lap.

His eyes twitched and opened slightly, a wound open on his head poured blood onto Joseph's legs, "Stay still, I will get help."

"Shhhhh. No more now lad, the day is done." His voice was quiet and shaky. "Did we do it? I see no one?"

"I think its over Redrick, I think we won." Joseph could not stop the tears now, they flowed out of him like a waterfall.

"That is good. But I would have you promise one thing to me."

"Anything."

"After this day, if you think of me, let the tears only be those you share in laughter or song, or over a good woman," his voice was getting quieter, "or if you're really lucky lad, a bad one." A tiny smile crossed his face and his final breath leaked away.

It took Parran and Arn a long time to prize Joseph away from Redrick's corpse, eventually the hunter managed with Speck's help, to lead him away.

Shouts again came from the ramparts as a further discovery was made, at the turn from the west wall to the north a pile of bodies was formed and at their centre stood Febra, in both hands the scimitars still held. Not a part of her from head to toe was anything but crimson, painted in the blood of her foes, she had stood against every attacker that had been dispatched upon her, at her feet the lifeless corpse of The Captain lay.

Arn moved to lead her away and into the hall, "Febra it's Arn, are you ok?"

She looked up at the concerned hunter, "I am Junas the Sword. Where is the King?"

Madistrin moved into view, limping from a wound to his side and the old pain from his leg, "I am here."

The girl, a picture of death absolute kneeled in front of him, "My Captain bade message to you my liege - The Sabre's held."

Joseph's nostrils were filled with the smell of burning as he looked out over the ramparts, "What happened out there Speck?"

"They happened." And he pointed to a group of men cloaked and dressed in leather, just as Cyrus had been. "They are the battle mages of Vedian and the fire was they're doing, co-ordinated with the Huskian's assault on the wall by DeFache it would seem. The enemy went into full retreat, those that did not run, were burned or captured.

"So we held?"

"We held Joseph and I have no one to thank more for that than you." Parran reached out a hand to him. "You have served this land like a soldier and yet you are not. You are perhaps more than that, a man from the Luff and you have my thanks for now and ever."

An hour later a commission sounded at the hall as three men were ushered in by Dance and the Huskian's. "We found these running from the camp."

"DeFache you know who I am. I am Scholatic, I wish to now return to my university." Shel-Toro held his head up, trying to remain above those around him.

"Your fate is not mine to decide my brethren, it is Madistrin to whom you must yield. It is he whom you have wronged, he and his people. What say you Madistrin?"

The Crown Prince, his armour now removed and his robes in place rested on his walking stick, a shadow of the man that had stood in the line just a couple of hours past.

"You have taken lands, incarcerated and killed men, you look to usurp the rightful crown and for what Shel-Toro. For this I would know more than anything? I knew you, or I thought I did and I would not counsel you for an evil man? Before I make my judgement I would know why?"

426

"You would know that which you can not accept. So in your hands the knowledge is meaningless. However I will perform my role as Scholatic, as teacher and try to educate. I have followed the path of man all my life, I have guided, I have debated and yet still you do not learn. You kill, you fornicate, you steal, I look at your cities and towns and I see the plague spreading. Year upon year I tried to guide, to hope for a change but each year I saw it worsen and then I came to the realisation, it will only get better, it could only change with a force as strong as that which steers its destruction. For listen now, all of you here! I tell you this, man will destroy himself, he will war and kill until there is nothing! There is no redemption without punishment! I sought to bring the strong hand to help the child. For that is what you are Madistrin. Like a parent I just wanted to protect my child and now the child seeks to punish? You have no right."

Madistrin moved to speak then held himself a moment, walking up the long room in thought. The hall stood silent waiting for his word.

"You have no evidence, no proof that we will end this way. Yes there is evil in men's hearts. I have seen it but it is tempered with our capacity for good. For every bad deed there is one that redeems us. You sentence us before we have committed the crime!"

"And what Madistrin if I could show you?" Shel-Toro leaned forward, his eyes striking toward the Crown Prince. "What if I could prove to you, the fate of your people?"

Madistrin waved his hands, "It is folly because that is not possible?"

"Oh but it is." Shel-Toro turned and pointed at Speck, "You boy have a book do you not. A very special book."

Speck was shocked, "Yes but it does not show the future. It can not help."

"In your ignorance you reveal yourself. The book shows what its living host would have you see, you have sought the past for your answers but MonPellia also unlocked a way to the future. Do you have the courage Crown Prince to test my words?"

DeFache spoke calmly, "You do not have to look. Nothing binds you to do so, would it change anything? Does knowing the future change your actions? "

427

"Boy bring me the book." Madistrin instructed Speck and carefully from deep inside his robes he drew it out, his most prized treasure, handing it to the Crown Prince.

Madistrin sat at the long bench in the centre of the hall and opened the book, its hard leather cover dropping open onto the table. Minutes passed and a heavy silence took the room, eventually Madistrin opened his eyes and looked at DeFache. "Does this vision hold the truth?"

DeFache held his head slightly to one side, "I have no reason to believe it would not, for if I read Shel-Toro correctly that book houses not the words of MonPellia but his very soul. However it may have given you just a segment, a moment in time, it may not describe the journey."

"So the future I offer my people if I cast down the council is war and famine and death. That is what as a King I offer them?" Madistrin's voice was strained and pain filled it.

Shel-Toro saw his opportunity, "You can offer them nothing because you are one of them. Men need the Scholatic, they need our direction our inspiration to ensure this fate is not theirs. Would you deny them that out of your hate for me?"

"No I would not, I have no hate for you Scholatic, only pity that you have lost sight of what is right and proper and many good men have died because of it. I stood in these halls shoulder to shoulder and I would be dead on its floor now if it was not for a man I had never met and who owed me nothing. A sole pikeman of Vedian that stands here now and I would make this decision for him. To save he and his family any more pain or suffering in their lifetime. I am perhaps not meant to be King, that fate was always my brothers. You are right, Vedian needs the Scholatic but it does not need you Shel-Toro, with your twisted ideals and god like self obsession, it will never need you. I will relinquish my title and leave the land to be guided by the council led by Umberto DeFache.

A fire lit in the eyes of Shel-Toro, "You have no right! You can not elect a Scholatic leader! That's is not your right!"

"Of course you are right, so I will offer you a different and simple choice, death or relinquish your post in the council. If what you say to be true and your love for man is of all importance, then you will take the latter option. Don't let your hate for me blind you Shel-Toro."

Parran interjected, "My lord, you would let him walk free after what has occurred?"

"More blood will not right his wrong Commander. He will lose what he holds most dear, the price of his ego. Will you take the charge DeFache?"

"You may not have your brothers instincts on the battle Madistrin but you would out manoeuvre many with your words. I seem to have no other choice and perhaps it is another opportunity to do right by my old mentor, for he truly loved both Scholatic and man. I will lead the council, until the men of Vedian no longer need our help and guidance." DeFache bowed to the Crown Prince.

"So Shel-Toro what is your answer? Do you accept my proposal?"

The Scholatic was angry and wanted to further vent his views on Madistrin but he looked around him and took the politic decision, "Yes."

"Then go now, leave Pluris and never return. You will find home in one of the universities, I leave the details to you DeFache."

Shel-Toro walked towards the door, he would leave with his life intact and the Scholatic still in control. He knew he had won in so many ways, he just needed for them to see it. He turned and began to speak.

"If my actions were guided by anything, it was the will of the people and when historians write and Scholatic debate, they will see the purity of my actions for the good of Vedian. This journey will be my final sacrifice...."

Shel-Toro's eyes went wide and a look of pain crossed his face. A thin blade protruded through the Scholatic's chest and as he dropped to his knees, his assassin was revealed.

Febra stood motionless, still clutching the scimitar that was impaled into the Scholatic.

"Your journey is over. So say the Sabre's."

Epilogue

The first days after the battle were the hardest, it was difficult to understand if they had truly won or lost. Madistrin insisted the four from the Luff stay in his halls for as long as they wished. He stayed in office just time enough to allow DeFache to unwillingly take the leadership of the council, his first act to remove the militia from every town and city in Vedian. In his first council vote he passed the removal of SanPollan from the council, retiring him to live out the rest of his days in Coralis university.

Remys and the other battle mages spoke with Speck and explained how they had seen the fall of Cyrus and it had acted as a catalyst they could not ignore, pulling them from the tower and onto the battlefield. They departed with Cyrus's body and made their way back to the tower, Remys made Speck promise to return to carry on his teachings when he was ready. While the young enchanter was polite and respectful in his heart he knew that was not the future for him, he could honour Cyrus better in the outside world.

Elder Orn departed a week later with the Huskian's and Commander Parran alongside the remaining royal guard. They found Bast'wa hiding in his Kanegon castle defenceless, his men deserted. As promised Parran offered Bast'wa's fate to the Huskian's but they could not see themselves to end his life. Rather they took him to work on their farms, to carry out recompense for his actions and there he remained for the rest of his days.

They all remained in Pluris for the rest of the winter and into the spring. Dance and Arn were married in the market square, Joseph his best man and Madistrin who grew close to the couple gave her away. They stayed for three more weeks but eventually Dance longed for her own family and the tribal life.

Arn approached Joseph and Speck as they sat in the market square, "I fear I am about to make a hat trick of broken promises my friends."

Joseph smiled, "You never truly left us Arn, your heart and courage have always been with us. I can see how much Dance longs for her home, it is time you gave it to her."

"Will you come to the Inpur both of you to visit us?" Arn asked sceptically.

"Of course we will. Although our first destination must be home. What shall we tell your father Arn." Speck enquired.

The hunter shrugged, "It does not matter, tell him I am sorry if it pleases him. Perhaps one day he will understand."

The pair left for the Inpur desert as the first blossom took hold on the trees. Joseph and Speck knew it was time for them to move on as well, the song of the Luff was calling.

Madistrin retired at the beginning of Spring, giving up any right to the crown, before he did formally, he undertook three final acts as Crown Prince: Firstly as promised to the party from the Luff he decreed a pardon for Rundell, which was announced at the pulpit with the help of DeFache. Secondly he granted the seal of royal approval to the bakery owned by the millers wife and youngest son. Finally he made every effort to find a relative of Lint, who had given his life to save Madistrin at Imanis, when none could be uncovered, he donated monies to set up a military school to be established in his name. The Lint Academy was for generations known to breed only the best and most respected soldiers that served in Vedian.

After the Huskian's debt was delivered Parran left his formal post but remained Madistrin's personal protector and spoke with Joseph on the eve of his departure.

"I am Commander no more. Just Parran a man of Pluris. But I would have you know this Joseph if ever you need a warrior, a man with limited skills, then call upon me. I will attend."

Joseph bowed, "You honour me truly. I can not imagine any situation so grave as to need a man of your fighting prowess and ability but if time came when I needed a man of impeccable truthfulness and honesty, then I would perhaps come calling."

Parran bowed, "There is one more thing before you depart." The soldier stepped aside and Madistrin walked forward.

"My liege." Joseph bowed low in reverence.

"Up please. There is no need. I am sorry to hear you are leaving buy I understand your need to return to your own home. There is one thing I would ask you do, If you will."

"Anything of course."

From his side he lifted up a long cloth bound item and handed it to Joseph. "Here the sword of my family, 'The Quelling Blade', I will have no line to pass it onto and no use of it in my dotage. With you, I believe it will be handled with respect and I can think of no other man that lives up to its words than you. For your actions Joseph made a nation strong that was weak, your words inspired men and for that you have my thanks and all of Vedian's."

"I do not know what I would do with such a gift?" Joseph was visibly shocked by the offer.

"I think you will do what is right." Madistrin bowed and left with Parran at his side.

Joseph and Speck returned to the Luff the next day, they tried to persuade Febra to accompany him but the warrior remembered nothing of her former life and saw no reason to leave the capital. They left her standing on the the west wall, staring out beyond the town, watching over the people.

The pair walked together on the long road and while each of them knew they had changed, in many ways they were still the young men that had left the luff.

It was months later that Joseph woke on the anniversary of winters night and realised what he had to do with the sword. He and Speck made the journey to Coralis and Joseph buried the blade with Redrick on the banks of the Medwere river that rolled up into the Rinslake Range. Every year after, they drank and laughed with friends and told stories of the great lover Redrick. Never to be forgotten.

If Vedian ever needed the sword again, he knew it was held safest by a man who knew the power of pacifism as well as domination.

As for Brine - the only Vedian soldier to survive the Battle of Pluris, his story is yet to be told.

Printed in Great Britain
by Amazon.co.uk, Ltd.,
Marston Gate.